This book is dedicated to my daughters
Kristin and Meredith. We have been through much
together. They have shown patience as
their mother embarked on one exploration after
another. Not all have been successful, but each
has taught its own lesson. *Silent Is The Magpie*
is as much their story as it is mine.

This book is also dedicated to all the would-be Jamies
out there. I have met you. We have talked. Shared
lunches, stories of family and friends, and sometimes
tears. I have heard your hopes and dreams and
frustrations. I know you are searching for the same
things Jamie is. It is not for me to say that you will find
them. But I do know that this four-year journey
has brought a greater understanding of what is truly
important in my life. So my hope would be that
through Jamie you might gain a greater sense of
what is truly important in yours.

Silent Is The Magpie

Acknowledgements

First, I would like to thank my editors, Kurt Landefeld, Paul Royer and Michael Olin-Hitt. They called themselves "The Three Stooges." I call them wonderful. I couldn't have done this without any of them.

Thanks to Mike Blanc who gave me endless ideas for a cover. He is a talented and fun artist.

Thanks to Brian Lewis, Reid Crosby and my husband, Jim, for helping me form my mountain man.

Thank you to some education majors at The University of Akron for their observations.

Thanks to my "Slices of Magpie" who got fed the book slice by slice as I wrote it. These great people are: Joe, Kristin, Carolyn, Suzanne, Mark, Martin, Sheila, Mike, Clarice, Margie, Josh, Jennie, Lee Ann, Ellen, Nancy and Cordell.

Thank you Gailmarie Forte for your good eye in proof-reading the book for me.

To Carol Landefeld for doing the final proofread.

Thanks to Elaine Mesek for helping me get this in book form.

To Jennie Levy Smith for getting me ready to print.

I especially thank Jim, for putting up with four years of my writing. He also helped me with the business parts of the story. He told people I was writing a story and I kill him off in the second sentence. I said, "This is fiction, Jim, and anyway you're dead in the first sentence. I just don't mention it until the second sentence."

Foreword

Silent Is The Magpie is about a woman who looks for and finds her identity, power and voice at an age when others might view her as completely defined (mother, grandmother, widow, usurper to her late husband's business empire).

Jamie Barlow refuses to let the death of her husband consign her to a life of meaningless lunches, countless hair appointments and anxious peeking from curtains waiting for infrequent visits from too-busy children and grandchildren.

Instead, she hops on her Harley and bolts suburban Pittsburgh for their small cabin deep in the Ligonier Hills to spend a year connecting – or reconnecting – with the life and creative forces within. In doing so, she learns more about herself, and others, than she could have ever imagined.

Her path, however, is not an easy one. In places it is blocked by others, some with murderous intent. In other places, however, the difficulty of discovery is rewarded physically, emotionally and spiritually.

Silent Is The Magpie might be described – incorrectly – as a "self-help book for senior citizens." But those familiar with American Indian cultures will see it first and foremost as something more profound, a vision quest. This quest is aided, surprisingly, by a young Cherokee man who has fled unspeakable tragedy in Oklahoma and found uninvited refuge of a sort on Jamie's property.

Jamie keeps a journal of her year in the woods. Her thoughts, insights, lines of poetry are reproduced on these pages. They become a tangible record of conflict and growth, of potential defeat and ultimate triumph.

Vanita Oelschlager has created a compelling character in Jamie Barlow. As lives stretch into our eighties and beyond, conventional notions of one's senior years are increasingly obsolete. Retirement at 65, followed by some period of "golden" years spent in semi-lucid repose, now seems as antiquated as a Model T Ford.

Jamie senses this as she flees the comforts of home for the rugged uncertainties of the hills. But it is not until she gets into those hills and starts her trek that she begins to understand why she came there. As with all quests, the journey *is* the destination.

We share Jamie's journey. We learn with her the connections between our "civilized" lives and the deeper forces of Nature that forge those connections. We come to know her relationships – and ours – with the eagle, hawk and magpie (a chatty bird whose mischievous ways belie something more.)

At the end, we celebrate Jamie's growth. We know that her journey to a final destination is far from concluded. And the Magpie falls silent finally when Jamie knows this too, deep in her heart.

It has been a personal joy to share Vanita's journey as one of her editors. From the start she knew where she wanted to go. All she asked was that we have the patience to help along the way. Though it took four years to finish, patience was the last virtue we needed. Getting to know Jamie and her friends was more than reward enough. I hope you will agree.

Kurt Landefeld
Editor

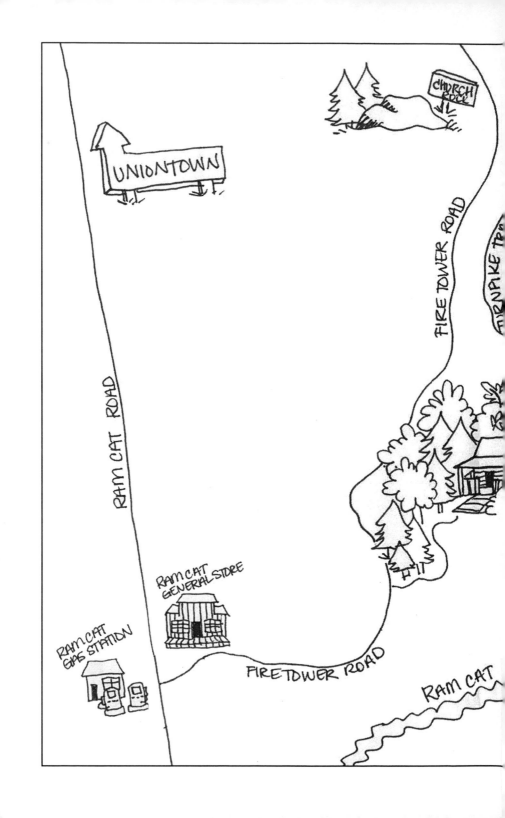

NORTH FACE
JAKES CAVE
NSET
OINT
SUNSET TRAIL
SALT PETER
HAYRIDE
GREAT WHITE OAK
LITTLE PINE
BEAR CAVE
NAKED BEAR
RAM CAT CREEK
TROUT TRAIL
EK

Chapter 1

On the Run

Jamie Barlow leans over the gas tank of her Harley, pushing it into turns at speeds significantly above the posted 50 mph limit. As the farmhouses and occasional trailers blur by the roadside, she knows a sixty-something helmetless widow ripping down these back roads like an escaped convict will cause some tongues to wag. She doesn't care. Let them talk. They always had. They always would.

She and her late husband, John, had been coming to Pennsylvania's Laurel Mountains for decades, usually in a van. Now she's coming alone for the first time a month after his death.

John had introduced her to these old hills. They had bought land, more than 800 acres, and built a cabin hideaway that still had most of the comforts of their Pittsburgh home. Even though they employed a caretaker full time and up to half a dozen men for various projects over the years, she knew they were still considered 'rich outsiders.' Many of these families could trace their lines back to the 1700s. But, outsider or no, this was where Jamie decided to go when she knew she needed time and space to plan for the next stage in her life. This time without John. Without her daughters and grandchildren too. And she left John's business behind as well.

She'd be back in a year. No less. They would manage just fine without her, she said reassuringly. Or hoped they would, she thought less assuredly.

Jamie had shocked them all with her announcement. But that was the way it had to be, because she knew something even more important was pulling her into these old hills. She couldn't quite put her finger on it yet. Still, she knew this was more than just another vacation ride. She knew this was the beginning of a journey whose destination was not yet known.

Jamie surprises even herself at her aggressiveness. She knows this bike well. The road too, having travelled it hundreds of times. She pushes herself and the Harley harder than she's ever done before. The wind bleeds tears out of her eyes and pulls her just-above-the-shoulder-length mane out behind her; in a backwash of all that lies behind.

What was this urgency rising from the hollow of her chest into her throat?

Was she feeling trapped by the burdens of John's business, a nationally recognized investment advisory firm? After a month, had she grown desperate to shed the "Widow Barlow" tag that friends (and not-so-friends) had so easily attached to her?

Not that those words were ever said. But she could tell already the difference in how her women friends approached her. She could also tell the difference in how John's men friends approached her as well. Was she shocked, despite his warnings, at how many were now calling and suggesting dinner? An evening at the orchestra? More?

Coming out of a long curve into a semi-flat straightaway, Jamie guns the bike past 65, edging to 70 mph. She loves the feeling of the deep, appreciative rumble between her thighs. Could she push it to 75? 80?

This was John's birthday present on her 65th birthday. An older model…a 1985 Sportster 1200. The "least dangerous" bike he could find. But still a Harley! She took six months learning how to ride it. She also learned what John meant by least dangerous. So, secretly, she'd had some custom engine work done that boosted its top speed to 140 mph. At least that's what the dealership said. She hadn't quite tested that limit yet.

When John found out he tried hard to be angry. "You'll kill yourself on this!" But Jamie knew he loved and admired her independence, even willfulness. He found it exciting, something that helped keep their sex lives active long after friends had lost theirs, or traded spouses looking for rejuvenation.

The Mail Pouch barn is coming up on the right. She glances quickly at the John Deere tractor mounted high above the doors. That was a story! But in letting her mind wander, the bike wandered too, suddenly spitting stones. Jamie corrected gently, regaining the road's bend to the left. She knows what happens when high-flying bikes and riders drift onto gravel berms. She was as bad as some of the locals. Bikers, usually young men, often pushed their cycles way past their driving skills or response time. Many paid the price in laydowns, broken legs and arms. Some with their lives, little plastic-flowered crosses marking where they tempted fate and lost.

At the end of the straightaway the road began a long up-and-down climb into the deeper, higher hills. Jamie slows some, but is no less determined to put Pittsburgh and all its chains and tendrils behind her. Way behind her. It is still forty miles to the cabin. Yet the miles and minutes seem to melt away. There is never much traffic on this road during the week. A little heavier on Fridays, Saturdays, Sundays and holidays when other weekenders like she and John would head up or back from their own sanctuary in the hills.

If you wanted to find these Pittsburghers, they'd be in restaurants and bars that catered to this elitist crowd. But John wanted to avoid them "like the plague." Their cabin was miles – and worlds – away from 'neighbors.' To Jamie, it felt closer to the mountains of North Carolina where her father's people had come from and where she'd loved visiting cousins. Where a smile was a smile – not cover for an agenda.

As she climbs, the road gets worse. She backs off on the throttle some. But even as the postings went from 50 to 45 to 35 and sometimes to 25 mph, Jamie has enough confidence – or is it compulsion – to stay over the limit a good 10 or even 15 mph. She is in a hurry!

As hillsides close in, rhododendron and mountain laurel are the only green in the still-brown April woods. It seems she is pulling a clearing sky behind her, the sun casting blinding shafts amid abrupt shadows of trunks and limbs crossing the road. She crosses some invisible line, and her shoulders fall at ease. Getting close!

John loved these last miles best. He told her this road had begun as an Indian trail. It was one of many that formed a pre-colonial network, smaller ones feeding into larger ones. The large trails led, inevitably, to the two great rivers – Allegheny from the north, Monongehela from the south – that joined in what is now Pittsburgh and became the Ohio. The Shawnee, who lived farther west, gave the "o-hi-o" its name, "beautiful river."

Jamie crests one last hill, then descends into a hamlet that sometimes had a name, sometimes not. But for as long as she and John had been coming here, it was known as "Ram Cat Run".

Jamie drops the 1200 into second gear and slows to a 20 mile per hour "waddle" while she makes her way along the three blocks or so of houses and a few commercial buildings that made up Ram Cat Run. From the corners of her eyes she can see heads moving to check out the rumbling sound outside. She can only imagine their surprise to see her instead of some tattooed and bandana-ed man. Now she downshifts and rolls crunching to a stop in front of the general store. This was her and John's usual stop for supplies before driving the final five miles to the cabin turnoff.

The building is a single story. Brick. Dating from the 1850s or '60s according to John. A wooden storage room was attached later, date unknown. Its large window fronts a buckled cement sidewalk. In a semi-circle professionally-painted lettering announces proudly:

RAM CAT RUN GENERAL STORE
EST. 1938

The font suggests the store was last 'remodeled' in the 1950s. Perhaps a centennial celebration of some sort. Below are the week's specials written from inside:

Jumbo Eggs 99c

2% Milk Gal $2.19

Chuck Roast $2.99/lb.

Even though hand-painted, the lettering looks experienced and sure, as though the scribe has been writing backwards for years and knows customers will jump at the weekly sales.

Jamie stretches and surveys the street again. Quiet, as usual. A few cars or pickups are parked as she is. The gas station at the end of town where she came in has the same Exxon-Mobil sign it's had for years. But wind knocked out the "M" two years ago, so from a distance it almost reads "Exxon −obit."

John always laughed at that, she smiles to herself. He really wanted it to read "Exxon- RIP." He'd never cared for oil company stocks, not trusting the quality of their management. She can hear his voice clear as day, "If I was a smart, young businessman why would I waste my career in a dying industry?"

It was this kind of short, direct analysis that drove John to seek out new, fast-growing industries where a few, well-managed companies would emerge as big winners. Just as the oil business had been when it was young, and a few − John D. Rockefeller most famously − had made fortunes and names that became household words. It had earned John Barlow a reputation on Wall Street as a "gambler" which he never liked. But his investment instincts had earned him and his clients untold millions over the years.

It had also afforded a quiet lifestyle that she and John both cherished. Which is why they'd bought the property and had the cabin built. He had loved these hills more than any other place on earth. And he and

Jamie had seen a lot of the world, despite his disability. She thought by coming to the place he loved most, she could escape the sadness and gaping emptiness brought by his death. Jamie reaches for her backpack. She has a short mental list of things she'll require to get settled.

Jamie depresses the door's handle and gives it a slight nudge. As the door gives way, the bell above tinkles gently. Familiar smells quickly greet her.

As her eyes adjust to the musty interior, she can hear stirring in the back. Two women, one early middle-age, the other just in her middle teens come out, wiping hands across towels. Both were inches shorter than she. The mother is pudgy but solid. The daughter slender, but rounded. Their bodies made taut from the hard work of minding a store six days a week. She always felt large next to them. But then she was taller than just about any woman she'd ever met.

"Well, hello, Missus Barlow!" said the older one, already looking past her to the motorcycle.

"Hello, Cora. Just stopping in for a few things."

After more than a decade, Jamie and Cora had finally 'introduced' themselves a few years back. Cora always deferred to the older, wealthier woman calling Jamie by her last name. Jamie was slightly embarrassed by this, but never insisted on a first name.

As Jamie makes her way down the aisles, Cora and her daughter, Ellie Mae, look at each other, eyes widening, saying nothing. A few minutes later Jamie puts a chunk of cheese on the counter, then a loaf of bread, a few sundries and a bottle of Jack Daniels.

"I'd like a pack of Marlboros, also, please. Hard pack."

Mother and daughter eye each other again, Cora directing with a nod. Ellie Mae turns to find the cigarettes.

"Beautiful day, don't ya' think?" asks Cora as she starts ringing up Jamie's purchase.

"Beautiful! Felt good to get out and ride."

"Here're the smokes, Mama."

"Thank you, Ellie." One more ring and "That'll be twenty-four thirty-one, Missus Barlow. Do you want a bag?"

"Oh no! Think I can get them all in here, thanks."

As Jamie puts the groceries, liquor and cigarettes into the backpack,

Cora tries to continue the conversation.

"Hank Fuller was in the other day and said your husband had...died. We're sorry to hear that."

"Thank you. Yes, about a month ago."

Jamie looks past Cora, eyes sad again at the memory.

"He was a very good man. He loved coming here."

Cora re-rolls the fallen sleeve on her frayed denim shirt and looks back at Jamie and tries a more personal tack.

"So, you holdin' down the fort all alone now?"

Jamie is a little surprised at the intrusion. Irritation rises quickly. What was she supposed to be doing, bringing a lover along? Somebody she'd kept on the side for years waiting for John to die? She hated it when women went digging for gossip. It was the thing that drove her to these hills. And here was this store woman asking her the same gossipy question as the wives of John's business associates! Instead she just answers coolly, wiping a loose strand of blond hair off her cheek, suddenly chiding herself: is that caution or paranoia?

"Yes. Just me. I wanted to get away for a little while."

"Hank said he was a good man, too. Paid fair. We're really sorry for your loss."

Jamie detects a sincerity that goes deeper than the woman's curiosity and softens to the gesture. She smiles and ends the conversation, "Well, time to get up to the cabin and make sure it's still standing!"

Outside, she straddles her sun-warmed saddle and eases backward while firing the engine. Expertly delivering a quick rev and a small spray of gravel, she leaves her parting comment behind: a snarl and a spit in the face of cloying shadows (or encroaching demons). Got to keep moving.

Chapter 2

The Resort of Last Resorts

Jamie kills the engine, drops the kickstand and swings off the bike. Stretching again, she surveys the landscape for any obvious changes since she and John were here the previous fall. The clearing itself is about half an acre. Smaller trees were removed to make room for the cabin and a side building for storage. It was ringed with large second-growth trees, many more than half a century old now. A broad drive wide enough for a couple of vehicles swept up to the buildings then completed a circle back to the entrance road.

A large white oak stands sentinel in the middle of it all. This tree has been spared from the earlier logging. It is easily a hundred years old. Staunch and majestic, its canopy is wide and inviting. Two breaks in the woods to the north announce the beginning and end of a large loop trail. Another break behind the cabin starts a trail to the south.

Jamie remembers how neither suspected last fall's trip would be their last one together.

Instead, he had talked of cutting another trail to branch off the north trail and loop around the northernmost edges of the property. John was always hatching a plan or dreaming and planning things bigger and more – despite Jamie's growing belief that less could be more. There were parts he had never seen. A ridgeline where two hundred year-old walnut trees had escaped the lumberman's saw. A spring that gushed out of a rock outcropping starting a stream that fed a larger creek below. There were even rumors of a cave where pre-historic Indians had lived now likely home to a family of bears. Jamie smiles sadly at her memories, then turns and looks back at the cabin.

Built a decade ago, its sparse design is unpretentious with a low-sloping roof and a large porch surrounding it. A double chimney dominates the roofline, wood being the only heat source. But it is extremely well built with thick walls and lots of insulation so even on their rare winter trips Jamie and John could be comfortable inside with a fire roaring.

One concession to John's disability was the ramps leading off each side of the porch so he could maneuver easily about with his battery-powered scooter. A ribbon of asphalt led to the storage shed so John could get in and putter around.

He had originally talked about having something truly rustic, no electricity or running water. But Jamie had drawn the line at that. And the one time when the scooter's batteries went dead and needed hours of recharging convinced John that having electricity was probably a good thing. Also necessary was a roll-in shower big enough for both the showerer and showeree. A year later a high-speed Internet line and fax machine were added so John could stay close to his business, even when he said he didn't want to.

Large windows on the cabin's north and south sides give the cabin an open, airy look outside and in. But John wanted the windows tinted so visitors couldn't see in and surprise them.

The windows were so large and thick that a crane had been needed to install them. But instead of renting, John had Hank Fuller *buy* one. Jamie thought that was a crazy expense. But Hank and the guys found other uses for it including lending it out to friends for their own construction projects. Like many of his other business decisions, John knew this was a smart buy. He figured Hank would earn a lot of good will by loaning the crane for other projects.

Hank Fuller had grown up in these hills. As had Hank's dad, his grandfather, and his great-grandfather, the original settler from the eastern part of the state. They had all been a rural Pennsylvania mix of logger, farmer, miner, machinist – whatever they could do to earn enough money to get by. Hank was also good at running crews. He had earned John's trust to the point where he managed their properties with little input from John during the great stretches of time when they were away.

She loved how John could relax here as he could no other place. And as he relaxed, then she did as well. Even when conversation drifted back to the company and its latest challenges, he could be easily distracted by a hawk perched on a limb or a doe leading two fawns from one trail to the next.

John hunted deer as a teenager and young man, but had never been a good enough shot to bag one. Of course, deer were far rarer then than now. Jamie suspected he might have missed on purpose more than a few times because he had taught her how to shoot and he didn't miss the lineup of coffee cans often. Still, he loved to tell his hunting stories and Jamie listened patiently no matter how many times he told them.

They kept the cabin locked, mainly to keep animals out. John had talked at one time of adding a security system, then decided he didn't want to make that compromise to their privacy. If someone found it and wanted to break in, well it was just things wasn't it?

John also knew people kept a pretty close watch on the comings and goings in their rural community. A local teenage would-be burglar would be found out pretty quickly. A drifter would be seen and found out even more so. Here's where they got some return on John's goodwill loans of adult-size Tonka toys. Such a network with people like Hank Fuller was far more effective than electronic eyes costing thousands of dollars.

Jamie opens the door and steps into the dark of the large living room. Letting her eyes adjust, she inhales the familiar aroma of wood and fireplace ash. She leaves the door open to the tastes and smells of spring. To let the moist, warming earth replace the dead winter air.

Jamie always called the cabin a "hunting lodge with a woman's touch." Curly oak floors and wormy chestnut walls give it warmth. A burled oak mantle is strong and massive framing the eight foot fireplace perfectly. Fronting the fireplace is a long, leathered sofa and a low burled maple table complementing the mantle. Made by one of the local craftsmen, it is museum quality. It is rare in a world of paychecks and budgets, but common in Jamie's life.

The rest of the room is fitted with shelves and an office space that includes a desk, computer, fax machine and other reminders of the business world they'd tried to leave behind.

Close to the south window is a seating area with an overstuffed chair, table and floor lamp. Here John and Jamie would often have their afternoon drink and take in the view of their ridge, the ravine below and the vista beyond. It was also where Jamie could snuggle in the early morning hours when she would sometimes wake early to read or write.

Hanging on the wall is a painting of her and John that she had surprised him with a few years ago. It had been taken from a photo of them at their Pittsburgh home, John seated and Jamie leaning over in a hug with both smiling at the camera. The artist had taken this image and re-set it in the clearing with the trunk of the oak tree seen partially in the foreground and their cabin in the background. John had loved it so much he teared up after she unwrapped it for him. Now, as she looks at his crooked grin and soft eyes, she tears up as well. "God, I miss you, John."

John and Jamie had travelled the world, but both had come to love this place best. John had dubbed it their "resort of last resort." A few years ago they'd come up for their first spring weekend to find that a medium sized oak had fallen nearly blocking the entrance to the cabin. Not wanting their privacy interrupted with a call to Fuller, John wanted to cut up the tree himself.

Jamie wasn't sure this was smart or safe, but John had insisted. So she got the chainsaw from the shed, an electric one that could be used for making kindling and handling smaller jobs like this. John sat on the ground cutting three-foot lengths, Jamie moving him to the next cut until the trunk was finished. Then he showed her how to use the saw and helped her cut up the branches.

She thought of the burden of carrying him. She could feel his warm gravity even now. The intimacy of his body against hers. His arms around her. His breath in her ear. The war that had robbed him of most of his legs had also bonded them in ways few others could know. At times the weight had been almost too much for either to bear. She could still hear him apologizing softly, "I know I'm heavy, baby."

Still, at other times, carrying him was effortless. As though they both had wings and could defy gravity. Many days she saw him stare at two hawks circling and could see the longing in his eyes.

As she reflected later, this had been a perfect example of the uniqueness and strength in their relationship. John taking on something that his disability should have ruled out. Then the two of them working as a team to get the job done.

During her middle years, years when most women became weaker and worried about brittleness, Jamie had become stronger. Stronger than she ever could have imagined.

John's doctors had watched in amazement as she moved him, something that usually took two men to do. Maybe it was just the everyday caring for John. Maybe it was something more. Now that he was gone, she was here to find out.

Jamie carries her backpack into the kitchen and starts to unload its contents. The kitchen is sparsely furnished. Electric stove and oven. A few cabinets. Sink – with a garbage disposal that Jamie had insisted on. Wooden block counters. Refrigerator. A small pantry. Mounted on the wall was a holder with chef's knives. Another rack held a cast iron skillet and a few sauce pans. This was not a kitchen for entertaining; it was strictly for the basics of weekend cooking.

A utensils holder next to the stove included her mother's wooden spoon. It was her only cooking spoon. Jamie guessed it was at least sixty years old. It had stirred countless batches of batter for cookies and pancakes. As a child it had seemed almost as big as the huge spoon Julia Child had waved on her cooking show.

How odd that, of all her mother's possessions, she wanted to make sure to hold onto this one. Her mother hadn't taught her much about cooking. But the spoon had served other purposes. More than once it had made her butt burn. So that even waving it once was enough to induce a young Jamie to obedience. Now, with her mother dead more than ten years, holding the spoon still brought back fresh feelings.

She thinks of her parents' marriage. She never talked to John much about it. But as an adult looking back at her parents, they seemed an odd fit. She loved her father's warmth and playfulness – unexpected qualities in an engineer. Her mother, despite bearing three children, never looked or acted comfortable with the roles of nurturer, teacher, nurse and the sometimes myriad other expectations society had of women. And Jamie never saw the small acts of affection that define people who have been in love for a long time.

She thinks how the children came to reflect the qualities of the opposite parent. She knows she has been perhaps overindulgent, making sure her own girls grew up with lots of love.

Jamie brings in the rest of her things from the bike. Then pushes it onto the porch. Later she'll park it in the shed. For now this will do. She is ready for a drink. And a smoke. A little early in the day perhaps. But this is her day. Her time. She can damn well do as she pleases.

She settles into the leather chair with the journal that will be her record of the year here. She sips her Jack Daniels and savors a cigarette, her first in years. The sun is sliding into the western sky casting sharp shadows from the still bare trees. Some have crossed the trail like a gate. The bars now seeming slowly to swing open; the way now beckoning before day's done.

A few falls ago Hank and a couple of the guys had lined it with daffodil bulbs for about fifty yards from the house. The following spring brought two brilliant long strokes of yellow practically commanding her and John to take their first John Deere Gator ride of the season. Now the strokes of color are there again, but broken in places where deer and other animals found welcome snacks. Maybe she'll plant some more. Tomorrow she will hike down to the stream that splits the two ridges. It will be the beginning of a hiking regimen she had promised herself as part of this year away. She wants to get to know this land more intimately than ever.

Despite the seductive warmth from the whiskey and the Marlboro, she can feel the evening will be cool enough for a fire. She remembers how John loved to sit with his drink close enough to stir the logs and embers, to thus keep the fire alive deep into the night. Those were the times when he sometimes talked almost in a stream of consciousness, ideas and observations flowing easily. She was a good audience, occasionally asking a question to spur another round of him talking, thinking, planning, looking ahead. Always looking ahead. That was John.

But he is gone more than a month now. And her whole life has changed, with no let-up in sight. Questions that could rest comfortably deep inside while John was alive now were dragged from their sleep and grilled rudely for answers. Who is Jamie Barlow? What does she know? What does she believe? In the years she has left on this earth, what does she want to accomplish? How does she want to be remembered?

Each question brings its own stab of fear. A panic that had begun somewhere in her core soon after John died. Then spread to her chest and throbbed in her brain. A panic that struck in the night when, half awake, she would reach for John and feel an abyss instead. A panic that struck in the middle of lunches with the wives of her husband's associates. A panic that would not go away even in the warm melting hug of a grandchild.

Another sip. A rising curl of smoke caught by a shaft of sunlight in its sensuous dance.

So she had decided in the middle of another empty-handed night that she would go to where she and John loved most, where she would feel closest to him, where maybe there might be answers to these questions, where the ghosts might be banished and a renewed sense of who she was might be found. Where a new Jamie Barlow might be revealed.

When she announced her plan, it set off its own round of panic. From family to employees to clients to business associates to associates' wives to even her hairdresser, the common question was 'You're going to do *WHAT?*' She knew there were even whispers about her sanity: a woman so overcome with her grief that maybe an intervention was required.

One board member, who had remained loyal to John to the end, asked, "How can you leave John's business like this? You really think it can hold up losing John and now you? You do realize you own the company now, don't you?"

One daughter, frightened at the idea of being left alone, covered her fear with guilt-baiting, "What about the grandchildren? What about their birthdays? They'll think Grammy and Grampy are *both* dead!"

The wives had given her those looks – equal parts calculating and clueless.

One friend, Marty, had been more understanding. A Jewish gastroenterologist, even he couldn't resist wisecracking, "What are you going to do about Christmas, for Christ's sake?"

But Jamie had surprised herself with her determination to go through with this plan. And the more others protested, the more certain she was this was the right thing to do. Even if she didn't know exactly what she would do with this year, this whole year, for herself. As John had said at times when he took chances with the business, "It's not the destination that's important; it's the journey."

They had had quite a journey together. And now that John had reached his destination, Jamie realized she had another distance to go. Hopefully a long one. And she realized too that she didn't want others leading her by the hand to places she didn't particularly care to go. She wanted to choose her own path, to explore. When she approached her own destination she wanted to look back and say "That was the real Jamie Barlow" and be pleased with the trail she marked.

She picks up her journal which she calls her 'lifeline'. She now sees the image of a palmist's reading ...hmmmm. The cover is worn, half its pages already filled. This "old friend" has saved her sanity more than once. She has inscribed her life's journey. The journey that has brought her to this place. And she now has new chapters to write out and struggle to understand. She needs to find the place inside called "home". Her center of gravity is gone. It is time to start the fire.

Chapter 3

A Start

Jamie wakes with a start. The clock on the mantle says six thirty. The sun has already slipped behind the ridge. Exhausted by the ride and lulled by the whiskey, she'd slept a solid two hours. A good shot is still left in the glass.

She gets up to stretch, standing by the window and watching the sky's deepening colors. They had always loved this time of day when John could let go, however briefly, of thoughts about markets, the political affairs that influenced them, and the fickleness of clients who somehow expected him to make them mountains of money by simply clicking his fingers. This time of day was when John could watch with a childlike wonder as dusk moved through its rapid metamorphosis from orange to pink to red to purple. Or when he would be the first to see a buck move out of the woods for his evening meal of spring grasses.

Turning back to the chair, Jamie picks up her journal, her "lifeline." The last words she'd written before falling asleep were the same ones she'd written at the end of each day since John's death, his last words to her:

"Love you, too, kid. I'm going home."

The first sentence was always his familiar reply when she said she loved him. The second sentence had been a bit of a mystery. "I'm going home" as in "I'm going to Heaven" was not like him at all. Not that John was an atheist, or even agnostic. John had believed in God, but not one who watched over and intervened into his daily affairs, or anybody else's. John's God seemed to be a God of Nature. Not a God you asked for help. Not a God you thanked when things went well. Nor one you blamed when things didn't. John didn't believe in Heaven or Hell, at least as places beyond here and now. He often told Jamie there were more than enough heavens and hells right here on Earth. That is why his "going home" words were both mysterious and comforting to her. As though, at the end of life, John had glimpsed something else. Something that was drawing him to another place and bringing him peace.

Somehow for a month now, that one sentence had pulled her back each time she whispered his name – and fell to pieces in the silence that followed. Somehow he was telling her that he was going to be safe. That he would be there when it was her time to "go home." He'd said it with such calm and clarity that she knew he wasn't saying it to make her feel better. Or that he was uttering words out of some drug-induced delusion. He'd said it because he knew it. And it had all the more impact because she knew her John was not a sentimental man.

Jamie crouches at the hearth to stir the ashes, as if scraping through remnants of her own inner fire, gathering the most hopeful embers beneath two fresh logs. Never troubling John with it, she had always worried she'd be afraid to stay at the cabin by herself. Now here, she doesn't feel afraid at all. She's not sure what she feels just yet. But for now the calm and quiet are welcome. She knows – hopes? – by this time next year, she will be a different woman. What "different", she can't say. But she is no longer John's wife. And while she will now always be John's widow, she doesn't want others to see her through a dead man's eyes. That is why she is here. To make the acquaintance of someone she's longed to meet: To find 'Jamie.' To discover what it means to be her. To meet and to tell herself – and others – about these discoveries through her journal and the life she brings back to family and friends. And perhaps to find whether anyone back home is still interested.

Dusk now succumbs to darkness. Outside it is pitch black. Jamie can see one bright star to the southeast. She knows there are other homes scattered on the ridges, but their lights are hidden. For both those in grand estates and those in tin-roofed hovels, privacy is plentiful in these hills. There is great wealth scattered throughout, but even the experienced eye would find it difficult to tell which graveled drive led to a twenty-room lodge and which led to a ramshackled cabin.

She turns on two floor lamps and gives some thought to making a simple meal. Walking into the kitchen she realizes this will be the first of many, many meals for only one. Not that she had ever prepared elaborate meals for the two of them. John had been an unabashedly 'meat-and-potatoes' man.

Despite its small size and limited use, the kitchen was equipped with all the modern conveniences, including a disposal under the sink, Jamie's favorite kitchen appliance – you could make much unpleasantness just disappear with a ½-horse Kitchen Aid. The refrigerator, small freezer and pantry were stocked with the foods she'd ordered and Hank Fuller had brought up last week.

She knows this won't keep her for a whole year. But the store in town will have most of what she needs to survive. She was even looking forward to trying out new recipes.

From the beginning their instructions to Hank had been clear: bring what they asked for and then leave them alone. She knows that his curiosity will get the better of him at some point and she will have to shoo him away. But once should be enough.

She opens the far right cupboard where she and John kept their "booze closet." There a half dozen bottles, mostly full, were arranged neatly side by side. Each had accumulated a thin layer of dust. She and John had joked about their bar. They only drank Jack Daniels. And they didn't entertain here. They said they ought to take the rest back to Pittsburgh, but they never did. Jamie puts the new bottle of "Old No. 7" next to the others. She and John had made an agreement to only bring one bottle at a time so they weren't tempted to drink too much. Still, they had had many fun times here begun with a drink or two.

John's full name was John Darien Barlow. Some of his friends called him "JD." She wondered then if he'd settled on Jack Daniels because of the initials. She wonders now if she will be tempted to empty her bottle as quickly as the two of them used to do. She closes the cupboard and opens another, reaching for a can of tomato soup. Soup and grilled cheese will be tonight's fare. Tomorrow she might do a roast for a week's worth of meals.

Jamie eats in front of the fireplace just as she and John did so often. The fire crackles making the large room toasty warm. It'll have to work even harder next winter to do the same. But thanks to the cabin's robust insulation, she hopes she'll make it through without getting into trouble.

She finds herself staring into the fire as John often did. She knew him well enough to leave him alone with his thoughts then. Often she'd occupy her time with a book. When John spoke it was often about some far off part of the business world where his mind ranged with ease. He didn't expect her to understand all of his thoughts. But he appreciated that she listened closely enough to ask a follow up question or two.

Often he just amazed her with his understanding of how certain political events would unfold. Or how quickly certain technologies would move from first generation applications into the economic mainstream, making untold billions for its developers and tens of millions for those who invested early in their companies. He wasn't right all the time. But he'd made enough money from his understanding of people and business that the major business publications and shows often sought his comments on the news of the day and on the futures of various markets around the world.

Now, though, she just stares. This fire will likely be her only evening company for an entire year. She looks forward to summer when she can be outside until 10:00 if she wants. For now, the room's silence is broken only by the occasional crackle of wood split by heat.

"John, I hope I know what I'm doing. And, honey, I hope you're close enough that if I get into trouble, you'll let me know or find a way to help me out."

Now she wants to turn in for the night. One more log on the fire then she pulls the screen across the hearth.

Jamie hesitates before entering the bedroom. The blow-up egg crate mattress is still on John's side of the big wide bed. He had to use that when he developed bed sores. Despite all her care, it had been one of these infections that finally claimed him. They had talked about Christopher Reeves who had died the same way despite his heroic efforts and the care he'd received. John had observed with an oddly clinical distance, that "all the care in the world can't help you if a bed sore gets hold of you deep down in the bone." And that's just what happened.

They tried joking about it, John calling her a "butt freak" because she needed to check there daily. Then she missed one. Until it was into the bone and too late. She felt guilty for not doing a good enough job when he needed her most. She felt guilty, too, at feeling relieved, never having to check for another bed sore.

At times, the weight of her caregiving had almost beaten her. It had been the hardest thing she'd ever had to do in life. Harder than birthing. Harder than parenting through the turmoil and tumult of children and teens – and adult children. Harder than helping her husband hold himself together when the business was teetering with other people's money on his back.

Despite her fatigue, Jamie decides the egg-crate must go away. So many things, meaningless now, like debris after a meal. "Is there a disposal for these kinds of leftovers?" she wonders. She lets the air out, putting each section carefully into the carrying case. She will donate it later.

Climbing into bed, it feels even larger and emptier than her one at home. Can this emptiness be filled? Should it be? Already men had been calling or visiting, suggesting lunches or other "neutral" overtures. Men who had known John. Men who appreciated what he had. Men who schemed to posses his woman – and his wealth, now that he was gone.

Laying back, she closes her eyes. Her mind drifts back to a time here years ago. A summer night. Moonless. When John had reached for her. Touching her in the way she liked best. An incredible tenderness from a man known for his rough ways around business. She tries to remember more, but her exhaustion takes over. Night. Silence. Finally, sleep.

Very much alone in the woods.

Chapter 4
Right Here

The next morning Jamie wakes to sunlight coming through the bedroom window. One other change John's death had brought was night after night she has relished complete, often dreamless, sleep. No caths, turns, dressing replacements, or ostomy disasters. No waking with flashbacks from Vietnam. Today she wakes feeling completely refreshed and alive, ready to begin setting out the pattern of her days and nights for the next year.

Jamie lingers in bed savoring the luxury of having no one and nothing to be responsible for except herself. Back in Pittsburgh her days were more crowded than ever with details of the business, making sure she made time for her girls and the grandkids, preparing for the string of lunches with well- and not-so-well-meaning friends and business associates. Now she thinks about getting out for a hike, the first of many she has planned as part of an imagined journey along the two thousand mile long Appalachian Trail.

She'd always toyed with the idea of walking from Georgia to Maine, but realized there was much of this acreage she'd never seen before. She even looks forward to getting lost. On the property. Inside herself. Finding her way back to the cabin. Finding her way to another Jamie. A Jamie defined by her choice. By what she believes in. By what she accomplishes. But she knows first she will have to outdistance her own ghosts, slip out of a self (grown) uncomfortably bound. Like a snake shedding its winter skin.

She will reflect daily in the journal, record thoughts, experiences, observations, feelings...all leading, hopefully, to simple truths about herself and maybe a few larger truths about how the scattered pieces of her self – and whatever new ones turn up – fit into some new reason to be...in some new reasonable world.

In the bathroom Jamie looks at parts of the past, now out of place. Sadly? Or thankfully? She shakes off the thought. She looks at John's medical armory. His catheters and urinal. An ungainly lifting contraption. Too many and too fallible ostomy supplies. A drawer full of paraphernalia just to fight bed sores. A pharmacopeia of pills, potions, and patches. Evidence of two lives lived in constant vigilance and challenge.

She wished for an aftershock, or some delayed tidal wave to come now and finish death's work; washing this all away. But then she picks up John's hairbrush, running her fingers over the soft bristles as she remembers the closeness while combing his hair. This she will keep for a while. His razor and shaving cream too. She wants to keep his smells close to her here.

Another shelf was reserved for her medicines. She had told her doctor of her plan to give up all medications while away. Doc Roseanne wasn't happy about it, worrying that Jamie's isolation could become life-threatening if her body needed help and it wasn't there. They negotiated an agreement: a promise to take a baby aspirin and a multivitamin daily – and a promise to call before doing anything stupid. The others would go in the trash.

Jamie looks at her thick, blond-streaked hair stylishly cut a few inches above her shoulders. John loved calling her "Blondie" or his "Tall Blonde." But she knows this has to go too. Another 'sacrifice' to her time in the woods – a gesture of welcome for some new Jamie.

She'd asked her hairdresser what would happen to it without cut or color for a year. After nearly fainting from the horror of the thought, he regained his composure long enough to warn of dire consequences. The blond would grow out and fade away, leaving her hair a ratty mix of gray and mouse-brown. "Honey, you will age ten years in three months. I promise!" She smiles thinking of his concern for her welfare.

He had offered to make a "cabin call" in a couple of months to "save you from yourself." Jamie smiles too at this memory. She had graciously declined his offer. She really wanted to see herself in all her mousey-gray glory! Who was going to see her anyway? The women at the Ram Cat Run maybe weekly and why would they care anyhow? She'd look just like one of them (*Hmm: maybe I've been just like one of them all along.*)

When it gets too long, she'll just pull it back into a ponytail, like it was when she and John were young and he would tug it like boys will to show he liked her. Still, she suspects her vanity will get the better of her and one of the first stops back into 'civilization' next spring will be her hairdresser's.

One thing not in the bathroom was the scale. She'd asked Hank to get rid of it. This was one morning ritual that was ended. First thing in the morning. Naked. Staring down at numbers that would then dictate much of the rest of her day. How much exercise. How many meals skipped. How many calories cut.

In John's world of business, she knew she had to look as good as she could. She knew wives who had let themselves go; wives who tarnished their husbands' success in an arena where image is everything. The judges and juries were the other wives. Their courts of opinion were the innumerable lunches or fundraising dinners or seasonal parties at one another's homes. Someone unfortunate enough to put on too much weight or wear an ill-fitting dress or slather too much make-up became an immediate target for others.

Jamie found it suffocating. Sometimes she would complain to John. He was dimly aware of the peer pressure and pecking order, but was clueless how wounding an evening of cuts, jabs, and smirks could be. And sometimes, while struggling for air, she'd notice John's eyes in lingering assessment of some swollen cleavage or sculpted behind. But in the same way, she could feel her assets under appraisal by John's competitors, his "friends." But after a few drinks, it got easier. It was just business, wasn't it? And she had to put up with it. For John.

But now that was all over. She didn't have to care about her weight. Or how much "boobage" she might show. She didn't have to dress for anything or anyone but herself. Hell, she could choose not to dress at all if she wanted! And if she didn't burn her bras, at least she could banish them. She could feel her shoulders falling, her neck softening, her breath deepening. This beginning moment of freedom was exhilarating!

To celebrate, she steps into a hot shower. Having hot water here was another of the creature comforts Jamie had insisted on. The shower was a roll-in, large enough for John to wheel himself in and out, although Jamie often joined him. It had two shower heads as well and a molded seat. More than once they had stayed in long enough even for their generous hot water heater to run out.

Dressing, she decides on jeans and one of John's polo shirts. She had started wearing them after his death, sometimes even to bed. She loved still smelling his scent on them. She was sure Hank wondered why she'd asked him to bring some of John's dress shirts up from their lodge. She had liked wearing them there as an occasional robe. She wanted to do the same here.

The morning is fresh with heavy dew. She can't wait to get outside and start exploring. While coffee brews, she surveys the great room. Hank had done as told and removed the flat screen TV, radio and telephone. He left the computer, fax machine and CD player with two racks of discs. He'd balked at taking out the telephone telling her, "You need that here for your own safety, Jamie. John would have my hide if I didn't say something about that." Jamie had thanked him for his concern. But she also told him that her plan would be wrecked with incessant calls from the office or her kids. She didn't include the possibility of other men calling looking for a free weekend with the Widow Barlow.

Hank had relented when she showed him what she affectionately called her "disposable" cell phone: "pay-as-you-go," couldn't be traced, no records were kept. Jamie decided to give him that cell number. He could call her only because of the strictest emergency. If she got a call for something less than that, then she would get a new phone and not give out the number. Hank got the message.

Jamie smiles now thinking of her unexpected assertiveness. She remembers how Hank straightened up and looked her square in the eye. Clearly, he was used to taking orders from John, not from her. But he heard the resolve in her voice. He was one of the first to see a new Jamie beginning to emerge though he didn't quite know it at the time.

She had decided on the computer with its Internet connection, along with the fax machine, as her only concessions – her "lifelines" – to the outside world. She could get emails from her children and grandchildren. She could check on news if she wanted. John was insatiable with his need for global information. Jamie wasn't. And if the Eiffel Tower fell over or aliens landed in Pittsburgh she'd hear soon enough.

She could also check on the weather. This would be needed information as she started taking longer and longer hikes. She imagined some lasting the entire day. And she wanted to be able to look up plants and animals online as well.

She smiles at the one trip she and John had made in the John Deere Gator. She would now retrace it on foot. One of the guys on Hank's crew had heard stories of an old whiskey still located somewhere on the property. After talking to a couple of the real old-timers still around, they had figured out where it might be. Sure enough they had found it one late fall day a couple years ago. The next spring they built a trail out to it so John and Jamie could see. It was tucked into one of the many stone outcroppings that dotted their ridges. John was especially excited, telling Jamie he thought it might date back to the late 1700s when the first English settlers appeared on this side of the Appalachians. Jamie wants to see it again and look closer for artifacts that might confirm John's hunch.

Before she tries her first hike, she decides to settle down with her coffee, muffin and, most importantly, her journal. The phone, fax, email: life support machines – lifelines...for a lifestyle that can no longer be. But Jamie is convinced these blank pages will be a lifeline...to a life yet to be lived. She discovered writing late in life, compared to most. In her sixties, this had become a consuming passion.

At first her writing was just words about feelings and random thoughts. Describing her life with John. Working out issues that her children or grandchildren were dealing with at any particular moment. But then feelings and thoughts began to shape themselves into more complete expressions. She wrote children's books and had friends illustrate them. She learned how to write speeches and deliver them, discovering a crowd-pleasing sense of humor in the process. This from the girl who choked on her words each morning on the school P.A. – and prayed each night for divine disaster upon those ancient electronics.

Jamie even "tried" poetry, although the words and lines seemed at times to flow with a power all their own. She didn't know if it was "good" poetry or "bad." What's more, she didn't care. If the lines captured a feeling or an experience, then that was good enough. Still, one of her goals here was to explore this kind of expression even more deeply. She was intrigued by how she might start writing about one thing and then something else altogether would appear on the page. She often asked herself "Where did *that* come from?" Jamie hoped she might have a better answer to that question when her year here was up.

She opens to the last entry, a line she must have written last night but looks strange to her this morning.

I want to be here because

She stares at the line for a minute. She thinks about all the "becauses." John's death. Getting away from the business. Letting her girls make decisions on their own. Running away from the men clutching at her and her wealth. From the raised eyebrows, clucks, jabs, and paranoia as the other wives nursed their neuroses. Jamie takes one more sip of coffee. Then a deep breath. Then she finishes the thought she started the night before.

I want to be here because

I need to be here.

I have the right to be. Here.

I am right to be right here...

I have to...Be

"Well, that's a start. Come on, girl; let's see what the wide world has for us today."

Chapter 5
Miles To Go

The morning is cool enough for a light jacket. When Jamie steps onto the porch she startles a cardinal that had perched on the seat of her Harley. It flies up to a nearby branch and starts a scold. She smiles and walks out into the oval clearing. The large oak is just beginning to bud out. It will be a couple of weeks at least before its leaves make a welcome summer shade.

She walks around the cabin looking for anything out of place or needing a fix. Hank has always kept it in good repair, though, truth be told, it still looked almost new even after ten years. But winters could be harsh and storms could bring unexpected surprises, like the tree that fell and John cut up.

A few years ago Hank had come over to get it ready for one of their winter getaways only to discover that a blizzard had been strong enough to knock out the bedroom window, leaving a shattered opening and a drift two feet high all the way into the living room. At first all suspected a break-in. But then Jamie fessed up thinking she may not have closed the window when they had last been there enjoying an Indian Summer weekend. From then on, John's last words before driving back to Pittsburgh on Monday mornings had been, "Did you lock all the windows?" It was annoying. But he was right to ask.

Today Jamie doesn't see anything out of place as she comes back around to the side where the shed stands. Normally, it was kept locked but Hank had taken the lock off at Jamie's request. There was a ramp up to a wide sliding door. Again, this had been done so John could have easy access to a workbench and his tools. He had learned a bit of carpentry in the Boy Scouts and liked to putter around.

Jamie slides the door open then takes a few seconds to let her eyes adjust to the darkness. She takes a deep breath of the building's masculine aroma of gas and oil and wood. She almost expects John to look up from his bench and show off his latest handiwork. The shed had also stored the Gator, one of a small fleet of maintenance ATVs. But this had now been moved to Pittsburgh. Jamie would keep the Harley here instead. For the winter months, she might have Hank bring a snow blower up as well.

She runs her hands over the bench's smooth, oiled wood. Cobwebs have gathered now at the edges. Touching the wood reminds her of how determined John was to keep doing the things he loved despite his injuries and complications. The bench had been built at a level where he could work sitting down, with clearance for his wheelchair underneath. All his tools were within arm's length. The ones he loved most he'd inherited from his father. A heavy, old plane. A T-square. A hand-cranked drill brace. Screwdrivers with wooden handles. A large ball peen hammer. Not that he used them all that much, but each held their own memories of a boy learning how to understand and work with wood, how to plan a project and end up with something of use. A chair. A table. A lamp.

He had told Jamie endless stories from his childhood. The father and grandfather who, like hundreds of thousands of others, worked in the steel mills and related companies in and around the "Mon," the Monongahela River Valley. Those men had made untold wealth for the likes of Carnegie and Mellon and Frick. They were in the mix of working class, later middle class, workers and managers who fed furnaces, poured metal, shaped slabs, cut ingots, wound coils and hauled their sweat-laden jewels to stamping and machining plants across the American Midwest. They were Germans, Czechs, Poles, Slavs, Italians, Greeks and blacks from the South. They all poured into this Valley and turned coal, limestone and iron ore into money that fed families, bought houses and cars, then sent many of their children and grandchildren to colleges and universities far away.

John had learned his work ethic from them. He spoke almost reverently of what it meant to grow up in that Valley during that time. Jamie had been fascinated listening to him, even when the stories made their tenth, or twentieth, round through after dinner discussions. Though both were from Pittsburgh, her background had been different. She had enjoyed an upper middle class life in a suburb far removed from the ever-blasting smoke and fire in the "Mon." Her father and mother were transplants from South Carolina. They had grown up in a South that tried to keep its antebellum posture by strict enforcement of a society segregated by race and class, one that lasted deep into the 20th century. Her parents didn't support those attitudes or condone a way of life that resisted the upheavals of enlightenment and modernity. They were firmly grounded in their Methodist ways and instilled the same in their children.

It was her father's engineering work that brought them to Pittsburgh. And while he was good at it and provided well for his family, somewhere in her teen years Jamie had sensed a disappointment hardening into bitterness from her mother. She never discussed this with either parent, or with John for that matter. She could only guess at her mother's lingering unhappiness, but for a long time believed she and her brother and sister were to blame. For what she couldn't know. Still, the children had grown tall, fair haired, healthy, and, for the most part, happy. Jamie sometimes saw their mother's darkness shadow her brother. But, again, she never asked and now the children themselves had children and grandchildren.

All this crosses through Jamie's mind as she lingers a minute longer in the shed. "John, I can feel you here, dear," she says smiling to herself. About to leave, she absentmindedly pulls open the one large drawer attached to the workbench expecting to find more tools. Instead there are four photos. Of her. Naked. In the woods. Taken by John many years ago. She laughs and cries simultaneously and remembers immediately where and when these were taken. They had been out on the Gator on one of the farthest trail loops on the property. There they'd found a spring coming out of the rocks that started a stream of water that became a creek further on down. John had brought the camera, a digital Nikon that he found easy to use, to take pictures of rocks, trees and whatever else he found of interest at a place they rarely visited.

The 'whatever else' turned out to be Jamie. And not for the first time. Still, it always surprised her when and where John's urges would come on. He loved telling her how to pose and she loved being his model. The sex afterwards was almost always enthusiastic and athletic without a hint of interference from John's disability. That day had been no exception. Her smile mixes with a tear as she tucks the photos into her back pocket. Not the kind of thing that Hank or any of his men need to stumble on. She thinks for a moment about what other "naughty" drawers or files there might be – those things we've all had friends swear to break in and dispose of so it doesn't make it into the news after we die.

Jamie steps out into the brightness and the day's gathering warmth. Sliding the door shut, she turns to see a flicker of red. The cardinal. Bolting again from the Harley to a safer branch. Again she hears the scolding as she considers which trail to start exploring. She decides on the easiest one for now. It runs below one of the ridge lines and stays level for almost a half mile before climbing to meet the top of the ridge. It's one that she and John travelled often. The trail is wide and worn, once an old logging road. She'll walk at least as far as the point of incline.

Jamie covers the flat distance easily. The woods are quiet and bare. She loves the muddy moistness rising up from the ground. Somewhere a crow caws and another answers. She pauses at a second growth maple where two summers ago her elder daughter's children had carved their initials with a bit of help from Grandma. There had been the usual squealing of "me-firsts" and "let-me's." John had watched laughing from the Gator.

It had been the only time any of the grandchildren had been allowed at the cabin. She had felt a little guilty for their selfishness. But John had not. They had both given children and grandchildren gifts upon gifts upon gifts. That they kept this for themselves was a selfishness John felt they deserved.

The climb to the ridge-top is steep, steeper than she remembered. The trail narrows a bit. Jamie is winded after a hundred steps or so. She stops and looks back through the woods below to the top of another ridge line several hundred yards away. Then looks back up to where this trail meets the next running the ridgeline. The burning in her legs and sweat on her forehead are reminders that she has not done this kind of hiking in a very long time.

She decides to head back, counting this is as a Beginner's Day. Jamie feels a vague sense of defeat, but also knows this is just one day, this hike one of many, many she will take. Twenty minutes later she is back in the cabin, sitting on the sofa, legs outstretched. She will mark her mileage in the journal. But first, a nap.

Jamie wakens an hour later to stiffness. Legs and back aching..

"Ooh! It's going to take a little time to get into hiking shape," she says stretching in front of the fireplace. She checks her pedometer: 1.7 miles. A start, but barely.

She fixes a lunch of soup and a sandwich, and settles into one of the large leather chairs that faces the south window. The sun is full through it now and she basks in its warmth. With the woods still bare she can see the long trail that leads down to her favorite creek. She can just make it out from flashes of reflected light. That'll be tomorrow's walk.

With a few hours of good sunlight left, Jamie decides to do a little more exploring. This time on her Harley. The cardinal that seemed intensely interested in her seat has left. Thankfully, he hasn't left anything behind. Jamie straddles the seat, turns the ignition, enjoys the engine rumbling to life, pushes back the kickstand and starts around the oval.

Coming down the hill, instead of the left turn that would take her back to Ram Cat Run, she turns right and shifts the bike comfortably but quickly through its gears until she's going fifty and her hair is pulled straight back behind her.

She knows she should wear a helmet, but the rush of air and sounds and smells is too intoxicating. John tried the first few times to coax her into wearing one, then gave up. She also suspected that he found her more exciting when she came to him after a ride, windblown and a little sore.

The road curves and curls hugging ridges and hills, occasionally breaking open into a valley. There are a few cars out today. For a minute she gets stuck behind a tractor pulling an eight-bottom plow. When oncoming traffic clears and the road offers a short straightaway, Jamie zooms around the farmer and moves back into their lane with a wave of her hand. In the mirror she sees the farmer raise a hand back. He's a young man that she guesses would much rather be on her Harley than atop his International.

This road leads to Uniontown, the county seat and home to about 10,000. About fifteen miles from the cabin, it has a nearly-regular grocery store, two car dealerships and a funeral home. Also a weekly paper to hawk cars, coffins and comestibles and chronicle the trickle of small-town community life.

Perhaps most importantly, it has a hospital that serves patients from a thirty mile radius. Several years ago John had donated money anonymously that helped expand their emergency care. He'd done this after needing help following an accident at the cabin. When he saw the decades-old equipment and room conditions, he arranged for a half-million dollar check to arrive on the president's desk two weeks later with a note stipulating that it be used exclusively to improve the emergency ward.

The biggest satisfactions he got from his generosity was the newspaper headline

Hospital Receives Anonymous Donation
To Upgrade Emergency Care

and the fact that he never required its services ever again.

There was a side benefit from his quiet philanthropy. The president was encouraged enough to launch a capital campaign to build a new ob-gyn unit. John's donation leveraged – or "guilt-baited" as he sometimes said – some of the other Pittsburgh wealth hidden in those same hills.

The county road dead-ends at one of Uniontown's three stoplights, this one on its eastern edge. Instead of turning right and going into town, Jamie turns left on the state highway and heads east. This road is a little more heavily traveled. It leads back up into other hills in the Laurels and some beautiful vistas.

Jamie lets the thrill of freedom seep in. This day is all hers. This ride is all hers. This road is all hers. No one to answer to. No meetings or dinners to rush back to. No worries about bandages or ostomy bags. The sheer freedom is exhilarating! She can ride for miles and miles and miles and no will care, no one will call, no one will carp or gossip.

Now the Harley pushes sixty...now sixty-five. "A woman and her Harley sharing an age and a speed as one." She laughs loudly at the thought. Anyone watching from a porch or a passing car might think maybe something is wrong with this picture. But there isn't. Or if there is, she doesn't care. The wind in her face blows away cares and memories and inhibitions. The sound of her chunky V-twin and the feel of its saddle are comforts known only to her.

The road is now open and straight, a broad valley between mountain spines. Farms and tractors and clothes on lines blur past. The land is brown with promise, speckled with dots of yellow.

Thirty minutes later Jamie slows for another town, this one lacking even one stoplight. Then, without giving it a thought she does a U-turn and starts heading back towards Uniontown. She knows a turn onto another county road might lead back to more familiar roads and the cabin eventually. But she's not ready to get that kind of lost just yet. She opts for the familiar ground of the return route.

With the sun in her eyes now, she slows just a bit. Seeing the sign "Uniontown 20 Mi" and a line of poetry – from her childhood? – pops into her mind, "Miles to go before I sleep." Yes, indeed!!

By the time Jamie makes the turn back onto the Ram Cat Run road the sun has moved from late afternoon to early evening. The shadows are long and sharp and short-lived by the time she makes her last turn onto the drive. Wheeled up to the porch and locked, she finally stretches and gives a shout into the silence of the surrounding woods: "It has been a good day! It has been a good, GOOD day!!" Now she's ready for a drink and a thought toward supper.

The night comes on quickly. Again the hills and woods fall black and silent. Jamie feels tugged at once between a lulling fatigue and an urgency for something more. Having finished a BLT and another Jack – not the best supper she knows, tomorrow will be better – she sits down in the leather chair and decides to spend the evening writing in her journal. She looks at her last entry again. Something different about those words. Not sure what yet. She turns to a blank page.

What to write about? The hike? The bird? The pictures?! The ride?

She closes her eyes and thinks. Then doesn't think. Thoughts float one way, then the other. If John were here he might interrupt with a question or a story. If John were here...If John...If...

Jamie opens her eyes. She glances at the clock. 9:30??!! What happened to the time?

She looks down at the journal. A single line stares back at her:

Tonight I want to write about   darkness

Where did *that* come from? Why is that word so far apart from the others? She stares some more. Then thoughts, now words, come to her and her pen begins to move across the page almost at will.

Chapter 6
Hearts In Darkness

Darkness....

There was a special darkness we shared...and another darkness that was mine alone.

So much of life with John happened at night. Not night after dinner and before the 11 o'clock news. Night after midnight. Deep night. Silent and dark. Not the evening; not the morning, but the part of night known only by those afflicted by day.

In the last years his handicap robbed him of sleep. Which meant it robbed me too. A catheter, a bag, a spill, a dressing, a war nightmare. Or I'd wrestle him to a more comfortable spot on the bed trying to keep those sores away. Caring for John meant watching over his slow deterioration; guarding against whatever might hasten the inevitable. It meant fretting whether he got the very best attention from his doctors. It meant wondering sometimes whom it would kill first: him or me. It also meant protecting him from others who thought his disability made him and his money easy prey. The schemers and the leeches in their thousand dollar suits. But they didn't know John. Or me.

Sometimes the business would keep him awake as well. More than once he made money in the day from what he learned about markets in Asia and Europe the night before.

Often we made love. Not the fun outdoors lovemaking we did here. Our deep in the night loving was quieter, more intimate. Like two people holding each other against life's storms. I needed it. He needed it. It became a bond that helped weather the betrayals of friends and business associates. A bond that also weathered the betrayal of his body... almost to the very, very end.

It seemed that as the strength in his body waned, the strength of his spirit became even more apparent. Even as he needed me to do more as his body could do less, I drew from him the courage to face another day. John had no fear. Of anything.

When he would slip into another few hours of sleep, often I would be left wide awake. Then that darkness became my own. Sometimes it was just minutes. More often it would be hours. It felt like stolen time. Time snatched out of the dark when I, too, should have been asleep. Instead it became time when something else awakened.

Out of that silence came the ideas for my children's books. The ideas themselves were often born from being with my grandchildren. Seeing their growing pains and their innocent joys.

I never took any creative writing courses, but I devoured others' work. My poems shaped themselves. They've been good enough for me, but I would like them to be good enough that someone else could read them and see some light in their own darkness.

My own works were born in isolation. Maybe they wouldn't have come but for the darkness. Not the darkness of night, but the darkness that haunted my days: Struggles and crises relentless and hungry for my sanity.

Still my own darkness wasn't silent. There were cries inside me. Still are. Me crying and not wanting to burden John any more than he already was. Me searching for something else and not having a clue. My poetry was sublimated crying – the only way I could bring my feelings into the light of day.

It was there in my deep night times when fears would rise up like ember-eyed hobgoblins. When sometimes I would shake and weep inwardly while they reached down through my brain and clawed at my gut. Sometimes I would clench my jaw, shake my head, even take a swat at my fears to force them away.

Fears of what I couldn't say. Losing John before I lost him? Living hourly with clearer knowledge of the inevitable? Living ever closer than others must to facing the certainty that this could not end well – and (the certainty) that our time before then would be a mounting struggle?

It was in that dark sanctuary with John sleeping dreamlessly next to me that something – or someone – started visiting me. A feeling, a sound, a touch, I couldn't say. I call it the Voice. Not mine. Someone else's. Or was it mine?

Maybe it was the answer to some prayer for relief, for some advocate, or maybe some part of me that was larger and stronger than whoever had submitted to a life that was not her own. Or was it the sound others have named "Hallowed Be?"

I started hearing it one night when the day's demons hurled about and I cowered deep in a living room chair. I call it a "Voice" but at first I didn't hear any words. Just a sound. A quiet sound. At once distant and near. Like a steady trickling song that seeped through all the noise.

It talked to me. Told me things that I knew were pure and true. About John. About me. About us. Even about the Vietnam War that first came between us. A war that everyone lost. A war that shaped our lives together by devouring them.

I guess the easiest way to explain is that it was a dream. Or a half-dream. But it seemed so real, so present, that I started talking back to it. And the conversations were a cool salve, a calming touch. So much so that later I could remember enough to write them down. My poetry was rooted in these.

At first I tried to tell a friend or two about the Voice. They would say it was just something in my head. But I would insist it wasn't. Then they would look at me funny and suggest sympathetically that maybe a doctor could help me figure out where "It" was coming from. I soon learned for my sake, and John's, not to say anything more.

It was then that I came to cherish my alone darkness. I'd crave the arrival of that Voice. Like a lover in wait. When the Voice came, I could feel its touch. I learned to love the quick shudder that ripples through my body. My mornings felt refreshed. Even John noticed the difference in my energy and attitude.

But it didn't come every time I faced the night alone. I wondered why. I felt abandoned. Then, almost in a fit of spite, I would sometimes wish for those other shadows to gather round and fill my ears with their wails so I didn't have to think about the Voice that didn't come. Whew. How sick was that?

The mornings that followed those nights were bad. They left me exhausted, and sore and snippy. I tried not to let John see that. But I know he did. And I know at times I hurt him. I didn't mean to. But the Voice spoke to me from somewhere beyond all the noise – somewhere I wished I could live. Maybe I made up an imaginary friend to share whispers of some happily-ever-after that waited soon as the gods realized their mistake. But I was addicted. And when I didn't get my fix, I went into withdrawal.

John would think it was him and the extra work his handicap made for me having to move and pick him up. He would apologize with "Sorry, baby, I know I'm heavy" in a way that never failed to melt my heart. And yet how could I explain that the weight I felt was far more than physical?

I would always tell him it wasn't him. But it was him. Our lives often seemed a blur. Complicated. Filled with crises large and small. The way his needs got in the way of the Voice. My Voice. (Hmmmm. My voice...?) How could I explain that? To him...or anybody else? People thought I was crazy enough at it was. Probably a lot of them still do. Best I just keep it all to myself.

That's why I'm here. To have all the alone darkness I want. And need. I want to coax that Voice into my room. Talk to me some more. Tell me more things that are pure and true. Maybe help me bring more words, more poems, into this journal and journey of mine.

Voice, I want you in the light of days and the dark of my nights. I'll be quiet and listen. Voice!? Walk these hills with me? I want you to come to me in the light of day as well as the dark of night. Voice! Come and join me as I walk these hills!

Jamie puts her pen down. She is exhausted. This is far more writing than she had planned on. But there it is. A preface, a proposal, a prayer. She reads her words, feeling a good tired in her body. It has been a good, full first day!

Then she has another thought and writes quickly:

P.S. John, I miss you. And I hate you too, honey. It's all so complicated. The way I'm missing you and so relieved at the same time. But I can't feel guilty. We gave it everything we had. It was just bigger than us. If you can see me, you can see where this page is tear-marked. Please, please I'm sorry if I hurt you. I was the one who was heavy, baby.

Today is Tax Day – your favorite! (Ha!) I know how you hated that day. But I will take good care of your business. Just not right now. You left it in good shape. It can stand with me being away. I just need to be here right now. I need to hear my Voice: find MY voice. G'night Hon. I guess we've got to "start" meeting like this. Let's talk more later, OK?

With nothing left to say, her head bobs and her brain slips offline. Blissfully, there is nothing in Jamie's world that will not wait 'til the morning. Her pen drops and rolls. And her eyes demand their privacy.

Chapter 7

Reflections

Noise, not sunlight, wakens Jamie the next morning. Some bird is scolding something. Cher-eep! Cher-eep! Cher-eep! Then the calls are interrupted by some kind of tapping and a rustling of feathers. Then another round of cher-eeps.

At first she doesn't want to get up. Daylight is a weak opponent to sleep's luxuriant arms. Feeling weightless, warm and eternal, Jamie is reluctant to surface. But the bird, whatever it is, is an incessant alarm clock clanging just out of reach. Jamie pulls herself out of bed, adjusts John's shirt and makes her way over to the living room window. There she sees a most unusual sight. A cardinal – the same one she saw yesterday? – is attacking her Harley viciously and relentlessly! It pecks at one mirror, then the chrome fenders, then the other mirror. After many successful dive-bombings, it flies to a branch and screams at the bike, then swoops in for another sortie.

For a second Jamie worries that maybe the bird is rabid. But then remembers that's a disease for dogs and raccoons and sometimes skunks. She moistens a towel from the kitchen, then she goes out to chase the bird away. "Shoo! Get off my bike!" The red bird stares for a moment, then flies off to the same branch and continues its tirade. She wipes off the poop-pee, then flails her towel to shoo the bird one more time.

She walks back inside to get a robe and slippers, John's shirt not being enough to keep her warm this April morning. When she walks back to the window, the bird is at it again. She watches more closely this time. Its anger seems directed at the mirror more than anything else. Why would that be? The bird seems driven almost to exhaustion in this fight with her mirrors.

A fight...a *fight*! This isn't bird raging against the machine. This bird is going mano-a-mano with other birds. Other males. His reflection in the mirrors. Defending his territory – probably with a mate nearby.

Now Jamie smiles and figures out a solution that will appease both parties. She grabs two old t-shirts and her towel and goes back out to the porch. Again the cardinal stares calculating before retreating to the branch and safety. She drapes the shirts over the mirrors and wipes the seat a second time. She looks at the bird and says, "Well done, Mister Cardinal! Your rivals are gone. Now we can both relax!"

When she walks back in, she goes to the window and sees the bird again on her seat. But this time his tormentors are gone. After a cocky little strut, he wings one victory lap, then lights back on the branch and starts another song. "Probably the cardinal version of 'We Are the Champions,'" Jamie chuckles to herself. Time for some coffee!

In the kitchen, she thinks of the men who came for her when John was alive. And the many others who came for her after he died. She had learned how to deal with the boys long ago. She could look them in the eye (often being their height or taller) and say no without bruising their egos too much.

But John was always on guard too. He'd fought off all would-be seducers, real and imagined. Jamie thinks back to when John swooped in and took her. Even though a year younger and an inch shorter than her self-conscious seventeen year-old six foot body, he had a confidence and determination that attracted her from the start. He was strong, smart and, well, cocky.

Jamie smiles remembering how their romance blossomed. Her shyness. His casual assertiveness. Her all-legs awkwardness. His all-round athleticism. Her big dreams. His bigger dreams. How he touched her differently from other boys. He wanted sex, of course. But he gave her pleasure too.

In that summer before she went to college, they tempted fate time after time. But he would not be denied the intensity of first sexual love. Nor would she. She came home every weekend during that first year so each could satiate the other. There was quiet talk between the mothers of marriage – after college. Jamie sighs at the memories. So many...so many...

She refocuses on fixing a large bowl of oatmeal made from steel cut oats. She adds raisins and cranberries. And honey instead of milk. She is *really* hungry! Yesterday's exercise had stirred her body. She wants to do more today despite a slight stiffness in her calves and quads. And she plans for an evening meal that will include a roast and vegetables. She knows that Jack Daniels and a can of soup do not a meal make!

Sitting down with her breakfast and looking out the south window, Jamie thinks how John loved to sit there and let the sun warm him as it moved from his left to right. Sometimes he would read. Sometimes he would stare deep into the woods looking for hints of movement. Sometimes he would just doze.

Jamie's thoughts drift to a talk she gave last year to a conference of caregivers. She was invited because of her life with John and the book of poetry that came out of those experiences. She told of how caregiving can seem to rob you of your own life. She saw heads bobbing up and down. She spoke to how the caregiver's days and nights are surrendered to the physical, emotional and mental needs of the other. Ordinary life experiences, going on vacations for example, just seem to slide out of reach. Even going shopping...or just going out with a girlfriend...become events that need careful planning.

But she told them life doesn't stop. And for caregivers especially, it was important for them to find those things that give them nourishment. Unless they did, both their spirits and bodies would starve and instead of giving care they'd likely just give out. She told them how John's disability had robbed them of their dream to hike the Appalachian Trail. So they had planned on Jamie's hiking the trails at the cabin and keeping track of her miles with a pedometer and a journal.

"It was something we both wanted to do. But it was also something I *had* to do," she said to knowing nods. "Do not, do *not*, feel guilty for knowing what you have to do...and then doing it. In a very real way you are taking in sustenance for two. If you don't get enough exercise or sunshine or other emotional 'food,' you will both starve. Don't think of yourselves as gluttons for punishment. Instead, be gluttons for nourishment. Eat lots of it wherever and whenever you can!" Her words of inspiration (and perspiration, too, she remembers!) had brought the crowd from their seats...and tears from their eyes as well.

But now John was gone. So, too, the responsibilities of caregiving. But not the desire to hike the Appalachian Trail. Nor the need for nourishment she hopes to get from her virtual trek. She and John had bought maps and books about the "A.T." as it was known by hikers. She'd also bought a backpack, good boots and hiking poles. He had encouraged her to do the hike, saying he'd follow behind sometimes in their John Deere Gator.

So today (yesterday didn't count!) will officially begin the daily hikes that will, at the end of her year, cover the equivalent of the entire A.T. All 2,174 miles. She'll do it on the more than twenty miles of trails that crisscross their 500 acres of hills and valleys, ridges and ravines. Only now she will do it alone. "Unless you want to come along, John." She says hopefully into the room he used to command. She'll have to average six miles a day to get it done. Which means she'll have to do a lot better than she did yesterday.

"Time to get a move on!" Jamie's 67 year-old body was perhaps more content to soak up the morning sun like a cat. But she wills herself into jeans, another of John's flannel shirts, a sleeveless sweater and her boots – the first of three pair veterans of the Trail say are likely to be worn through on a stroll of this sort.

She adds a canteen of water, hunk of rye bread and some sharp cheddar cheese, plus John's hunting knife to her backpack. As an after-thought, she tosses in a couple bandages, a small roll of gauze and tape. Just in case. Then Jamie heads out the door. To "Trout." Her favorite trail. The one that starts on the backside of the cabin with a long, gentle slope through old woods and on down to a creek.

Chapter 8
Gators and Trout and Men, Oh My!

"Trout" was the first trail Hank and his crew cut for John and Jamie. The ridgeback here was broad and covered with second growth trees. Its gentle slope led to a delightful creek at its bottom about half a mile away. The fish in the water gave the trail its name.

Initially, it had been a rough trail that the Gator could maneuver over without much trouble. The men had cut a turnaround at the creek that first season. Then the next spring they'd continued the trail up the other ridge, eventually making a loop of several miles back to the north side of the clearing. In subsequent years other trails had been added looping off this first one. In time, each had gotten its own name, some after a distinctive landmark, others because they reminded John and Jamie of someone or something. Trout had become well worn over the years because of its relative ease and both John and Jamie loved checking out the creek for trout and other wildlife. It was often the start of a daylong adventure that could take them miles and miles away from the cabin.

John loved to drive the Gator. It had been equipped with hand controls for the gas and brake. A shoulder harness and seat belt stabilized him. He and Jamie would go "Gatoring" for hours at a time. As they bounced over trails, through streams, up and down ridges, Jamie realized how much strength he had in his arms and hands. John was like a teenager with his first car as he pushed the Gator up steep sections of ridge, Jamie holding on for dear life. "Hang on kid!" he'd shout. And Jamie would scream like she was eight years old again and clinging to a Kennywood roller coaster. Then both would laugh with deep glee and relief when they'd crested and come to rest on level ground.

Later, John's disability robbed him of those arms and hands. Then Jamie took over the driving while John was strapped into the passenger seat. She was never as adventurous as John, driving more cautiously and less muscularly than he had. Still, the Gator rides remained the highlights of their cabin weekends. But now the Gator is in Pittsburgh.

The morning air is cool, almost crisp. Traces of frost in shady spots are a reminder that spring comes unevenly in these hills. Snowfalls into late April are rare, but not unheard of. The top of the ridge is covered with hardwoods. Farther down is a glen of white pine with some spruce mixed in. At the bottom, hardwoods reclaim the ridge and provide shade for the rhododendron, flowering dogwood, and various flowers that thrive in the moist soil and filtered light near the creek.

Jamie sets her pedometer to zero. She checks her watch: 9:30. Her legs are still a little stiff from yesterday, but not bad, she thinks to herself. As she stretches, she decides on a plan: down to the creek then over and up the other side of Trout for a half mile. Then turn around and back to the cabin. She guesses it'll be a little over two miles round-trip, maybe an hour, hour and a half at most. Not nearly the six she needs to average daily if she wants to cover the A.T., but she knows she's not in shape yet to do that. She'll give herself a month to work up to the six, eight and ten mile hikes she plans on making in warmer weather and longer days.

Legs stretched and body warming, she's ready to go. Standing under the oak, she does a girlish pirouette and laughs at her silliness. She's glad that John or anyone else isn't there to see this sixty-something woman shed six decades of life, jumping at her freedom.

She breaks into song and mimics skipping over the tight twirl of yellow bricks as Dorothy and Toto start their trek from Munchkin Land to the Emerald City.

"We're off to see the Wizard!

The Wonderful Wizard of Oz

Because because because because...

Because of the wonderful things he does!"

She laughs thinking how her daughters would be mortified seeing their mom behaving this way. Then laughs again knowing her grandchildren would squeal in delight.

Jamie steps into the woods behind the cabin and starts down Trout. The walking sticks are a little awkward at first. But within a hundred yards or so she gets the feel of where and how to place them. The trail is muddy in spots. But the walking sticks keep her from slipping and maybe landing on her butt. Tree roots become natural stairs as she makes her way down a few of the steeper parts. About halfway down Jamie pauses amidst the white pines to listen. "These woods are lovely, dark, and deep," she recites from one of her favorites, Robert Frost. Not a sound except her breathing. Then a zephyr plays through the soft five-needled clusters and Jamie hears a whispered welcome from the trees... and senses a willingness for this sanctuary to take her into its confidence.

She closes her eyes and another memory wafts through her mind like a playful breeze through the trees. Of all people, it was John who had taught her the 'sounds of silence.' As impatient as he could be with companies and markets to move and make money, still he loved to get out in these hills, turn off the Gator, encourage Jamie to close her eyes and tell him what she heard.

At first, she heard nothing. Just the silence of the wood. They would wait, willing the merciless tick-tock of the world to go away. Then sounds would begin to emerge. A songbird call here. An answer there. If they were close enough, the creek would speak. Even the air, the sun, clouds...they all had their own 'voices', some seeking a reply, some simply saying "I am." John amazed her with the ways he would reach out to Nature even when he could go no further than the limits of his scooter or the Gator.

Now she opens her eyes and feels memories and the peace of the morning and the memories settle over her. She can see the stream glistening ahead and she's anxious to be near to the energy and sound of its lively flow. Her strides are quick and purposeful. Even though yesterday's hike had tired her muscles some, she can feel her legs rising to the workout. A few minutes more and she's reached the bottom of the ridge.

The creek is full and happy, carrying winter's melt downstream a few miles more where it will meet another and become a river. Now it's about six feet across and two to three feet deep in many places. Upstream a few yards is a pool that stays about four feet deep even into late summer. There the trout go to stay cool and where she herself had splashed more than once while John watched and took pictures.

Jamie leans close to the water looking for flashes of color. There! Was that one? Closer.

There! Another? Yes! The fish, having seen her, dart for cover in the deeper water. It makes her heart sing to see these rainbows again. Like they were colors brought down from the sky, a promise fulfilled of Nature's restarting life again in these hills.

Hank and the guys had placed several large stones as a sort of bridge across to where the trail continued up the other ridge. The high water laps at their crests making Jamie hesitate to chance it.

"Go for it, babe." Jamie straightens and turns quickly. It was John's voice. But he isn't here! Yet she heard it as clearly as when he'd urge to take a summer dip.

"OK, John! Here I go!" She steps onto the first stone, the first of six to get to the other side. A second step. Then a third that slips and launches her into a "do or die" fourth-fifth-and-sixth dance that lands her on the other side still gyrating and flailing. She erupts with a "Whoa Wooooo WeeHaHah Made it!!!!!" like a teenager laughing aloud in church as she imagines watching this comic routine from somewhere safely outside of herself.

Jamie is proud of her nimbleness. "I'll be back," she says to the trout; maybe to John too – and definitely to the bridge!

She closes her eyes, breathing in the cool, earth-moist air. The forest is silent, except for the excited babble of the stream. She feels the kind of quiet that she had only felt deep at night, when John had found his few hours of rest. She likes this quiet better.

"May peace be with you." Jamie opens her eyes. Where did that come from? She heard it clear and distinct. She looks around to see if somehow, some way another person had crept up on her. No one.

"May peace be with you." Weren't these the closing words at John's memorial service? Was this her Voice speaking again? Rather than feeling alarmed at "hearing voices," as her friends sometimes teased, she is comforted by them.

"May peace be with me," she says softly. "Lord, I certainly hope so!" And laughs at her self-directed joke. Time to get moving again.

A couple hundred yards up the trail she pauses for a breath. Her eye is drawn to something farther up ahead. At the top of the ridge line she sees it. A human figure. Silhouetted between leafless trees and blue sky. It looks like a man. Has he been watching her? Something else moves. Lower, in the undergrowth. A dog? The figure doesn't move. Makes no gesture of recognition. But she is sure he sees her. Her heart races at this – intrusion?

What is a stranger doing on her property? It butts up against a state park on its eastern boundary. Sometimes she and John saw evidence of people wandering over. But this figure – this *man* – is miles from that end of the property. What *is* he doing here? Should she walk ahead and confront him? Threaten to have him arrested? Maybe he's an escaped convict! What then?

Surprise quickly deepens into panic. She wishes John were here. She stares a little longer. No movement. Half a step back. Still nothing stirs. Another step. Then another. How far away is he? Close enough to run her down before she gets back to the cabin? Maybe.

She turns to hurry back down the trail. First the stream. Then the half mile or so to the cabin. Could he watch her all the way? She doesn't see him coming down the trail. She gets to the stream and looks back. Not there. Scans the ridge. No signs. But is this good or bad? She is not comforted.

The half mile back leaves her gasping and leaning against the cabin. After a couple of minutes, she ventures back to the trailhead. No sign of him. OK. Maybe it's OK. Still she hustles, slips inside and locks the door. Slowly her heart returns to something like normal. She looks out the back window. Again nothing.

What good is being here? She only imagined being *alone* in these woods. Her woods. Maybe share them with the occasional bear, coyote, or copperhead. Didn't think to add a Sasquatch and his dog to the list.

She checks the door one more time. She feels safe in this fortress. Still, she goes to the closet to make sure the shotgun is still there. It is. A Parker. With shells neatly lining their boxes next to it. She has used this gun before. But only for target practice years ago. She wasn't sure she could still shoot it, but if she had to? Jamie promises herself tomorrow nothing will frighten her back home. That is a pledge. But for today – safety. She would rather take on the demons indoors than the demon she saw on the ridge.

Bathed in sweat, Jamie decides to shower and try to keep her heart inside her chest. Before she steps in, she walks back to the front door and one more time makes sure it's locked. And does the same with the sliding doors on the other side of the room.

After the shower she pulls on a sweat suit. She resists the temptation to call Hank. She stares at the computer and resists that temptation too. She settles on music instead. She puts on a favorite...an Anne Murray CD. She begins to settle down. Jamie grabs an old magazine and leafs through it. Slowly she relaxes. Fatigue replaces panic. As she falls asleep the magazine slides to the floor.

When she wakes the sun is already casting a long, sharp shadow across the living room floor. Jamie pours herself a Jack Daniels and lights a smoke. She draws deeply on the Marlboro as if to displace the anxiety over that stranger in the woods. The cigarette doesn't taste as good as she thought it would. But she likes the feeling of exhaling deeply, as though she could blow away today's trauma. The Jack is better than she remembered. Jamie forgives the fear she let confiscate her day.

She replays the CD. She is always moved by Anne's songs. Something about them makes her sentimental. Even sad sometimes. "Snowbird." "You Needed Me." "A Little Good News." "Could I Have This Dance?" When the CD is over, Jamie sits to write her own version of "A Little Good News."

Jamie stares at the last line. She really could use a little good news today. But for the next year all the headlines she reads will be the ones she makes. That's what she wants. If she wants to hear a little good news, it will be up to her to find it and write about it.

April 16, 2008 – 4:00 PM

My second hike. Trout Trail. My favorite. Hiked not even two miles. Scared by a man. Should I call Hank? This day ruined. Well not exactly ruined. There was the cardinal protecting his family and fighting off invisible foes. Maybe the man I saw was not there at all.

8:00 PM

OK. Better now. Napped. Just finished dinner and dishes.

I ate better. Scrambled eggs. Cheese. Toast. Coffee and JD.

Don't know how much I'll write tonight. But want to write something.

Won't call Hank. But will take phone with me tomorrow.

If someone finds me murdered, look for a pretty tall guy. Dark hair. I think. Might have a dog. Have no idea who he is or why he is on our property. Maybe just lost from state park. Maybe he came out of the Youghiogheny River that runs through the state park close to our property.

Promise to myself: If I see him again, I'll call the sheriff.

Scared before. Now more determined.

Came here to get away from people.

Now have to worry about some vagrant wandering around.

"I Ran"

I saw a man
I didn't know him so I ran.
Through woods, over stream I ran.
Down hill and up hill I ran and ran.
I listened through my heart and through my lungs.
But I couldn't hear him. Or see him. Or smell him.
Did I see a man?
Was that why I ran?
Is that who I am?
Man or no man?
Running from... or
Running for
My Life?

Grateful for the Voice during the day: "May peace be with you."

No Voice tonight. Get a grip Jamie! Enough ghosts around here! Scaring yourself half to death!

Ok. That's it. Going nowhere.

Lost to the day. Better to the morrow.

Miles to go, but first: sleep.

Chapter 9

A Different Path

Jamie wakes from a restless sleep. Lots of dreams. Or maybe one long dream. Whichever, she doesn't feel rested. The previous day preys on her. Not just seeing that man in the woods. But how she panicked and felt like she was running for her life. Then locking herself in and gulping down a whiskey and cigarette seemingly in one breath.

She feels ashamed for her cowardice. Some, maybe many, women might have understood. But John would have teased her. Like other successful men, he'd had the courage to face down enemies seen and unseen. After years of marriage, she learned that he counted on her to not only be physically strong but to be as fearless as he was. She wasn't. But she tried and was able to put on a good face most of the time. Yesterday she was unmasked. And she hated it.

Jamie kicks off the covers, walks out to the living room and stares out the back window, half expecting to see that man (and his dog) walking with purpose up her hill. But she sees no one. Just a gray dawn. Then she walks to the other window and looks for the cardinal. No sign of him either. Then she unbolts the door and sticks her head outside, just to make sure. Not a sound anywhere. She closes the door and leans against it for a second, trying now to relax and get a grip on herself.

"Darn it, Jamie! You've got to do better than that!"

She walks into the kitchen and starts the coffee. She is also determined to make up the part of the three miles she didn't cover yesterday. While the coffee brews, she pulls out her Appalachian Trail binder. It's a three-inch thick mix of maps and other information retrieved from the A.T. and other websites. Organized by state, it's a complete catalog of what anyone would need to know about hiking from Georgia to Maine.

Jamie opens to the first tab, "Georgia," and the map showing the trail's southern terminus at Springer Mountain. Behind it is a printout from the Georgia Appalachian Trail Club's website. It reads: "Springer Mountain is 3782 feet high. A bronze plaque marks it as the southernmost post of the A.T. A nearly nine mile hike is needed to get to this point from a parking lot south of here." Jamie runs her finger along the map tracing spots she would've 'covered' if she'd walked six miles from Springer Mountain. A couple of shelters. Some breathtaking vistas to the west. And Three Forks, where Noontootia Creek forms from three smaller streams.

"Noon. Too. Tee. Ah." She says the word carefully. What a crazy-sounding word! Guessing it must be Cherokee. An instant reminder of her own not-so-distant ancestry.

"Time's a-wastin'!" Jamie jumps up and smiles again at a favorite phrase of her grandmother's. Something else she hadn't thought or heard about in years. Where *do* these things come from??? She gets a mug of coffee and makes some toast. Coming back to the map, she plots her day, running her finger along that first southern stretch of the Trail.

Long Creek Falls. Elevation 3120 feet. Hawk Mountain. 3130 feet. Gooch Mountain. 2775 feet. (Another crazy name!) About seven miles altogether. Good! That will be her goal today, rain or no rain.

Clouds and cold had slipped in during the night. Rain would come later, she knows. When is hard to say, so she'll remember to add a poncho to her daypack.

She decides to start in the opposite direction today, heading north from the clearing. It's a short but fairly steep grade up the ridge to a connector that John dubbed "Vertical Reality Trail." Not as strange as "Noontootia," but unique in its own way. This trail continues climbing the ridge, then bends back to the west. Along the way, it passes one of many rock outcroppings on the property. Because it was larger and deeper than most, Jamie named it Bear Cave, thinking it might be a comfortable place for a bear to hibernate. None had ever been seen there, but the animals were not unknown in these hills. And with spring they would be awakening to hunger and the urge to explore.

Jamie and John had actually seen them on other parts of the property. So much so, they'd gotten somewhat used to them. Still she knows to keep her distance. Especially now when a mother might be out with cubs. But...no fear!! No more of that.

No lions. Or tigers. Or bears. Or a man with a dog.

"If I'm going to make it here, I can't do it living afraid. Jamie girl, you've got to go out there and face the world! You wanted this. Now go and do something!"

Fortified by her own words, Jamie finishes her coffee, throws on a light wool sweater over her flannel shirt and slings her backpack over her shoulders. Grabbing the hiking poles at the door, she looks back into the corner where the shotgun leans unloaded. She hopes she never has to use it. Still, she's glad that John insisted on showing her how.

Now she's out the door and strides across the clearing to the trail that ascends quickly up the ridge. Even though it's just a couple of hundred yards at most, Jamie pauses at the top out of breath. Vertical Reality Trail is just ahead.

"Whooo!" Jamie pants, already breaking into a sweat, and hoping maybe this was the hardest part of her hike.

The trees here are also second-growth hardwoods. Not a lot of green yet. She walks slowly towards the turnoff. Then she stops and closes her eyes. Her mind slips back to a hot afternoon late last summer. Her final Gator ride with John. Here. John was weak and getting weaker. But he'd insisted on one more weekend at the cabin. One more adventure over the river and through the woods.

Jamie didn't know then just how bad John's health was. She didn't have a clue that this would be their final ride together. "Of course we never know which of any of the day's events will be our last, do we?" she asks herself. At first she thought it was just to get away from the pressures of the business. Later she came to understand this trip was more than that.

John would never admit to being religious. He was too smart and saw through the hypocrisy of too many organized churches to ever feel comfortable inside their confines. He was also too smart to think he had answers to all the universe's mysteries. Which meant he was skeptical of anyone else who claimed they had. Yet he never thought of himself as a "spiritual" person.

This man who had beaten so many at the game of stocks and bonds and money took his real joys from his experiences in nature. His wealth had allowed them to travel the world. She'd seen him grin excitedly as eagles and grizzly bears plucked fat salmon out of an Alaskan river. She shared his childlike wonder at the dancing colors of the Aurora Borealis. They'd even arranged a special high wire mountain-to-mountain swing through the canopy of a Costa Rican jungle.

But it was here where John felt closest to whatever he believed in that was greater than himself. Jamie never broached these larger life questions with him directly. She had tried once or twice earlier in their marriage, but he seemed annoyed that she even asked.

At first, she took this to mean that he only believed in what he could see and hear and touch. And she felt some disappointment that for all his talents perhaps John was more superficial than she initially thought him to be. Then she felt some guilt for even thinking this, reminding herself of all he had gone through as a young man in Vietnam, horrors buried so deep that she knew not to even go there. If he felt no need to acknowledge a God here maybe it was because God had abandoned him there.

But then there were the times here, when he might say something or more often than not, say more by saying nothing. She could tell he was thinking about something beyond the here and now. He'd made his mark on this earth, no doubt about it. And his mind was restless enough to wonder if there was a place for him beyond *this* place. But he did it in his own way, just as he had with the rest of his life. Looking up past the bare-limbed trees to an unsettled sky, she hopes now that he had found his place out there, somewhere. If so, she hopes she might join him there one day. Jamie had sacrificed a lot waiting for him to answer his own questions, wanting to ask her own and falling silent instead. She had yearned to explore spiritual matters with John...with a friend...even with a minister from the church of her youth.

This cabin was John's church, these hills and valleys and starlit skies his sermons. And as the restlessness in his spirit pushed him outward, Jamie's drove her inward. It was there she had found The Voice. Or The Voice had found her. She doesn't know which. Maybe by year's end she will. Maybe she'll be able to share her discoveries with someone. Maybe even John...

CRAAAAACCKKKKKK!!!!

Jamie jumps a foot in the air and spins to her left at the same time.

"Ahhh!" she screams.

The image of the man from yesterday replaces John. A man charging at her – stopping short – then retreating...But instead of a man, a large limb hangs swaying back and forth on a still larger limb twenty feet from the ground. It sounded like a rifle shot. But the woods returns quickly to its morning silence.

"My God...," Jamie says, catching her breath. She stares at the limb coming to rest and laughs at herself, a bit nervously. "You're nothing but a scaredy cat. Won't have to worry about some mountain man getting you, you'll scare *yourself* to death first!"

Why do limbs fall like that? Why do seemingly healthy trees fall without so much as a breath of wind to push them over? There is much about nature's ways she doesn't know. And now without John she wonders if she'll learn on her own. Or maybe she'll pass through these woods time and time again blissfully ignorant of the whys and hows of life and death surrounding her. But she doesn't want to be "blissful." Or "ignorant." She is here to learn. Somehow. Some way. Jamie turns back toward the turnoff. Time to get moving again!

The Vertical Reality Trail is narrower and rougher than Trout. It's a clearing through the woods, just wide enough for the Gator to squeeze through. Following the ridgeline roughly to the northwest, it quickens into a steep ascent and just as quickly, Jamie's breath spends itself. But Jamie plugs on, planting one pole and one foot, then the other in a determined upward march. Even though these too are second growth woods, they are heavier and thicker here. John hoped in time they would match the original giants that had been logged out long ago. In a month their leaves will block most of today's lowering sky.

Jamie keeps her eyes on the ground in front of her. She feels her body settling into the hiker's rhythm. Four steps and a breath. Four steps and a breath. Four steps and a breath. Onward and upward. "A good Christian soldier," she smiles to herself remembering the Methodist training of her youth.

A short flattening of the ascent is a good place to stop and rest. She looks back down the ridge only barely able to make out where the trail began. Turning a complete circle, she hopes for some sign of wildlife – well, except maybe for a mama bear – but sees nothing. Her slowing breath is the only sound she hears. Jamie takes two large gulps from her water bottle and checks the pedometer. 1.2 miles. Not bad! Further than she thought she'd gone. She looks ahead to the top of the ridge. Only a couple hundred yards more. She plants a pole in the ground and sets off.

She reaches the crest once again out of breath, but knowing the rest of her hike will be easier. The trees have thinned out some and now she can feel a breeze stirring. She keeps walking, not wanting her sweat to cool into a chill. Her legs begin to protest, but she ignores them for now. In time they will accommodate her determination. Until then she has to push through the twinges and aches.

Here the trail winds back and forth across the ridgeline. At different points the trees part and reveal a wonderful vista. In the distance Jamie can see other ridges. They look like a rolling wilderness that might go all the way east to Harrisburg. But in reality they only hide other homes large and small. And tucked in the valleys are small clusters of homes, some grown large enough to become hamlets or villages like Ram Cat Run.

Still, she and John used to love imagining they were pre-colonial pioneers exploring a continent still new and fresh and full of promise. Both of their families were parts of 19th century waves of immigrants mostly from England and Germany. Eventually his had settled in Pittsburgh among immigrants from all over Europe and, increasingly, from the American South as well. Hers were among the southern root system, only coming to Pittsburgh with the onset of World War II.

But Hank's people had come a century before. They had fought a war for the right to come west. Then they had fought the first Americans for the right to stay there. And they had been among the first Europeans-now-Americans to raze the sylvan giants that had grown there for millennia and were then gone in less than a century.

She had seen the stump at Hank's house one time. A massive oak almost four feet high and nearly five feet across. It had been handed down from one generation to the next, beginning with Hank's great-great-great-great-grandfather. It was *the* family heirloom and Hank talked with deep pride about the man who had brought down that tree. The stump was nicked with generations of initials including Hank's. He had mesmerized her and also John one afternoon, talking through the initials as though they were a litany of English kings. She then understood better Hank's tie to these lands even though much of its wealth had been cut and mined long ago. He'd been able to make enough from what was left to avoid leaving and having to find work in the mills where John's and her forbearers had begun their American lives.

Thinking about Hank and the rolling ridges has helped Jamie slip into an easy hiking gait. The relatively level ground, cool air and woodsy silence combine to help her eat up miles across the ridge. Even the yelping in her legs has quieted. The trail is wider here, too.

The breeze has picked up a little and she can feel the rain coming with it. But her hike is on the backstretch now. She begins her descent. But then she stops, heart pounding in a panic, realizing where she is. This is the backside of Trout Trail. Looking down she can't quite see the creek, but she knows it's there.

She is almost on the spot where she had seen the man and his dog yesterday. She looks around thinking he may have followed or that both were waiting behind a tree, ready to pounce. Nothing. She looks again. Nothing. Then she looks down and she can see his boot marks in the ground. And the dog's paw prints too. Both look large. But the edges are soft and the earth is springing back a bit from the imprints. She turns again and sees marks headed back the way she just came. Again, not recent.

Jamie looks around furtively one more time, then walks carefully down the trail eyeing the other prints. Another fifty yards and they stop. Jamie does too. Again she looks back half expecting this stranger to be upon her. Nothing. She looks down and can now just make out a bit of the creek. She can also hear it, barely, above her own breathing.

"Settle down, girl. There's nothing to be afraid of. If he was coming after you, you'd have known it by now." Jamie talks a shot of courage into her body. A deep breath, one more turn, and she forges ahead to the bottom and the creek. She makes it to the stepping stones and across in less than ten minutes. She turns back one more time and looks back up the trail. Again, nothing. She even looks down into the soft ground for footprints not her own. She makes out deer hooves. But no man. And no dog. OK. For now at least.

It begins to rain.

After holding off this long, she'd hoped she'd make it back before the skies opened. Not today. It starts as a sprinkle. But within a minute or two it's pouring. Jamie thinks about putting the poncho on, but she's almost home and the rain isn't as cold as she expected. It almost feels good against her face and forearms. She's extra glad now for the poles as they help keep her from slipping on the increasingly muddy trail.

She stops in the copse of pine trees to catch her breath and look one last time for yesterday's intruders. Nothing again. She feels a small sense of victory. Not sure why, but she feels...*better*.

Her sweater is soaked. Her flannel shirt too. In a fit of...something... emancipation, maybe... she decides to take them off. Dropping her backpack, she pulls off the wet wool and stuffs it into the pack. Then she unbuttons the shirt and ties it around her bare waist. She slides the pack over her equally bare back and makes ready to finish the final quarter mile of hike. Jamie turns and marches back up to the cabin. Others had said that John marched to a different drummer. Well maybe she can march to one now too. Trespassers be damned! Spring rains too!

Chapter 10

More Questions Than Answers

Back at the cabin Jamie is thoroughly soaked, but exhilarated. Standing under the porch roof and watching the rain continue, she lays her hiking poles against the cabin, sets her backpack down and checks the pedometer. 6.3 miles. A good hike! Her watch reads a few minutes after 12:30, about three hours.

Maybe she could've gone a mile or two more, but Jamie can feel her legs beginning to tighten. They'll want a hot shower soon! At least they didn't give out when she was miles away on the other ridge, or when she had to make the last climb up from the creek. Still, she's glad she didn't have to test them while being chased by some wild man and his dog!

It strikes her then: why was she so exhilarated with her nudity, with feeling the touch of the world on her skin? Was there some primal zest – the way kids want to run naked and free – more powerful than the fear that should rationally have displaced it? Or maybe there was something even more feral, like maybe her hormones – with a man in the "room."

And while she needed to stop to catch her breath a few times, she didn't feel exhausted by the longest walk she's taken in many, many years. Maybe tomorrow she'll feel sore. But for now she's made her first trek along her A.T. (Her "Aspiration Trail," maybe?) a successful one, something she'll mark off on the map. John would be proud!

Thinking of her husband, she looks down to realize what a sight she would be to him now. She laughs thinking what he'd say about this soaking wet crazy woman standing half dressed in an April rain. Actually, she knows *exactly* what he'd say. Or, more to the point, *do*. He loved to cast Jamie as some Earth Goddess scantily clothed in the woods – and she loved how he'd lust for her. "Oh, John…John…John…" So many good times here. So many…

Jamie hugs herself and with a quick shiver now realizes both legs and breasts are ready for the pleasure of hot water rushing over them. But not before promising herself warm girlish dances in warm summer rains and...and...what?

More to explore. More to find. More to know. About this little part of the universe for sure. But also about this other universe within. Yes...a world apart. A world where someone lives that she wants to know better.

Brrrrrr!! Inside!!!

After her shower and a nap, Jamie wakes feeling a little stiff. But not as bad as she thought she might be. Still, if her masseur, Tomas, had been close by she might have asked for a rubdown. But the only rubbing she's going to have for the next year will be with her own two hands.

She dresses in jeans and another of John's flannel shirts. It's still raining. Maybe not quite as hard as when she got back to the cabin, but it feels like it's settling in for the day. Jamie settles in too. She starts a fire to chase away the afternoon damp and chill. Then she makes a bowl of soup and a sandwich. Setting them down on the large, low burl table between sofa and fireplace, she gets her A.T. map and spreads it across the rest of the table. Then she carefully marks off the day's hike: 4/17. 6.3 mi. About a mile and a half past a trail on the map that leads to Long Creek Falls. She wonders what that looks like. Tomorrow she'll try to go at least that far. But if her legs scream too much, she'll just make it shorter. There's no hurry. Just keep moving. That was something John liked to say, especially when times were tough. Just keep moving.

On the map her finger traces another six and a half miles. Over Hightower Gap. Horse Gap. Sassafras Mountain. Cooper Gap. Justus Mountain. She imagines those vistas, being able to see tens of miles over land where maybe some of her ancestors hunted deer and buffalo and where too, they may have been hunted by mountain lion.

Jamie looks ahead to the Georgia/North Carolina line. It's 75 miles from Springer Mountain. If she keeps up her pace she can be there in less than two weeks! Just keep moving.

She gets her journal and makes short notes:

April 17

Cool. Rain.

Hiked 6.3 miles on Vertical Reality. Back around to Trout.

About three hours.

Didn't see anything or anyone.

Boot prints and paw prints on far slope of Trout. Stopped about third of way down.

Feel good. Legs a little sore.

Tomorrow aim for another six miles.

Jamie finishes the afternoon checking on emails. She had promised everyone that she'd never go more than a week without answering. Thankfully there are only a few that really need attention. Stella asking whereabouts of some business correspondence. Her girls checking to make sure she's alive. A luncheon invitation. She clicks off and settles into her chair with a cheap novel while the rain drums a steady beat on the roof. The wind powers in crescendos, the rushing downspouts raise their voices when the wind draws its breath.

The next days are a disappointment. The rain doesn't let up. Jamie tries going out, but only manages a mile or two each time. The trails are muddy and slippery. Even with the poles she ends up on her butt more than once. The poncho keeps her fairly dry. But she can't see anything more than the few feet of trail ahead of her. It's all mud and roots and rocks. Not even a foreign footprint. Still, she marks progress in her journal.

April 18: More rain. Still cool. 1.8 mi.

April 19: Still raining. Maybe little less today. 1.4 mi.

April 20: Raining! Didn't want to go but did. 1.2 mi.

April 21: Rain on and off – mostly on. C-c-c-old. Damp. Miserable. Shivered through 1.3 mi. Ugh.

The next day marks the end of Jamie's first week at the cabin. What began with high hopes has already settled into an almost suffocating disappointment. The days are long, longer than she ever imagined without anyone to talk to. She finds herself checking the computer several times a day and feels an added disappointment when her mailbox isn't full of people needing her...replacing what just days ago was irritation at their dependency!

Her hiking has been a disappointment too. What she planned on covering in a day has taken four. She can't even take the Harley out for a diversion. She feels trapped in the very place she came to seek freedom. What is going on? No John and no Voice come to distract the attention of two uninvited guests: boredom and panic.

Jamie is too depressed to even try to hike. Instead she settles close to the fireplace with a mug of tea and her journal. She will try to write herself out of this funk.

April 22

My first week done.

It's been nothing but rain, rain and more rain.

And cold. The kind that bores into your bones and won't leave.

Trails too slippery.

Not going out today.

Maybe this whole thing is stupid.

Haven't seen a hint of sun in days. I need sun. When John started taking me to Florida for weeks on end in the winter I thought it was a silly luxury. No more.

I need sun. I need it here. I won't last long if this rain and cold don't get out of here.

No joy. No John. No Voice.

Just wet and cold.

Have got to shake this, but how?

Maybe all springs are like this, but I was inside and too busy to notice.

I've tried walking a different path each day. One foot in front of the other. Just keep moving like John said. But the pace is too slow. Frustrating.

I don't want to get so caught up in 'hiking' the A.T. that I forget why I came here in the first place.

I came here to find ME. I came here to build my own personal space. I came here to say goodbye to John. And say hello to this...this...whatever it is that speaks to me.

But what is this Voice? Is it real? Is it me? Is it someone else? God? God's counterpart? Where does the Voice come from? Inside my head? Or outside...from the Universe?

I wish I knew. Maybe if I keep writing I'll find something that helps me understand.

Keep moving. But I feel panicky. Like I'm running out of time. Missing something. Missing what? I don't know.

Jamie gets up and looks out the window.

The rain is letting up. But clouds have sunken down over the ridge so the world beyond her clearing has fallen behind a seamless and featureless shroud. She can see nothing. She hears nothing. Just silence and gloom. Maddening!!

Jamie shuffles back to her journal. Reads what she's written. Closes her eyes and imagines the warmth of the Florida beach where she used to walk. She raises her face to the sun in her mind's eye, feeling its rays embracing and warm. Then the image fades and she opens her eyes to the fading fire and again looks down at her journal. With a sigh she picks up her pen and starts again.

Ten Questions

1. *What do you do when your life doesn't fit?*

2. *How many times have I put on a dress that's too tight?*

3. *Am I really willing to try something different?*

4. *Do I want a life that fits comfortably into society?*

5. *Am I like a snake shedding skins of past lives as lover, wife, mother, grandmother?*

6. *What does it mean to 'get a life?'*

7. *What can I control? What can't I? What difference does it make?*

8. *Who was I when I met John? Who am I now? Who do I want to be?*

9. *Am I walking (running?) away from something? Or towards it? Both?*

10. *Am I moving out of something? Or into it?*

Lots of questions. And I'm here to find answers. I can't go back to the old ways. To the old me. If I do, I will die. Simple as that. End of story. Or start of a new one!

Jamie closes her journal with a vague feeling of satisfaction. Something came out. Even if only questions. It hurts. But a good hurt. Like a deep massage. A massage for the inside of her self.

The day is spent and so is she. She checks the door and turns out the living room light.

Walking into the bedroom, she disrobes, then turns down the covers. But before climbing into bed another light draws her to the window. The moon. Full and ripe. Somehow in the lost hours of writing, clouds had drawn away to reveal night's beautiful sky-goddess...one of the most sacred lights of all.

Moonlight casts a strong shadow of the shed against bare ground. The trees stand strong, etched against the night, their limbs now bursting with sap and reaching...reaching. It's as though other worlds, other lives dance there. Unseen. Unheard. Yet every bit alive as the rain-filled world that had brought her so low these last several days.

"Well, we'll see how it goes. Maybe I can answer those questions. Maybe you can help, too, Mister Man in the Moon! Or whoever's out there – or in here!"

"Yes we will," something in the distance answers back. What? She heard that distinctly.

Who said that? The Voice? The Man in the Moon?? Oh Jamie girl, time for bed!!

Her goose bumps aren't all from the room's chill. She jumps under the comforter and satin sheets. Maybe tomorrow the sun will shine again. Maybe.

She snuggles down and hears the first sound in days. "Whoooo. Whooo."

Her owl! "Whooo. Who are you?"

"I don't know. But I think I'm finding out."

"Whooo. Whooo."

Then a slightly different call.

"Whooooooah."

But Jamie is already drifted beyond the reach of caring.

"Whoooooah."

Someone answering the owl? A night watcher? Another voice in the dark?

Chapter 11
I Know I'm Heavy, Baby

"I'd like a double mocha cinnamon swirl latte. Grande. With 'Mount Everest' whipped cream. But make it lite. And you can skip the maraschino cherry. Yes, that's all. Oh! And that cheese Danish over there."

Jamie feels a little giddy and a tad girlish at indulging her weaknesses. Double mocha lattes and cheese Danishes are two of her favorites. It feels good to be out among people again. The cabin's isolation was almost getting to be more than she'd bargained for. Still she doesn't remember seeing this Starbucks when she stopped in Ram Cat Run the week before. And she doesn't remember the hamlet being busy like it seems to be today. But she feels some kind of comfort here, snuggled into a bit of nameless busy-ness.

"That'll be $6.01," the woman behind the counter says cheerily. "If you want to grab a seat, I'll bring your latte over." She reminds Jamie of a younger, happier version of Rosa, her assistant.

Jamie sits near the window. The grocery store is just up the block on the other side. She can see Cora, or is it Ellie Mae?, painting specials on the inside of the window. But she can't make out the businesses across the road. There's a blur of activity outside, people walking, cars and pickup trucks going back and forth. She's never seen Ram Cat so busy! Is this Saturday? She smiles to herself. Her week has shrunken to three days: Yesterday. Today. Tomorrow. She recalls once hearing that the Navajo language draws no tense distinction – so everything that was or will be *is*. Hmmmm, she wonders. Maybe there really *is* only today.

It's quiet inside the Starbucks. Empty, except for herself, Rosa and a man sitting at a small table across the room. He sits facing her and the doorway. His face is half concealed by a book he appears to be reading. Something about a fish made of water. Jamie has a vague sense he's watching her. Why would he do that? Maybe he's just waiting for someone. But the dog at his feet seems to be looking at her too. When did they start letting dogs into Starbucks? Jamie looks back out at the blur on the street.

Rosa brings her latte. It *was* her behind the counter! Maybe it's the light, but now she looks older. She sets the mug down carefully, making sure not to topple the mountain of whipped cream. Jamie mouths a "thank you." Strangely, she turns without saying a word. Jamie spoons into the whipped cream. Buried inside is a cherry! Didn't she order without? Oh well. Plop! Into her mouth. It tastes good. Naughty, actually. John always said it was OK to play with your food – in the bedroom! The tip of her tongue traces a line of cream from her lip as she smiles at the memory. Such good times with him...

The traffic on the street seems to have thinned out, even vanished. Maybe it was just a flurry of activity. She glances around to ask Rosa about that, but she's gone. Maybe into the back room for a minute. The man is still there. Reading. Watching? Even though most of his face is hidden, something looks familiar. The eyes? She looks back to the street. Jamie spoons out another dollop of whipped cream. Then dips into the warmth of the latte. Yum!

She came down from the cabin for some company. Days without end of rain and utter silence had really gotten her down. Even her journal had stopped becoming a refuge. She thought just being around people, maybe even a minute or two of conversation, would do her good. So when the morning had dawned brightly, she jumped on the Harley and sped to town. She parked it right in front of the Starbucks, although it doesn't seem to be there now. Maybe she parked down by the grocery and walked over. She cranes her neck to see, but it's not there. Probably behind that old pickup truck. Whatever...More whipped cream!

She brought her journal with her in case she had a chance to write some more. She pulls it out now and opens to the last entry. Strange...she doesn't recognize this handwriting. Large, childlike letters scrawl across the page.

Compliant   Complicit   Illicit

Where did these come from? This is not her handwriting. What the heck did they mean?

She tries to say the words quietly. "Compliant...complicit...illicit." Then below, almost too small to read, was her own handwriting again:

Mask up. Save yourself first.

Another slurp of whipped cream. Another cherry. *Another* cherry? What's going on here?

Jamie turns the page and tries to write. But her pen makes no marks. Out of ink? She didn't think so. She shakes and scratches it across the page to coax the ink back out. No luck. The other words, not hers, seem to undulate on the page. Jamie squints trying to refocus. Instead, she hears a voice. Not hers. Singsong. Childlike.

"When you eat the cherries, you can taste the illicit."

What? The voice continues. Innocent. Charming. Vexing! Jamie flashes back to the playground, girls with big teeth and pigtails taunting her to join in their jump-roping chant.

"And if you're compliant, you're also complicit."

Compliant. Complicit. Illicit.

Lick up the cream and then you can drink it!

Mask up! Mask up! Save the only one you can."

Grasping for anything real, Jamie pins down her latte with both hands as a shudder wracks through her body. The cup is empty. She nearly attacks her journal, swatting it closed and sweeping it into her bag in one motion. She doesn't want to sing the song. Compliant. Complicit. Illicit. Silly words. Who put them there? Not her!

It's time to go. Time to go. Time to go.

Save the only one you can.

She shakes it off and gets up to look for Rosa. She'd like to say goodbye before she goes. But Rosa's nowhere to be seen. Maybe next visit. Jamie turns towards the door and the man stationed at the entrance across from it. Something familiar? He looks at her. Then puts the book down calmly. It's John! His mouth opens.

"I....know...I'm...heavy...baby."

The words seem disembodied like a soundtrack gone very wrong. Jamie means to cry out expelling some long-denied wail of hurt and loss and of desperate confusion. But the din in her brain has robbed her of breath. Her mouth moves, but no sound can emerge. She lunges for the door trying to open it. It won't budge.

"I...know...I'm..." John calls again, but Jamie wants out. *Now.*

In desperation, Jamie takes one step back and throws herself through the window and onto the street. But instead of being showered by glistening daggers, it feels as though she stepped into a bath of pure light. It's blinding. She stands outside. But the street is gone. No glass. No blood. And all she can feel is just the light. And silence. She can *feel* the silence. She escaped and now she's...*free*!! She tries to look back... nothing...ahead...nothing. Nothing but light. And...peace? No. Not yet.

Jamie sits bolt upright in bed, the morning light streaming across her bed. A dream? A dream! She looks around trying to get her bearings. But, it was all so...real. Rosa. The latte. And John. John! It was him! Calling to her?

"John?" She calls into the air. "John!" She calls louder. No answer. She looks at the clock. It's late! After nine. Late!

Despite the air's coolness, Jamie throws back her covers almost as if willing the night, and the dream, away. Her body is bathed in sweat and quickly chills. She jumps out of bed and rushes into the living room and her journal. She wants to write down as much as she can remember.

Compliant Complicit Illicit

Taste illicit

Starbucks Rosa

Grocery store cherries

When you eat cherries taste illicit

Man dog who?

John I know I'm heavy baby

Jamie stares at the words. What do they mean? What did the dream mean? Anything?

Quickly she adds:

Lonely

People

Song child

Mask up

Starbucks

Happy relaxed scared

Free

Light   everywhere

Now she stares at these words trying to make sense of it all. Was that man the same one she saw on the trail? How could he be? Too far away to actually see him. But the dog seemed familiar. How? And then John! It *was* him! Looking right at her and speaking to her. She heard him! She was happy to see him. And she wasn't. Why? She'll try to sort all this out later. Maybe it means something. Maybe it doesn't. For now she's cold and wants a hot shower.

The water feels good over her body beating the last of her dream/ nightmare away. But when she closes her eyes the image of John staring at her over his book returns. She opens them again quickly! He frightened her. It couldn't have been him. Not really. Just a dream. Maybe because she misses him still.

"John, honey, you have to go." The words come tumbling out. And she's sorry as soon as she said them. Maybe because she knows it's true... too true. She tries again, leaning her face into the stream and concentrating on the day ahead. Now the image of sunlight floods her mind's eye. She is happy to see the sun again. Today will be perfect for a long afternoon hike. But first, she wants to go to town and get some groceries. Something more than soup and frozen dinners. If she's going to survive a whole year here, she's going to have to do some real cooking!

Dressing with jeans and flannel shirt – and bra for town – Jamie's anxious to get on her bike and into Ram Cat Run. Throwing on her backpack, she heads out the door and over to the Harley. She's glad to see the bike's clean. No more attacks from Mr. Cardinal. She looks to the limb where he'd sat and scolded her, or his 'rival', that morning. Gone. Hopefully he's bedded down with Mrs. Cardinal and making plans for their hatch.

Jamie straddles her ride and turns the key. She loves feeling it rumble to life. Even though it's been parked for a week, it starts easily as though anxious to be of service again. She revs the big V-twin a couple of times, pushes back the kickstand, stomps into first gear and easing the clutch, half-walks her machine across the opening to the drive.

In ten minutes, Jamie is pulling into Ram Cat and parking outside the grocery. She pulls her hair off her face and looks up the street remembering her dream. The hamlet is quiet like always. She looks across where the Starbucks might have been. But there isn't one. And now she laughs a little to herself. Why would there be a Starbucks in a sleepy little place like Ram Cat?

She walks into the grocery. Cora is behind the counter writing on a pad. She looks up at Jamie and her eyes widen. "Good mornin'. Didn't know you were still here."

Cora, Jamie is learning, is nothing if not direct.

"Good morning to you," Jamie says shutting the door behind her. "Surprised to see me?"

"Why shor'! Not used to seeing you twice in the same week."

Jamie smiles back at the woman as she walks closer to the counter. "On my calendar it's been a whole week since I was here. And I might be back again in less than that next time!"

"Why? You sucked up that whole carton already? Them things ain't good for you! I only keep 'em 'cause people want 'em and there's nowhere else close by to get 'em."

Jamie laughs a little at this and replies, "No, I'm not here for more cigarettes. Truthfully, I've only smoked four or five. Not even sure why I asked for a whole carton."

"Well, you can't bring 'em back! You bought 'em. They're yours."

Now Jamie laughs again. "Oh, no! That's not why I came today!"

Cora straightens up and looks more closely at the taller, older woman. She, too, is wearing jeans and a flannel shirt but a couple sizes smaller than Jamie. Jamie can see she's eyeing her up and decides to ignore Cora's probing. Besides, she has nothing to hide!

Though young enough to be Jamie's daughter Cora looks older than her years, which Jamie thinks to be early forties. Maybe it's from having borne the burdens of keeping a store together and raising a child by herself. Jamie guesses Cora is used to a world taking things from her and not giving much in return. She wants to like this woman. Jamie pulls a shopping list from her pocket.

"You want some help with that?" Cora asks gesturing. Then, without waiting for an answer, "Ellie! Up here! Miz Bar-lo needs some help!"

"Oh no, really, I don't mind..."

Ellie Mae appears from the backroom, wiping her hands across her coveralls.

"I got that all straightened up, Mama. Hi, Missus Barlow!"

"Good," her mother answers. "Here, take her list and get what she needs." Cora pulls the list from Jamie and hands it to Ellie Mae.

"It's not all that much, really."

Ellie looks it over and starts reading, "Baked beans. Two cans. Creamed corn. Two cans. Carrots. You want the fresh ones? Pound of bacon. Mama got some nice thick-cut in yesterday, you want that? Loaf of bread. Whole wheat. Four apples. Pork loin. How big?"

Cora jumps in, "There's a real nice piece back there. About two pounds. Bring her that one." Ellie disappears down the aisles with a basket.

Turning to Jamie, she continues, "I try to do a good job with my meats. Folks here know I give 'em quality and don't charge an arm 'n' leg for 'em. Helps me from losin' customers to the Giant Eagle down in Uniontown."

Jamie replies, "I imagine it must be a constant thing trying to keep the store going."

"Tell me about it! You want some coffee?"

Pretty sure it's not Starbuck's, Jamie smiles and says brightly, "Yes, I would! I got up late and headed down here without making my breakfast."

Cora pours from the coffeemaker behind the counter. A new mug for Jamie and a refill for herself.

"Black?"

"Yes! Perfect."

"Missus Barlow, you want the Van Kamp's or the A and P brand?" Ellie's voice rings out from the back of the third aisle.

"The Van Kamp's 'll be fine, Ellie! Thank YOU!" Jamie is liking this a lot, a reminder of how much she really has missed being around people in just this first week at the cabin."

Cora eyes her steadily as both sip from their mugs. "You fixin' to be here a while?"

Jamie looks back at her, measuring quickly how much she wants to confide in this woman who seems intent on fast becoming her friend, or at least knowing her business!

"I'm planning to stay a year."

"A year! Up *there*? By yourself?" Cora seems truly impressed. Or just amazed.

"Yes. John and I always loved coming here. But usually only for weekends. I wanted to try being here for an extended period of time. Maybe I'll only make it another week! But I hope it's a lot longer."

"What're you gonna do?" Cora asks genuinely interested now.

"I've started doing a lot of hiking." Jamie notices Cora's eyes widened as she said this. "And I want to continue the writing I've been doing for several years now."

Jamie sees that Cora is studying her closely now and decides to plunge ahead with something close to a confession.

"Losing John was hard. But afterwards I knew some of the emptiness I felt was not being his wife anymore. People looked at me differently, almost like I'd been the one who died. And then I realized my whole life had been being somebody else. A wife. A mother. A *grand*mother! And before that a girlfriend. Or a daughter. So I decided now was the time to be me. Or find out who I am. I hope."

Jamie looks back at Cora for some hint of understanding. And she can see Cora's trying to take it all in, yet not quite absorbing. "Well, I guess there's all kinds of lost souls trying to find themselves, not that I had that trouble myself."

Now it's Jamie's turn to have trouble taking in Cora's words, never having thought of herself as a "lost soul." Cora fills in the pause quickly.

"Of course, not sayin' you're one of them lost souls, Miz Barlow! But summertime I've seen my share passing through. Usually college kids in some beat up ol' car tryin' to find the state park. Or once in awhile someone hitchhikin' to God knows where. Not like they're gonna find any good rides around here! Lucky to get one to Uniontown!"

Then she adds, almost wistfully, "Never understood why someone felt like they had to go clear cross country just to remember their name or who their family was."

As Jamie considers replacing Cora's "remember" with "forget," Ellie Mae comes around the corner with a box full of Jamie's groceries and sets it on the counter.

"Here ya go, Missus Barlow! I think I got everything!"

The three women peer in. "It looks like you got everything, Ellie. Thank you much!"

Cora reaches in for the pork loin. "Ellie, this isn't the one I had in mind. This is a three-pounder. Look back there for a two-pounder. I think it's a little better cut, too."

She hands the meat to her daughter and the girl walks it back to the meat section.

"You didn't have to do that, Cora."

"Three pounds is a lot if you're just cookin' for one, Missus Barlow..."

"Jamie! I thought we settled that last time," Jamie says smiling back at Cora. "That'll be the last *Missus Barlow* I want to hear in this store!"

"Well, alright...*Ja*-mie." Cora smiles now too and Jamie can see she seems pleased with her insistence on first names. "I just didn't want any of that good pork going to waste and you feeling like you spent money you shouldn't have."

"Is this the one, Mama?" Ellie Mae hands a smaller piece to her mother who nods in satisfaction.

"Yes, that's the one I wanted." Then remembering who the customer was, she hands it to Jamie.

"Does that look alright to you? You can see it's a nice cut, not too much fat. That should roast up fine."

"Yes, that looks wonderful! And you're right, it's a better size for me. I'll cook it tonight with some potatoes and carrots."

"I didn't see any potatoes in that box. If you got any leftovers up there from last year, they probably got potatoes of their own by now. How 'bout some onions?"

Jamie starts laughing, "Great! Forgot to add those to my list. My backpack's going to be plenty full."

Cora turns to Ellie, "Get Miz Bar-, Jamie, a couple potatoes from that bag that ripped open yesterday. And onions too." As Ellie disappears into the back room, Cora turns back to Jamie, "They're good Idahos. No sense letting them go to waste."

Before Jamie can say 'thank you,' Cora leans close and says quietly, "Listen, you be careful up there. A stranger's been comin' in here since last fall. Has a dog." Jamie hopes Cora doesn't see the shiver that just went up her spine.

"Doesn't have a car or nothin'. Just walks in, gets what he needs. Pays and goes. Polite. Doesn't say much. Sheriff knows and is tryin' to keep an eye on him. Thinks he might be living up there in your hills."

Ellie returns with the potatoes and onions. "Thank you, Ellie." Unsure whether to continue this part of the conversation, Jamie looks at Cora for direction.

"She knows."

"Know what, Mama?"

Cora hesitates a second. "That man who comes in here with his dog."

Jamie watches Ellie's eyes get wide and a smile break out. "I think he's cute, Mama."

"He is NOT cute, Ellie Mae! And you have no mind talkin' about things you know nothin' about!"

Jamie wants to agree with Cora, but remembering her own daughters' teenage years she's not so sure. And looking at Ellie, she sees the familiar problem of a girl coming to grips with a woman's body. In her mid-teens Ellie is already her mother's height or a fraction above. Her ripeness and promise is a contrast to her mother's early middle age.

Cora turns back to Jamie. "She's gotten total boy crazy the last year or so."

Jamie smiles back at her, then at Ellie who's looking at her for some support. "I know what you're saying. I went through that ten years ago with my girls. Ellie, I'll tell you something my mother told me and I told my daughters: Men won't pay full price if the sign says for 'Free.'"

Cora laughs at this warning in language she knows. Jamie can see Ellie is still trying to sort it out.

"My boyfriend, Billy, he pays most times when he takes me to the movies," she responds hopefully. The older women just exchange knowing looks.

Jamie thinks it's about time to get back to the cabin. She wants to hike, although she's certain now that the man she saw and the one who's been coming into the Ram Cat are one and the same. She'll think about extra precautions when she gets back.

"How much do I owe you, Cora?"

Cora speeds through the register while Jamie and Ellie watch. "That'll be nineteen forty-six. 'Taters are on me."

Jamie hands her a twenty and then eyes the rack of jerky on the counter. She had told John once this was the only store she knew where were twelve flavors of "chew" and only one of Tums! Same with the jerky it looks like. All sorts of choices! She pulls a pack of Slim Jim's off. Cora's eyes widen slightly at a choice she wouldn't have expected Jamie to make.

"That's another seventy-nine cents." Jamie hands her another dollar and Cora makes change.

As Jamie loads her backpack, "I'll be back next week for more. And I'll let you know how I did with that roast!"

"We're glad for your business, Jamie. It's been nice talking with you," Cora adds sincerely. Jamie can feel the woman warming to her and is glad for it. "If you see that man on your property, you call Sheriff Bob right away! He'll make sure to find him and have him hauled away for vagrancy."

"Thank you for the warning. I'll let you know next week!" Jamie swings the backpack over her right shoulder and heads towards the door. Then she stops and turns.

"Cora, has there ever been a Starbucks in Ram Cat?"

"A what?"

"Starbucks. Coffee shop chain."

Cora looks at her confused. "Long as I can remember," she turns and pats the urn behind her, "this has been the only 'coffee shop' ever been in Ram Cat! Why you askin'?"

"Oh, it's nothing. Memory's confused. Getting old! See you next week!" She turns as another customer walks in.

"Bye, Miz Barlow!" Ellie calls after her. Jamie smiles one more time and steps into the midday sunshine.

Chapter 12
Jake

Back at the cabin Jamie unloads groceries and plans the afternoon's hike. She's glad for the chance to get to know Cora and Ellie a little better. She's also concerned about Cora's warning, certain now that the man she saw and the one who's been coming into the store are one and the same. Still, the sheriff's onto him. If she sees him again on her property, she'll report him. Maybe. Maybe she'll also tuck her cell phone into a pocket hoping it works if he, or something else, causes her trouble out on one of the trails. Of course, it could be weeks before anyone could find her carcass if they didn't know where to look. She adds an entry to her journal below her notes about the dream – and what a dream! – telling where she's headed today.

Today: Sunset, Turnpike Trails

Taking cell phone 412-987-3344

Cora warned about stranger

Tall with dog

Think he's same one I saw

Sheriff knows

Not afraid

I am not afraid

I am not!!

Satisfied with her declaration, Jamie adds a little map showing the cabin and the trails marked clearly. Just in case. "It's silly. But if anything happens at least I left a record. Make it easier for the sheriff to find what's left of me, John!" Jamie echoes John's gallows humor she'd learned to love.

Jamie then stuffs a lunch into her hiking pack. Pepper jack cheese. Bread. A Macintosh apple. Water bottle. She grabs her poles, slaps on the pedometer and is ready to go. Today will be her longest and most difficult hike. But she wants to do it, despite the slight apprehension lingering from Cora's warning.

Sunset Trail runs off to the west on a slight downgrade. The day has warmed nicely and Jamie breaks a sweat within the first couple hundred yards. She's glad she left the sweater behind. The sun makes her squint and Jamie loves how the sunlight feels on her face. She imagines browning to an adolescent tan later during the summer months, her hair highlighted *naturally.*

Jamie remembers a childhood photo taken by her father when she was seven or eight on a family camping trip in another run of the Alleghenies a hundred miles to the north. She squints back to the camera and sun, like today, her tow-head blonde hair cut short, head cocked and right arm raised to block the sun and see her father better. In her one-piece suit she was already beginning to sprout the legs and arms that would define her later height. Her smile shows her gap-toothed innocence.

The photo had become one of her father's favorites, so he said, and therefore one of hers too. He'd had it enlarged and framed. It had occupied a central place on one of her parents' living room bookshelves, next to others of her brother and sister long after the children were grown and gone from home. When he died, it disappeared with the rest. She had always meant to ask her mother about them, but by then she was in the middle of raising her own children and, truth be told, she was afraid to. Afraid? Yes, it seemed. But why? It was like a creaky sound while alone in the house. It was a question she was always afraid to broach...with anyone. Even John.

When her mother died, she asked her brother one day when they were sorting and packing family belongings. He couldn't remember the photo. Later she asked her sister, but she answered somewhat distractedly that she thought their mother had given it to Jamie. *Did it matter to no one else?*, she wondered. Now as she continues climbing another ridge Jamie feels the sadness and loss of that moment. Moments, really. Those individual experiences that, years later, one looks back on and feels the broken bonds: sees a family that no longer was.

Jamie yearns to be that girl again. To be smiling back at her father, trying to please him and the camera. To feel the hot of the sun, the cold of the lake. To squeal when he picked her up and let her do a backward somersault off his chest into the water. A bead of sweat, no, a tear slides innocently across her left cheekbone and curls towards her lip. She recalls there are five kinds of tears, each chemically identifiable with its emotional well. Her tongue reaches for it, and wonders at its flavor. Jamie keeps climbing.

She reaches a stand of trees that protects a gathering of ground pine. The cover looks like miniature pine trees each about two inches tall. Jamie bends over to look at the small needles that form a circular pattern. Each "tree" is actually part of a larger organism, its roots connected to neighboring runners. Jamie tries not to step on them, as their green carpet has crept onto this part of the trail. Hank told her and John how people here made them into Christmas wreaths. Maybe Cora knows how. She'll try to remember to ask next time she's at the store. Maybe they can make a couple of them together next fall.

Jamie climbs on to where the ridge crests and bends to the south. Here is a substantial outcropping that she and John named Sunset Point. They watched many sunsets here, panoramic spectaculars ending long summer days. The view stretched out miles and miles across a valley and to another ridge and another ridge beyond that. John said he could fantasize being in the West with a vista like this.

Hank and his crew constructed a deck large enough to wheel the Gator onto. It includes a railing and benches built into it. Jamie slides her backpack off and sits on one. A perfect spot for lunch and a rest. She looks at the pedometer: 3.1 miles! Longer than she would have remembered! A good start for today. The distance ahead was greater than what lay behind, but most would be downhill. As she pulls out her lunch, Jamie looks down and sees initials carved into the bench.

J B
+
J B

Weathered now, they'd carved those the first summer this trail had been opened, their third at the cabin. John had enjoyed leaving their names behind in odd places. There were others scattered across the property. Some obvious. Some not. Jamie runs her fingers over the letters thinking again of the many times they'd Gatored up here. She looks down the bench and sees the less sure scrawls of her grandchildren's initials. One afternoon, they had insisted on adding theirs as soon as they'd seen John's and Jamie's. She wonders if the next owners of the property will wonder who these people are, or care. But maybe they'll add their own carvings of immortality.

The view across the valley to the next ridge is beautiful. She can see where it's starting to green up along the stream that winds through, making its way south to join others flowing on to the Youghiogheny. Higher up the green fades. On the ridge, miles away, only dabs of color can be seen. In a few weeks when the leaves are out, the stream will be mostly hidden, betraying itself only when sunlight catches it just right. The ridge will be hidden, too, the few roads slicing between and across its eastern face along with the equally few houses.

Jamie thinks on another summer day in two or three months she'll plan to spend the better part of it here. She'll bring her journal and write. Maybe a letter to John. Maybe one to her grandchildren. Maybe one to her daughters, too. Maybe one to herself.

But for now lunch is over and she needs to get going before she cools down to a chill! A breeze has started in from the west and she realizes it's warm enough to hike without a sweater but maybe not to sit around and dawdle.

Jamie stretches her legs and lower back. Oof! She sat too long and they've tightened up. A few more bends and Jamie grabs her poles. "Miles to go before I sleep," Jamie says, calling up a familiar line from a Frost poem. A sigh and a push off down the trail. Sunset follows the ridge for a few more miles. It then loops and connects to other trails that come back eventually to the cabin. That loop is several miles longer than she wants to – or can – finish today.

However, about a quarter mile down, another trail – Turnpike – cuts in and leads more directly back to the cabin. It's still about four miles, but she remembers it as fairly flat most of the way. John had named it Turnpike because it became the shorter and faster way back home. Actually, it was originally a logging road and so it's also wider and smoother than the trails Hank and the others cut through other sections of their property.

By the time Jamie gets to this turnoff, her muscles have warmed up again and stretched some. She knows she's going to be really sore by the time she gets back, but it will be that kind of 'good' sore of a body responding to getting into shape. A shower and a glass of wine are already calling: good motivators for a couple hours more hiking. Turnpike Trail leads through an immature second and third growth forest with openings here and there where trees had not yet recaptured their rightful places. It's rutted where years of trucks and tractors had scarred the forest loam.

As with other parts, Jamie and John could only imagine what these forests looked like originally. Huge, ancient stands of hardwoods creating canopies broken only by descending streams and rivers. As she walks along looking at maples and oaks and beech – six, eight, even twelve inches in diameter – Jamie tries to imagine their ancestors standing two, three, four feet and more! Limbs more robust than the whole trees here now. She and John had talked often of preserving the property so that their descendants a hundred years hence might get to see some of these trees approach middle age. *That* would be a legacy! With John gone, the responsibility is now hers alone. She would do her best.

Jamie walks about a mile on Turnpike where it now takes a sharp bend to the south. A quarter of a mile farther the old road splits a pine forest. These trees stand uniformly apart. It's clear they were planted as quick growth replacements for the original hardwoods. Someone planned to harvest these too, probably soon, judging from their size. But now they just continue to grow, many of their lower branches interlocking, so that this forest within a forest has become dense, almost impenetrable. Jamie pauses and peers down the rows into darkness. She breathes in the pine smell and relishes the special quiet of their quiet sanctuary.

She closes her eyes and another scene from that childhood movie, "The Wizard of Oz," pops into her head. The one where Dorothy, Toto, Scarecrow and Tinman enter another deep forest wary of its surroundings. "Lions and tigers and bears, oh my!" She laughs to herself. Jamie turns and looks the other way into the pine darkness and calls out "Lions and tigers and bears, oh my!" And again, "LIONS AND TIGERS AND BEARS, OH MY!!" Oh, Lord, if her daughter and grandchildren saw her acting this way now! But she wants to feel like a girl again! And why not?

She remembers how scary this movie was the first time she saw it. How she started watching it on the floor in their family's living room with a bowl of popcorn for her and her brother (their youngest sister not yet into the world). And how she ended up crawled into her father's lap, almost too frightened to watch another scene. How her brother teased her for being scared. But then how the flying monkeys sent even him to the security of the family sofa.

Years later, when she had become a mother and her girls were old enough to watch, she remembered how amazed she was when Dorothy landed in Munchkinland and stepped out into a world of blazing colors! She had always seen the movie on her parents' black and white TV set. Her wonder was lost on her daughters who had known only color television. She remembers too the mixture of relief and disappointment – was that the right word? – when her girls weren't frightened by the Wicked Witch or flying monkeys or even the Wizard himself. Was that just her? Or had their generation grown numb to both wonders and horrors? She just wasn't sure...she makes a mental note to write down this memory when she gets back.

Coming out of the pines, Turnpike again turns to the east and starts a gentle slope down. A rock outcropping crowds the right side of the road. She steps past it and....and... a MAN! THAT man! Sitting on a rock as though waiting for her. Jamie lets out a little scream. She stops right in her tracks, pulling her walking poles against her in self-defense. She stares at him. He looks back at her. She doesn't know what to do. At a glance she can see he is one of the scariest looking men she's ever seen. Dirty. Long black hair parted in the middle, hanging below his shoulders. Worn boots. Threadbare jeans. Flannel shirt open at the chest, folded up along muscular arms.

She continues to stare expecting him to lunge. She'll do her best to fight him off, stab him with her poles. And for some crazy reason her mind already jumps to the newspaper headline: "Decaying Body Found On Trail. Believed Missing Barlow Widow." Defiantly she says in the loudest voice she can summon, "Stay where you are!!"

"OK." He replies calmly. Too calmly.

"I mean it!"

"I believe you."

"Who....who are you?? What are you doing on my property?? I have a gun!" Jamie spits these out in rapid fire as though the faster she talks the braver she feels and the easier it might be to fight him off.

He smiles at this last bit of bravado, which unnerves her some. "I won't move an inch."

Jamie steps slowly to the far side of the road and a bit to the downhill side as though it might give her advantage if she has to make a run for it.

The man leans back and crosses his arms. A half smile creases the right side of his face. Good teeth.

Just then Jamie's bluster abruptly dissolves with the menace of large black beast charging into her peripheral view – she flashed on the byline: "Woman mauled beyond recognition by dog or bear." As it bolts to within six feet, Jamie covers her face, gulps one last breath, and whirls away, ready to scream.

"ARF!"

She tries to scream again. But nothing comes out. Jamie half turns and lowers one arm in time to see her attacker drop to its haunches and with a tilted head, offer a querulous "Arf?" The dog, a lab mix of some sort, is panting with smiling eyes and a tongue too big for its mouth.

"Easy, Job." The dog looks at his master and wags his tail. Then back at Jamie. Jamie looks at him still waiting for a lunge. She's a goner for sure now. 'Say your prayers, Jamie.'

"It's OK. He won't bite. Unless I tell him to."

Now she looks back at the man. He's smiling. What kind of smile is that? It looks friendlier than it ought to be. Maybe she can stall him with conversation. Maybe…

"Job?"

"Yes. That's his name"

"Like in the Bible Job?"

"Yep. Like in the Bible."

"Why did you name him that?"

The dog, sensing they were talking about him, decides to stretch out on the trail.

The man laughs and says, "Because of all the trials his master puts him through!"

The stranger has a way about him that makes Jamie relax a little. She shouldn't. But she does.

"Like killing people?" She tries to sound glib, but the ebb of adrenalin has left her with a tremor causing one pole to jump from her hand. A spastic attempt at its recovery swats the staff off the trail and into the brush.

"Oh, he's never killed anybody. Scared a few deer. Maybe he'd try if some crazy woman pulled a gun and tried to shoot me." He smiled as he said this.

"Who said I'd try to shoot you?"

"Well, you said you had a gun. I guess that means you intend to use it if you have to."

"Who said I intended…" Jamie catches herself not wanting to surrender her bluffed advantage. "Well, I will if I have to!" she tries to finish, aiming for dangerous but nailing hapless.

"And I don't doubt that you would."

Jamie now begins to notice that he sounds better than he looks. He might look rough, but there is some polish to him. She wonders where that might come from.

There's a pause. Both look at each other, then they glance at the dog which is already dozing as the humans chatter. When she looks back, her heart jumps again! The man has pulled out a large knife and an apple that looks a lot like the ones at Cora's store.

He sees her alarm. "I was just stopping for a bite of lunch. Do you mind?"

"No. No, I don't mind," Jamie answers carefully eying the knife. It looks like the hunting knives she's seen Hank and the others carry.

In a couple quick moves the apple is stemmed, cored, and sliced. Before he pops one in, he extends one to Jamie resting easily on the blade. "Would you like one?"

Luring her forward. The moment of truth.

"No. No thanks. I just a…"

Then she changes her mind not knowing why. A test. Her last?

"Well, OK. I guess I will."

She steps across the road and reaches slowly for the apple, lifting it carefully from the blade. Then she steps back to her side as she puts it in her mouth. It tastes good.

The man smiles and lifts a wedge to his mouth.

"Looks like one of Cora's apples." Trying to keep her mind off her own vulnerability, Jamie tries again with small talk.

"That her name? Woman from the store in town?"

"Yes."

"Yep. From her store. Seems nice enough. Little scared of me. Can't say I blame her. Don't always look my best when we stop in."

Jamie summons her courage again. Their eyes meet. She wants to get a good look at him. In case by some small chance she does get away and gets a chance to report him to the Sheriff.

"What's your name?"

"Jake."

"Short for Jacob?"

"Yep."

"Another Bible name."

He laughs softly. "Yes. My dad was a preacher and he wanted to give me a proper Christian name."

"What's yours?"

Jamie is startled by this. She really hadn't expected this kind of conversation before being attacked. "What?"

"Your name. Or would you prefer I just call you the one I decided on after seeing you a few times?"

"What?!" That last sentence sent a shiver down her spine. She felt somehow exposed. Violated.

"I've seen you and your husband on that little green jeep. Seems like you were always yakking about something or other. So I decided to call you 'Magpie.'"

"Magpie?!" Jamie almost bursts out laughing. "Why would you call me that? Isn't that a bird?"

"Yes. One that just yak yak yaks." Now Jake is smiling with genuine amusement.

"I don't talk *all* the time! And how would you know that anyhow? Do you snoop on our lives as well as live on our property?" Jamie tries to summon some indignation, feeling roles reversing slightly.

"And my name is Jamie Barlow. John Barlow is my husband. Maybe you've heard of him."

"No I never heard of him. Where is he?"

"He's dead."

That sentence stunned both into silence.

Jake's voice softens after a minute. "And I'm very sorry for your loss. He seemed like a brave man to not let being crippled keep him from coming out here."

Now Jamie stares hard at Jake. This is much more of a conversation than she'd ever imagined from this man. But now all she wants is to be done with this unwelcome interview. Just make her getaway. As though she really could ever get away. At least get closer to her phone. And her gun.

"I...I...have to go."

"OK. Sorry. Didn't mean to upset you."

"Yes." She thought better of saying what she really thought. "I understand. But...I have to go."

Jamie looks over at Job. She'll have to walk past him to continue on down the trail.

She looks back at Jake.

"OK. See you. Do you mind if I stay here a bit longer?"

Jamie wasn't sure if he meant here on the rock. Or here on her property. Right now she didn't care.

"No. It's fine."

She starts moving away. Job sits up, tail wagging, wondering if this new human was joining them on their hike.

"Come here, Job."

"Thank you." She gives them a slight wave and takes a step towards home. She hopes.

She takes another step. Then another.

Then Jake calls out, "What are those poles? You cross-country skiing without snow?"

She stops and turns. "Walking poles. They help me keep my balance."

Jake chuckles. "You don't need to *buy* a walking stick. Just pick a branch up and shave off the bark. And if you need more than one, you shouldn't be out here alone."

Jamie notices Jake's walking stick...beautifully carved with a hawk on top with his wings spread in flight, and maybe a snake on the side. "What's the difference? A pole? A stick? They all do the same things."

"No, Magpie, they don't. Your poles are man-made and you can't feel the ground with them. A walking stick is from nature and you can feel the earth as you walk along. Not just with your feet, but in your hands also. And, ONE walking stick. Not two. Learn balance."

"Well, I really have to go now."

"OK. Well, nice meeting you...Jamie...Barlow."

"Yes. You too...Jake."

She turns.

"See you again?" he asks.

"Maybe." She answers without turning back.

"And get rid of those poles!"

She doesn't answer this gibe.

'Maybe indeed.' She says to herself. 'Just keep walking Jamie girl. One step. One step. Don't look back. You're going to make it. You're going to make it.' She's sweating profusely now. From fear and exercise. She does look back after five minutes. But he's not following. At least that she can see.

Jamie relaxes a little, but not completely. She finishes this hike in a half sprint. And slows only when the cabin's in sight. Then, looking one last time, she darts inside, closes the door and leans against it to catch her breath.

"I made it."

Chapter 13

I'm...not...heavy

Jamie is physically depleted and emotionally drained. Tired. The kind of tired that comes from exertion, compounded by the fear of confronting that man – Jake – and his dog. She looks out the window one more time just to make sure she hasn't been followed back to the cabin. Not that it would make any difference. She knows he knows where to find her.

Promising to practice with the shotgun tomorrow, Jamie coaxes herself out of her worry-closet. Right now she just wants a shower, to read, write in her journal, and have a Jack – in that order. Today she ran straight into her fear and faced it: That dark trespasser and his hungry black dog. Either or both could have made sport of her. She'd felt afraid, yes but *angry* too – pumped for a fight.

Jamie felt...a warrior inside? And this warrior felt ready. Today was a beginning. It will not be her last bout. She will face it again. And again if she has to. Until there is no more fear. Of strangers. Or of even darker things. She will do what she has come to do. Alone. No white knights to the rescue for Xena any more.

The shower feels like a lover's embrace. Water cascades over newly-taut muscles relaxing slowly into a satisfied ache. The pounding from the showerhead slowly settles the pounding in her heart. Snuggled in sweats, with two fingers of Old #7, Jamie settles into her chair to read the A.T. trail guide. She gulps at the whiskey anticipating its familiar jolt. The alcohol helps her slip from this day, this place, 'til her imagination leaps from these Laurel Mountains to their Smoky cousins hundreds of miles to the south.

Over the past two weeks of hiking, she's made good progress up the Trail. Adding the miles in her journal, Jamie has "walked" more than halfway to North Carolina. In the guide, her fingers trace over each map's details. She tries to feel the stone and clay, the gravel, the grasses and vegetation underfoot; to "see" the trail before her: where it climbs to sweeping vistas and tumbles into sleepy ravines. Some of the names in the guide speak to the area's violent history. Slaughter Gap. Blood Mountain.

"God," she thinks wryly to herself, "maybe someone will rename one of our trails after I get murdered out there." She reads about Blood Mountain. Site of a battle. Not between whites and Indians. Between Creeks and Cherokees. Cherokees...the tribe of her mother. With the blood of her great-grandmother – her own blood. Not talked about by later generations ashamed of their less-than-full Anglo-Saxon-blood.

As a child Jamie had found this great-grandmother's photo at the bottom of a box of family memorabilia. She remembers asking her mother who this was. "Someone you don't need to know about," she said at first, trying to hush the child's curiosity. Then, after repeated questions, her mother relented with a sigh that seemed to release the weight of generations. She said more quietly, "She was my grandmother. My mother's mother. She was an Indian. Cherokee. But we never talked about her. I never knew her. I remember my mother telling me she was beautiful. A princess."

"A *real* princess?" Jamie remembered asking.

I don't know, honey. Maybe she was..."

"She looks beautiful, Mama."

"Yes...but that's enough. She's gone." As her mother's memory ended, so did the conversation.

Young Jamie stared at the picture. Seated, the mid-nineteenth century woman gazed back at the mid-twentieth century girl. Dressed in blouse and floor length skirt, she looked like the women of her time. Her hair pulled back and tied. But her skin was dark, her cheekbones high. She sat erect and had the formal, severe look of early photographs.

It was her eyes that stayed with Jamie for years after that brief conversation. Dark. Commanding. Unashamed of *her* history. Or, better yet, *unafraid* of it. And unafraid to be *who* she was. Maybe she *was* a princess.

From time to time afterwards, Jamie would stare at her own face, its blond hair and light-colored eyes not giving a hint of that more colorful heritage. Especially in summer when she tanned darkly herself, she would run a finger over her cheekbones searching to feel the resemblance, a great-grandmother reaching through the generations to touch her.

Jamie drifts out of memory and returns to today. She has that photograph somewhere. Back home. She made sure to find it when she looked among her mother's things when she had died. She wishes she had it with her now.

Leafing through the trail guide. But thinking other thoughts. A sip. The warmth of the mid-spring sun spread across the living room feels good. Almost toasty. She likes the quiet. Peaceful...Jamie's head falls back, heavy. Her arms relax, and the map drops from her hand.

She finds herself in yet another place. A woods. Surrounded by ancient trees. Older by centuries than the second growth she knows at the cabin. The path she was on led deeper into the forest. Worn. Made by animals or humans? She can't tell. But the forest commands quiet. She walks. Silent and respectful. Proud that not even her footsteps can be heard. Like an Indian. Like a *Cherokee.* She stops by a shag bark hickory that crowds the trail. Its roots rising six inches above the worn dirt. Jamie runs her hands over the bark. She tries to look up to the crown. But the top is beyond her sight. She tries stretching her arms around it. But they don't cover even half of the massive trunk. Why is she hugging this tree?

Then a man steps from behind the other side! The man from the trail. Jake. She tries to scream, but can't. She backs away from the tree as he steps around it and stands imposingly within her space. He seems even taller than he did when they first met.

She tries again to scream, to scare him away. Instead, he is the first to speak.

"What are *you* doing here? What *are* you doing here, Magpie?" he demands accusingly. His words seem to echo through the forest. "Magpie...Mag...Ma." Breaking the ancient silence, threatening a lifetime secret. Yet the forest embraces them. It leans forward, listening for her reply.

Jamie – Magpie – launches into an avalanche of words. She can't hear what she's saying as usual. Often what she really meant to say is even in there...in among all those words. Words of apology. Of explanation. Of feelings held in. Fears confronted. Talkingtalkingtalking. Like a magpie. It may be a good way to talk. Open the floodgates and let it flow. Let it burst. Let it pour all over the walls that have held it all in. "I don't know. I don't know. I want to be. I don't know."

Jake stares impatiently and asks again as though he hasn't heard a word she's said, "What are you being here?"

"I don't know. I have no idea. I just know I need to be here. I feel called." Called. Calling. Calling. Calling.

Is he mocking her? Mocking the Magpie? She looks up towards the sky, but all she can see are tree limbs and branches and leaves. One green canopy. Here and there points of light strike through. Jamie holds her arms out and starts to twirl, just as she did as a girl. "I just need to be here. Here. Be. I just need." The green becomes a swirl closing out the rest of the sunlight. "A-gi-li-si. A-gi..."

Jamie awakes with a start. Oh! Just a dream! She starts to relax, regaining her surroundings. But the strange sounds hang in wisps caught on the threshold between dreams and the day. Panic? No. Urgency? Yes!

She reaches for her journal and begins to write, to somehow complete the dialogue with Jake in her dream:

"I don't know. I have no idea. I just know I needed to be here. I felt called. ahgeeleesee"

What I said in my dream. To Jake. Man living on our property. Asked me what I was doing there. I should have asked him!

Maybe it seems like time for a 'walkabout' like the Aborigines do. When it's time they do it. They can't tell you when it's time. They know it's time. Just go and see what you find. See what you see. See what finds you outside the box you live in.

I've gotten caught up in all the doing. None of the being.

Dream message: See what you see, Jamie. See what you find. See what finds you.

The sun has slipped behind the hills. Evening has come on. This day feels more like a dream than the dream itself! Then one more urge to write. Something else from the day. Memories pulled out from deep inside. Pen moves effortlessly across paper. Words flow. Sentences congeal.

Remember when you took my picture

The one where I could barely see you

Because the sun got in the way

And I had to close my eyes real tight?

That was your favorite,

I remember. You said

I looked like Shirley Temple

And I smiled because of you and the sun.

You said "Stand still!" and I did.

Holding one arm up so the sun

Wouldn't blind me while you stood

Holding the camera and said "Cheese!"

Then I twirled away and ran down to the river,

Where you helped me turn somersaults

Off your brown chest

Blond head over heels

Blue sky and yellow sun a blur before

Cold green water rushing.

That photo stood frozen in time

On the living room shelf

Next to my brother and sister

For decades it stood still

While our lives rushed on.

Until one day you were gone.

And then it, too, was gone,

I was afraid to ask Mom where.

Where did the light go?

Where did you go...

Daddy?

Jamie Stares at the words. Then the tears start to flowdown her cheeks. Several dripping onto the paper before she wipes them away. Where did these come from? She hasn't written like this before. All the memories. All the feelings. "Where *did* you go, Daddy?" She pauses. Then writes "Daddy" at the top, a title crunched in. "And where am I?" The question lingers unanswered. For now.

Jamie closes the journal for the night. Maybe the Voice has returned in a strange way. She feels like someone, something is talking to her. If Jake is involved, maybe the devil is too. Maybe he *is* the devil. She doesn't care. The Voice has come back and is helping her write. Helping pull her forward. Each uncertain step.

Jamie pushes herself out of the chair and aims her weary body and mind for the bedroom. She isn't hungry. And despite the nap, she is fatigued. And she is too tired to eat. Even though it's just evening, she wants her bed. She will think about all of this in the morning. It seems like she has lived through a new day in a new skin, and it seems to fit. She will see if she still feels that way tomorrow.

It is warm enough to open the window a little. The cooling air feels good against her body. There is movement near the barn. A doe and two very young fawns. This is good. She doesn't know why. Yet. But turning away, she is ready. As Jamie falls into a deep sound sleep, her body lets go and effortlessly alights into a warm and wonderful space. Like a warm jell. It surrounds her. Comforts. Heaven. "I'm...not...heavy..."

Chapter 14

New Beginnings

Jamie jumps out of bed. Something had wakened her. A sound? A dream? A sound from a dream? She jumps not out of fear, but anticipation.

The sun rises confidently over the next ridge, bursting into her bedroom. Yesterday's warmth has stayed the night. Today promises to be warmer still. Jamie feels like she is ready to conquer something.

She walks out of her room and straight to the door. Locked! Of course. But today the lock was more of a source of annoyance than a bolt of safety. Maybe the time would come when she wouldn't feel the need to lock the world out. Jamie steps onto the porch to bask in the morning warmth. She feels good. A gathering of what it is she's exploring…a next chapter of her self discovery. There was a surge of wonder…that sense of newness…the smell of pine in the morning air. If she didn't need boots she would be ready to take off hiking now.

She looks toward the barn, half hoping to see the doe and her fawns. Not there. But she knows she will see them again. As a mother and grand-mother, she knows there is nothing quite like the beauty of youth. From wrinkly newborns to diaper-clad toddlers to holy terrors on tricycles, then bicycles, she loves the energy, the wonder, the sheer thrill of being alive that is being a child.

She never understood those adults who shut off their own youth, and who shunned the youth of others. She soaked up their energy and radiated it back out in love. Even in the moments of her own deep despair, the squeal of a child was like that bright ray of sunshine that now warmed her body. Jamie wants to feel more of this light, this warmth.

She decides to get dressed and get going…setting out for maybe her longest hike to date. She can feel she's getting into shape. A quick breakfast and a look at the AT guide for a visual of where she is "hiking" today. She's about to go inside when she sees IT. The walking stick. Leaning casually against the side of the cabin.

Her initial reaction is curiosity. Then fear! Combined with a sudden realization that she's exposed – literally – to someone who has been to her – HER – cabin in the middle of the night. She shivers, even in the morning warmth.

The stick could only have come from the scary man stalking her hills. Jake. Should she run in and lock the door? Should she get the gun and take wild target practice? Get on her bike and tear off across the hills? Does she take Jake's stick with her on her walk today? A lesser woman would have called the cops and had him hunted down and shot like a rabid dog.

Jake still creeps her out, but there is something about him that makes her want to know more. Maybe it's the storyteller in her. Maybe she wants to know the story of a man who could live in the woods with his dog. Virtually no contact with people. No amenities. Is a dog enough? What does he carry inside himself to be able to do that?

Jamie picks up the stick and looks more closely. It has weight. Walnut? It is as tall as she is. Straight and thick. But her hand fits around it comfortably enough. Smooth, drawing down to a slight taper at the end. This wood has been worked by skillful hands, not a machine. She can't help but admire the craftsmanship. Her hand moves up and curls around the staff's thicker top end. It, too, has been worked into the shape of a hawk's head. It looks like the one she saw yesterday. Why would he give her his walking stick?

Jamie starts to take it inside to have a better look, but she knew this stick had never been inside so she left it against the cabin wall. Respecting its nature. Jake's nature. She was sure now. She would take that gift with her today. A gift. That is what she would see it as. Fears and gifts cannot live together.

A slight rumbling rises inside of her. What is it? She hasn't felt that feeling in months. Maybe a year. Where is that coming from? When she looks at the stick, it comes. She runs her fingers over the head again, pausing at the grooves of the hawk's hook-tipped bill. Her breath shortens. Jake's manhood is in that walking stick. How can that be? He is the devil, or worse. Is there something about him that excites her? Where did that thought come from anyway? She looks around, trying to peer deeper into the woods, wondering if he has been watching this play between his creation and her nakedness. She sees nothing. The shiver has passed. Replaced by another kind.

She needs to get going or this will drive her crazy. This dichotomy. Jamie decides to hike White Oak Trail today. She knows it is hard and long. But she knows she has the stamina, and desire, to do this easily. She gets to White Oak, by starting south on Trout Trail and the Bear Cave. The fear she felt half an hour ago is distant memory.

This back and forth between brazen courage and crouching fear is the kind of thing that would have drawn sarcasm from John. He who never felt fear. Not even at the end.

But John is not here now. Just her. And this wild man who knows her habits. And now her home. "John, babe, I will practice with the shotgun. I promise."

For some reason, she is not worried about meeting Jake. She *should* be. The women at the store said as much. Maybe she'll say something to the sheriff next time in town. Maybe. Anyway, she figures it'll be days before they meet again. Why? She doesn't know. She just *feels* it. Like he made his point. And will wait to see how she reacts.

"OK, then. Let's see how I react. Let's see if I'm afraid of this…this… man!'

The walking stick works like Jake said. She has to practice balance, but she feels everything. It pushes confidently into the moist soil. She descends Trout quickly, hardly noticing the swamp marigolds gathered in small fields along the creek bottom. "They like their feet wet," Jamie remembers reading.

Jamie gets into a rhythm that feels trance like. A song from her past bubbles up. She sang this years ago when she was in the church choir. Of all the songs she has sung, why this one? She even remembers who wrote the words. Brian Wren…1970 something. The song fills her mind:

> "This is the day of new beginnings,
> Time to remember and move on,
> Time to believe what love is bringing.
> Laying to rest the pain that's gone.
>
> Then let us, with the Spirit's daring,
> Step from the past and leave behind
> Our disappointment, guilt and grieving,
> Seeking new paths, and sure to find."

Jamie arrives at the Great White Oak tree. That tree had marked the property line years ago. Hank had told her and John that an oak tree takes one hundred years to grow, one hundred years to live and one hundred years to die. One day when she and John had taken a ride to the Great White Oak, they were saddened to see it had fallen. Probably the victim of a bad storm. Three hundred years. What this Great White Oak tree must have seen in those years. It was already beginning to rot, with plants and bugs making homes here now in the decaying old king of the forest.

Jamie rests on the old tree for a while. Listening to see if it has a story to tell her. She runs her hand across the bark-less trunk. The quiet of the spring forest is intoxicating. A cardinal flits through the trees. A male. Soon his song croons to whoever can hear. Hopefully, a female will join him. Jamie listens to how his song repeats over and over. Clear and straight.

"Magpie"... "Magpie"... What does a magpie sound like? What a jerk! What right does he have to call her that? Who the hell is he? Who is he to tell her she talks too much? What does he know of my life? The cardinal calls again. Jamie relaxes again. Maybe she *should* listen more. But hadn't she been listening all her life? To her father? To her brother? To John? To all the hangers-on around John and her?

She had always heard of people who talked too much. Never someone who *listened* too much. She lays face down on the big old carcass. She nuzzles a bit of moss with her cheek. Her body is atop the three hash marks the owner had used to mark the corner of his property. She presses her ear to the now-dead trunk. A sort of embrace of something in nature that had done its job and could now rest in peace. She wants this Great White Oak to tell her one of its secrets. If not today, another. She will come back.

On her way home Jamie sees all three colors of her beloved trillium. This was truly spring. The trillium, once considered endangered, were in no danger here. There were thousands of them. People had tried to transplant them to their domestic gardens. Trilliums have a very long tap root. If you cut it at all the plant cannot survive. No one took the time to dig deeply enough. Was there a lesson there for Jamie? Had she ever dug deeply enough?

Jamie finishes eight miles effortlessly...loosening her clothes as the exercise and warm air work their magic. Somewhere on the way back she crossed from Georgia to North Carolina at Bly Gap and entered the Nantahala National Forest. "Nantahala"...another Cherokee word... "land of the noon-day sun." Perfect for today's hike, where the sun was nearing its zenith. A happy, warm day. Jamie estimates today's hike ended at Wateroak Gap. Coming down the hill to the cabin, she sees the doe and her fawns moving down Trout Trail. She is happy.

She leans Jake's walking stick against the cabin. She runs her fingers along the shaft. It served her well. She will use it again. She takes the two metal walking polls, compacts them to put into storage. For the rest of the day, Jamie answers emails that won't wait. When she finally gets her work done she opens her bird field guide to look up the magpie. She puts the descriptions she finds into this day's journal entry.

April 24 – Magpie – large bird. White wing patches in flight. Green iridescence on the wing.

Song: mag-mag-mag or yak-yak-yak

Nest: cup nest with thorny branches – double intense and placed in bush or tree.

Eggs: 6-9 greenish blotched eggs.

Magpies are frequently shot because they steal grain, but the most important part of their diet is insects and small rodents. They are more beneficial than destructive to agriculture. In captivity a magpie may be trained to imitate the human voice.

The French painter, Claude Monet, painted **The Magpie** *in 1869. It is a lovely winter scene with a Magpie perched on a wooden gate. Monet painted this when he was coming out of a very depressed period of his life.*

"So," she thinks to herself as she closes the guide, "Is he calling me Magpie because I talk too much or because he's in a depressed period of *his* life? Or...both?"

She opens her journal and writes quickly:

Jamie: yak yak yak

Jake: black black black

Now she is ready for bed...and tomorrow.

Chapter 15

Shooting Practice

Jamie wakes thinking of the date. April 25th. She has completed ten of her 365 days here. She can either move forward into them or let the days come down on her. She knows it's her choice. Will she seek these days out, or will fear stalk her and keep her penned in? "Get going, girl," she thinks. "The answers are out there. Not in this nice warm bed!"

Today, target practice. Then a walk.

Jamie dresses and has some breakfast. Toast slathered with peanut butter. Banana sliced on top. Breakfast has always been Jamie's favorite meal.

John taught her to shoot, but she wonders if she remembers. Is it like learning to ride a bike? Will it come back to her? She remembers the kick of the rifle stock in her shoulder, and she takes a small pillow from the rocking chair to soften the jolt.

Jamie takes the gun and ammo onto the porch and opens the barrels with ease. Remembered one thing. She slips the shells into each barrel and closes the gun. Ready to shoot.

Jamie remembers John telling her all she needs to protect herself is this shotgun. She can wildly fire it almost anywhere and one or more pellets will hit the object she is shooting at. He said anyone who knows guns, gets out of the way of a woman with a shotgun. He also told her not to aim it if she wasn't going to shoot. Another person could read her eyes. They would know if she would use it. Or not. Then they would take it and use it on her.

The gun is heavier than she remembers. 'OK, Jamie. Just shoot the sucker!' She lifts the rifle, edging the pillow between the gunstock and her shoulder. Takes aim. Pulls the trigger. Nothing happens. What could she have done wrong? Woops...forgot the safety. It's probably a good thing guns have safeties on them. It protects us from ourselves. After taking the safety off she tries it again. The rifle fires with a wild kick that jerks the barrel up and throws her footing off. The blast stuns her, and her hearing is dull, as if her ears have cotton in them. As soon as she can hear again, she hears uproarious laughter coming from somewhere in the brush. It has to be Jake. Is he stalking her?

She wants to aim at the bushes, but then she remembers. Don't aim unless you are going to shoot. If she aims he might come out and call her bluff. Jamie continues to shoot and reload four times. She puts Jake out of her mind. Could Jamie shoot an animal? No. Could she shoot an animal if she was starving? She doesn't know. Could she shoot a person? No. Could she shoot a person if they were hurting someone close to her? She doesn't know. Could she shoot a person if they were coming after her? Probably not.

Target practice ends. She has remembered how to do it. Maybe Jake will be a little afraid of her for a change. Those were her goals. See if she remembered how. Scare Jake. She had thought he would simply hear the blasts echo through the hills, but he'd done more than that. He'd seen her shoot.

After making sure the shotgun is empty and cleaning it like John showed her, Jamie puts everything away. She never understood why the two barrels on the same rifle were different diameters. Wouldn't it have been easier if both barrels were the same? Oh well. Maybe it was a guy thing. Jamie heads out on her hike. She has moved across Georgia and is making her way toward North Carolina on the A.T.

In reality, on her property she will hike "North Face Trail" to "Salt Peter Rocks". There she will pick up "Upper Salt Peter Trail" and take it to "Hayride Trail" which will bring her back close to the cabin. On the porch, she hesitates and looks at Jake's walking stick. She holds it in her hand. Feels the solid, polished wood. She likes the stick better than her poles, but she isn't sure why. She is no longer scared of Jake and resists the pull of attraction she can't understand. Is it because he is mysterious? The next time she meets him, she'll test him. Ask more questions.

Today is cloudy. No rain in the forecast. Still not warm. "North Face" is steep and rocky and cold from lack of sun. She still gets winded on the steep trails, but regains her breath again on the flatter trails. "North Face" gives her a beautiful view of the trillium. Still in full bloom. A sea of white faces just begging her to stop and enjoy. She does. They spend 49 weeks of the year gathering in food and getting ready for their next big show. How simple their lives are. How complicated hers is. When the weather warms up, she will bring a notebook or her journal on hikes and stop often to see what she sees.

Every time she sees Salt Peter Rocks, she is amazed. How did these huge boulders get here, all piled up together? John said it had to be the glaciers that pushed and carried them here. The Salt Peter of the rocks was used in making gun powder during the Civil War. And because these rocks were close to the Mason Dixon Line, they were convenient to get to. This was another spot John liked to take Jamie's picture. As she climbed them for the photo she always watched for snakes that might be sunning themselves on the warm inviting rocks.

Today as she walks the narrow path through the rocks, a voice says, "Been huntin'?" Jamie's heart leaps from her chest again. Just how many heart leaps can a person's heart stand? She will use the rest of hers up for sure with Jake. At first she doesn't see him, but then, there he is sitting atop a boulder, his feet dangling down over the edge.

"You scared me," Jamie says. Her breath is short. She takes a long inhale.

"Sorry," says Jake. "Were you hunting this morning?"

"Just target practice," Jamie tries to sound calm. "You some kind of stalker or voyeur getting your kicks?" She looks straight up at his eyes. "You're lucky the rifle is too heavy for me to carry on my hikes. Keep in mind you're trespassing."

"I'm not stalking you" he says, calmly. "I'm just watching the new creature in the woods. I know what to expect from nature, but I don't know what to expect from you. And I had quite a laugh seeing you fire a gun. Have you ever gone hunting?"

"No. Look who's a Magpie today," says Jamie. "Where do you live, Jake?"

Jake nods toward the woods. Jamie notices that his hair is clean today. Jeans not so ragged. Did she just get him on a clean day? Or did he clean up a little for her. She wonders why the thought excites her. Quandary.

"Do you have a house?"

"Not like your house."

"By the way," Jamie remembers. "Thank you for the walking stick. What will you use?"

"I have more."

Jamie notices his accent. A soft southern accent, maybe. The sound of it almost makes her feel comfortable.

"Do you carve them?" she asked.

"Yep."

"You're a good carver. I like the smooth top." She is embarrassed about mentioning this. She hopes it does not show in a blush. "May I keep it?"

"Yep."

Jake asks, "What are you doing here by yourself, Magpie?"

"Sorting my life out. What are you doing here, Jake?"

"Same."

"How long have you been living here, Jake?"

"About a year," he answered. "How long are you staying, Magpie?"

Jamie hesitated. "If we're going to run into each other a lot, you can cut the Magpie stuff. If you can't call me by my real name, at least call me Maggie."

"You staying up here by yourself? No helpers? No family? No men?" His question should scare her but doesn't. His gentle way of talking calms her fears. His eyes are soft. Hardly the eyes of a killer. He speaks as if educated and not from the area. His teeth are good. Straight. Like he'd had braces as a kid.

"All by myself," she says. Jake's face remains calm and inviting.

There is a rustling in the brush. Job comes bounding up. He must have been chasing something in the woods. When he sees Jamie, the dog walks towards her, his tail wagging so much his rear haunches swing. "Hey, Job. You been playin' in the woods, boy?" She pets him on the head. He licks her hand.

Jamie tries to think of something else to ask Jake. Some kind of test. He doesn't seem dangerous or even weird, despite the fact he lives in the woods somewhere. She realizes it isn't the questions she asks that are the test, but the way he responds and acts. He keeps his distance. He is calm and polite. A little quirky with the Magpie thing. She is beginning to understand he has a dry sense of humor, but his laughing at her does not seem cruel or dismissive, only good humored.

"Well, I had better get going," says Jamie. She can't help but ask a question that rises to her mind with a calm, unexpected comfort. "Will I see you again, Jake?"

"Do you want to see me again?" he asks.

"It would be nice to have someone to 'yak' at once in a while," she tries to be funny.

Jake smiles. "I'll see you down the trail and around the bend then."

As Jamie starts off, Jake says, "Hey Maggie."

Jamie turns, pleased he honored her request to call her a human name.

"I hope you find what you are looking for. And I hope you look at what you are finding."

"Me too, Jake. Thanks. And thanks again for the walking stick. It works great."

"No problem."

"Bye, Job. I'll see you soon boy." Job's ears perk. He pants a smile, his tongue jutting.

Jamie finishes her walk thinking of Jake. She is less afraid today. She won't be stupid, but it might be nice to have someone to talk to once a week or so. Maybe he knows the answers to some of her nature questions. Having Job around is sort of fun too. She can't quite put her finger on what it is about Jake that draws her in. She has a whole year to figure it out.

This day, Jamie enters the cabin unafraid. She leaves the door ajar. It is a nice feeling. How to keep the peaceful, safe feeling is the question. She puts a red dot at the 60 mile marker of the A.T. An accomplishment. Checking the computer, there are messages she has to answer. It takes several hours. Already Rosa has property questions. Jamie isn't going to worry about downsizing her properties until this year is over. She has left Rosa with the job of making sure they were all used in a charitable way until she gets back. The company has some urgent questions too. When she finishes she goes out on the porch to watch the sunset and eat her dinner. It is cool, but she has pulled a blanket around her. She wonders if Jake is watching, surprised that she hopes he is. In the fading spring light she writes in her journal.

April 25 – Today I conquered my fear of Jake. I look forward to another chance meeting. "I hope you find what you are looking for. And I hope you look at what you are finding," he had said. What am I looking for?

What am I supposed to be finding.

I seem to have a foot in two different worlds. The world that has been my life.

This simple world. Exploring myself. My surroundings.

Have I lost a self? Found a new self? If I keep a foot in two worlds, will I ever know where I live? Which world will I choose? The business world? The world of self discovery? Can they ever merge?

Jamie looks toward the barn and watches a doe and her fawn as they graze the field for a long time. Clouds hide the moon and stars, yet she can see every spot on the fawn clearly. When they finally wander off, Jamie goes in to bed. Sweet dreams, Jamie. A year away is not going to be a mistake.

Chapter 16

Church Rock

Spring slides toward summer. Jamie enjoys all of it. May is beautiful. The May-apples with their umbrella leaves. Jack-in-the-Pulpits everywhere. Preaching to all who will listen.

She finds a patch of wild asparagus and picks some for her supper. Hank taught her how to find morel or sponge mushrooms. They grow on the dark side of the ridges. She finds a few and uses them sparingly in her soup or omelets. Dandelion greens are plentiful. Jamie's grandmother had taught her to cook and enjoy these with a little oil, vinegar, salt and pepper. Jamie hasn't had any for years. Everywhere she lives, the dandelions are not good to eat with all the weed killers used on lawns. Her children had missed this delicious natural food.

For over a month, Jamie and Jake meet on the trails. Not every day. Perhaps twice a week. Jake would walk with Jamie, keeping pace with her without being winded. It perturbed Jamie that he could talk calmly while she panted for air. Last week, Jake asked why she always just walked the paths. Jamie said she didn't want to get lost...that her sense of direction is bad.

"Don't be afraid of getting lost. Would you listen to a poem I memorized? It's one of my favorites. I ran across it when I was in college. The preface to the poem invites the reader to hear a Native American speaking to his grandson and reminding him of what's important."

"I'd love to hear it, please."

Jake motioned for Jamie to sit by him on a large flat rock. He closed his eyes. "Wait," he said. "Okay, now I remember how it starts." And he began to recite the poem, slowly.

"Stand still. The trees ahead and bushes beside you

Are not lost. Wherever you are is called Here,

And you must treat it as a powerful stranger,

Must ask permission to know it and be known.

The forest breathes. Listen. It answers,

I have made this place around you,

If you leave it you may come back again, saying Here.

No two trees are the same to Raven.

No two branches are the same to Wren.

What a tree or a bush does is lost on you,

You are surely lost. Stand still. The forest knows

Where you are. You must let it find you."

That day Jamie learned much about Jake. He had told her that his mother was a Cherokee woman named Anna whose family had followed the Trail of Tears to Oklahoma. His father was an Irish preacher who had come to preach and save the heathen Indians. Robert Kelley had fallen in love with Anna. They were married and Jake was their only child. Jake's father had wanted Jake to go to school. Jake's mother and grandfather had been against white man's schools.

Jake said he had always wanted to work with wood. He knew that's what he'd do. He did agree to school to please his father. Whenever he could he would sneak off with his grandfather into the woods to learn the Cherokee ways and stories. In college he studied literature, philosophy, religions of the world, languages and history. When he graduated he opened a cabinet shop.

Jamie shared the sketchy details of her Cherokee heritage with Jake. From what she had heard, her family didn't travel the Trail of Tears, but settled in Tennessee.

One thing was off limits to talk to Jake about. If Jamie asked him why he was here, his eyes would cloud over and he would be silent. He had a sad secret, she knew that much. Maybe he would tell her. Maybe they could share their stories with each other and try to heal.

One day on the trail, Jake said, "You live by one of Pennsylvania's most beautiful state parks, Maggie. You should try to enjoy it."

"Will you go with me to explore it?" she had asked.

They did. It was rough terrain. There were no cleared paths. Only trails etched out by the deer. One day Jake took her to a beautiful overlook. The outcropped rock seemed to overhang the entire valley. The view was beautiful. Jamie had Jake take her twice so that she could find this place on her own.

She called it Church Rock. That is where she started to go on Sundays. Church Rock became a spiritual place for her. She would take her journal and talk to God and whoever else would listen. If she got there in the morning it would be filled with sun. By noon, the large oaks and maples covered it in a canopy of shade. Some Sundays she would lay naked on the massive rock. The sun warmed it to a perfect temperature. She would take her lunch and stay until she was afraid it would get dark before she got home.

In these ways, Jamie worked on her project: Herself. Jamie V. (Vogel) Barlow discovering herself. Who she always was. Despite what people told her she was. Or tried to make her. Or tried to be for her. Or she tried to be for them. When she reflected...when she took time to be silence to think... to feel...then she could think with her heart.

It is a Saturday in early June when Jamie wonders why she is driven to finish the Appalachian Trail. Maybe it is because the day's hike has been a hard one. Maybe she just needs to take a day off. She can't put into words why she needs to get to the end. What is at the end? Maybe she is starting at both ends. Maybe she will meet herself in the middle. Maybe she will become what she is meant to be.

That makes a nice closure...completion. When you embark upon a journey of change, the self you are changing into embarks from some other end point to meet you. Jamie wants herself and everyone to get there. All reach their journeys end and realize it's just begun and this is God or Spirit or Love.

Sometimes when Jamie lets her mind go where it wants...she thinks of John and their life together. She and John had been high school sweethearts. Their love seemed to be sweet and infinite. They had four joyous years together and two beautiful girls before he was called to Vietnam. What happened to him there she could only imagine. He came back a different man. Someone she had never gotten to know again. It took years for him to finally tell her the story. He swore her to secrecy. Their children had never really known the other Daddy. This was the Daddy they had always known. He loved them very much, but sometimes his mind would go to another place where none of us were allowed to visit.

About a year after his return, gangrenous complications from the aftermath of the crash led to the progressive loss of his extremities. This added an additional horror. For three years he fought to keep his legs. When the nightmare ended, John had lost everything below the knee.

Sometime along the way, Jamie became aware that she was in it for the long run with John. He was not the John she had married. Why did she stay? Do all the work? Invest in herself to that degree? To the end?

And here she goes again with the Appalachian Trail. She wants to go the distance. What is that? What moves and pushes her? Is it coming from the inside or outside? Maybe it's like her old saying: *Men do what men gotta do. Women do what needs to be done.*

Chapter 17

Indebtedness

On June 3, Jamie sits on Church Rock. Instead of seeing tree tops or chipmunks, or hearing birds, all she can do is remember when John finally told her about the helicopter crash. He had told her the events of that day in Vietnam three full years after he had returned home. He made her promise not to share that horrible memory with anyone. Not their girls. No one. It was a terrible promise to keep. And on Church Rock, four months after John's death, the memory was haunting her.

She walks the trail home from Church Rock and cannot get the images out of her mind. John in his wheelchair. Telling the story with no indication of its horror in his voice or on his face. Sometimes she could see the events, as if they'd happened to her, as if Jamie had been the gunner on that chopper. As if she bore wounds so deep, they would never heal. She decides to tell the story to her journal, just like she remembered John telling her. She won't break her promise, but she needs to get the story out and lay it to rest. She can't carry it for John any longer.

Jamie sits in her favorite chair for writing. Two fingers of Jack and a fresh pen. She closes her eyes and sees John as he was when he told his story so long ago; when his soul seemed to bleed out and into the cracks in the floor. She had thought that if he told her the story, he might then be able to start healing. Now she knows she was wrong, but then she thought her love would help him around this obstacle. She never knew him again. Never again saw the man she married.

First some background. Then the story.

John and Tom had been best friends. John had met Tom when he was in grade school at the age of eight. They were inseparable all through school and college. Like Siamese twins, if one was out, the other was there.

Tom had been a part of both of our lives when we started to date. Best Man at our wedding. Me sworn to find him the perfect girl. At the hospital with John at the birth of both girls.

When John received his draft notice and decided to sign up for Army helicopter training, Tom went with him to try for the same. With a friendly competition through flight training, they placed number one and two in their class. They asked to be assigned together and the request was granted. They shipped out together to Vietnam to be assigned to an AH-1 Cobra helicopter unit near Khe Sahn.

The two saw action together for almost eight months flying normal fire support missions. They both flew with other pilots but enjoyed it most when assigned together. Each mission meant a turn gunning from the front or piloting from the rear. John had explained that the ship was the priority. When the plane flew, personnel had a chance. And so the gunner was also a target drawing fire from the pilot and the flight machinery. Teamwork was essential. And on this chopper, the team's name was Rattlesnake One.

John's eyes clouded over when he told the story, but no tears – only distance ensued. As I listened, tears poured down my face – and remembering they still do…yet not one of his words has been washed away:

"It happened after the fire fight. We flew low over lush vegetation. Rolling hills. Dense foliage. Barren cliffs jutting from nowhere. Rice paddies dotted the country side below. The air hot and humid. Large puffy clouds contrasted against hazy blue sky above.

It always comes back to me clearly.

'Rattlesnake one-one is off. Leaving the scene of the fight.'

'Where is one-five?' Tom asked through the intercom.

'He's at our five o'clock,' I answered from the gunner's position up front.

'Nice shooting up there Johnny boy.'

'I bet those medevac pussies have us around for protection,' I had said. 'Get us the fuck out of here.'

'You going to keep flying after this police action is over, John?'

'If this is police action I'm not going to be a fucking cop. Shit, the only flying I'm going to do is in the back of my private jet. I'm gonna start a business and become filthy rich.' I had said. 'I'm telling ya, you should come work for me.'

'Thanks anyway, pal. I am going to get as far away from civilization

as I can. I'm going to buy a farm in the hills and the only fuckin' bullets I will hear will be from my hunting rifle.'

I keyed the intercom button. 'Fucking turbulence.'

It felt like we had flown into a storm cloud. But the sky was clear.

'What was that? Fuck me. I think we're hit!' Tom said.

'Where is he?'

'There at 10 o'clock, by the rice paddy!'

'Where? I don't see him!'

Several bullets riddle through the engine and transmission with a hard thumping sound.

'Fuck. Fuck. We're going down John' he had shouted.

'Head for that hill for cover if you can, Tom. I can't get the gun around to get those gomers!'

'No good. Shit! Hold on to your ass. It ain't gonna be soft.'

The helicopter hit hard on an angle on the side of the hill. Dirt, rocks and debris exploded in all directions. I raised myself in my seat just before the impact but must have blacked out for a minute as we rolled inverted into the rice paddy.

I awoke to find the canopy filling with water from the side. I quickly pulled the release to open what was left of the canopy.

'Tom, we got to get out of here! The VC are coming!' I yelled as bullets kicked up water next to him.

'Go John! I can't move. I think my fuckin' back is broken!'

'Fuck. You should have just put it in the water!' I yelled.

'Get out of here, damn it. One-five was right behind us. He'll call in a medevac.' 'I'll be fine, you stupid fuck. Take the radio up that hill and see if you can get a signal.'

Here John's voice got softer. I could hardly hear him but he still talked on. I had to move closer to him to hear the next part.

"I moved around the front of the chopper. In a few steps I was on the hill heading for some large rocks at full speed trying to unsnap the cover of my .45. As I dove behind the rock I turned in time to see four VC arrive at the remains of our chopper. Two raised their AK's and pumped too many bursts into the body of my oldest and best friend.'

It ended with: "I'm alive, Jamie. And he's dead. I should have been with him."

John's loss was not a physical loss like losing an eye or an arm. Instead it was a sacrifice, pure and simple. It got down to the buddy or John. Only one was going to be gone and one was going to have a chance to live. "I'm alive and he's not." It was a debt John could never live up to or live down.

I'm alive and John's gone. Did one need to leave? One need to stay? The horror is playing itself out again. Is a choice forced on us when there is no choice at all? Seems I've faced this before. Maybe it's become so routine we don't see it at all...

John was doing his job, doing the right thing. The outcome was less than what he hoped for. Always thinking he had done the wrong thing. Indebtedness.

The gangrene he suffered after he was picked up. Sacrifice and indebtedness. Doing one's best and having it blow up in one's face. What's worse than losing your legs...losing a friend and feeling it's your fault? Doing one's best when the best wasn't good enough? Trying to do things right and losing a friend? Trying to make right something that can never be made right?

John fulfilled his promise to himself. He became very philanthropic when he started making money. I think he hoped it would make up for something. But maybe a gift with a burden attached is no gift at all; it's a 'dredit' card statement...with, likely, a 22% interest rate.

Sacrifice...indebtedness – two concepts that have a false reality and an artificial value attached: two conditions that seem everywhere to confront us, personally and culturally. The "sins of the father", "The sacrifices of the Father", "Women and children first", "Survivors' guilt", "Jesus died for YOUR sins", "After all I've done and given up, this is the thanks I get?"

Indebtedness to our parents; mistakes with our children; both selfish and selfless acts impacting others who never deserved it or could never repay it...when, where the truth lies, is that we all feed upon each other – literally and figuratively: plants and animals, parents and children, current and past, world without end.

God, please let me learn something here. Let me, with the time I have left, do it right. Let me find what I am to do now.

The sun eased its way into the western sky. It didn't force its way on the night. It quietly but persistently set...like yesterday and tomorrow. No fight. No struggle. A voice came to her again. She picked up her pen.

Sunrise – sunset

Sure, as it rises:

It will set.

Sure as it sets:

It will rise.

Let me be as the sun

Suffering no yesterdays

Fearing no tomorrows.

Let me rise

And rest

As the sun

Jamie will not fight the story. She will learn from it. Days stretch out before her. Days on end where she can learn how to live out the days ahead – not the ones behind.

Jamie starts to close her journal. Only one page left. On it she writes:

That story is done. That burden laid down. John died long ago. I couldn't save him from his past. It buried him. It's haunting me. His life is past. My life is ahead. The past ends here.

As if to cement her resolve, the voice again steps forward penning her words; guiding her hands: *"Let the dead bury the dead."*

Jamie tears this last page from the book. Takes a match from her pack. A strange calmness, a new lightness grows in her heart while a small pyre turns to ash in her hearth.

"Done."

Chapter 18

Ancient Stones

It started quietly, easily. Not an argument at all. It was more of a teasing Jamie began over wanting to see Jake's 'home.' On their walks, she slips in comments about his all-natural dirt floors, or his sand rock shower. Or she'd ask if his place was more like the 'Little House on the Prairie' or 'Fred Flintstone's house.' "You know where I live, why can't I see where you live?" she asks. "After all, you ARE living on my property, aren't you?"

But it is not teasing that finally brings Jake around to showing Jamie his place in the woods. It is a day Jake joins her unexpectedly on Naked Bear Trail. That is his way. To show up unannounced with Job. She has gotten used to it, although it still rattles her a little bit when "her Indian," as she sometimes calls him in emails back to a friend, just appears out of nowhere. "I feel like an animal you track down in the woods," she says. "Why not come over and knock on my door?"

"Because you might call the sheriff and have me arrested," he says, walking beside her, his eyes to the ground.

"Well, two months ago when you appeared out of nowhere and scared me half to death, I might have, you're right! John would have just shot you on the spot. But I think we've gotten to know each other. And... maybe I trust you. So, I'm not likely to call or shout at this point" she chuckles. "But I still wouldn't let you in. You're definitely a porch visitor." He nods with a laugh. She likes to make him laugh. It is rare to see him smile.

The trail slopes sharply downward to the southwest, a turn that leads, eventually, back to the cabin three miles away. The trail narrows a bit. Jamie leans forward to get a glimpse of Jake's face, but she trips on a root, falling forward and down off the trail. She slides twenty feet screaming before a small tree stops her from sliding further. Jake is just a step behind, trying to catch her. "Mags! Are you all right?"

"Owwwwww...I....think...so." Jamie sits up slowly, leaning against the tree that has broken her fall.

Jake kneels beside her; Job sniffs. Jamie's knee has a good sized scrape on it; blood begins to ooze at the surface. Her forearm has a smaller one to match.

"God, that was stupid!" Jamie says.

"You said it, not me. But once your mouth starts moving, sometimes the eyes stop seeing."

She looks at him, ready to be angry. But he is smiling. Their eyes meet. Something changes. She is not sure what it is, but the smile is like an offering, a gift. They hold each other's gaze several moments before the sharp sting of Jamie's leg make her look toward her wound.

"Is anything broken?"

At this, she laughs. "Noooooo...I don't think so. Help me up?" Jamie grips Jake's arm and he pulls her up. She winces. "I think I sprained my ankle a little."

"Can you walk? Hold on to me. Try to keep your weight off it."

They climb back up to the trail. The pain isn't that bad. Still Jamie needs a minute to catch her breath. She is beginning to feel the soreness in the scrapes, too.

She puts a hand on Jake's shoulder and slowly balances herself.

"How does it feel?"

"Sore. But I think I'll live."

"Can you walk?"

She removes her hand and walks slowly in a circle. "I think I'm alright."

Jake looks at the small trail of blood making its way down her shin. "Well, I think we should get those scrapes cleaned up."

Jamie looks down and sees the blood. The blood doesn't bother her; all the years dealing with John's emergencies, large and small, had steeled her with the calm of an emergency room RN. "I guess so. Can't stay here. I think it's about three miles either way. Might as well finish it out."

"Maggie, I'd feel better if we could bandage those."

"Sorry, Jake, I don't have any in my pack."

"You wanted to see where I live?"

Jamie's eyes widen. "You live close to here?"

"And, believe it or not, I have bandages, too."

She looks around, trying to see signs of habitation. "How far is it?"

"Closer than you think," he smiles.

She smiles back, grateful to see sides of him than he has not shown before.

"OK. Which way?"

They walk a hundred yards back the way they came. There, a deer trail branches off to the left. It is hardly visible, but with Job leading the way, Jake steps off the wider trail and into the forest undergrowth. Then he stops and turns. Jamie is a few steps behind.

"I'm sorry, Maggie. I'll walk more slowly. Can you make it OK?"

"Yep." She doesn't mention that her leg is beginning to throb. "How far is it?" she asks again.

"Not far. You'll see. Just follow me. No big roots here."

He looks down at her leg. The blood has begun to dry. He looks back up at her shirt and she feels his eyes on her breasts. Jamie wishes she was wearing a bra. She was wet with sweat and mud. Everything shows. His eyes catch hers for an instant. Job barks expectantly. Jake smiles and turns. Job takes off for home. Jamie follows Jake.

The trail crosses the far side of the ridge line. The slope on this side is gentler. It is a part of the property that Jamie has never seen. But there are many parts of the property she has never seen because she and John never strayed from the trails that had been made for them. The trees here are older, taller. The underbrush thinned. Jake has moved thirty yards ahead, but she doesn't call after him to slow down. Her leg hurts. Still, she doesn't want to show weakness.

The deer trail disappears as the forest opens. It dips more sharply as a rock cliff emerges from the side of the ridge line. Jamie tries hard to keep up. But Jake strides confidently, as though he's forgotten she is even there. Job has gone far ahead.

She looks down for an instant to make sure of her footing. When she looks up, Jake has disappeared too. A shot of panic moves from her stomach to her heart. Is this the trap? Is this the end? Has she been stupid to trust this man? He seemed so genuine. So trustable. Why is the old fear coming back? She slows.

"Jake?"

She walks a few more steps. The cliff now looms over her. She feels like she is in one of those B-grade horror movies where the audience knows he is behind the tree with a chain saw. They are all spilling their popcorn and saying, "Don't do it!" Where has he gone?

"Jake?"

"God," she thinks to herself, "maybe he's one of those Indian shape shifters, changing himself into a crow or an eagle."

"Jake!" Suddenly Job bounds out from the rock, tail wagging. What is this?

She leans down to the pet the dog. When she looks up, Jake is standing a few feet away. She screams startled. "Jesus! Where did you go? Why did you scare me like that?"

"Sorry, Maggie. I realized I needed to straighten a couple things up. Didn't mean to frighten you."

"But, where did you go? Where did you come from?"

"Two very different questions. Two very different answers. But, here's the answer to the first." With that he steps back a couple steps and beckons her forward.

As Jamie moves closer to the rock face, what had been solid reveals a crack. Actually more than a crack, a crevice, about two feet wide. But barely visible at a distance of even ten feet. "You wanted to see my home. This is the front door."

With that Jake steps back into darkness; Jamie follows, mixing curiosity with dread.

The crack opens into a large room. As her eyes adjust to the darkness, objects start to appear. A wooden bed with blankets. A circle of rocks for a hearth. Other things farther back that she can't make out yet. Even with its midday June sun, the room remains cool and dark. Jake lights a kerosene lamp. "Here, Maggie, sit down." He gestures to the bed. Jamie walks over and sits down, still trying to take it all in.

Job follows and settles easily near the entrance.

"You *live* here?" knowing the question is stupid even before she finished asking.

"Home sweet home." He brings the lamp closer to look at her knee.

"Is it sore?"

"Pretty bad."

Jake takes the lamp and steps deeper into the darkness. The room... a cave really...is larger than she first thought. All she can see is the light. She hears him picking something up out of the blackness. Then something dripping. A medicine man's pouch of potions and miracles? "I think I can patch you up."

He kneels in front of her with a moist rag and a large bandage. He sprinkles the rag with what looks like herbs. "I'm just going to wipe off the blood and clean a little around the scrape. Is that OK?"

"Yes. How long have you lived here?" Jamie's curiosity starts to take over as her fear subsides.

"Long enough." He starts to wipe off the blood starting by the ankle.

"Do you like it here?"

He shrugs.

She knows by how he answers that the questions annoy him a little. She knows they are dumb questions. She can't help herself. But the way he holds her calf and gently wipes the blood away relaxes her some. She resists asking anymore questions.

"Ouch!"

"Sorry, Maggie. I was trying to wipe some dirt away from the wound. And these are herbs my grandfather taught me about. I always keep some on hand."

He moves the cloth around the edge of the scrape, and gets the worst of the dirt away from the pink flesh. Then he blows on the skin to dry it. His breath feels cool. He rubs her calf almost unconsciously. It seems like ages since anyone has 'cared' for her like this. She feels the bandage cover. "There, I think that will hold until you get home. Let me look at your arm." She leans forward and extends her arm.

"This doesn't look as bad. How does it feel?"

"Sore. But not as bad as the knee."

"Do you have bandages at home?"

"Yeah."

"OK. I'd still put one on. You may not need one after today."

"Thank you, doctor."

She coaxes a small smile out of him with that. She likes the way he moves easily, confidently around her.

"You have goose bumps. Are you cold?"

"A little. It's cool in here."

"Yes. The cave goes back a ways. We are not the first to have made a home here."

"What do you mean? Have other people been trespassing here, too?"

She regrets the word as soon as she says it.

Jake straightens up and moves away without replying. He comes back a minute later. He extends his hand. Jamie holds the light up to see better.

There are a half dozen arrowheads in it. She squints to see the detail. They look smaller and not as finely chipped as the ones John had in his collection.

"These belonged to the other...trespassers."

She feels the sting, but doesn't let him see it. "Did you find them here?"

"Maggie," with more than a hint of exasperation, "sometimes you can find answers before you ask questions." He pauses, letting her embarrassment sink in. The old teasing had come back. If she could only get him on her turf, she could turn the tables. Until then, she'd always be the dumb one.

"Yes, I found them here. But these are not of my people. I don't know for certain, but I think these are from my people's people's people. The first people."

He hands them to her. As Jamie feels the small, ancient stones, Jake again slips into the blackness. He returns holding something large, like a stick. It is black and curved.

Jamie is still staring at the arrowheads.

"This was with them."

"What is it?"

"Rib bone, from the look of it."

"From a person?"

He rolls his eyes and signs. "The grandfathers of my grandfathers were hunters, not cannibals! But this is a bone I have never seen before. I want to learn more of the animals that were here with the First Ones."

She reaches for the bone. He hands it to her reluctantly. Jake is probably thinking, this rich white woman is too much. Yet he takes her arm and looks carefully at her skin. Jamie doesn't ask what he is doing.

Jamie runs her fingers along the long bone. She shivers. But not from the coolness this time. Something else. She doesn't understand what or why.

They slip into a long silence. Finally, Jamie says, "I'd better go."

Another pause. "Yes, Maggie."

She moves to get up, winces and stumbles slightly. Jake catches her arm. She reaches for his other arm.

"Maggie!"

"It's OK, Jake. My ankle got stiff while I was sitting."

They hold on to each other for a moment more. Then he releases her, embarrassed slightly that maybe he had held her longer than he needed. "I guess I never realized you were so tall...only 3 inches shorter than me," said Jake. "And you are strong. Stronger than I would have guessed for an older woman."

"This old woman has spent years carrying her man."

"I didn't mean to call you old."

"Don't worry about it Jake. I don't feel old."

Job stirs, wondering if they are going for another walk. Tail wagging, he disappears through the crack. They follow him into the warm air and dappled sunlight.

"I'll walk you back to the trail. And then you're on your own. Is that OK?"

"Sure."

Another pause as Jamie squints into the woods. Then she turns back, looks at him again, searching for something in his eyes. Whatever it was, she didn't find it. Maybe next time. Still, she takes a step forward and gives him a quick hug. "Thank you for not killing me."

"Sometimes you are *too* much, even for a man as patient as me."

"You mean as patient as Job?"

This causes Jake to chuckle.

Something else stirs inside Jamie. She had felt the fullness of her breasts press against his shirt. Something she had not felt for a long time. "You and Job, my very own Hole-in-the-Wall Gang."

"What's that?"

"You never saw 'Butch Cassidy and the Sundance Kid?'"

"No."

Job barks. "I'll tell you another time."

"Well, let's go then."

By the time they reach the trail, Jamie's ankle has loosened up. She can finish the miles back to the cabin at almost her normal pace.

"OK, you're on your own, Maggie."

"Jake, thank you. I'd like to see more of your home. Another time, OK?"

"What more is there to see?"

"I have a hunch that there's more. Maybe a lot more."

"Oh, Magpie, as much as you talk, I doubt you would ever see more."

"I take that as a challenge! I think I will come over sometime. Unannounced. Just like you do with me."

"Well, I can't stop you. But I can't promise that I'll be there."

"Good! Then I can snoop as much as I please!"

He smirks, but with humor in his eyes.

"I am not a pest! But you try to be this man of mystery. So naturally you arouse my curiosity. And now you show me ancient arrowheads and dinosaur bones..."

"That was not a dinosaur bone!"

"How do you know?"

"Because I do. Now go."

Jamie turns to head back down the trail. She stops after a few steps and turns.

"Thank you, Jake."

"You're welcome."

"Oh, Jake. One more thing. Do you like to dance?"

"Why would you ask me that?"

"Well, I'm having a dance on my deck some night for the neighbors. Would you like to come?"

"Who are your neighbors?"

"Well, I'm inviting you and Job and any other animals that want to come."

"When?" Jake asks with his hands on his hips and a slight hint of a smile.

"Soon. Oh, yeah, I'm making dinner too."

"I'm not coming in your house, Maggie. I might like it."

"The whole thing will take place on the porch."

"We might be there."

"Great!"

Jamie walks the way she had come. She has no desire to finish the trail today. She wants a hot shower. NOW. As she walks, she wonders if Jake might follow. Just to keep an eye on her. But she doesn't turn to see. Instead she likes the thought and smiles at the comfort it gives her. Another hundred yards and she begins to work up a good sweat. Then she laughs out loud at another thought. She can take off her shirt and finish the hike topless. THAT would give Jake something to spy on! Men always loved her breasts. And she could tell in that instant when they hugged he had responded as well. She likes knowing her breasts can still work their magic on a younger man.

But she decides against it. Maybe another time. Maybe when he can see them closer. Maybe when she knows more about this man. For now she is glad that she is the one to set up their next meeting. What possessed her to say she is having a dance? Dinner? She can hardly cook something decent for herself. He may come and he may not. It will be fun to think about. She was almost to the door. "Did he call me 'Mags'. Hmmm."

Chapter 19

Where Fear Ends

The next day the therapeutic levels of adrenaline, Jack Daniels and a good night's sleep had worn off. The soreness in Jamie's ankle and knees has spread across her body. No walk today. She has walked every day since her arrival...through rain and mud...in cool weather and hot. More than three hundred miles. On the AT she would be at the North Carolina-Tennessee border. But today she will give her body a rest.

Limping out of the shower, she takes a good look at herself in the mirror. Two months of walking and no junk food have done wonders for her 67 year old body. She examines herself for a while, proud not only of the tightness, but of what her body can do.

'Think I've lost ten maybe fifteen pounds.' She says to herself, hands sliding down her body pausing to appraise the reappearance of her waist.

For a moment, Jamie closes her eyes and touches her breasts. She tries to remember how John's hands felt when he touched her there... insistent, demanding, like all men. But a tenderness too. John, for all his rough business ways, knew how to touch her in ways that made her feel wanted...and loved.

The moment passes. Opening her eyes, she looks down to her knees and ankle. The abrasions are nearly gone. Medicine Man Jacob has *some* herbs. Maybe she will ask for the secret recipe. But the ankle is swollen, having turned an ugly mix of black and blue. She will need something for it.

Jamie combs out her hair, now longer than it has been in years. The bleaching and highlights have moved out to the ends, like memories slipping away. She stares at its natural color...dark, heavily sprinkled with gray. Not an attractive color in the world she came from. Her mother, grandmother and great-grandmother had been happy with it. Or if not happy, content. Jamie sees a glimpse of her mother's face in that mirror. Long ago she read a book that said she would be just like her mother and there was nothing she – or any other woman – could do about it. She hadn't liked that book. Jamie wonders if her girls want to be as different from her as she did from her mother.

Jamie pulls her hair back into a loose ponytail. Dresses. Eats a breakfast of oats, raisins, and dried cranberries. Her ankle reminds her of its need for attention. She will take her Harley to the store to shop and see if they have Epsom salts for her ankle. It will be a short trip. Once home, she will sit and read and soak her ankle.

As she rides to the Ram Cat, she thinks of how her relationship to Cora and Ellie Mae has changed over the past two months. Funny how they have become protective of her – almost motherly.

It started one week when she asked what to mix together to make a meat loaf. "Forgot my cookbook," she had said. They gathered what she needed and wrote out a recipe for her. They would ask which vegetables and fruits she liked best and have a delicious looking selection the next time she came in. If she needed pens or barrettes or copy paper...the next week they would have it for her. Once they offered her coffee. Now each visit meant a fresh pot. The store was never too busy for a cup of coffee, it seemed.

Jamie gets off her bike and limps stiffly inside.

"What happened to you?" asks Ellie Mae.

"Little hiking accident, that's all. Sprained my ankle. Do you sell Epsom salts? That was my mom's cure-all."

"We don't sell it," said Cora, "but we only live two blocks up the road. I'll go get you some. Take a load off. Nurse your coffee and your pride 'til I get back."

"Thanks," said Jamie. She watches Cora's skirt sway opposite her wide hips pumping away with purpose. She settles into an old wicker chair by the door that looks as stiff as she feels.

"How's you boyfriend, Ellie Mae? You still in love?"

Ellie Mae's large green eyes tear up. "He's gone Miz. Barlow...gone."

"Please, Ellie Mae, call me Jamie. Gone where?"

Now the tears flowed down her pail cheeks. "He just up and left when he heard I was late," she said.

"Are you pregnant, Ellie Mae?"

"Yes, I...I think so. I haven't told Mama yet 'cause I only missed one period. Please don't tell her. She'll be mad. We can hardly take care of ourselves. If I have a baby, it will be too much."

"What are you going to do? You have to tell her. You'll need your mama...and a doctor."

"I know", said Ellie Mae as a wall of tears washed down her face. "If I miss again...I'll...tell...her. I will."

Her sobbing was uncontrollable. A timeless wail from young women around the world. Alone with the greatest gift...and burden...of all.

Jamie puts down her coffee, stands up and hugs Ellie Mae for a long time. Ellie Mae's body sinks into hers, her head sunken between Jamie's breasts.

Comforted, she regains herself slowly. "Miz Barlow...I mean Jamie, I'm 'a-scairt'! Glad I could finally tell someone."

"It will be OK Ellie Mae. Things have a way of working out for the best. I'd like to skin that Billy though. Nail his hide to the barn door. Running off on you like that."

Ellie Mae smiled at the idea of Billy's come-uppance framed by a barn door. She had never heard Miz Barlow talk like that. She felt closer to her.

"Mama's coming! No more talk." Ellie Mae wipes her eyes and tucks her shirt into her too short shorts.

"Just what the doctor ordered," says Cora swooshing in with a sandwich bag full of salts. "Oh, and by the way, Ellie Mae and I was making ham loaf and fixed some for you too. We froze it, 'cause we don't know when you are coming. Just warm it up. We'll make extra when we's cookin' and freeze 'em up for you. No problem."

"That's so nice. I love ham loaf. I'll need to pay you extra for your time to cook it," offers Jamie.

"You can pay for the supplies, but we love to cook and that part's on us," said Cora, smiling at being able to give something to this wealthy woman who seemed so much like folks now she'd gotten to know her a little better.

"Wow!" said Jamie. "You two are spoiling me. Thank you sooo much. I'll get my groceries and get going. I can't wait to have dinner tonight."

"Soak that ankle at least three times today," prescribes Cora, "It'll be better right quick."

Jamie leaves feeling sadness for Ellie Mae and warmness for the feminine friendship she can feel taking shape. Three women thrown together by chance who would otherwise never have known each other. Their ages are like grandmother, mother and daughter. *And now maybe granddaughter.*

Life with John had always been a man's world. She had learned how to live with men. But she kind of likes this sisterhood thing too. "Oh that poor baby," she says out loud.

The June day is perfect. Jamie has ham loaf to look forward to. Life is good. She is content. By 6:00, Jamie is on the porch reading and soaking her ankle for the third time. The sweet smell of ham loaf fills the house and snakes its way out the door. The potatoes are ready to mash. Fresh broccoli, clean and ready to cook, al dente.

"How's that ankle?"

Jamie jumps up, kicking over the bucket and almost falling on hers. There stand Jake and Job in the yard. Job wagging. Jake trying hard not to laugh.

"God, Jake! You scared me! Couldn't you break sticks or something to warn me you're coming? You remind me of my brother who used to jump out of nowhere and scare me as a child," She sits back down carefully.

"Old...Indian...trick. Sneak up on white women and children," Jake talks in broken 'Indian'. He takes a step closer. Job sees that as a sign to bound up on the porch and give Jamie a licking in exchange for a couple of good scratches.

Jake has clean clothes on and actually looks very good standing in the late afternoon sun. "I didn't think you'd be walking today. But I want to check on your ankle," he smiles irresistibly.

Jamie laughs. "Well, come on up and have a look."

Jake dabs the remaining drops of water off Jamie's ankle with his shirt. He gently turns it side to side in his immense muscular hands. "Not too bad, what were you soaking it in?"

"Epsom salts. I went to the store and Cora brought some from home for me."

"Looks good. Glad you took the day off." He looks up at her with his intense blue eyes. She could look at that blue forever.

He looks back to the ankle. "You'll have to rest it a couple days. But I'm guessing you heal fast."

"Look at my knees! Your potions worked wonders!"

Jake ran his hand up the back of Jamie's calf, extending her leg slowly. He smiled at this handiwork.

"Yes, I agree." Unconsciously, his fingers massaged the back of her knee. Not like a lover. More like a doctor. Or a healer.

Still it was having an effect on Jamie that she hoped he wouldn't see. "Now that you're here, pull up a chair and sit a spell."

"Thanks. Actually, I want to share this day with someone besides Job. It's my favorite day of the year."

Jamie looks puzzled, "What? Did I already forget your birthday?"

"It's June 21st...summer solstice. Longest day of the year."

"Oh, I'd forgotten that. I'm glad you came. Will you have supper out here with me? I have enough to share."

"I thought you couldn't cook," Jake teases.

"I can't," said Jamie. "Cora and Ellie May have taken pity on me and ever since I asked them what ingredients go in a meat loaf, they have made me something each week."

"They don't do that for me," Jake whines.

"It's 'cause you're too scary, Jake."

"Are you still afraid of me, Maggie?"

"Hell, no! But having Job helps you out a lot."

They both laugh.

Jake says, "Well, you want to talk about scary...I was at the Ram Cat Run store last month. There were two guys at the table having coffee. It was early morning and they were having 'possum jerky with their coffee. One guy said, 'Yum. Yum!! T'ain't nothin' like 'possum jerky to make a man stand up straight!' mimics Jake, slipping into the local accent. "The other guy said 'Yassir...'possum jerky...couple bites an' you can last all day. ' 'An' I like ta finish it off with some of mah fav-or-ite 'pep'mint snuff. Leetle pinch 'tween yo'r tongue and yo'r cheek is all ya need.'"

Jamie laughs at his affected performance.

Their eyes smile at each other.

"I'll have supper with you if you have enough," Jake replies to her offer.

"How much do you eat? I think I can handle you – with leftovers for Job."

"Ruff," Job seems to understand and agree.

"I've wondered about your Harley, Maggie. It just doesn't seem to fit you. I don't see you as a 'Harley Mama."

"It's the essence of riding a bike, Jake. It's the real taste of spring or summer or fall. The world is really on your skin. You're absorbing it in fast forward. The chill...the warmth of the sun...the smell of the trees: The difference in air pressure as you go up and down a hill. You feel that stuff, you taste it, and you smell it.

"That's why you see a dog with his head out the window in a car and it's just, 'Arr-rowf-barrr-awkawrrrooof-awroo! (ssshlorp-skalurp-eh-he-eh-heh-eh-heh)'"

Jake throws his head back and lets out a laugh that seems to come from some place deep inside – neglected too long. Job barks, loving the 'dog talk'!

Jamie goes on. "Going fast forward through all those smells. Dogs have a thousand times greater sense of smell than we do. That's why they look the way they do. Next time you pass a pick-up truck and a dog's nearly falling out, remember, he's getting canine crack cocaine!"

Jake, still laughing asks Jamie what the dog is saying.

"Something like, 'Look at me! I'm Wooon-der Dog! And I'm flying! Eat my hairy spit you under-mutts (sniff). Oh wowoo, get a load of the bark-y-cue six blocks over this way this way – No. Wait! (sniff) Oh-my-Dog-oh-my-Dog!...Two borders and a poodle all in heat! This way, this way, this way (snorffle) No! Wait. Stop! Untouched 'treasure-can'. Stop stop STOP! (shlurff) Beef bones! Kitty litter! Maxi-pads! Mine, all MINE!'"

Jake laughs so hard he almost falls out of his chair. Jamie likes to make him laugh. He always seems so sad.

While they share dinner Jamie tells Jake about the cardinal attacking the mirror of her bike. She says she thought he was protecting his territory from a presumed threat. Jake says she is right.

"When I covered the mirror he stopped. So I keep the mirrors covered now. I don't think he would have stopped the attack if I hadn't," Jamie offered.

"He wouldn't have," Jake confirmed, somber now and serious. "The bird was seeing the reflections of his own fears in the world. Don't you? Isn't that what you see? Does the world have anything to do with what you see in it? Or is it a reflection of your fears. What the bird saw in the mirror was the reflection of the thing he was most defended against and the ghost that he would fight to the death. Battling his own reflection to the point that he would smash his beak, break a wing and die. Beaten by an enemy he could not defeat – himself."

Jake's eyes flash and his voice intensifies. Jamie has a pang of fear in her gut. "Scary," is the only response she can muster when the silence grows uncomfortably long and Jake grows dark and distant.

"Well, if the reason you came outside is because you saw a bird attacking your mirror, I'm out here too, because of a bird. There was a woodpecker years ago pecking on my chimney. When life was very sure and my family was attaining the American dream in our new house in a new development. The woodpecker 'moved in' and was pecking the shit out of the chimney.

"Rather than kill it, I talked to a naturalist friend of mine. He said that though developments go up and trees are all cleared, the birds still try to live there. 'They are still trying to live by doing the thing that they are wired to do, and that is peck at things that look like trees to get their food. That 'pecker is looking for food where he is never going to find it. He needs to be in the wild – and his wild is gone,' I was told."

"Somehow, it hit me: Even though it seemed I should be happy, having a new home and my acre of the American dream, I realized I was living where life could not be found.

"There's a wilderness back there made of concrete and steel. But the food I need to survive is in this world made of woods."

Jamie is in shock at the power of Jake's sharing. She is moved too.

"What happened to you Jake? Why are you here? Why are you so sad?"

"Jamie, I can't share that with you now. Maybe never. If I could share it, you are the one I would trust with my pain. But for now, let's just enjoy the summer solstice together."

Jamie and Jake sit. She has a Jack and he has a beer and they listen to the sounds of nature...the sounds of their hearts...the sounds of their souls, hurting together, but in different ways.

As it begins to get dark, Jamie asks "Aren't you afraid to walk home in the dark."

Jake laughed. "Why would I be afraid of the dark?"

"I am," confesses Jamie.

"Maggie, there is nothing to be afraid of. The world wants to share itself with you. It wants to embrace you. It wants to love you. Don't be afraid of it."

She wonders if he hears his own words, but instead says "But I'm afraid I might get lost in the dark."

"It is never dark outside, Maggie. Only place it's dark is in your closet of fear. There is always some light to see by. The darkness you see is where your fears block the light. Maybe life only begins where fears come to an end."

Jamie, thinking many things at once, says, "Life begins where fear ends, 'huh? Mind if I quote you, next time that dark cloud of yours storms across that face?"

Chapter 20
Summer Solstice

Jake and Job walk into the darkness. Another measure of this mountain man's skills. Jamie had offered a flashlight. But Jake refused, almost insulted. She'd forgotten that he'd spent a lifetime living in darkness. This night, the shortest of the year, light lingered in the sky. And Job would never let him get lost, she thinks to herself.

Jamie limps inside. She is glad Jake came by. Job, too! Now Jake's presence feels reassuring. As someone who quickly trusted men, and just as quickly seemed disappointed by them, Jamie feels a satisfaction that her belief in this man has grown slowly. Maybe he will not disappoint her.

She sits down next to her journal...opens it...reads what she has written so far. Where is her Voice? Still distant. Going over the pages again, she notices one thing. In April, her words were written tightly together, one thought hurried along to another. Almost as though something were chasing her.

Lately, the entries are more open, obviously more relaxed. The words looked stronger somehow. She picks up her pen and begins to write:

June 21. Longest day of the year. Shortest night! My ankle feels better. Still sore. I won't hike again for a few more days. Jake stopped by with his dog Job. I was glad to see them. Jake tells me I'm healing fine. We are becoming friends. But he keeps a distance.

Why this growing attraction to Jake? He's as young as my girls. Is it because he is the only man around? Because I want to know his story? Just raw desire?

Why do I feel conflict/guilt over these feelings and John? Is it Jake's lighter side or his dark side that attracts me?

Jamie lays the book aside and disrobes, her thoughts turning to sleep. She pulls the sheet to her breasts. But the night air is warm. The owl hoots in the distance. Sleep comes easily.

Then she is awake. How long has she slept? Her clock says not quite one. A little over an hour. Jamie lies listening for the owl. The night is still. An occasional breeze moves the curtains ever so slightly. The moon is above the cabin eaves and beyond her view, but the long shadows in the woods draw her up. She kicks the sheet aside. Her body does not chill but warms. She remembers how John would wake her in the middle of such nights, reaching for her, wanting her, satisfying himself...and her.

Suddenly she gets an urge to go outside. She doesn't bother to put on a robe or even throw a blanket around herself. She needs to get over her fear of the night. But it's more than that. As she steps onto the porch, she can feel the thrill of it. The night air sweeps over her flesh. Every part of her is exposed to it. Her body is electric, alive with the sensations sparked by John's touch, now eons ago. The breeze is cool. The darkness is all embracing, pierced only by shards of moonlight. Jamie has the urge to face the dark, to feel it on her skin like she feels the night air. Jamie wants to experience the dark with nothing between her and it. The ground is moist and cool. She puts each foot down gently before shifting her weight. With the moist soil she can also feel pine needles like a welcome mat laid out just for her. The occasional movement of air feels like a caress on her legs, her arms, her breasts. She closes her eyes and when she opens them, she is surprised by how well she can see.

She decides to walk...placing each foot down to feel what she is touching, before she puts her weight on it. She doesn't want to step on something and twist her ankle again. As though it too wants to feel the darkness, her ankle does not bother her as much as it did just a few hours before.

Even in the moonlight, the opening to the path towards Jake's retreat is dark, shaded. She pauses a few steps into it, waiting for her eyes to adjust. Her flesh tingles. What if Jake sees her? But of course he can't. He's home in his cave. Asleep, she assumes. But if he did, would she feign modesty? Or let him survey her aging beauty?

She senses her way along the trail, pausing for sounds, looking back to make sure she won't lose her way. A swift darkness erupts. Thumping, buffeting her face and shoulders – quickly followed by a pounding in her chest and ears. What was that? Then the hoot. Closer than ever before. The owl. Her owl. Perched ahead. Its looming shape against the lighter sky.

Ok. Enough. She turns back. Then pauses and looks back up the trail. She imagines Jake seeing her. Coming to her. Touching her gently. Running his fingers over the curves of her body...another hoot. The spell is broken. Back to the cabin.

Inside, feeling a chill, Jamie covers herself with one of John's shirts, knees to her chest, wrapping herself in her own arms. Warmer. The journal seems to call to her. She picks up the pen to write again:

I walked in the night. In my skin. Alone. Into the darkness.

I could feel my body embraced by the warm air, the cool ground,

the soft leaves, the moon light.

Something happened. I can't describe it. Yet

The longest day of the year = the shortest night of the year.

Like night in Midsummer Night's Dream, it reveals a lot.

I had the courage to step naked into the night.

To walk into the woods. To reach for something I can't even articulate.

I have rumblings of the subconscious...some primal urges.

Did it happen? Is it just a dream?

As Puck signs off at the end of Midsummer Night's Dream...

> *If we shadows have offended,*
> *Think but this, and all is mended,*
> *That you have but slumbered here*
> *While these visions did appear.*
> *And this weak and idle theme,*
> *No more yielding but a dream,*
> *Gentles, do not reprehend.*
> *If you pardon, we will mend.*

Jamie sets her journal aside. She hasn't thought of a Midsummer Night's Dream and Puck since the high school play. Where did it come from so suddenly and so clearly? It could only be the Voice visiting again to help her realize her life is changing. Picking up her pen again she writes:

My life was not my own – consumed by the 'busyness' of my husband's dreams and nightmares. Put that chapter to rest. A sea-change is coming. I will face it. I will manage whatever comes.

Maybe life has different chapters. Maybe this is a later chapter in my life. Maybe later chapters are about thoughtfully responding, rather than

hectic   reacting.   ...growingupgettingmarriedhavingkidsgettingremarried-
havingcrisesmakingupmakingoutgettingaheadgettingscrewedandburned-
climbingtheladderdefendingyourturfbeatingthecompetitionguardingyour-
investmentsfightingcellulitewrinklesandrustetc.etc.etc...

Am I now a 'retired wife and mother'?

My question: Is there life BEFORE death?!?

The fax machine whines. Jamie jumps and spins her head towards it. What time is it? Three? She has gotten several faxes, but none while she was around and none this late. This can't be good. Page after page spews from her machine. It is typewritten – how odd.

When the cascade stops she sees the letter is from Stella...the woman she charged with the care of Barlow Associates while she is away. The person she trusts above all people.

Jamie,

I am sorry to bother you and I wouldn't if I didn't think this was very important. I will stay home from 8 am - 9 am tomorrow morning to wait for you to call me. I couldn't write this on email. I dragged out my old Underwood and am faxing it to you tonight so that it won't be seen by anyone but you and me.

You know I followed John's investments as an accountant, and a trader.

John frequently invested in start up ventures and didn't always keep records. There were so many, he didn't remember them and didn't really even care.

He selected people and causes he thought might be viable and then got out of the way and dismissed it from his mind. Tracking them down would require a lot of digging through records. Adding to the complexity was the fact that start-up operations frequently needed multiple infusions of cash. John was a deep pocket, where everyone stuck their hand. His investments in any given venture were likely to be serial and frequent.

He would make contributions in exchange for either equity, or as a loan, or for options, or for warrants.

Do you recall when he made several contributions for different forms of securities in a start-up company named Nexsentury? One of the contributions was in exchange for warrants at $.01 a share. Each warrant was exchanged for 1 share of stock.

To be specific, I recall the exchange was for 20,000 warrants tacked on to equity payment...meaning: they gave him equity but as a kicker, they gave him warrants at a low price.

Some warrants in this type situation expire worthless. However this company's dramatic success treating Alzheimer's made the company and warrants extremely valuable.

By my calculation, the warrants are now worth $10m. As you know, I got somewhat involved in John's will and trust at your request. My recollection is that all of his different securities and options in Nexsentury were to go to Children's Hospital.

Because I am on the investment committee on the board at Children's, I have seen all the records of securities in Nexsentury being transferred to the hospital with the exception of the warrants now worth $10m.

I checked with the CFO at Nexsentury and the warrants were converted to stock two years ago, meaning the $10m went somewhere, but not to the hospital. He indicated that the warrants were signed over to a corporation in the Grande Caymans.

The CFO tried to track down the company that the warrants were signed over to and it seems it vanished or never existed. It would appear that a dummy corporation was set up for the sole purpose of receiving this money.

Children's did receive several certificates representing investments in Nexsentury and would have no way of knowing that these warrants existed. Not knowing, the hospital wouldn't miss them.

I hate to see $10m destined for the hospital diverted through chicanery and I know you feel the same.

The warrant document appears to be forged, because it purports to have John's signature. You and I know he would never direct money to a front in the Caymans...or anyplace.

On the surface it looks like John exercised the warrants for someone other than the hospital. We both know that is not true, but we can't prove that he didn't.

No one knows this but me and now you.

Please call tomorrow and we will talk about where to go from here. I will do what you want. I can't even imagine who would do such a thing, but it must be someone with access to the physical documents.

Again, forgive me for intruding, but I knew you would want to know.

As always, I am here to help you and to preserve John's memory and legacy.

It will be great to hear your voice. Sorry it won't be over better news... I miss you. We all miss you.

Sincerely yours, Stella

Chapter 21
Dance Like Nobody's Looking

By 8:00 the next morning, Jamie has her coffee and her charged phone ready to go. She uses the code that keeps her number from being on caller ID.

"Stella," Jamie says softly. "How are you?"

"I was better before this discovery."

"I'm sure," Jamie answers.

"What do you want me to do, Jamie?" Stella's voice cracks like she is holding back tears. "My mind is so full I can't see clearly what I should do."

Jamie, with a steady voice, says, "First of all let's stay calm. I'm sure your head is spinning like mine, but we'll figure this out together. I've read your fax, and I have a question. Have you seen a copy of the warrant with the signature?"

"No" said Stella. "I didn't see it myself."

"Start with getting a copy from the transfer agent. They'll have a copy of the endorsed warrant. Have them fax you a copy...both sides. The back side will have when the transfer occurred and the signature. The agent will be happy to comply. It's in their own self interest. They don't want to have handled a fraudulent transfer." Jamie takes a deep breath to get herself together. She is sitting at her desk writing notes on Stella's fax. She writes things like, "Stay firm. Don't get pulled in. Stella you can do this."

"Okay," Stella says. "Okay."

"Stella, I want you to check the signature and the date. I have a feeling if someone forged John's signature, they made it look like the stamped signature. John's handwriting deteriorated in the last three years and is nothing like it used to be. Get a recent signature and compare them."

"Right, Jamie, I will do that today."

"Stella, keep it low key. This is very important. I'm not sure what we should do, but we need to keep this between us for now." Jamie looks out the window and realizes how far she feels from the office.

"I understand, Jamie. I just wish you were here to help me."

"I'll help you. Don't you worry about that," said Jamie. "But I can't come home yet. I am just starting to heal. Please, Stella, just do as I ask and type and fax me what you get. Trust me on this. I won't leave you alone. I'll touch base with you once a week and you can fax what you find."

Jamie sees the possibility of a huge cascade of cold water being flung over everything. Will she be hurled back into the old reality?

"Are you OK, Jamie? We worry that you have cracked under all the pressure that was your life...and then to have John die...." Stella starts to cry.

"John would be proud of you, Stella. I am grateful to you. Whoever did this has to be a person we know well, which leads me to acknowledge that someone close to us is actually a stranger to us.

"I need to stay here, Stella. I know it may seem like I'm running away from my life, but I am coming to know myself...learning the truth about myself. I am learning that this is the most important thing I can do right now."

"Jamie?"

"Yes?"

"Will you promise to call me each Wednesday at 8:00 like today? I think if I knew we would talk, I could do this thing."

"I promise," said Jamie. Jamie is surprised at how calm she feels. Perhaps it's because she has to stay strong for Stella. Or perhaps it is the distance she is forming between herself, her true self, and the company. She wonders if she should ask about the company. She wonders if it would put her back into being enmeshed with it, but finally the words came out of her mouth before she has consciously decided. "How is the company doing without John?"

"We've had some people pull money out as we suspected would happen. But the kids – I still call them kids – are rising to new heights with this responsibility you gave them. Keeping the company going keeps his memory alive."

"Good, Stella. I knew you were the one to lead Barlow Associates into its new identity. Where can I fax you something if I need to?"

"I'll always put the number on the fax. Evening is the best time to fax me here at home. Thank you for your help with this. I never imagined anything like this could happen. Take care of yourself, Jamie. We wish you were here, but we understand that you need time."

Jamie glances down at her notes and then back out the window.

"Take care, Stella. And thanks. Give my love to everyone will you?"

"Sure, Jamie, we all love you. Good-bye."

Jamie flips her phone closed and holds it, massaging it with her fingers for a while. She pours herself another cup of coffee and sits by her journal to write.

June 22nd

I am strangely calm about the Nexsentury news. It seems so far away from where I am. I know I can't live locked away from the real world...forever. But I have a choice. I can let this be a roadblock for me, or it can just be a speed bump. I can try to figure out who betrayed me or I can move forward.

Letter to myself:

Get on with what you are here for, Jamie. You've worked hard and struggled plenty. Now, you need TRAINING, Maggie.

Get your ducks in a row, Blondie. Line yourself up behind what makes you feel most alive. Your passion is your engine. Be like a train: all in one direction; all in a row; staying on track, no effort spent but what serves the goal. Line up all that you are behind why you are here and where you are going.

All the goods moving in one direction. Like a train. All those valuables on board – commodities, assets, raw materials and manufactured goods – mean nothing 'til they get where they're going.

Do you think a train looks anywhere but ahead? Got it? Get it!

When everything goes crazy, get back to your mission statement and have a Re-View.

WHAT

AM I

DOING

HERE!

Jamie decides this is the last day she will stay in and baby her ankle. She needs to keep moving along her trail. She will go to Church Rock tomorrow and just meditate for the day. A whole day just being: In nature. With the birds and the breeze in the trees. Small, unseen furry things rustling about. Clouds. Sunshine. Shadows, coming and going. Smells of the earth and all it holds dear. The self that she's been waiting to meet, waiting inside for her turn to come out.

Jamie remembers something she saw in the shed while she was recovering. They are the little metal stakes for naming plants in the garden. They could fit a small saying and hold up through the seasons.

She remembers driving along a road in the spring and in the middle of nowhere saw a clump of daffodils. Well, she knew damned well they didn't get there by themselves. Somebody planted them there. Someone got out of the car with a trowel in hand and put bulbs into the ground that they might never see. But how fun and wonderful is that? Random acts of gardening.

Today she will write on two of the metal stakes. She will plant messages on the stakes. Tomorrow, on her way to Church Rock, she will post them along the way. Maybe someone someday will see them. She needs ideas small enough to write down...large enough to carry with you the rest of your life. She will spend the day digging through her writings and books to find her first two sayings. This will be what she will think of instead of thinking about the theft.

When Jamie looks at her trail map, she sees she is just crossing into Virginia. She has always loved that name, her mother's name being Virginia Dare. She reads the write-up for the first town you come to in Virginia...Damascus. It is called "the friendliest town on the Trail". If she ever goes to one of the towns she has passed on her virtual journey, it will be Damascus she decides.

By the end of the day Jamie picks her first 'signposts.' She wants sayings of no more than three lines that will uplift and empower those who read them.

On the first one she writes:

>Dance like nobody's looking

>Sing like nobody's listening

>Love like you've never been hurt.

On the second she writes:

> Only as far as I stretch can I reach
>
> Only as far as I look can I see
>
> Only as far as I dream can I go.

Jamie is ready for tomorrow and the rest of her journey.

Chapter 22
Lifeline

Jamie is walking a new trail when she feels a oneness with all that is out there in the woods. She feels more like she is loved than simply a lover to the world. She feels earth, woods, and sky drawing themselves closer around her in an aching and sensual way. The trees reach toward her, arching over the path as if to enfold her. They breathe into her and she breaths into them. They find life within each other's breath. She feels the earth press up into her feet yearning to touch her, to know her and to live in her skin. It says, "Love me, please don't hurt me, I'll give you all that you need." She wants to yield, to give herself over and say, "Yes. Yes! I've always been yours!"

With these words, all that is urgent and needful gathers up into the warm shape of a man, like the long shadow of a tree stepping toward her. As he comes closer, she smells the wood smoke on his flannel shirt. He stands against her, chest to chest, before his arms fold around her. His hand takes authority over her sacrum and cool behind. Fingers part the feeble resistance of soft inner thighs. He pulls her to him. Crushing himself to her. Fingers then retracing their path on a slow thorough search of her own middle ground...chancing upon...then slipping from ...locating... then losing...maddeningly taunting her sweetest of spots. She grapples, grasps an unbearable firmness, planting it deep inside her.

A deluge of shuddering, shimmering, floating, exploding again and again where the boundaries of self and the edges of other fly away with all that is sane and insane. Two become one, and one becomes all and ever and ever and ever...'til, ecstasy fades to bliss. But the man dissolves, the shadow fades, and Jamie again finds herself walking, trying to recall...a face...a name?

Jamie's eyes open to the morning sun. The bed sheets are a ridge at the foot of the bed. She is on her back. She can't move. She doesn't want to move. She wants to go back to the dream. She lies enjoying the feeling of being filled, fulfilled and throbbing in the aftermath. She knows that she will never be able to go without a man. As much as she would like to do that, there is nothing quite like taking a man deeply inside her. But the scene where she is intertwined there on the mountain with nature, tells her she is never alone. She has been searching for this embracing nature for sixty-seven years, and there it was. But the shadow in the dream. It was more than simply nature. It was every bit of a man. She could still feel him, almost smell him. Strange that dreams sometimes don't give you a face to remember.

Jamie gets out of bed finally. The Fourth of July and a Saturday. Jake has started showing up on Saturday afternoons. He has figured out that Jamie visits the grocery store on Saturday and always has a great something cooked by Cora and Ellie Mae. Better yet, she will share it with him. Jamie loves these Saturday nights with Jake even more than the chance meetings on the trail. After a beer or two, he opens up...sometimes the dark side...sometimes the fun side.

Jamie is hungry from her ravishing night. She cracks three eggs for an omelet and uses up the last of her sweet onion, red pepper and sharp cheddar cheese. A little hot sauce. Perfect. The last slice of rye bread with Cora's homemade strawberry jelly finishes off the meal.

Riding the bike to the store, Jamie thinks about Ellie Mae. Still no period, but she hasn't told her ma yet. Every week she looks at Jamie with those sad eyes. Jamie can tell as soon as she walks in what the status is.

The meal of the week is a chicken pot pie. It looks delicious! They always give her plenty for several meals. They don't know that it is gone by 7 PM every Saturday night. Jamie stays for coffee. Then she gathers her groceries and heads back up Fire Tower Road for home. Jamie can tell that Cora and Ellie Mae are starting to like her a lot. It has become a pleasure for all three women to chat the way women only will. They hug each other like old friends or close relatives. Cora lingers with her hugs and when she touches Jamie's arm afterwards, it is a special touch. They will need each other if a baby is on the way.

Jake arrives about five. Jamie has had her walk and a shower. Dinner is warming in the oven. Job is asleep by Jake's rocker within minutes. Two hours later, Jamie's had a Jack and Jake two beers. The dinner dishes are in the sink. They sit back to talk as they do on these special nights.

"Maggie," Jake says, "I killed my baby boy."

Jamie freezes in her chair. She looks at Jake. His head is down, looking at the floor boards on the porch, hands together like he is praying.

Jamie goes hollow in the chest. She can feel the weight Jake has just released.

"Was it an accident, Jake?"

"Yes."

Jake's shoulders are hunched, and he continues to stare at the floor, without moving. Without even breathing. Jamie waits. His breath will come back. He will tell more when he is ready.

Jake rubs his hands together. "Daniel is dead and it is my fault," he says. He glances up toward the trees, eyes squinted as if the sun stung. "That is why I bought a dog and started east." He bends over, rests his forearms on his knees, hands still together in a clasp. "My wife left me. She couldn't forgive me. I had nothing then, so I left, too." There is a slight shrug in his shoulders, but no expression on his face. "I was headed to the Appalachian Trail and when I got to your property, something inside me told me to stop here. My grandfather taught me to listen to myself, and I knew this was where I needed to stop running. I explored and found the cave and stayed hidden from you."

Jamie's chest aches. Her stomach goes heavy. "Oh, Jake, I'm sorry. I can't imagine what that must feel like." She puts her hand on Jake's arched back and leans toward him, as if to see his face. "How old was Daniel?"

"He had just turned five. My wife, Clair, wasn't the outdoorsy type, and she said when Daniel was five, I could take him camping with me. For months before his birthday, it was all he wanted to talk about. I told him camping stories. I found a book of children's poetry about camping. We even roasted marshmallows at the fire place. He and I waited anxiously for his fifth birthday so he could go with me. He turned five on December 24, and the next week we went winter camping."

Jake glanced at Jamie and caught her eye. Then he gazed off toward the forest. "He wandered off while I was asleep. The next morning, I looked everywhere for him, and I found him frozen to death." He hung his head and took a long breath. "I wasn't going to ever share that with you, but my whole body told me I needed to."

Jamie rubbed her hand along Jake's back. She felt his ribs, then moved her hand up to his neck and let her fingers rub him gently. "I'm glad you did, Jake." A breeze sweeps through the trees, and Jamie feels her hair flutter against her cheek. "What about your parents and your ex-wife. Do they know where you are? Do they even know you are alive?"

"No."

Jamie reaches out and takes his hand in hers. She just massages it with her fingers, not knowing what to say. His hands are rough, but warm. Jake leans back in his chair. His head falls back in an exhausted pose. She takes his hand gently to her mouth and kisses it. What were her troubles compared to losing a child and it being your fault? No words come to her. She wants to take him inside her like in the dream. But all she can do is hold his hand in hers. They sit like this until the shadows deepen and the trees take on the dark green of evening light.

"I need to go Jamie. I need to go." Jake rubs his hands against his thighs and leans forward as if to stand.

"OK, Jake. You go, but first you need to wait here until I get something for you."

Jake sits lifeless in the rocker waiting for whatever she has for him.

Jamie goes into the house. She unplugs her phone and takes it to the porch.

"You need to listen to me, Jake. This is my cell phone. It will keep a charge for five or six hours. Just turn it off when you aren't using it and it will last longer."

"Why would I need a phone?"

"You need to call your parents and your ex-wife, Jake. Either tonight or tomorrow morning." She holds the phone out to him. "Just dial the number and push Send."

Jake is quiet for a moment, then he says. "Keep your phone, Maggie. I don't need to call anyone."

"You listen to me, Jake. Are you listening?"

"Yes, Maggie, I'm listening."

"Your parents are aging. They could get sick and you wouldn't know. The stress of them not knowing where you are could kill them. Don't let another person die while you're looking away."

Tears flow down Jake's cheeks. He gently takes the phone from her... gives her a long hug...walks off into the gathering darkness.

"Jake?"

"Yes?"

"I need the phone back on Tuesday sometime."

"Sure," he says. "You'll have it." He turns toward the trail. "Thank you," he says without catching Jamie's eyes. "Come on Job, boy. We need to go home."

"Jake!"

Jake stops but doesn't turn.

"I love you."

A whisper comes back to her. "I love you too, Maggie."

Gone.

Chapter 23
Reaching for Roots

The summer days seem endless, until July slips quietly into August. Jamie walks earlier now, to stay out of the humid heat. She is up before the sun, putting on her walking boots and as few clothes as she can: shorts, socks, bra, t-shirt.

It is August 2nd, and she is 630 miles along the Appalachian Trail, according to her mapping. She's on the Virginia-West Virginia state line at Peters Mountain. The air is still. Leaves from the trees are not cascading in a breeze, but instead stand full and still. Jamie's stride is quick, her arms pumping. To think that in April she had walked with two poles. It makes her smile.

Jamie walks out of the woods and into a field of tall grass. Grasshoppers leap as she passes. Brown grasshoppers, larger than she had ever seen. In the field, the sun hits her face without mercy. Sweat runs down her forehead, drops from her nose. The heat prickles her arms and legs, as if it had become like bugs. Heat bugs. Jamie pulls her shirt up and over her head. She sweeps it off and swings it in her right hand, without missing a stride. She has walked in her athletic bra before. There is a kiss of cool air on her stomach and chest, but it lingers only a moment before the heat is back. She doesn't worry about somebody seeing her. The bra holds her comfortably, and her body is firmer than it has been since she was 40. The walking is thinning her of excess weight, both physical and emotional.

Jamie walks into another woods, the field behind her, her arms still pumping, her breathing deep and steady, four steps to each exhale, four more for each inhale. She steps onto a ridge in the trail, the hill slopes upward to her right and plummets steep to her left. There is a tickle in her stomach. She has learned to trust this feeling. It always precedes seeing Jake on the path, as if there is a telepathy between them. She smiles at the word. Tele PATH y. Her life is literally a path now, and it has crossed Jake's with consistent twists.

Sure enough, Job bolts out of the woods from its steep edge, tail wagging, tongue hanging from the side of his mouth. He wags so with such vigor, his haunches sway. He bobs his head upward, as if asking for Jamie to pet him, even while he is five yards away. Jamie stops to greet him. She leans over. Job walks between her legs, still wagging. He turns around and sits in front of Jamie.

She pets him with long strokes. "Yeah," she says. "You just need some lovin'. You just get no attention at all." Job looks up to her, as if he understands what she says. He lies down, rolls belly up, and waves his front paw, inviting a rub.

Jake pulls himself onto the trail by climbing roots. "What a baby," he says.

"You expected him to climb up roots?" Jamie asks, as she marvels at the strength in this man. Jamie has thought of herself as strong. Jake is a different kind of strong...mind and muscle.

"Job and I are hunting for just the right root for a project we're working on.," explains Jake. "You don't know the right root unless you feel its strength."

"What kind of a project would you need a root for?" Jamie is interested. Jake does some unusual things. But roots?

"We are going to make a tool the Indians used to make. It's called a head knocker. It's hard to explain, but we'll show you when we have it finished."

"A head knocker?" Now Jamie is really curious. "Do you knock heads with it?"

"That's the idea," Jake says matter-of-factly.

"But Jake, whose head do you want to knock? There is no one attacking you and the bears don't want to get near you."

"I told you before, Maggie, I am a carpenter and wood worker. Every week I do a different project. Sometimes a project takes two weeks. In the summer I gather up supplies for winter projects. This is the only way I can keep my sanity out here away from people. It helps me forget." Jake squats beside Job as he speaks. He doesn't look at Jamie. "Seeing you every Saturday and the other times we just meet, has made everything much more bearable."

Now Jake stands and looks her in the eye. "I'm glad you're here,

Maggie. I'm glad to have a friend to share things with."

Jake moves uncomfortably. It seems the intimacy of sharing a feeling makes him nervous. "Come on Job. We are on the hunt here!" Jake smiles over his shoulder. "Only two more days until Saturday. See you then."

"Hope you find your root," Jamie calls after them. She feels a different kind of warmth now. It comes from Jake's sharing a sentiment and his smile. Jamie finishes her walk thinking of this strange, sweet alliance. She showers and gets to her journal to put these reflections into words. Jamie re-reads an entry from a month ago.

June 30: Evening. Feels like the end to the hottest day of the year. There was no breeze at all. Up at 6. Put on sandals, put ice in the water bottle and started hiking at 6:30. Took the White Oak trail down to the creek. Within 15 minutes was so sweaty took off shirt and shorts. Creek low. Enough water to sit in and cool off. Gravel on my bottom. Gurgle between my legs. Closed eyes and listened to the silence. Total peace. I feel a freedom I have never known. I am me. Not John's wife. Not my girls' mother. Not Stella's boss. Just me. Me. Jamie. Ja-ME. I know things no one else does. I feel things no one else feels. I like who I am. I like who I am becoming. Even if I can't explain it. Yet.

As the day cools into evening Jamie moves onto the porch to write. She has her Jack and some veggies to munch on. A slight breeze stirs the leaves and the sound is relaxing.

August 2: Evening

Jake continues to be my 'wise old Indian' teaching me all he has learned from his grandfather and mother.

A bit eerie. Exciting. I have developed a sixth sense about when Jake will show up. Got the feeling today, and there they were. Job first. Jake to follow.

He called me his friend. I can feel the trust building between us. He respects my privacy. Seems to have a sixth sense too.

Jake's intimacy with the natural world is truly impressive. He senses shifts in weather hours before they occur. Knows which plants are edible. Which are medicinal. Which are poisonous.

I gave up my favorite appliance, the disposal, and am composting waste now. The daffodil bulbs in the shed will have fresh compost when I plant them in sunny spots around the grounds this fall.

Never known a man like him. The men in my world were the men in John's world. Businessmen. Professionals. Highly educated. Successful in their own rights. For all their worldly successes, something was lacking. Maybe it was just that their worlds were full of THINGS. Their conversations were about THINGS.

Jake is different. Better? Perhaps. I haven't decided. The hurt he runs from and can't escape gives him a vulnerability that touches my maternal side. Unpolished. Yet poised. More disarming than dominating. His physicality is raw. Unpracticed. Unpredictable. I am unexplainably drawn. He has a modesty...a shyness that he wears like a second skin. He never stares at me. Doesn't make me feel like a thing. Reticent with his feeling as every other man I have known.

Head knocker! If he's made something every week or two, he must have quite a collection. In the cave? Will he show me?

Chapter 24

Job

It's the first Saturday in August...overcast, but warm. Jamie will go for her grocery run...looking forward to the evening with Jake and Job.

She eats the last of her eggs and toast. Makes a quick grocery list. Fires up her Harley. Looking at her watch, she notices that she is a little early. The store opens at nine. She will fill up with gas this morning and heads for the Marathon Station a few miles south of the Ram Cat. Mike, the young man who works most days, said he would go over her bike for her before winter to make sure it was in good shape.

"You should ride this baby more," he had told her the first time she got gas. "Harleys need rode to stay healthy." When she was early on Saturdays, she would drive the roads full speed to "clean the carbon."

This morning she rides free in the August air. The shadows are long on the road. August smells different than July did. Was it different plants in bloom? Summer pushing toward fall?

Jamie's foot hits the first step of the Ram Cat as the hand-lettered sign flips from "Sorry, Closed," to "Open," – smiley face for the "O".

Jamie knows the news had been delivered as soon as she sees Cora. Both women look like they have been crying. Cora reaches both hands toward Jamie. Jamie envelopes her in her arms as Cora's soft plump body seems to relax with one long sigh. Then Jamie reaches one arm to Ellie May, pulling her into the warm circle of women. The three women just hug each other – no words – for a long time.

Cora disengages first. She motions for them to sit at the table and pours coffee. The red checked tablecloth reminds Jamie of her mom's picnic cloth when she was a child. Mercifully, the bells on the door remain silent. No one comes in for a while.

Ellie Mae speaks first: "I told Mama, Jamie."

Cora sips her coffee, her chubby hands shaking a bit.

"I figured something was up," said Cora. "She couldn't seem to keep anything in her stomach."

Ellie Mae fidgets in her chair, then looks straight at Jamie. Jamie notices for the first time her beautiful blue eyes and long lashes.

"Mama told me she was pregnant with me when Daddy married her."

"It was more shot gun wedding than love match", said Cora. "My Poppa was really upset and took things into his own hands. I'm not sure Ellie Mae's daddy ever forgave either of us."

"I never knew that," said Ellie Mae. "But it sure does explain a few things. Mama was so nice about the whole thing. We just cried and are trying to figure what to do now."

Jamie's eyes glaze over and she seems far away. Slowly she remembers her own long ago. "I remember a time in college. I was dating a boy I liked, but he wasn't someone I really loved. I was about 19 and I thought I was pregnant. Something inside me told me that if I was, I would need to kill myself."

"Why on earth would you have to kill yourself?" asks Ellie Mae. She leans forward with interest. She is so tiny in her tank top and short shorts. Her sandals look like a child's.

"I wasn't sure why, but years later when one of my friend's daughters got pregnant in high school, my mom said to me that it would be better for the girl's mother if that girl were dead, rather than disgrace her mother like that." Jamie takes a deep breath and another sip of her coffee. She has never told anyone that.

Jamie straightens up in her chair. "Well then, what have you decided to do Ellie Mae?"

"Mama and I talked. I can't have an abortion. But I can't raise no baby without a husband. And Billy, my boyfriend, or was, is nowhere ready to be one. I want to get married someday and have children with someone who loves me. We were wondering if you would help us think of what to do. You live in the big world out there. What's other folks do?"

"First of all you need to see a doctor and make sure you make the healthiest baby you can." Jamie takes Ellie Mae's hands into her own. They are soft and her nails are shiny red. "I'm proud of you for doing this. There are lots of people out there who want babies. You need to make a healthy baby to give as a gift to someone. Do you know a doctor you could go to?"

Cora spoke up, "We don't have a doc ourself, but if we get real sick we go to the Urgent Care Center in Uniontown where there is a hospital. We could go there. We got no insurance is the thing. Babies cost lots."

"Go there this week if you can," Jamie advises. "Tell them your situation and they will find you some help. In this country they won't turn you away. Sometimes they have a different charge for people without insurance."

Jamie tries to sound reassuring. An idea is perking in her head. But time to think about that later. "Do you eat healthy food, Ellie Mae? Lots of fruits and vegetables, meat and milk? Take a B-complex?"

"Yes, ma'am, I do, most times, except for the B thing. Probably this coffee don't do me much good."

The women agree that after the appointment they would talk again about the possibilities. The three relax into their uncomfortable chairs.

"How's business been this summer?" Jamie asked.

"With the hot weather, we've sold lots of Ram Cat beer!" Cora laughs. "Yep, I'd say we're having a pretty good summer." Ellie Mae agrees. "We cooked you up a great ravioli dish," offers Ellie Mae. "With spicy marinara sauce. Ma made you fresh bread to go with it. Ma makes great homemade bread. I told her we should sell it here, but she's too tired after work to do that."

Jamie gathers the week's groceries. The women have customers, but each gives Jamie a hug before she leaves. Ellie Mae's tiny body melts into hers. A child having a child, Jamie thinks to herself. Jamie sits on the bike, feeling in her heart that everything will be all right for Ellie Mae. Jamie really loves these two women. Their lives are growing together. From such different walks of life, now bonding in feminine instinct to welcome a baby. Unalike in many ways. But now sharing the fate of a new life.

Jamie feels an urgency to get home. She gets a desire for speed, a little anxiety even. She tries to talk herself down. She knows she is going too fast for Fire Tower Road conditions. She lectures herself after losing track of her speed several times on the way home. Why the sudden need for speed?

Quickly unloading, she crams new groceries in front of the old, then hurriedly readies again for the trail. She catches herself rushing, and then has a laugh: "What's the big hurry – you're not hot for the trail, are you girl? You're on fast forward for your dinner date tonight. Tell the truth!"

Snugging the last double tie to her hikers, she thinks she hears something. She pauses. Is that Jake ?

"Maggie. Maggie. You home?" His voice is tense.

Suddenly shrill, "What happened, Jake?!" chokes out Jamie, now afraid for the reply. As she rushes outside she sees Jake carrying Job. No blood. Job is a little limp. When Jamie comes out he lifts his head slightly in greeting. His tail makes a few wags.

"Bit by a copperhead! We gotta get him to a vet. Can you help us?"

"Sure," Jamie jumps into action. Now with a strange inner calm...and knowing why the rush to get home. "Get on the back of the bike with him. We'll ask Cora where to go."

Jamie knows Job is heavy, yet Jake seems to carry him effortlessly to the bike. Jamie gets on and starts the engine. Jake easily put his leg over the back seat and gently lays Job between them. "Can we ride like this?" Jake asks.

"We'll see. Try to sandwich Job in between and hold him with your legs. Then put your arms around my waist if you can. I don't have time to teach you to ride, but do what I do. When I lean, lean with me. If I go left you go with me. OK?"

"Got it."

Jamie bikes quickly but safely down to the Ram Cat.

"Just stay here and I'll ask. Don't move Job."

Jamie rushes inside and explains things as best she can.

"Where is the closest vet?" Jamie asks.

"There's a vet place about five miles from here," Cora says with a disapproving look on her flushed cheeks. "We'll have to take you in the truck. You'll have to go along Jamie. That man and his dog can ride in the bed."

"Fine, let's go," Jamie hurries back outside.

Cora and Ellie Mae come out after her shortly. Cora's hips sway with this fast pace. Ellie Mae walks slightly behind her mother, as if hiding. They are still in shock that Jamie would be anywhere near this man.

"Ellie Mae," said Cora dangling her keys, "you take the truck and drive them to the Clinic."

"Of course I'll go."

"Take care Ellie Mae."

"Yes, Mama, we'll be fine."

As Jake climbs onto the back and braces Job and himself against the cab of Cora's pick-up, he says, "I can't believe he got bit. Dogs can smell that cucumber scent of a copperhead from a mile away."

Jamie gets in front and slides open the cab window. Jake nuzzles his face into Job's fur, muttering to him. Jamie offers reassurances. Ellie Mae drives in disapproving silence.

Jake jumps out of the cab with Job before Ellie Mae brings the truck to a halt. The clinic is a small, non-descript, gray cinderblock building. A sign hangs over the door on chains: ANIMAL HOSPITAL. Underneath in smaller letters, 'All animals welcome.' There is a faded drawing of a brown dog and a black cat. Jake runs for the door, sets the sign swinging with his height, and disappears inside.

Ellie Mae looks distressed. "What are you doing with that man? The sheriff is really worried about him!" She continues in a whiney voice. "I heard the sheriff say they think he killed someone. They are checking wanted posters. Say they can't arrest him until they have a warrant or until he does something else." Now Ellie Mae whispers. "If you want to know what I think, the sheriff is afraid of him too."

"Well the sheriff can stop worrying. Jake would never harm anyone."

"You know his name?"

"Yes. And his dog is Job," Jamie answers calmly.

"Mama would say to stay clean away from the likes of him."

"If I had done that, Ellie Mae, I would have missed knowing a good man, a good human being. I took the chance to look beyond the gruff exterior, and saw a man who lives at one with nature. A man who has been deeply hurt by life. A man who is trying desperately to heal in the only place he can heal – alone in nature."

"Well," frets Ellie Mae, "does he have to heal in your nature? Tell him to get to some other nature to heal. Besides, you don't know nothing about him, really."

"Before we go in, let me tell you something I learned long ago from my husband." Jamie puts her hand on Ellie Mae's as she talks. "He said that if you hear the sound of hooves in your back yard, you will think there is a horse there. But maybe you should have a look. It might not be a horse at all, it might be a zebra. People aren't always what they look like, Ellie

Mae." Jamie talks softly now leaning toward her. "When you start to look pregnant and people see you, they may think of you as a 'bad girl' who got pregnant. In truth you were a girl in love that trusted that your man loved you too. You won't be the horse they think you are, but a lovely zebra instead. Let's go on in."

Ellie Mae follows her inside. The two women sit and wait. A curtain hangs down over a doorway. Jake and Job must be back there. They hear muffled voices in the back. Craving a smoke, Jamie renews an old habit of working at her cuticles. Ellie Mae seems lost in her own thoughts.

When Jake comes out carrying Job, they both look better. Jake says with obvious relief, "The doc says Job will be all right by tomorrow morning. I really don't want to carry him home. Could we sleep on your porch tonight?"

Ellie Mae sucks in air. Jake looks at her. "And thank you, young lady, for the ride. Be sure to thank your mama for us too."

Ellie Mae turns for the door. Her sandals march across the gravel lot with a crunching sound. She starts up the truck. Jamie knows this isn't the end of the discussion with Ellie Mae and Cora too, but she needs to get Job back to her place where he can lay down.

They thank the women again for the help, get on the bike, and ride up Fire Tower Road toward home. It is late afternoon when Jake lays Job on a towel on Jamie's porch. "You can sleep inside if you like. I agree he should just rest and recover."

"We'll sleep out here if you can spare a blanket. As I said, I'm not coming inside. I might like it in there," Jake smiles.

Jamie remembers John's blow-up-egg-crate mattress. She brings it out and Jake pumps it up. They ease Job into the center and within moments he sleeps peacefully.

"Do I see a pack of 'Boros on your side table?" Jake asks.

"Would you like one?"

"Please." Jake slumps into the rocker. "You smoke?"

"I did years ago. I said if John ever died I'd take it up again. I bought those the first day. Had two so far. Weren't as good as I remembered. What about you?"

"Same. Years ago. It just seems that I might relax a bit if I had one now. What's that they say, 'One's too many when a hundred's not enough'?"

Jamie fetches the pack and a light. Jake fires up, inhales deeply, coughs once, takes another deep drag, then sinks deep in the chair.

"How about a beer?" Jamie offers. "I don't think either of us is driving anywhere else today. Hey, how'd you like the ride on my Harley?"

"Next time without Job. I got a little of the feel for it, but want to do it again when I can enjoy it. And, yes, I'll have a brew with my smoke."

Jamie sets dinner to warm on her run for the beer. "We spent lunch at the vet's, so dinner's early today," she muses, returning with some crackers and sharp cheddar in one hand, two longnecks in the other.

"I saw the garden stake you wrote on the other day," Jake looks at her appreciatively. "What a nice idea. I was having a bad day and was walking along, and there it was."

"Which one did you see?"

"You mean there's more than one of them out there?"

"Well, yeah, only two. But I plan for lots more. I got the idea when things were going badly at John's company – well I guess it's my company now – and I was about to get sucked back in. It was when I had the sprained ankle. I wanted to get my mind cleared, so I decided to leave some notes along the trail."

"Could I do one, Maggie?"

"Sure. You want to do it now? I can get you a stake."

"I'd like to write a poem on one. It's got five lines to it. Would that fit?"

"Funny, there is one larger than the rest. It's yours. I'll get it for you and my permanent pen to write it with. But only if I can read it now and don't have to hunt for it." Jamie smiles a teasing smile. "Deal?"

"Deal."

Jake takes the stake, thinks for a minute, and begins to write:

> There is a pleasure in the pathless woods,
>
> There is a rapture on the lonely shore,
>
> There is society, where none intrudes,
>
> by the deep sea, and music in its roar:
>
> I love not man the less, but Nature more.

He turns it on the back and writes: George Gordon, Lord Byron (1788-1824)

He hands it to Jamie. "One of my favorite poets. I brought a book of poetry with me when I came east. This is in it. Have you read any of his poems?"

Jamie reads it twice and looks on the back. "That is beautiful, Jake. I'm sad to say I can't remember a thing but the name, Lord Byron."

"I'll lend you the book, if you like. If you've got one to trade. I would like one of yours to read while you have it."

"I'll be glad to lend you any of my books. I have two by Mary Oliver. I love her poems. Have you read her?"

"No. Read me one now, Maggie."

Jamie brings both books out on the porch and reads Jake a few dog-eared pages. "This one's called 'Praying.'"

<blockquote>

"It

doesn't have to be

the blue iris, it could be

weeds in a vacant lot, or a few

small stones; just

pay attention, then patch

a few words together and don't try

to make them elaborate, this isn't

a contest but the doorway

into thanks, and a silence in which

another voice may speak."

</blockquote>

"I like that." Jake says smiling. "In our culture, your weeds are often plants we use to heal. And silences are as important as words."

"You may take these with you. When you bring me your book, though, you must read to me – that's the deal."

"How about two of my favorites right now?" Jake asks. Jamie nods.

As he recalls more passages by heart, she feels a closeness to him that she has never felt before. Here is a man of few words. Who feels the words. Who loves words. And when the words come they are emotionally charged. This big wild-looking mountain man. She is so happy she has the time to look inside him. She realizes in that moment she has never stopped to see with her heart and it feels good.

The two eat and talk into the night. Then they hug. She lingers a second longer in his embrace. When Jamie goes to bed, she leaves the door open. Jake lies beside Job on the mat that had belonged to John. He looks like a child with his dog. Jamie feels warm all over. In the morning, Jake and Job are gone. The mat is flat and folded with the blanket by the door. The stake and the books are gone too. Later, when she gets back from her walk, she finds the book of Byron poetry leaning back in her rocker.

Chapter 25

Wood Smoke and Honeysuckle

August 26th

Some morning thoughts before I walk.

Today feels different. Feel a self emerging. A self beyond the socially defined goals of wealth and success. I've slowed life down. To a walk. I'm sensing what lies ahead. No knee-jerk reactions lately.

I've seen that trust can be misplaced. I feel safer with a man who lives in a cave than with business partners.

And who would have thought Cora and Ellie Mae would become friends? Cultural divides and social taboos hold no sway when a baby's on the way. It doesn't matter whose baby. How old you are. Feminine instinct is to work together for the birthing of new life.

I am finding a self I like. Feel drawn to go 'off road' today. Maybe Church Rock for lunch and some sun. I feel a change in the air. In myself. Maybe fall is coming.

Jamie packs a blanket and some lunch: cheese, Cora's left over crusty bread, deep purple grapes and a red pepper. She will pick raspberries on the way if the birds and bears have left any. It isn't Sunday but she feels drawn to Church Rock.

As she walks she tries to see things with her heart. She gets a warmth and trill in the chest when she opens to nature. She notices everything. The trees and plants seem more vivid today. The rocks underfoot appear spaced perfectly for her stride.

By the time she reaches Church Rock it is 10:00 and warm, the sun rising towards the noon sky. She looks out at the vista. Jake told her that you can see five miles to the far ridge line. There are two ridges between her rock and the farthest ridge. All she sees are trees. The ridge line is

30 miles long. There are probably a couple thousand people in that view range, yet they can't see her and she can't see them. Will she see houses when the leaves fall? This rock, the size of a barn, was it pushed here by glaciers, or did God put it here for a few special people to have one of the best views on earth?

Jamie isn't the only one who uses this rock. More than once, there has been a black snake sunning itself like she was going to do today. Once she came and there were two black snakes intertwined like they were braided together. She has meant to ask Jake what that was all about. She poked them with a stick and they slithered away, leaving the rock to Jamie for a few hours.

Jamie takes off her clothes. She positions the blanket so her body will be in a direct line with the sun. She lays down feeling the hardness of the rock beneath her. A cool breeze kisses her skin. The sun warms her all the way through. A shiver of excitement passes over her when she thinks of her exposure in front of all those people who can't see her. Complete freedom.

Three sides of the rock are exposed. Lots of places for critters to hide.

She remembers some things Jake had told her. At the base of the rock, thirty feet below, is an overhang. Cave like. He told her there is a porcupine living there. She asked if he had seen it. He said, "No, just the droppings." That was the day she got her lesson about the many varieties of spoor: coon, deer, bear, the whole works. He had also told the old joke about how porcupines make love. "Very carefully."

Jake also told Jamie that this rock would have been a great place for Indians to send smoke signals to the surrounding valley. The park system realized the same thing and built a fire tower nearby.

On the rock, Jamie fades in and out of sleep. When the sun goes behind a cloud, the air is cool, but the rock holds the heat. Her skin bristles with the breeze, and she feels as if she sinks into the rock for warmth. She does not know how long she has been on the rock when Job appears as a beacon. "Hey, Job, don't you bark before you enter a lady's room?"

She doesn't move to cover up. She doesn't even lift her head, but tenses slightly when Job sniffs her face, then her chest. "Careful boy," she says. She pushes Job away.

She hears Jake's footsteps and what must be a knock on a tree. "You decent?" he asks playfully. "Depends on your definition of decent," Jamie replies, eyes still closed. Job comes back, tail wagging, and Jamie sits up to pet him. Job is pleased to provide for Jamie's modesty in exchange for a scruff-rub and back scratch with her un-manicured nails.

She turns to see Jake. He is sheepish. "May I come in?" Jake asks, looking straight at Jamie. She pushes Job away again and lies back down. The rock now seems harder under her spine and she shifts slightly to relax. "This isn't 'Church Rock' today," she says, half annoyed, half playful. "It's 'Naked Rock'. If you want to get naked, you're welcome." She shuts her eyes and tries not to be affected by this man. She hears Jake take off his boots. There is no relaxing now. Only a desire at once familiar and strange. How long had it been since she felt this way?

Her breath goes shallow. The trill is back in her chest, but stronger. Her nipples taut as nerves. She rises on her elbow to see Jake take off his shirt, then his jeans. He has no underwear. The sight of him ignites every molecule in her body. He seems both nonchalant and shy. She likes that. Their eyes meet. Then he looks away.

Jake snaps a branch from a bush. The noise seems to snap the tension as well. He steps onto the rock with an athlete's grace. She smiles gently, admiring the tone of his muscles. There are no tan lines on his Native American skin, the summer having given him a darker hue all over. He looks down at her and smiles. "Nature has been kind to your body. Your time here has healed much already." How does he know such things? she asks herself a bit nervously, feeling more co-ed than grandmother.

"May I?" he asks, gesturing to the blanket. "Of course!" Her mind and mouth are disconnected. He comes and lies beside her on the blanket. Job moves to the fern- covered bank behind them, a self-appointed sentinel. Or maybe he was thinking, "I'd rather be in soft ferns than on a hard rock." Jake swings the small branch in front of Jamie. There are flowers on it.

"Do you know what this is?"

"No Jake. What is it?" She is glad to have something to think about besides the cool edges of Jake's skin. She hasn't felt like this about a man in a long time. It's not just desire. There is a thrill inside her, rising from a part of her she'd forgotten about.

"Honeysuckle." Slowly he picks off a blossom. There is a drop of liquid on the stem. He dabs it on his finger and rubs his moist finger gently on her lips. "Tell me what you taste?" Jake instructs.

The taste is subtle and sweet. "Tastes like honey." She licks her lips again. He slowly pulls off another blossom from the branch – a sweet drop of nectar rises to his finger. This time he puts it on his own lips.

Jamie rolls toward him and kisses his honey lips. It was an impulse, not planned, not anticipated. An erotic jolt shoots through her body. If she lives forever, she will never lose the animal part of herself. She will never tire of the feel of a man's warmth growing in her hand. Jamie feels his teeth, takes his tongue. Jake, Jake, Jake, Jake. In the future, she will try to say his name enough, but she never will.

Jake draws her to him. She feels his belly tighten under her, hard as a board. Her wetness slips on his skin. Jamie pulls his head to hers. Kisses him fiercely. She is on the edge of losing control. It is the moment of vulnerability, the point where there is no turning back. No thinking. Only the animal part of her wanting to get as close as she can to him.

Then she leans away from Jake, rises to her knees, and faces him. She gently, but insistently pushes him onto his back. Then straddles his body and lowers herself onto him. He puts his arms around her. His warm face meets her breasts. He takes her nipple in his mouth and cradles her other breast in his callused palm. Velvet and sandpaper. No words. None needed. Only awakenings. Her eyes meet his, and she studies his youth, his manhood. She smiles down at the wonder in his eyes, the secret she has unearthed.

Somehow she takes Jake within her deeper than she has taken any man. He breathes heavily and lets out a low moan as he pulls her toward him one final time. Jamie kisses Jake and he kisses her and from that moment on she will never be able to separate the smell of wood smoke and honeysuckle from this moment in time.

She lies against him. Their bodies slick with sweat. She feels him drop away. His breath becomes more regular. His eyes begin to clear. He strokes her hair. Gently he turns her over on her back. He lays over her, careful not to put his weight on her. The hardness of the rock presses into his forearms. He kisses her eyes. Her ears. Her breasts. Her belly. Her gall bladder scar that she always thought of as ugly. The line of soft down that leads from her navel to her dark triangle. The inside of her legs where the skin is softest.

Then his carpenter's hands lift her hips and his tongue touches her innermost part. He drinks long and deep from the bowl of her. She pushes against him, shuddering with pleasure over and over. Jake puts her gently down. He positions his head gently on the softness of her belly. The sugar maple tree shades the rock now and they lay in cool silence. Her hand runs through his dark hair. There is nothing to say.

On that sacred rock. On the rock she has missed for so many years. Jamie lives. The silence is not empty but full with wind, sun, shadow and peace. Just as she thinks Jake must be sleeping, he asks, "In this area, do you know when most Indian babies were born?"

Jamie smiles. "No, Jake. Tell me when the babies were born."

"In very late fall or winter or early spring."

"Why then, Jake?" Jamie asks coming back to earth, almost annoyed at this bit of conversation. She doesn't want his quizzes. Only him.

"Well," he explains. "The Indians lived in 'long houses.' The man went to live with his wife's family. Everyone slept in the same room. You had your mother-in-law, her sisters, and nieces and nephews as close as three feet from you at night. It made things hard to handle. So with spring and summer and early fall, the couple could go somewhere in the woods and they had some privacy."

Jamie smiles at this.

"Also, in the winter, the young braves didn't want to have to walk all the way to the Ram Cat to get a rubber," Jake waits for her to realize what he has said.

Jamie smacks him on the shoulder. They both laugh until they have tears in their eyes. They share Jamie's lunch and Jake's deer jerky and dried crab apples. As evening cools the air, they dress. Jamie watches him. She realizes how natural it is, even the getting dressed. They walk together to their separate paths.

Jake puts his arms around Jamie. He puts his hand under her chin. He lifts her lips to his. He kisses her softly. In her ear he whispers, "Today, I felt alive for the first time in a long time. I felt more alive than any other time in my life. Thank you."

"I felt alive too, Jake. I thank YOU."

"Job and I will see you Saturday, if not before," he flashes his Jake smile. Jamie watches them walk off toward their cave. She starts for home. Life will never be the same.

Chapter 26

Haiku

It's close to dusk by the time Jamie gets back to the cabin. She is tired but wants to write some in her journal before sleep. She looks back at her hurried entry from this morning. Now she understands why she felt different today. Why she was drawn to Church Rock. The change she felt coming. Was that the voice inside her like a sixth sense?

August 26th cont.

I want this day suspended forever. This is a day I never want to let go of. A day that contains nothing else but itself, no intrusions. I was naked. Felt wonderful. A 67 year old woman naked outside? Why not? I was naked alone. I liked it. I was naked with another. I liked that too.

Sometimes Jake can be fierce. Like he is fighting off a demon. Today he was gentle. I am a generation older yet I felt like a fawn. Jake reached for me. Then through me. Like he needed me to help him go somewhere else. He was with me closer than any man has ever been. And then I felt him fly away. Not leaving me. Not abandoning me. No. More. Can I find words?

Jamie falls asleep. The pen drops quietly to the floor. When she awakes the following words are right below the others...she doesn't remember writing them. It is a poem written in haiku style. Jamie remembers studying haiku in college: five syllables, then seven, then five again. It's her handwriting and her pen, but she feels sure she didn't write it. Is this the Voice again? "Please let it be", she whispers to herself.

Two unite to heal

sex taboos God does not know

souls are one...God sings.

She reads it again and again. Exhaustion takes over. She drinks some milk and goes to bed. No shower tonight. Jamie wants the smell and feel of this day to last the night. She falls into an exhausted sleep. The day extends into her dreams. A fast merging and purging of images. Snakes wrestling, then lifting into the sky becoming hawks circling and twirling and the weight and weightlessness of Jake on her, in her. Rolling together in a blanket of honeysuckle. John appears and disappears from behind a cloud. Reaching and touching nothing. Hearing Jake call her name. She calling his. The two swooping over that valley, the ridge, the rock.

Jamie wakes early. Refreshed. Alive. She steps outside to greet the morning. On her chair a rock holds a piece of paper. She picks it up. Jake's handwriting. Her heart speeds ahead when she sees he too has written a haiku and left it for her:

> Life loving itself
>
> intimacy...privacy
>
> soul to soul healing.

Chapter 27
Alone Again

For the rest of the week, Jamie is busy with the business and works through problems with the life she has put on hold. With faxes and emails, she tries to keep the business at arm's length, knowing if the threatened calamity gets any closer it will overwhelm her and everything she's trying to do here. It *must* be kept away. And Stella's going to have to handle things. She just *has* to.

As Jamie had suspected, the signature on the warrants wasn't a two-year-old signature. It was more like John's signature had looked 10 years ago. Stella was busy collecting sample signatures from everyone who could possibly have been involved in this two year old mystery. She had talked to the FBI at Jamie's instruction to see what she should do next. The FBI said they would talk to her, but she would have to go to Washington, D.C. to a handwriting expert. Stella would have to wait two months for an appointment with the expert she had finally hooked up with, Ken Branson. Jamie still called each week as she had promised.

In the reality that Jamie wants to stay in now, where is Jake? Even though she is used to him showing up unannounced, still she thinks after what had happened on Church Rock he would come to see her. If Jamie has learned one lesson about men it is when they've had a woman once, they'll come back for more. Sometimes a lot more. At least at first! Each day she hikes as usual, hoping Job will come bounding up at the next turn in the trail, with Jake following. But with each day that passes, she gets a strange feeling in the pit of her stomach. She recognizes it, as women do, when they wonder if they have made a mistake with being intimate.

She tries to dismiss the feeling with a renewed interest in the Appalachian Trail. Studying the map, Jamie sees she's 830 miles from Springer Mountain. That puts her in the middle of Virginia. At Humpback Mountain. Perfect. About twelve miles from Shenandoah. Just before she starts her walk in the mornings she opens the guide book and studies the area where she would be along the trail. One morning, a quote from her guide jumps out: "Take nothing for granted. Not one blessed cool mountain day or one hellish, desert day, or one sweaty, stinky hiking companion. It is all a gift." That describes life here at the cabin. With Jake. *Or* without him.

By Saturday, thoughts of Jake have settled down. Almost. She looks forward to her ride down to the Ram Cat. She gives the Harley an extra long revving, feeling its throaty response as she clicks into gear and roars down the road.

Ellie Mae is full of talk about going to the clinic. They have offered a sliding payment scale and said that she is healthy, but gave her a paper with things she needs to do. Jamie notices a glow to her skin. It is a healthy glow she has seen on other pregnant women when their bodies carry new life inside of them. Jamie wonders when these short shorts and small t-shirts will be too tight for her to wear.

Jamie sits with Ellie Mae and looks over her instructions, mugs of coffee steaming between them. The musty smell of the store has come to be a comfort to Jamie. Her time with these women something she looks forward to. Memories of pregnancies and birth flood into her consciousness again. Every birth is a miracle. Every life is precious. Every mother-to-be deserving the best of care, no matter how she conceives.

Ellie Mae tells how the clinic doctor talked to her about adopting out her baby. She said she could see the baby and then decide if she wanted to put him or her up for adoption. At that point she would sign papers and they would take the baby to a family who could really take good care of her/him. Ellie Mae seems comfortable with the whole thing. But Jamie senses her uncertainty. Jamie looks into those young blue eyes and sees something more. That unspeakable fear every first-time pregnancy injects into a woman's being. Jamie says nothing about this, yet.

From behind the counter, casually, Cora asks, "That fella, Jake, was that his name?" Cora is waiting on customers who all came at once this morning. She is just getting around to putting on her brightly flowered apron. Her hair is what Jamie calls 'wash and wear', always the same, always neat and easy.

"Yes," says Jamie, her heart headed south to the pit of her stomach. The word 'was' seemed to start the cascade. "Where'd he go?" asks Cora.

"What do you mean, where did he go?" Jamie feels her face heating to the color of her red shirt. She had dressed for her hike today with special care to look good. Her favorite red polo shirt, jean shorts, hiking boots.

Cora rings up the last person in line. A local woman with her two small children who have been playing hide and seek in the isles. Cora realizes that this is news to Jamie. Her eyes soften as she moves to the table to sit with her and Ellie Mae for a minute.

"Didn't he tell you?" asks Ellie Mae.

"No." She tries to sound casual. But Jamie knows her throat tightened into a higher pitch, betraying more of their relationship than she wants to share.

"He was by on Thursday, and used the pay phone," said Cora softly. "We heard him say he needed picked up here and needed taken to the Morgantown airport. A cab showed up thirty minutes later, come from Uniontown I think, and he and the dog got in and disappeared up the road."

Jamie starts to shake. She thinks the shaking is on the inside but she's not sure.

"Did he say anything else to you?" Jamie asks trying not to sound panicked.

"He was polite as usual, thanking us for everything, but that's all, Jamie. He looked cleaned up. Like he was going somewheres special."

Jamie wishes for this to be a dream. She wants to wake up and know that what they told her is not true. Tears begin to well up in her eyes. She doesn't want to give herself away right now. She needs time to think about this. Jamie shops quickly. She can't remember what she had been planning to buy. Nothing looks good to her anyway. Coffee, she is almost out of coffee. Jack Daniels for sure. She'll just eat some of the stored foods if she gets hungry. Jamie puts her things on the counter and takes the delicious looking fried chicken and potato salad they have made for her. She knows she is going to cry and she wants to cry in private. She packs everything into her backpack. She sees that her hands are shaking. Got to go.

Again, she guns the Harley. Not the happy revving of just a few hours ago. She waves feebly to the women. And roars out of town so loud that more than one head pokes out a doorway or window to see who is causing the stir. She is tempted to ride and ride and ride. To ride this man out of her life. But she knows, too, what she really wants is to hide. To crawl into a small hole. And try to forget about this man a generation younger who has gotten what all men want anyway. Even at 67, she feels as used and spit out as Ellie Mae must feel at times. How can he do this to her? Why has she been so naïve? Well…good riddance! She roars up the hill.

Jamie puts the food away. Tears burn in her eyes and spill over, continuing the burn as they roll down her cheeks. She dressed for her walk early this morning. She dressed for the possibility of seeing Jake. God damned men! She grabs water and her walking stick and heads out quickly. She walks like a woman possessed by something…fast and deliberate and longer than any hike so far. By five o'clock, she has cried all the tears she thought she had in her. She pours herself a Jack Daniels and heads for the porch. She knows she can't eat the great meal Cora and Ellie Mae have prepared with this genuine love that has developed among the three women. It will just have to wait. Like her. Waiting…for what? Not a man she has no business being with. And who has no business being with her.

She has wanted to be alone for this year, hasn't she? She has needed to find herself and she is. So why is Jake's leaving hitting her so hard? Is it a woman's ego? He had sex with her and then left. Left without a word. Maybe he went back to his old life.

She knows eventually they will go back to their separate lives, but this is too soon. They are both helping each other heal. Or so she thought.

The fax machine whirrs to life. Nothing good ever happens when that machine starts spitting out paper, demanding Jamie's immediate attention. She wants no part of it now. So she just yells, "And screw you, too!"

Another JD and her day is over. Maybe her life as well. John is no help now. He is too far gone. And so is she. She falls asleep in her chair. No interest in her journal tonight.

Chapter 28

Blue Highways

Sunday morning feels no better. Jamie wakes with a headache served up by too much booze and too little food. Her body is stiff from a night spent in the overstuffed chair. The slant of the light tells her it's early yet. But the air feels like midday. It is going to be a scorcher. She thinks about a shower. Then says no. Not sure what she's doing or why, she puts hiking boots on, picks up her backpack and stuffs her notebook, a bottle of water and an orange inside.

She marches up the hill, walking stick digging angrily, wanting to feel a sweat start quickly. The doe and two fawns she startles a hundred yards later don't faze her. She knows that in Pennsylvania there are more deer with twins than in other states. She doesn't stop to marvel or enjoy. She is on a mission. Her legs feel strong, even if her head and stomach are no match. Soon the beads of JD-cleansing sweat begin their trickle down her cheeks. Dampness gathers under her arms and breasts. This is better.

The slow climb to the ridge seems to match the sun's equally steady climb into the morning sky. Thirty minutes later, a full sweat on, she reaches the turn off to Church Rock. She pauses for a minute, not even long enough to catch her breath. She thinks about just removing her clothes and finishing the hike the way he'd found her less than a week ago. But again she says no; today she doesn't want to see him, especially *that* way. She has a better idea.

Another fifteen minutes and she turns to the right and follows the lesser marked path to Jake's "cave." A few minutes later and the ledges come into sight. A minute after that, she steps into the cave's cool darkness. Now she takes time to catch her breath and let her eyes adjust to the darkness. Slowly the details of the space, *his* space, reveal themselves. When she's been here before, she noticed how he took care with his housekeeping. Now things seem out of place, as though he's left in a hurry. Well, he has, hasn't he?

She has to bend over to look in spaces she only peeked at before. She thinks maybe she'll find some inkling of why he has left, if he intends to come back. She worries she might be the reason for his leaving. What can that be? Drugs? A weapon? A sign that someone else had been here too? She doesn't know...there are clothes. Winter ones. Folded. He's left books too. There aren't many. But as she picks up one after the other, she can tell they have been read thoroughly. Two catch her attention.

One has an unusual title: *Zen and the Art of Motorcycle Maintenance.* What could a religion have to do with taking care of motorcycles? Did he have this before they met? Maybe she'll ask next time she sees him. She catches herself with that thought. If she sees him? Thinking this, she forgets the headache and notices more of an emptiness that won't go away in her chest. "You shit!!" she yells into the rock walls.

She puts the book down and picks up the one next to it. *Blue Highways,* by a man with a Native American name, William Least Heat Moon. Not knowing why exactly, she stuffs this one into her backpack. Yes, it is stealing. But not if its owner never plans to claim it. She's had enough. Plus, the cave's cool air is giving her a chill. Just as she is about to step back into the light and heat, she notices one more thing. Two neatly stacked piles of freshly cut limbs. On closer inspection she sees the wood is cherry. She has learned what different woods look like from John and from Jake. Some thick limbs. Four inches in diameter. The others about two or three inches thick. They are standing as if being dried out. All the bark has been carefully pealed off. She wonders what those might be for. Not firewood, she knows that. But he had been planning to do something with them before he left.

Her walk back to the cabin is easier, more leisurely. She knows no more now about how or why Jake left. But she feels better for having made the effort. This time she takes the turn to Church Rock. Jamie slips off the backpack. She pulls out her water and the orange. Taking a sip, she then does what she'd done less than a week before, removes her clothes and settles onto the coolness of the limestone. She lays back and closes her eyes. She does not want him to discover her this time. This time she wants this space for herself. Only for herself. No Jake. No John. No Ellie Mae. No Stella. She runs her hands over the wetness of her sweaty body, almost like checking to see if she is still alive. As a soft, warm breeze dries her slowly, she falls into something she's needed for days...a deep, deep sleep. When Jamie wakes, she is covered in shade. But the air is still warm and she stretches her body, happy that she now feels rested. Part of that feeling comes from the fleeting images of a dream. She reaches for her journal, hoping to capture something before she's left with just feelings.

Me on a horse. Someone next to me. Riding fast. Through a field. I think. Hugging horse's neck. Taking me somewhere. I think it's going to be alright.

She looks at the words, trying hard to capture other details. But the dream is gone. Maybe the fragment from her dream means something. Maybe it doesn't. Still, for some reason, she feels better than she has in days. Since she last saw Jake really. Maybe it all will be alright. Jake. The business. John. Her.

She takes the orange and peels it slowly, now reluctant to leave this place. As she separates rind from the fruit, she thinks of how she would section it like this for her children, how she taught them to do the same. As she slips a section between her lips, she remembers how she would do that for John in the final months, helping him with this sweet bite of life, once so easily taken for granted, now savored with each drop of juice.

The final section in her mouth, she looks down at the slow river of juice sliding between her breasts. She closes her eyes and thinks how just a week ago Jake had stirred her own juices. Will she ever have that feeling again? Or will it be a memory to savor like this day, this rock, and this orange? She has decided to embrace their time, not regret it. If their moment here helped him to escape from his cave, then that was good, wasn't it? If she never saw him again, still there was something gained from their 'relationship' – if that's what it was – wasn't there? She wished him well. Now she was ready to go back to the cabin.

Chapter 29

Nuts!

Monday morning announces itself with another whirring from the fax machine. Jamie looks at the clock. 7:30. Faxes this early could only mean more problems. Still she refuses to go near it until she's made coffee and starts on one of the rolls she'd bought at the Ram Cat. There is a chill in the air that seems early for September. She puts on one of John's shirts. Then, carrying coffee and roll to the machine, she looks down cautiously at the larger-than-normal stack of paper. The cover note from Stella is crisp, and efficient, if not entirely correct grammatically:

Jamie, you must look at this and respond TODAY. Ted said Rich is moving against you with the Board. If you loose Board support, you will loose control of the company, too. Ted said to tell you that you have to come back NOW. If you don't, you may come back later to a disaster.

Jamie couldn't figure out if that was Stella's opinion or Ted's. Not that she cared. She knows she doesn't feel the urgency to maintain control of the company (whatever that meant) that they did. Still, she feels an obligation to their clients and employees. She knows she can't just leave them under new management. She sits down with papers, coffee and roll. It will be a not-business-as-usual Monday, she sighs.

The papers are a letter from Rich to the Board outlining what he believes to be a series of missteps John had made in the final year of his life. And, with Rich's usual Machiavellian flair, he intimated that perhaps John's mistakes were part of a plan to suck money out of the company for personal benefit. A single tear trails Jamie's cheek as she arrives at the real business of Rich's manifesto: the company needs a thorough going-over, a restructuring and new direction before all is lost. What's more, it is plain that Jamie, "the dear, deeply grieving widow," is too far gone in her own loss to provide the leadership John has left to her as chair of the Board.

Rich's proposal was this: remove Jamie as chair ("and allow her the dignity of grieving without the fearsome burden of running a company for which she was ill-prepared in the best of times"). He further proposed electing himself as chair with a promise for a "full accounting and revised strategic plan within 90 days." He asked for their responses by Wednesday.

Jamie's hands tremble as she puts the papers down. Not from fear, from anger, "That little shit!" she says to herself. She considers her options. The first, going back, is *not* an option. She still controls the company. Rich would need 75% approval to remove her. At best, he might get 35 to 40%. If someone else from the Board, say Phil, had tried to make this move maybe she would have more reason for worry. But Rich was a weasel and the Board knew it. John had regretted putting him on from the first day. He justified it only by saying that Rich was a self-made billionaire who usually got good press from reporters fawning over his rags-to-riches story – which he never tired of re-telling.

Jamie owns all the stock. But this is the first time since John's death that she will have to use it. Ted is watching out for her, and she knows she can trust him completely. But John also said Ted got nervous in a fight and tended to "make his way to the back of the crowd." Ted was worried about personal liability. Her only option is to stand firm. But she will do it from her own position of strength – which now happens to be here.

She starts writing a note back to Stella. Then she remembers something John had said about negotiations, "The more you say, the more you give away." She crumples the note and tosses it towards the waste basket. She walks around the cabin a bit. Gets another cup of coffee. Tries to think how John would have dealt with this. She would not let the company go under. But neither would she give up what she came here for. She needs to write back something that lets Ted and Stella know she is still in control for as long as she wants to be. Something that would give them the courage not to cave in when other members of the Board started putting pressure on Ted to follow Rich's agenda.

She stands in front of the bookcase. These were John's books mostly. A lot of military history. Especially World War II. Patton was one of his favorite generals. She had even tried to find him a pearl-handled revolver like the one Patton carried. "What should I tell them, John?" Jamie waits for the Voice or some kind of answer to come.

She stares at the books a little more, then walks outside where the sun has chased away the early chill. Jamie wanders over to the ancient white oak, so large it creates its own clearing. Looking down she sees its acorns. "Mighty oaks from little acorns grow!" she had learned in school, smiling at the thought and comfort she feels being next to this tree. John's tree. Then it hits her. Jamie walks back quickly inside, grabbing another piece of stationery. She writes in very large letters, filling the entire page:

Dear Stella and Ted,

Here is my answer to Rich's proposal:

NUTS!

Love,

Jamie

She stares at the page, laughs at her cleverness. She stares at it once more, making sure this is what she wants to say. Convinced that it is, she feeds the fax a light snack.

The answer came from a story that John loved telling about one of World War II's most famous battles, The Battle of the Bulge. "Nuts" was the same answer the American general defending the French town of Bastogne said when the Nazi general demanded his surrender, saying he was completely surrounded. "Nuts" meant "Go to hell!" and John loved telling that story to whomever he thought hadn't heard it before and some who had. It was how he felt at different times in building the business when he'd been surrounded and his competitors demanded surrender. Everyone on the board had heard the story. And having it come back to her this way, she knew it was just what she needed to say.

Jamie feels good. Really good. It is a not-business-as-usual day. And she likes it.

Tossing the now-stale roll up on the roof for the birds, Jamie packs for her day's hike. She is starting to get her appetite back. This is the first day of September. She is going to pay attention to see if she notices fall approaching. She heads out back, down to the trout stream. Her pace is energetic, but not frantic. She will get through whatever is put in her path. She crosses the stream and heads up the other trail, the one where she had stopped cold when she saw the man and his dog looking at her. The day when she ran back to the cabin. He won't be there today. She wouldn't care if he was. This is *her* land. This is *her* journey. And no one, *no one*, is going to take that from her.

Jamie reaches the ridgeline a little out of breath, but not winded. She is proud of her fitness, her femaleness. She knew that if John were here, he would want her. He loved wanting her outdoors. And she loved his wanting her in all the different 'private' places they had made for themselves across the property. John's disability didn't hinder his libido, or his imagination. Jamie loved his great appetite for life. She closes her eyes and thinks of him taking her in his arms. How sure and strong and confident he was in holding her, touching her. She drew strength from him in life. Could she be doing the same now that he was dead? Could her journey somehow still be a shared journey? She is comforted by the question, although she doesn't have a ready answer.

A hawk's cry opens her eyes. Arcing across a patch of sky, it soars quickly out of view. Then a second hawk traces the same arc and disappears. Jamie smiles thinking them a pair, the thermals rising along the ridge giving them an easy ride for miles and miles. Her reverie ended, Jamie sets out to finish her hike. There is a shortcut back to the cabin. But today she decides on the longer loop. Almost ten miles altogether. She knows she can do it, if not easily, without taking all day.

Hours later and back at the cabin, Jamie loves how she powered through the rest of the hike. After a shower, she settles on the porch with a tumbler of Jack Daniels and the book, *Blue Highways*. She will eat Cora's dinner early tonight. The thought of fried chicken and potato salad sounds great. Just thinking about it makes her stomach rumble.

Jamie thumbs through the book somewhat absentmindedly. Why did Jake have this particular one? Well, of course, because of all his travels. This book is about the writer's driving a long circle around the United States. He'd lost his job. His wife left him. He had nothing better to do. "Sounds a lot like Jake," she says to herself. The author was also part Osage. Jake is Cherokee. An early passage was heavily underlined.

"On the old highway maps of America, the main routes were red and the back roads blue. Now even the colors are changing. But in those brevities just before dawn and a little after dusk, times neither day nor night, the old roads return to the sky some of its color. Then, in truth, they carry a mysterious cast of blue, and it's that time when the pull of the blue highways is strongest..."

She wonders how Jake got here. Hitchhiking, he said. By the interstates? That was illegal. Or the blue highways? Did he come here straight from Oklahoma? Or did he and Job travel the country before settling here? She takes a sip and ponders these questions.

She turns the pages more slowly, then pauses on another.

"It isn't traveling to cross the country and talk to your pug instead of people along the way. Besides, being alone on the road makes you ready to meet someone when you stop. You get sociable traveling alone."

Jake certainly wasn't sociable the first few times they met! She smiles to herself thinking they did get *very* sociable later on. Now he was gone. And the "pug" too. She misses Job almost as much. She flips through more pages. Another marking stops her.

"Still waiting on the weather, I started reading a book I'd bought in Phoenix, 'The Sacred Pipe,' Black Elk's account of the Oglala Sioux. In contrast to the straight and red road of life, Black Elk says, the blue road is the route of 'one who is distracted, who is ruled by his senses, and who lives for himself, not for his people.' I was stunned. "Was it racial memory that had urged me to drive seven thousand miles of blue highway, a term I thought I had coined?"

Jamie is stunned, too. Maybe this book was speaking to Jake. Speaking to his life in Oklahoma. Speaking to his life on the road. Speaking to his life here. Or the life that was here. How she longed to know more about this man she didn't know at all. She finishes the JD. What a day this has been! One man trying to take control of her company. Another man dead, yet closer to her than ever. And this man, a stranger, and a lover, gone yet leaving behind a map into his soul. Maybe. She would have to write later.

A car door slams. Abruptly, she is alert to the world. Muffled voices. So lost in her thoughts she never heard the car's approach up the gravel road. She looks in the direction of the sound, but she can't see through the dense foliage. This is why she loves this place. Secluded. Hidden away. Private. Still, fear creeps in. Fear has been a stranger for months. Now it is returning. Why?

She stands up trying to see something. She spots what looks like a taxi driving away. Who is coming for her? Hit men with orders from Rick? Just as she is about to go inside and lock the door, Job comes bounding, tongue dripping, straight for her. "Job"! Jamie hugs him and buries her face in his soft warm fur. She is crying uncontrollably again. She looks up and there is a tired-looking, dirty, Jake in city clothes. Wrinkled and filthy. Hair unkempt. Even his face is dirty. Like he has been in a fight and has slept on the ground. She can't talk. Jake comes to her and wipes her tears with his fingers. She pushes his hand away. "Where the HELL have you been?" Jamie asks in almost a hiss.

"I'll explain if I don't die from hunger! Do you have anything I could eat first?"

Jake looks hollow and hungry. Jamie looks flabbergasted. Stuttering through the preface of six different tirades, she takes a breath and manages: "Cora and Ellie Mae made me fried chicken and potato salad on Saturday. I shouldn't feed a bum I don't know, and right now, I don't know you. Leaving me without a word is not the Jake I've come to know." Jamie, now realizing that it had been days ago, days since she's eaten, days since Jake disappeared, adds, "I suppose you want a beer, too?"

"Please! Please."

Jamie silently swings twice more between fury and glee, then heads for the kitchen. Her body won't stop shaking. She carries dinner out on a tray with a beer. On the porch Jake has two helpings, sharing the meat with an equally ravenous Job, before he says a word. Jamie eats quietly, still not sure about what is happening or how she feels.

"Jamie, something happened on that rock the other day. Something much more than what it seemed to be. I felt the burden of blame lift from me about Daniel's death. It was something I can't explain to you yet, but it was so real. At the funeral I couldn't say good-bye to Daniel. Couldn't let go of my own self-hatred. But Thursday I felt the uncontrollable urge to say good-bye. I didn't want to worry you or explain it, so I took Job to the kennel up the road and went to the airport. I had to wait all night for a plane to Oklahoma City. When I got there I bought some flowers. I took a cab to the cemetery. I told the cabbie to wait. But after a few hours I knew I couldn't leave. I had to spend the night with Daniel. I asked the cabbie to come back in the morning. I slept with Daniel and I cried. I whispered. I screamed. I prayed. I finally mourned, Jamie. I set Daniel free of my own grief and regret. Now we can both move on."

His tears flowed as freely as hers had when she thought he had gone. "I wanted to be back to you for Saturday night, but I couldn't get a flight until today. I knew you would think I just ran off if I wasn't here on Saturday for dinner. I'm sorry, Jamie, but it was something I had to do."

Jamie looks into Jake's eyes. She is beginning to understand. After a few minutes, Jamie asks, "Did you call your parents?"

"No, Jamie. I told them I would be home in the spring and I will be. I needed time alone with Daniel. Can you understand that?"

"Yes. Yes. Yes." But she held back her emotions, not sure whether he was telling the whole truth yet.

"Something else I must tell you. Something very important for you to understand about yourself. Many people are healers in this world, Maggie," he said. "My people notice who among them are healers and they use their gifts. White people are given talents too, but if they see it and don't believe it they go on with their lives not using one of life's best gifts. You, Maggie, have that gift. You healed me on that rock and I will be forever grateful."

Jamie has a feeling that she has somehow always known this. "I guess I have noticed that sometimes I am able to help people with just holding their hands and listening. Is that what you mean by being a healer?"

"Exactly," Jake answers.

"Why wasn't I able to help John with his huge burden? I wanted to help him most of all."

"It's not for you do decide, Maggie. You just need to be open to it and let it happen if it is to happen. Sometimes the ones closest to you, you can't help. Do you understand that?"

"I think I understand, Jake." Jamie is softening now. No anger. No rage. No fear.

Looking at Jake, she says, "You need to take a shower and let me wash your clothes. Will you come in and do that?"

"I'm afraid to want more than is already mine. Afraid I'd want to stay. A shower would feel great, but I can go to the creek tomorrow."

Jamie takes his hand, pulling him up from his chair. "Come with me. I promise to kick you out. You can shower and I'll wash your clothes. We can sit and wait for them to wash and dry. Then you can go back to your cave. Come on."

Jake lets himself be led into the house. Jamie turns on the shower. Jake half turns away and slowly undresses – watching for Jamie's reaction. Jamie tries not to stare at his lean, sinewed body. Then he says, "Maggie, come with me."

Jamie raises one eyebrow, says, "You're filthy!" and whisks his clothes to the washer. But she returns naked, saying, "If you're clean, I'll reconsider." Immediately he pulls her into the shower with him. Their embrace lasts an eternity. In a silence too full for words. Jamie adds soap to her search through the muscles of his back, then holds him at arm's length, cleansing and appraising him like fine, fragile porcelain. Jake, in turn, worships each part of her and touches with reverence. Slowly, sacredly, like she is a goddess being worshiped with cleansing water.

They wordlessly dry each other and Jake takes her hand and guides her to the living room. She stands in silence as he puts kindling and logs in the fireplace and starts a fire with a single match. Then he turns and again taking her hand pulls her down to the rug next to the hearth. Without words and without really knowing the steps in between, their bodies entangle. Two fires: one without, one within .They lie together, and make such sweet love, that she feels her heart is about to burst. All of the most extreme emotions wrapped in one day. Their words a babble, the language of lovemaking speaking volumes of passion and forgiveness, of regret and redemption. All emptying into and around each other.

Later and finally satiated, Jamie and Jake put on robes and sit on the porch to talk until his clothes dry. He eats again. Just before dark, Jake and Job walk off to the woods.

At the edge, he stops. "Maggie, I thank you for helping me forgive myself. I will always love you for that."

"You're welcome, Jake. Life is not always what it seems to be. Thanks for helping me see who I am. You have been a gift to me too. We found each other for a reason. I believe that things happen for a reason, don't you?"

"I do."

"I love you too, Jake."

Jamie watches as they are engulfed by the darkened forest. Now the setting sun leaves a fire in the sky until finally day succumbs to night.

September 1

My emotions had the best of me. I need to try to not let outside forces shape who I want to be. I need to do that for myself. The Voice came to me to help me deal with John's business. "Nuts" came to me clearly when I relaxed and opened my mind to whatever was ready to come in. Then, Jake came back.

Jake said something that moved me more than many things in my life have moved me. When we were intimate, he felt the burden of blame lifted from him and he felt light and free. He said I have the gift of healing. He told me he thinks many of us are healers in some way. We just need to be open to whatever comes.

We talked about the book I took from him, Blue Highways. *I will ask him more about this. I learned much in less than a week. I am open to learning more.*

Jamie goes to bed with a kind of exhaustion she hasn't known in a while – an emotional exhaustion. Her owl calls out and another answers back. That mating call of nature. We are all the same, she thinks. All life is one life. And it loves itself, celebrates itself, through each of us.

Chapter 30
Vision Quest

September goes by too quickly. Jamie plants the daffodil bulbs she has in the shed. She plants them with splashes of color in mind for next spring. She knows the deer may find and eat some of them before they ever have a chance to bloom, but it's a chance she's willing to take. After nearly six months here, she's learned how to take from and give back to the land and its animals. She has learned much from Jake about survival and taking care of the land. Jake has been gathering food for the winter. He shows her how to follow the deer to where they find crab apples. She's watched fawns lose their spots and grow into yearlings. She learns of walnut trees and their bounty. She loves the taste of nuts like hickory and beech that are new to her. She has gathered blackberries. Of course she can buy as much food as she needs. But she is learning to enjoy the richness of the land itself. What it can offer her. The appreciation she can offer it. Jake tells her that last year he had enough to last through the winter...only visiting the store once a month or so. She tries to imagine living that way and can't. She would be willing to try.

Jake wants to ride the Harley again. They plan to go the first Wednesday in October if the weather cooperates. The leaves would be great then. She wants to take him someplace special and wants it to be a surprise. She's taken short rides and long ones alone throughout the summer. Sometimes she feels guilty leaving Jake behind. But then she realizes the guilt she feels is part of falling back into that old pattern of being some *thing* for some *body*. She doesn't want to go from being Jamie the Housewife to Jamie the Girlfriend. She just wants to be Jamie. On *her* bike. Alone.

As summer gives way to fall, warm days are followed by cooler nights. Then cooler days too. By the end of the month, hints of frost start to show higher up on the ridges. Leaves begin their show. Jamie is happy with the mix of independence and interdependence she and Jake have developed. He puts no demands on her, she none on him, although if several days pass between visits she can feel twinges of worry. More than once she has set off for the cave to look for him when Job, then Jake come loping from the other direction.

Here is the day of their ride, the one with the surprise destination. It follows one of those stretches when she hasn't seen Jake for days. Still, Jamie starts packing a lunch. She wonders if he will even come. He never seems to do much on a time schedule...except maybe Saturday night dinners. Searching the refrigerator and cupboards, she finds the wild blueberries Jake showed her how to dry. They are delicious. She lays those out. There are four crusty rolls and some aged cheddar cheese. Jamie cuts the cheese into slices so she won't have to pack her knife.

As she walks past the table to get her backpack, she stops to look at the calendar and realizes today – October 3rd – is special for another reason. It's John's birthday. How could she have forgotten? He would have been 67. He always teased about being younger than her. A pang of guilt shoots through her chest; it's John's birthday and she's going on a big adventure with Jake. "Happy Birthday, John. I'm sorry you're not here. But I hope you like the woman I'm becoming. I do."

Jamie then runs her fingers over the A.T. map. She has now walked more than one thousand miles. Along her Appalachian Trail journey, she has symbolically crossed Georgia, North Carolina, Virginia, and Maryland. At the Maryland-Pennsylvania border, she crosses the famed Mason-Dixon line that once divided a nation between states where slavery was permitted and those where it was outlawed.

Jamie takes her pack to the kitchen. She halves some hot peppers. Every time she works with these peppers that she loves so much, she coughs from the strength of the fumes. But by getting rid of the seeds, they are not too hot to eat raw. She then fills each half with some horseradish bar cheese and puts the halves together. She includes some crisp new apples that Cora got in last week. Jake has eaten most of them. Jamie loves this man's appetite...for apples, for her body, for life. Jamie tosses in a couple of Cora's brownies for dessert. She wraps everything carefully and puts two frozen water bottles in to keep their food cool.

Jamie enjoys the depth of her relationship with Jake. From their first sexual encounter, they have been greedy for each other's touch. She is shocked at her own desire for him. He too seems to harbor a craving and each time they come together they make love. She quickly lost any shyness about their age difference. She can tell his hunger is genuine, deep.

An earlier twinge of guilt over John's memory has been washed away by waves of pleasure from a union, pure and real. Experiences with this Indian – this "cave man" – taste authentic and are far more satisfying than the scheming businessmen of her husband's world and their never-ending quest for wealth.

The October morning is brilliant with sunshine and leaves in full color when the 'boys' show up. She puts food and water on the porch. The dog seems to understand he must wait for their return. Jamie hugs Job, "We'll be back before dark, boy. Take care of things for us." Job licks her face and lays down in a sunny spot, content. Jamie has told Jake about the Indian mounds belonging to the Monongahela, a tribe believed to be descended from the earliest group of human inhabitants of western Pennsylvania. Many burial sites and villages have been unearthed during the settlement and development of western Pennsylvania and northern West Virginia. That's where they're headed today.

"It's about a forty-five minute ride, but I need to make one short stop along the way," Jamie explains.

"I'm putting myself in your hands, so wherever you take me will be fine," Jake says. "Just don't go too fast. Remember, I've only done this once." Jamie shows Jake how to ride with her. She pulls him close with his arms around her waist. If she leans left, she tells him to lean with her. If she leans right, he must match her lead. They head gently down the long gravel drive to the road. Jamie could have turned right towards Ram Cat Run and taken the highway through town to the intersection that would have led to their destination. She turns left instead, knowing a back way to the same road. As she accelerates, Jake holds her tight. After the first couple of turns, she can tell he is a great student and dance partner. He moves with her gracefully, two bodies, one machine.

Jamie pilots the bike first to Uniontown. She stops at the Clinic where Ellie Mae goes for her check-ups. She tells Jake she will just be a moment. She disappears inside the clinic and returns within 10 minutes... saying nothing. The ride to the park is a true experience of the feel of fall and atmospheric pressure. Jake takes it all in. He says in her ear, "I see what you mean about feeling the world on your skin. I love this two wheel ride." Jake kisses Jamie softly on the neck and gently tightens his grip on her. Heaven.

After nearly an hour they arrive at a barely noticed signpost and pulloff – a small marker that starts the trail leading to the burial mounds. The mounds are several miles away, far enough to discourage all but the most determined seekers. When Jake and Jamie have hiked for two hours they still haven't reached their destination. But they're hungry and decide to break for lunch. The aged cheese has softened just enough to bring out the flavor. She is glad she packed extra rolls. Jake likes her cheese filled hot peppers. After they eat and talk casually, Jake picks up a leaf and is lost in thought. Finally Jamie asks, "What do you see there?" Jake's head pops up from miles away. Jamie notices his eyes in the filtered light of the forest. That blue just makes her melt.

Jake says, "I was just thinking about the old saying, 'as above, so below.' In each leaf is an image of the tree." Jake picks up another leaf for Jamie. As she looks at it he takes his leaf and outlines her face. "The image of the tree is in the leaf and the image of the leaf is in the innumerable branchings – main branches from the trunk and smaller branches and smallest yet branches up to the tiniest branch which is the stem of the leaf. You look into the woods and see an old tree that has come down – been uprooted – and you see beneath the ground: the branches and twigs above, so below." He pauses. "Are you listening, Maggie?"

"I'm mesmerized" says Jamie, as she looks at the beauty of this man beside her. His hair shiny and black falling in his eyes. The intensity yet playfulness of him. Assured, Jake continues, "The leaves on the tree are like individuals, live persons. They bud…they leaf…they die. Each of those is an individual life that seems to think it is some separate part. Each leaf living an individual existence, grabbing all the sun and rain and CO_2 it can, exhilarating in its own existence. Seems to think it is isolated. Seems to think that its life is like no other life, like each leaf and snowflake is individual, unique and alone. Each snowflake comes from the water and returns to all water. Each leaf comes from a tree and returns to the soil and that becomes a part of the tree again and that is the ONE THING."

Jake lies down and puts his head in Jamie's lap. Jamie smoothes the hair out of his eyes. His hair is wavy and softer than it looks. She likes to rub her fingers through it whenever she can. "Look up there, Maggie, do you see that spider web?" The light is just right on the almost perfect web to show it off. How does this man notice everything? Jamie thinks to herself. She so wants to notice the world around her. She has gotten better, but watching Jake inspires her to keep her eyes open to the world. "I see it, Jake."

"The spider web appears overnight. This by a critter with a brain no larger than one of my hair follicles. No blueprint. No training. No equipment. Beautiful and efficiently functional and stronger than steel."

"Jake?"

"Yes, Maggie?"

"I have learned so much about nature and life from you. I've learned more in my few months with you than in my whole sixty-seven years before. Where did you learn all of this?"

Jake looks up at her. "I was lucky enough to have a grandfather who knew nature. He taught me a verse from your Bible's Book of Proverbs: 'Go to the ant, observe her ways – and be wise.' He taught me to be silent and watch." Jake pulls her face to his and kisses her. "I think maybe you just were never quiet long enough, Magpie," Jake teases. "There is something I've wanted to ask you. You walk your trails. You mark your progress. You count the miles. You measure them against this Appalachian Trail. Are you accomplishing something? Are you getting somewhere? Maybe instead of walking all those miles you should let the world pass its way through you."

"I don't know, Jake. I just feel better when I walk until I am tired. I guess I hope that's substantial enough to sustain me...till something deeper demands I take the next breath, move the next step, to look up once again and keep on moving. Now these trails seem as familiar as my backyard at home. Of all the places I've learned about on my imaginary journey across the A.T., a few remain alive in my mind. Where it crosses the Mason-Dixon Line seems to be one of those places."

Jake takes her hand, running his finger along her life lines, and asks, "Why do you think that is?"

"I don't know that either. Maybe because it's closer to the land I know. Maybe because there's a chill in the air now. As the A.T. winds its way north, I, too, feel the passing of seasons, the coming of a winter I don't feel quite prepared for. Maybe it's something more."

"I think the answers are coming to you. Maybe they're not here yet. But they are close." He kisses her again. "I guess we could talk all day, but if we are going to see these mounds you want to show me, we had better get moving." Jake unwinds his long body and pulls Jamie up with him.

They had only walked another ten minutes when Jake stops. "We are on sacred ground," Jake says. "How do you know that, Jake? Did I miss a marker? I thought they were farther away."

"I feel it, Maggie. I want you to feel it too. The way to best honor this sacred ground is in silence. Thank the spirit of this ground for having waited for us and welcomed us."

In front of them are several mounds of dirt with no trees on them. It looks like there are three of them, maybe more. They stand still for a moment. Then Jake walks slowly uphill. Jamie follows. She knows not to say a word. Soon her senses sharpen. She smells mold. Dry leaves under foot, crunch. Cicada chirp louder than she has ever heard them before. The floor of the forest is dappled with sun…beginning of fall when light comes through. She feels a cool breeze on her skin. Jamie feels the presence of another…not just Jake. She looks around. No one.

They walk slowly to the highest spot. No trees for cover. Warm sun touches them gently. Jake motions for her to sit. They sit back to back, each with a different view in front of them. His strong back holding Jamie up makes her feel the strength of him in her.

They sit for a long while. Jamie feels like she and Jake are one person. She feels part of the earth she is sitting on. Everything she sees in front of her seems to come close and enfold her. This feeling is something new to her. It is like the strongest kind of love. Like a total love of herself and everything around her. She wants to sit here forever and not lose this feeling.

Jamie stares into the woods. At first, all she sees are trunks of trees and their branches forming a forest at once impenetrable and forbidding. There is no trail. She closes her eyes and when she opens them she stares into the eyes of an eight-point buck staring right back at her. How could she have missed this magnificent animal, not twenty feet away? She realizes now it was always there, but she didn't see it at first. It was invisible until she could see with a different kind of sight. Where does this sight come from? No answer from Jake who remains silent as a rock.

She senses the animal is a kind of sentry, deciding whether she can be trusted to be shown another world invisible to an outsider's eyes. Suddenly the air starts vibrating, the trees are breathing and she can feel the blood in her capillaries filling the skin on her face. The air and the ground, the wind and the water, the sky and the stones and the ground and the spirit of all that surrounds her doesn't stop at the edge of her skin – but that her skin simply envelops her like the tissue of an organ in the body of all that is. Jamie is and is not. The buck is and is not. Jamie is the buck. The buck is Jamie. All are the forest.

Then the vision passes. Jamie feels at once fulfilled and disappointed. Jake gets up and takes Jamie's hand. She wants to stay, yet knows she must go. He leads her slowly back along the path they came on. As he takes her down the side of the mound, she looks back to get it grounded in her mind. She never wants to forget the curve or it…the treeless mound so important to the Indians – and now to her. Walking back she doesn't feel like the same person who came into the woods. She doesn't want to go back to a life that no longer contains her. She isn't afraid of going forward any more. She is afraid of going back, maybe. Back to a life that seems too small. She is no longer a citizen of the world inside of herself, but a citizen of the world around and within, entirely connected and whole. This small thing that she calls herself is a piece of something vast. Today she is part of the whole tree...roots, trunk, branches, stems, veins and leaves...air, earth, water.

They ride back to the cabin in silence. There is nothing to say. Jamie thinks Jake must have been moved too. The rumbling of the motor between her legs. Jake flat up against her, holding on tight. She feels a kind of alive that she wants to remember forever. Can she get that kind of alive feeling when she goes back to face her life? Could this aliveness be her new life?

Chapter 31

Night Moves

Jamie stirs, vaguely aware of a man lying next to her. He is strong, alive – someone deeply sexual. In her half-sleep, she reaches for him. In her dream he has come to her bed. She closes her eyes, trying to drift back into the dream. His look. His scent. His words. His passion. Is he John? Jake? Who? He is a man and a ghost. At once a stranger and someone so intimate that as two they seemed like fused souls. How could that be? And what about the other ghost, the man who made this cabin and her life here possible? Where was he? Ready from beyond to wreak his revenge on his faithless wife? But he is eight months dead. Is Jamie still his wife? Can she be faithful to him – or at least his memory – even as she explores something new with a man half John's age...well, almost half *her* age! And what exactly is she exploring anyway?

Sleep will not return. She is awake. More than awake. It is that time. She can feel it. Time when it seems like her very soul floats out of her body and fuses with someone – or something – else. Everything that happens seems to move her more into another world. Her times with Jake. The hike to the Indian mounds. Everything propelling her forward. To what? Jamie pulls John's polo shirt off over her head. She throws it on the floor and steps away from it naked. She moves noiselessly out to the living room, reaching for the table light thinking she would write, then stops. Instead, Jamie turns to the door and into her October night. Although cooler now, she wants to feel the air on her skin again. Stepping into that moonless night, still she can see the forest's outlines, stars vibrating against their canvas, John's solo oak tree, sentinel of the ages.

She closes her eyes to better feel the air, to better hear her world. It is quiet. Not even the owl breaks the silence. She enjoys the slight chill raising bumps along her skin. She listens to her own breathing...steady, easy as though coming from some deep meditation and releasing into another's breath. Jamie stretches her arms, holding them out from her sides, tips of fingers reaching into the darkness. She lifts her head slightly, taking in the scents of pine and fallen leaves and damp. Jamie turns a semi-circle slowly now facing toward the road, almost as though she awaits the embrace of people and things far away. No images cloud her mind. Only the senses of smell and touch and hearing connect her to the world. Then...something else. A slight stirring.

"*Go. Your time. Heal. Strong. Deliver. Savor. Your time. Your time. No fear. No fear. No fear.*"

The words come as a whisper. From where? No panic this time. She knows. The Voice. It is back. She hugs her arms across her breasts, embracing the friend who had helped her through John's last months. The Voice who had spoken to her on other, more troubled nights. The Voice, now back, sounds different. Embracing and releasing.

"*Go. Your time. No fear...no fear.*" Her body rocks back and forth in cadence with the words. "*No fear. No fear. Go on. Go on.*"

Now she stops. "I will go," she says in reply, not knowing exactly what that means. But she doesn't care. She knows her path will show itself. And that it will take her, and others, to places where they will be challenged, maybe even overwhelmed, but ultimately rewarded. She knows she will take her steps into an unknown with strength and confidence, looking forward to a life not yet fully lived. "*No fear.*"

The light comes ever so slowly into the eastern sky. Jamie knows she can't go back to sleep. She starts a fire. Dresses for the day's trip to the Ram Cat and her hike, to visit Jake and Job by evening. She makes some coffee and gets on her Mac Book to write. She has another children's book done. She is working on something for Jake. She has several poems that she is working on, too.

At 8:45, Jamie hops on her bike and heads out for the week's groceries. She looks forward to her time with Cora and Ellie Mae. Ellie Mae is four months pregnant and positively glowing. "You look beautiful." Jamie gives the girl a big hug as soon as she walks in. Ellie Mae is definitely showing. Her tiny body carries this baby front and center. Unlike women in Jamie's day who wore maternity clothes, Ellie Mae just wears regular clothes a size or two too big for her. Still shorts and tee shirts...just larger.

Cora, dressed in her usual skirt and denim shirt, comes by for a hug also and looks admiringly at her daughter. "She is finally feeling good," she says. "The doc at the clinic is really pleased with her and the baby."

"I'm taking good care of myself, Jamie. I always remember what you said. "Make the best baby you can to use as a gift to someone else," Ellie Mae says as she gently rubs her belly.

"Come sit," says Cora. "Something weird happened this week. I'm afraid I didn't realize how weird until I had blabbed too much." Cora and Jamie sink deep into their chairs with their coffees. Ellie Mae has a glass of milk. "What happened?" asks Jamie.

"Well," starts Cora. "A stranger walked in. He was all friendly like that. Talking about the weather and hows he'd heard of our Ram Cat Run beer. He ordered up two cases plus some other supplies. Then he started asking questions."

"Jamie," says Ellie Mae. "We didn't catch on to what he was a doing for a while."

"What exactly was he doing?" asks Jamie.

Cora and Ellie Mae exchange worried glances. Ellie Mae pats her stomach again and Cora pulls at her sleeves as she always did when she was nervous. "He asked lots of questions about you, Jamie," says Cora searching Jamie's eyes for a reaction.

"What kind of questions?" asks Jamie puzzled.

"He wanted to know what you were like. If you lived alone. If you did anything weird…like that," says Ellie Mae fidgeting in her chair.

"At first, because he was so friendly, we joked that you drove a Harley and hung out with a scary mountain man and his dog some," Ellie Mae explains.

"Yes, she's right." Cora says. "Then he asked some questions that made us look at each other and wonder if maybe he might be stalking you or up to no good."

"Like what?" Jamie asks.

"Well," says Cora. "He wanted to know where your cabin was? How long you planned on stayin'? How often you came for food? If you had talked about your plans? Me and Ellie Mae clammed up right quick. We could see he was up to no good. We sure are sorry, Jamie. We would never do anything to hurt you. When he left we saw his car…one of them fancy Lincolns. We got his license plate number if you need it."

"Keep it," says Jamie. "We might need it later. But I'm not afraid of someone like that. A couple people at the company my husband owned, and now I own, want to prove I'm crazy so they can take it from me. I'll handle this. You didn't do anything wrong."

"Oh, yeah," says Cora a little relieved now, "We saw he had a camera. He was no tourist! When he left, he didn't go up Fire Tower Road. If he had, one of us would'a followed him."

"Not to worry," said Jamie trying to be cheerful. The three women again hug each other warmly. Jamie towers over them, but when they are close like this she feels their equal. Maybe they have learned to blend into each other as close friends do.

"What's for dinner?" asks Jamie, wanting to switch the subject.

"We did a pork roast with potatoes, carrots, turnips and onions. Ma made you one of her famous cherry cheesecakes. The baby and I REALLY like that lots," Ellie Mae says, continuing to pat her belly. The women have calmed down and are back to business as usual. Cora and Ellie Mae feel Jamie understands and has forgiven their mistake in giving this stranger information he shouldn't have.

"Something else really exciting," gushes Ellie Mae. "The doc says I don't have to pay any more…that the baby and the birthin' is all taken care of. Can you imagine that? Don't know how that happened, but we are so happy."

"That is good news, Ellie Mae. "I told you there are ways of getting care in this country. That makes me feel good. Now you make sure you go to see them when you have a scheduled appointment or any time you have a question. You hear me?"

"Yes, ma'am. I will do what they tell me to do. I'm so glad to have someone who knows what to do. I don't know nothin' about babies."

Jamie takes the week's groceries to her Harley. She rides up Fire Tower thinking of the man who was asking questions. She is not going to let it scare her. Let them send a detective with a camera. She is not crazy. Well…maybe a *little*.

After her hike and a shower, Jamie writes this in her journal:

October 15th

I think if I am going to go back to my world, I might need a credo to live by. Something simple. Something I can remember. Something I can live by. This one has been wandering around in my head lately: "Just Gotta Love 'em." Meaning someone who's reached the point where they realize that all along they've been reacting to others' attempts to control fate, control the world, control life and the lives of those around them. And thus they themselves have become one of those trying to ride herd over fate, the world, his life, and the lives of those all around them...and has come up realizing, after trying for 50 or 60 years, it's like trying to hold three handfuls of sand to keep back the incoming tide. It has brought me only illusive rewards trying to accomplish that which can never be done.

I wonder what would happen if we gave up their adversarial "win or go home" posture and resolved to only ever respond with love; to only ever look for the good; to only ever see the best in people and events; to only ever return no man evil for evil, but always move onward and upward asking others to join them ahead of and beyond the fray of squabbling to become the one to die with the most toys.

Seven months into my journey, I have decided these will be the words I live by: Just Gotta Love 'em. That's it. I can never PROVE this path right or wrong but to myself. This is my decision, my choice. These are the seeds I wish to plant, so if there is life beyond this, I can look back and smile upon where my love grew. Everything I have learned points in this direction. I will say it over and over to myself. "Gotta Love 'em'"... "Just Gotta Love 'em.'" Amen.

Jamie is resolute. She settles in and waits for Jake and Job to arrive. Life is good.

Chapter 32

Trick or Treat

It is October 31st...Halloween. The phone rings just as expected. 9:00 on the dot. For Stella punctuality is the 11th commandment. Her fax had come through at 7:30 saying "0900, URGENT." Jamie can pretty well guess the subject. Still she is anxious to hear what Stella has to say. Stella respects her privacy and always faxes that she would be calling and at what time. Small talk dispensed, Stella gets down to business. "I met yesterday with Ken Branson," Stella talks quickly and in a hushed tone. She'd flown to Washington yesterday to meet with one of the nation's leading handwriting experts. Jamie turns the speaker phone on and leans against the counter. "And?" she asks.

"He showed me how they enlarge the writing to compare signatures. As I suspected, and I'm sure you did too, it wasn't John's writing. It was Larry Moyer's writing for sure. Ken said he would testify to this in court, Jamie!" Jamie paces in front of the phone, remembering Larry's sudden death from a heart attack. John had not felt up to the long trip for the funeral, but they had talked to Larry's wife several times.

"Stella, I feel better knowing this. But it makes it harder with Larry dying just before John did. There's nothing I can do to make him confess and pay it back."

"But Jamie, I can take it to your lawyer for you," offers Stella. "Ken says that's the next step. We – I mean, *you* – have a case that can clear John's name and save the company!"

Jamie's mind begins to wander as she stares out the window. During John's last years a nasty culture of rumor-mongering at and around the company had become part of the air they all breathed. Some of it was directed at John because he couldn't wave a magic wand and make the markets do things they weren't prepared to do. Much of it was directed at

Jamie, coming from those who thought they were much better prepared to run Barlow Associates than she ever could be. A lot of it was posturing for position in the eventual transfer of ownership to the Associates. As John's assistant, Stella too had become fair game for prying eyes and whispering lips. Now her comings and goings had become fodder, fueling speculation over Jamie's next "maneuvers." It is a shame, Jamie thought. John had been so extremely generous to his employees when times had been good. Then, when his health failed and times weren't as good, some repaid his kindness with laziness, recrimination and, now a palace revolt.

Stella's anxiety, touching on fear, is evident as she tries to whisper and push her urgency at the same time. Her voice twitches up to a slight rasp. "Jamie, are you listening to me?"

"Stella," Jamie returns with a calmness born of respite from the company atmosphere she has come to cherish. "We're not going to do anything yet. I want to sit on the information. Fax me a copy of the signatures and his report. Maybe you're right. But this isn't something I'm going to start without some idea of where it's going to end. I need some time to think this through."

"But Jamie," Stella sounding more like her mother. "We have to get that money back from his estate. This is a criminal case now."

Jamie knows Stella is worried. She really has no idea what Jamie's been doing all these months in the mountains. She is alone. Maybe she even thinks Jamie's grieving for John has left her alien to the real world. Jamie can always tell when Stella is probing, looking for one question to answer another. She doesn't have the patience to put her fears at ease, although at times she tries. She needs Stella to be loyal eyes and ears. At the same time, she doesn't expect Stella to understand fully what this journey – *her* journey – is all about. Maybe someday. But not yet.

"Stella, here's what I want you to do. Send me Larry's records and any news articles about him that we have. I'll go online to see where he gave big amounts of money. I want to know if a large deposit came in after this event. I want to know about all gifts and bequests before his death." Alive, Larry had been a substantial account for Barlow Associates. Then the family changed advisors. Not knowing John as well, they weren't comfortable with his aggressive and unconventional philosophy. John never held a grudge when someone did this. He had a very accepting view of human behavior, something Jamie loved dearly about him. Although, he might not be very accepting knowing his former client and friend had stolen $10 million intended for Children's Hospital, using his name.

"Jamie, this is dangerous and I don't like it. What if Children's Hospital finds out about it? What if Rich finds out? He was slowed a little by your email, but people are watching and talking." As Jamie continues to pace in front of the phone, she thinks of Rich and his ambitious efforts to displace her. What about the man at the Ram Cat?

"I think Rich sent a private investigator up here to spy on me, Stella. I'm sure he won't give up. But you have to stay calm and act like all is normal. Remember, it's Halloween. So put your best Barlow mask on. And don't treat them to anything they don't deserve to know about!"

"Jamie, Rich really scares me. He would do anything to get control of Barlow Associates and you know it. Anything! I worry for your safety. You would be much safer here and you know it, and that's all I'm going to say."

There is a pause. Jamie feels her words can settle Stella. Jamie continues to try to calm herself with movement. She makes one more try at helping Stella shed her fears.

"I can take care of myself, Stella. When Rick comes here he's playing on my turf. I have the advantage. And you need to trust that I will take care of Children's and Barlow Associates too." She thinks about reporting her target practice with John's shotgun, but knows Stella enough to know that this would only add to her worries. And any mention of Jake was out of the question.

Continuing in the same calm tone, Jamie says, "The Nexcentury warrants were the crown jewel and that is why Larry took them. He knew their real value. No one would have swiped them to hang on their wall. That would be like swiping the Mona Lisa and hanging it in your living room."

"But if he took it to make a philanthropic gift with, that just seems too crazy to me," insists Stella.

"Larry made great philanthropic gifts, Stella. But so did Al Capone. It didn't matter where the money came from, the beneficiaries lauded his gift." Stella's silence means her words might be starting to have an effect. Jamie takes it as her way to wrap up the conversation.

"Stella, the next few months are going to test both of us as never before. Even though I am away, I'm not far away. No one is going to take Barlow Associates from us. Send the information I need. I will figure out how to handle the Children's situation."

Jamie stops her pacing and faces the phone squarely. "Stella, I need you to be strong. And act strong. That's the best way to keep Rich and the others in their places. You are my proxy. When you need something done, it's OK to use my name. That way, they'll know we talk a lot.

"John taught us this great lesson: our world, in many ways, is still a jungle. He ruled his part of it with great success and great kindness too. That's how I will continue. If we show fear or act hurt, the scavengers will look at us like lunch. As long as we show we're in charge, they still might circle, but they won't dare attack. OK?"

"OK." The voice sounded calmer. Reassured.

"So let's get back to work and shut up all the naysayers!"

"OK, Jamie. I'll get that information for you right now." Stoked with a bit of Jamie's courage, Stella is ready to head back into the battle for Barlow Associates. "Bye, Jamie. I feel better!"

"So do I. Get back to me as soon as you can."

"I will! Bye for now."

Jamie clicks off the phone. She'd been pacing through the call. Now she sits down, slightly winded. Small beads of sweat gather across her forehead and at the nape of her neck. She's taken care of Stella's hobgoblins. At least for the moment. But the real ghouls were still out there. And she has to figure out how to get to them before they get to her. Trick. Or treat. Indeed! Jamie laughs to herself.

Chapter 33

Giving Thanks

November 26th – Thanksgiving morning.

My first Thanksgiving without John. A year ago I could not have imagined it.

Jake has invited me to dinner in his cave. I guess he shot a wild turkey. I wonder how different it will taste from our store bought ones?

Funny. Thanksgiving in a cave. Not even the pilgrims had that experience. Hiking there soon. I'm thrilled. Should write more but want to get going.

She closes the journal, then closes her eyes for a minute. What a swirl life has been in the seven months she's been here. Just the opposite of what she wanted or expected. John's death. The coping. The crowding around of givers. *And* takers. The courage to leave that life behind in search of another. Expecting solitude and finding anything but.

Cora and Ellie Mae...just shopkeepers in her life with John; now becoming dear, deep friends. And new life on its way. Always new life. Pushing the old out of its way. Demanding its day in the sun. Sunrise. Sunset.

And Jake...Jake! Where and how did this man come into her life? Had God put him here just in time to take her to places she had never been? Or had God put her here just in time to take *him* places he'd never been? She smiles at both thoughts.

Jake...her wounded mountain of a man. Healing now. Not completely. But much better than their first time together. She knows their bonds have grown deep and true. What the future may bring belongs to the future.

Perhaps it is the gift of aging. Or maybe the gift of being in these hills and getting intimate with the trails and streams, woods and rocks, animals and flowers, but Jamie knows time – her time – is no longer an abstract, cutting each day and night into artificial slices. She has learned to savor each moment in each day. Not in the sense of being aware of each breath she takes. But in how she has fit into the rhythm of daylight and sundown, or moonlight and another sunrise. Maybe if she stayed here for the rest of her life, she would feel as bonded to this land as the first generations of humans did. Getting to know its gifts, and its dangers, with as much love and respect as one did to your elders, and the elders before them, and the elders before them.

She hears herself whisper a silent word of thanks. To whom? To what? To all? She doesn't know. The word is enough. An offering of grace to all she has learned in her own new world. Jamie settles almost into a trance when one of the 'policemen' of the modern world – the alarm clock – crashes through to her consciousness. She had set it the night before because she wanted to be up early enough to write and do some chores before setting off for Jake's. She had forgotten to turn it off when she got up early.

What to wear? It sounds silly, but she always dresses for the occasions in her life. This was one that didn't take much thought...no one to impress. Well, *almost* no one. But she does want to look nice for Jake.

She pulls out a better pair of jeans that Jake will probably sneer at because of the label. She smiles at what she'll say in return. And a nice wool sweater. Red and black. With a v-neck. It looks great but will also keep her comfy, she hopes, in case her idea of warmth differs slightly from Jake's.

She takes an extra long shower. Again, she closes her eyes and thinks about their showers together. His insistence. Her yielding. Dried and combed, Jamie pulls her hair back and holds it with a large barrette. It now reaches almost to the middle of her back. She has never had hair this long...not even as a child. Dressed, she fills her backpack with a few goodies of her own. Two bottles of wine. Glasses wrapped in a towel. And an opener. She is sure Jake has none of these. Plus some crackers and a wonderful cheese left from his last visit three days ago. Has it been three days? 'Time flies...' she says to nobody. And a flashlight. Just in case. Darkness comes early now in these hills.

As Jamie opens the door to start her hike, she hears the all too familiar buzz of the fax machine. A fax? On Thanksgiving? Might be important. But not today. Tomorrow. She closes the door behind her.

It's cold as she starts out. The early afternoon sun doesn't feel any warmer than it had at sunrise. Morning sunlight and clear sky have given way to high overcast. The sun is on its descent, but still high enough above the hills to give some warmth if it wanted to. Today, it apparently does not. Despite the cold, every cell in her body is hot in anticipation of this dinner. She hopes he asks her to stay the night, or at least walks her home. She is still not completely comfortable in the dark. Within a couple hundred yards she has settled into her familiar pace. In April she would have been reaching for her second wind at this point. Now, her body is relaxed, leaning easily into the ridge's incline.

All the leaves in the woods are down now. Except for a few spruces and fir, everything is brown and bare. Though Jamie walks in silence, she makes enough of a presence to send a doe and her two fawns moving away from her, down towards a stream and underbrush. The mother knows what the young ones are just learning; this is the deadliest time of year for her kind to meet the two legged animals. At a bend in the trail, another tree clings tenaciously to its now brown leaves. A pin oak. Why so long after the other oaks and maples and beeches and sycamores have given their leaves to the forest floor, does the pin oak hang onto hers? Jamie doesn't know. John would know. Maybe Jake does too.

The hour-long hike goes by quickly. She pauses at the turnoff to Church Rock. How many times had they been there since that first encounter? Jamie thinks that for her and Jake, maybe that should be the holiest of places. A shrine to their love. 'Maybe we should carve our initials into the rock,' she thinks with a smile. 'If Jake doesn't think that would be a desecration to Nature,' she says again and laughs lightly.

A hundred yards from the entrance to the cave, Job comes bounding out as a one-dog welcoming committee. Amazing how he can know she is coming. She bends down for some dog kisses and returns the favor by scratching his ears. 'This dog is so smart and loving,' she thinks. ''Just like his…master?' The word doesn't feel right. Maybe just 'human.'

With Job leading her she arrives at the entrance to the cave. There's no door, so she calls out, "Knock, Knock", as he leads her inside. Jake is busy cooking but comes to welcome her with a hug and a kiss. His hair is clean. He is wearing a red and black flannel shirt tucked neatly into his boot cut jeans.

"Right on time," he says. They laugh at the joke. Punctuality where none is needed.

"Do I need to take my shoes off to come into your home?" Jamie teases.

"Not unless you take your clothes off too."

"Jake! Is that any way to talk to a guest in your...cave?" They both laugh.

"Something smells really good," she says as she removes her backpack and coat, placing them on a handmade rocking chair.

"My special wild rice and the herb stuffing," Jake says.

"You look really nice, Maggie. You didn't have to dress up for me. Especially in those expensive jeans. They probably cost five times what I would pay for a pair."

"But they are the ones that really fit well, don't you think?" As she turns slowly around, so he can look closely at her backside.

"Well, I do give them that. But..."

"Oh shush! Now...how can I help?"

"Did I hear something clink in your backpack?"

"A guest always brings a good bottle of wine to their host. Or maybe two!"

As she unpacks and uncorks the first bottle, Jake checks the turkey. "I shot this turkey three days ago," he explains. "A lucky shot, too. I cleaned and dressed the bird and had him smoking ever since. The aroma drew a couple of coyotes close enough that Job had to charge them. He's fearless. By the time I emerged with my gun, they had moved across to the next ridge line. Still, it was a warning to be careful. Even Job at his size could be tricked into a deadly fight if there were a larger pack around."

Jake has the cave lit up so well that she can really see the whole of it for the first time. The first thing she notices is that there is a full size bed where the small one had been. She looks at the wood. It's the same wood she saw stacked when she came to the cave while Jake was in Oklahoma. It is beautifully done. She runs her hand over every part of it. "This is beautiful. Why did you make it?"

"Just in case you spent the night. I wanted you to sleep in a bed I made for us," he said softly.

"But what if I hadn't come?"

"I made it with the hope that you would." Just as he was about to explain further, a burning smell hit them.

"The rice!" he said, moving quickly to stir the cast iron kettle before more of it burned.

"Is it OK?" Jamie asked.

"A little burned at the bottom. But that's all. It's what I get for letting you distract me, Maggie." He teased. "Wine, please!" Jake stands up tall. Most of the cave is high enough to accommodate his tall body. He wipes his hands on his pants.

"Coming right up, sir!"

She hands him his glass. Jamie's eyes move around the room. She sees woodworking projects everywhere...walking sticks, head knockers, a beautiful table and chairs, and what looked like totem poles.

There was a bookshelf and a table with a newspaper. "Jake, why do you have a newspaper?"

"I bought it to remind me that all the news is always the same, just the names change," he said. That makes sense to Jamie. She has never thought of it that way before. Sunrise, Sunset. Something to ask about later. Not now.

"What will you do with all this beautiful furniture when you leave here, Jake?"

"I don't know," said Jake. "It doesn't matter. I made them to keep my sanity so they have already served their purpose." She runs her hands over each piece. Trying to imagine the time it took. The knowledge of the wood and the knife. The anger and the grief pushing into each shaving. Each piece holding a part of Jake's life. Her heart heaves a brief moment. Another something to ask about later. Not now.

"Dinner is served, madam," he says with a properly fake formality.

"Thank you, sir." He holds out one hand-made chair for her before settling into his own.

"A toast," Jake says, raising his glass. This time with a seriousness that gets her focused again on his eyes. She raises hers and smiles. "Maggie, to a very special giving of thanks for all you have brought into my life. I came here for solitude and loneliness. Instead I discovered a bounty and companionship beyond anything I could have imagined, or felt. I have new life. And I have only you to thank for it. Happy Thanksgiving."

With tears in her eyes, Jamie takes Jake's hand and kisses it gently.

"Thank you, Jake," she says through soft sobs and between kisses. "You have brought so much into my life that I can't even begin to explain or say. You have powers I thought no man could possess. I, too, have new life. And I have only you to thank for it. I love you, Jake."

Now it was Jake with tears. But he pushes them back with a kiss to her cheek.

Jake says quietly, "Maybe we should eat before Job gets the idea this is all for him."

The dinner was delicious: wild turkey with herb stuffing, wild rice, gravy with dried mushrooms, heavy homemade bread, dried fruits, and broccoli he had asked the Ram Cat to get for him. They sit by the fire after dinner, full and satisfied.

"You will need to stay the night," said Jake.

"Oh, yea? Why is that?"

"There is a bad storm coming tonight. Rain, then ice, then snow."

"And how do you know that?" she asks. "Have you got the Weather Channel up here?"

"I just know. I learned how to know what the weather will be. My grandpa taught me that. It isn't just a line to pick up chicks."

They both laughed. "I didn't bring extra clothes," Jamie replies.

"Well then, Maggie, you will see how I live day to day. It is time you learn to live on and off the land. May I teach an old dog new tricks?"

"I'm ready to learn, but I'm no 'old' dog," Jamie says playfully punching Jake's arm.

"Sorry."

"You can make it up to me by taking me to that new bed with you. It needs broken in and this 'old' dog just might have a few tricks to help do that."

In the early minutes of dark an owl seems to be just outside the cave. She bounces her hooting call off bare branches in the valley. Jamie hopes someone answers her call.

Chapter 34
Nature's Way

Jake had been right. A cold drizzle started not long after they were in bed. It turned quickly to a sleet that made the woods crackle. Jamie and Jake listen in silence, burrowed under blankets. While Jamie might have preferred the thick mattress of her bed back at the cabin, she is surprised at the comfort of this one. The early beds had ropes woven back and forth in checkerboard fashion to hold the mattress. Jake has made their mattress using wool blankets that he sewed together the same way. A set of flannel sheets and two wool blankets on top make for a warm and cozy nest. She also appreciates the deep cover of his cave. Despite being outdoors, not a drop of rain or sleet finds its way inside. Jake keeps the fire roaring so the entire space is comfortable. Job sleeps peacefully at their feet.

They are content as they sleep into the night. Then several hours later Jamie awakes. Jake is gone. So is Job. She feels a rush of panic, suddenly vulnerable in her nakedness. "Jake?" she calls into the space that now carries a chill. "Job?" The fire has settled to a deep glow of orange embers. Where would they have gone? She looks for his clothes. Of course, they are gone too! Then she laughs quietly at the silliness of thinking he would have gone into the woods without them.

Just as she is climbing down from sheer panic to plain worry, she hears a stamping of boots. First in is Job, tail wagging, then Jake with big snowflakes melting on his black hair and across his jacket-covered shoulders. She sits up, blankets slumping to her waist. She reaches over to receive Job's licks on her hand and gives him a scratch around his ears in return. "Where did you go?" she asks half angry, half relieved.

"I heard nature calling," Jake says laughing. He removes the coat and starts stoking the fire.

"You what?"

"I had to use the 'facilities.'"

"Oh," says Jamie, as the reality of her own needs make its presence felt. "I think I need to go also."

Pausing for a second, she asks, "Jake...where *is* your...bathroom?"

He looks at her with loving, teasing eyes, then thumbs toward the entrance, "Out there."

"Out where?"

"There," he says laughing. "In the woods. Watch your step. Snow's not bad, but ground's a little slippery. Job will go with you. Better take my flashlight. And my thermos of water. It's warm."

"But..." The reality of life in the woods finally dawns on her, "Where do I go?"

"Anywhere you want," he laughs again, not wanting to relieve her obvious mental discomfort. "Just don't let a raccoon bite your backside."

"Jake!!"

"Sorry, he says teasingly. You'll be fine. And Job'll make sure no raccoons or anything else disturbs your quiet time."

Jamie struggles back into jeans, sweater, socks and boots. She isn't happy about this new 'adventure,' but she has no choice.

Jacket on, Jake hands her the flashlight and thermos. Job is alert, tail wagging, ready for his new assignment. Jamie doesn't know exactly what the thermos is for, but figures it must be to clean up.

Kissing her, Jake says, "Go about six yards back on the path here. Off to the right is a deer run. There's a tree down about ten yards from there. It'll be a comfortable enough seat."

As she turns uncertainly towards the entrance, Jake pats her backside.

"If you're not back in fifteen minutes, I'll alert the Mounties."

"Thanks...a lot," she says with more than a bit of sarcasm, as Job leads her into the snowy darkness.

Later, it is Jamie's turn to stamp her boots. Relieved, in more ways than one, she has negotiated the trail, found the downed tree, shivered through her own call of nature, and then realizes what the thermos is for. She thankfully also discovers a few gently used Kleenex retained from her last walk. Job had kept a respectful distance. But once again was ready to lead her back to the cave.

Jake welcomes her with a big hug and kiss. "Feel better?" His arms enfold her like she is in a cocoon.

"Yes. But Jake, I don't think I can make a habit of this. It's not the 'au natural' I seek!"

"Well, come back to bed and let me warm you up." She feels herself warm to his arms and melts to his chest. Yes, she wants to be back in bed.

She finds his lips and kisses them. Feeling drowsy again, she says, "Yes. That would be nice. That would be very nice."

Jamie wakes the next morning to the smell of coffee. Jake has been up a while, judging from the fire's blaze. "Good morning," she says stretching her body and pulling hair back from her face.

"Morning sleepyhead," Jake smiles. He is fully dressed. Same shirt and jeans as yesterday.

"What time is it?" Jamie doesn't have her watch. She had decided not to wear it a few months ago so that she could live by her biological clock.

"Oh, about eight. Breakfast?"

"Yum!" she is surprised at her hunger. She rises from the bed to accept her first cup of coffee that Jake has dipped from a large pot over the fire. A second pot is filled with leftovers.

Bare feet on bare ground is a reminder of her nakedness. She feels the cool air around her body. She moves to put clothes back on. Jake regards her with some disappointment. "What?" she asks. Looking into his always compelling eyes.

"Oh, nothing. I just hoped to admire the décor a bit longer."

Jake!" she says as she pulls clothes from the pile next to the bed. "Honestly, you are the horniest man I've ever known!"

"And there've been so many..." he teases. She pulls on the jeans but waits on the sweater.

"No!" She delights in this banter. No man, not even John, has been so openly sexual with her. There had not been many in her life. Two before John. None during their marriage, though quite a few offered to loosen her vows. Even if she had been interested, which she most definitely was not, she knew these men smelled money, not love. And now Jake.

Jake makes her feel free and easy with sex. He is comfortable in his skin and makes her feel that way in hers. She loves that. She steps towards him to get more coffee and give him a kiss. "Ok, big guy, what's for breakfast?" She pulls her sweater on slowly.

"How about turkey stew and some biscuits?"

"Sounds delicious! Can I help?"

"The turkey stew's about ready. I'll put biscuits on and we should be ready in about ten minutes."

She relaxes with the coffee and watches him move comfortably around his 'kitchen.' His movements are fluid...almost graceful.

"Have you been out?" she asks.

"Yes, but not far. I think we only got about three inches of snow last night. But it's still coming down." He pauses, and then says, "Maggie, I think it would be safer if you could stay here today...and tonight."

She smiles back at him. "I think that could be arranged. Are you sure the inn's not full?"

He laughs. "It will be if you make your reservation now."

"You take plastique? Or just cash?" She reaches into her pocket as if looking for payment.

"I think your signature will do – it's a relaxed operation."

"It didn't feel very relaxed last night!" she banters, remembering his waking and wanting her again somewhere deep in the darkness.

"We only aim to please," he countered. She laughs, now blushing slightly.

"Breakfast is served!" They enjoy the meal together. The humble fare made delicious with appetites unleashed.

The rest of the morning is spent talking and lounging. Jamie asks about the book 'Blue Highways.' Jake tells her it was written by a Native American, William Least Heat Moon. It's about his travels across the country along the small, two lane roads, blue highways in the travel atlas, to small towns with unusual names. Ninety-six, South Carolina. Dime Box, Texas. But it's more about the travels in his own mind, with his own spirit. And now Jamie begins to understand why Jake has carried it with him across his own travels. She senses the author was looking for something, maybe just peace. Just like Jake. She touches his hair as he tells her about the book. A man so open. Yet full of mystery too. There is more to learn.

The spell is broken as Job stirs himself and looks at them, tail wagging, obviously wanting to lead them out into the snowy woods.

"What's on the menu for dinner tonight?" Jamie asks playfully.

"You have a choice between brown and rainbow trout."

"Jake, I'm not in the mood for one of your fish stories."

"It's not a fish story. I get them from the fresh fish market."

"I've never seen fresh fish at the Ram Cat...maybe frozen fish sticks. And if you're catching them yourself, where is the fishing pole? I don't see one. It's an 1800 foot drop from here to the Youghiogheny River. And that's miles away. John said it would be literally impossible for fish to make their way up here as this is near the summit of the ridge and the streams tend to be shallow and small. Bear and raccoon would get any that somehow got this far."

Jake added, "And don't forget the mink. They are pound for pound the meanest animal I know. They make wolverines look like lap cats. So John should have been right. Except the Indians proved him wrong."

"What do you mean?"

"We could start all the way back with George Washington and Fort Duquesne."

"Hey, Jake," Jamie teased. "I could starve to death while listening to your protracted fish tale. The suspense is killing me."

"OK," Jake laughed. "Follow me. It isn't far. And it's open 24/7, 365 days a year...even Thanksgiving and Christmas." They set out from the cave, Job leading the way, as always. Snow is falling, but not heavily. And it is a wet snow that makes hiking easier.

Still, it is almost an hour into their trip when Jamie says, "Jake, you're making this tedious."

"I apologize. We're almost there," he says with a wink.

Finally, they come to a ledge where Jamie can hear water.

Jake points to a spring coming out of some rocks and pouring into a trough. Jake explains that the water comes out of the spring and stays about 45 degrees, year 'round.

"The Indians didn't have thermometers," Jake explains, "but they knew trout only survive in cold water. So they dug a trough fourteen inches wide, five feet deep and fifteen feet long. The heat loss to the air would be minimal compared to the water in the trough...because it was much deeper than it was wide. I tried to measure the exact dimensions, but they didn't fit very well. So the Indians, like 95% of the rest of the world, must have used the metric system."

Jamie takes a swing at Jake. "I'm hungry!" she insists.

"Patience, young lady, the truth is about to be revealed. You can see the cat tails in the trough. The Indians probably planted them along the edge for the fish to hide from critters. The trough is deep enough to keep out bears, raccoons and mink. The Indians probably planted the hemlocks. They would keep the sun from warming the water. Their low branches kept out the Great Blue Heron."

"Jake, I know you eat trout, but I've never seen you with a fishing pole. How do you get them out? With your hands?"

"I catch them like the Indians caught them, Maggie. I built a couple of traps…twenty inches long and six inches in diameter. One is a cone with the narrow end emptying into the trap. The wandering fish goes through the opening and can't get back out. I put one trap in two days ago." With that Jake gets the line tied to the branch. He pulls out the trap. There are three beautiful trout. "We want fish. Voila! Here's dinner."

Later, Jake places the fish over the open fire on wet cedar slats. Jamie marvels at how delicious they are…cooked to perfection.

By the time they have cleaned everything up it is dark again. Jamie says, "I could probably walk home tonight if you went with me."

"Please stay," Jake says. "Just one more night. I'll walk you home in the morning after breakfast. Promise." Jake takes Jamie's hand and leads her toward the bed. Slowly he takes the clothes from her newly taut body. She never feels shy or embarrassed any more…only excited.

Jake lays Jamie on the bed and gently pulls the covers over her. She watches as he takes his clothes off. Every part of his body is beautiful to her. He nods as if asking for her permission to get under the covers. His dark eyebrows have that questioning look of a child. He is always polite in these matters…never assuming anything. How nice is that? Their love making is sweet and they fall into a deep sleep wrapped in the blanket and each other. Just before she does, Jamie wonders why this man has to be only starting his life, while she is finishing so much of what he has yet to encounter. She will have to let him go. Why does life give you these dilemmas? She will just enjoy what she has for now. Tomorrow will be another day.

Chapter 35

Break In. Break Through.

The next morning, Jake and Job walk Jamie home. Snow has blanketed the mountains during the night. A late fall snow, wet and heavy. Already the air feels warm enough that it will start melting as the sun pushes towards its shortened zenith. Jamie knows she has to get back and let Stella know she is alright. Jake senses her anxiety and asks if everything is OK.

"The rule with my friends and family is, if they email me and I don't respond in three days, they can come to see if I'm alright," Jamie explains as they make their way down the trail. Job bounds ahead. Then, as Jake tries forging ahead in the snow, Jamie follows behind, sometimes stepping into his tracks, sometimes making ones of her own. "Not my idea, but theirs."

"You seem to have kept them away from the door so far," Jake says.

This hike takes almost twice as long because of the snow. Jamie is glad when she can make out the cabin through the trees. She is sweating and both she and Jake stopped twice to catch their breath. She could see how someone would get in trouble in these mountains if they were caught by a storm and had no shelter. When they are almost at the cabin, Jake stops…frozen. He is alert, like she has never seen him before. Stiff, erect, leaning slightly forward, almost in attack mode. Job is at the door, sniffing anxiously.

"What is it Jake?"

"Someone has been at your house while you were gone, Jamie."

"How can you tell?"

"Job has got a scent. And I don't think it's bear."

Jake looks around warily, eyes focused for the slightest movement, for something out of place. Jamie's heart starts pounding. She hasn't felt this way since that first day when she saw Jake and Job on the far ridge and practically ran back to the cabin. Job circles around the back side and, finding nothing, returns to the porch, nose close to the scent in the wood.

Jake motions for Jamie to stay put. He steps quietly onto the porch and noticing the door ajar goes into a slight crouch. Her heart still in her throat, Jamie is thankful Jake and Job are with her. She thinks any intruder will come out the worse if they get tangled up with those two. She, too, looks around for...what? A man? But there's nothing here. No car. No tracks. She looks back to Jake and he's gone! And so is Job. Her moment of sheer panic dissipates when both step out from the cabin.

"It's OK Maggie. No one's here."

Jamie finishes the last few steps to the porch and instinctively throws her arms around Jake. The embrace lasts a long time. She hates feeling vulnerable. Yet right now that is exactly what she feels.

"Are you sure?"

"Yes. But someone was here. Did you leave your door unlocked?"

"Yes. I always do. Who would bother me up here?"

"Well the door wasn't forced open, so I guessed that was the case. But there are mud tracks inside."

"I want to see."

She pushes past Jake to assess the burglary damage for herself. Letting her eyes adjust she looks for overturned chairs or papers strewn across the floor or bedding shredded. But she sees nothing. Just boot prints muddied and dried on her floor. Even the refrigerator is as she left it, but she looks carefully inside to be sure.

"Jake, I don't see anything missing."

"Well whoever was here came and went before the snow. Maybe when it finishes melting we'll see tire tracks or something." Jake looks like a detective, collecting clues. He is almost animal-like in his search of her place. There is nothing he leaves unnoticed.

"Maybe it was just someone who got lost, Jake. Or some kids fooling around."

"You could be right. But only one person came in the cabin. And judging from the boot marks I'd say he wasn't a kid. Are you sure everything is where you left it?"

Jamie scans the room again, looking for anything that is not as she left it. "Yes. I think so." She pauses, then decides it's OK. Whoever, or whatever, came to the cabin for her, or just a place to stay dry for a bit, is gone. Even Job has settled onto his familiar place, the rug in front of the fireplace.

"Oh, Jake, let's not worry about it! Come on. Get your coat and boots off. If you'll start the fire, I'll warm up some soup. And I have Cora's corn meal muffins here. They're huge!" Jamie starts working quickly, wiping the boot mud off the floor, trying to wipe away fears she thought had been put away forever. Ten minutes later, Jake has a fire crackling. From the kitchen, Jamie watches him try to settle into the couch. But his senses are alive too. His eyes dart around the room looking for more clues. She appreciates his desire to protect. Yet she also senses a need to protect him from the details in her other life. She hopes he doesn't start asking a lot of questions.

Jamie is glad she can break the moment with food. "Here we go," she announces too brightly. She hands him a big bowl of beef barley soup and a muffin. Jamie settles in with her own soup and muffin next to him. Job, looking expectantly, gets half of Jake's muffin, gobbles it down, taking a half turn around the rug before curling a half step closer to the fire, ready for a well-earned nap.

They eat in silence, absorbing warmth from the soup and fire. The hike had been tiring. And the moment of panic had sapped the last of her morning strength.

"More?"

"I would, if you have some. Job might like a taste too." On cue the dog, eyes closed, wags his tail. Jamie stands. But before she steps to the kitchen, her eyes settle on the small desk and the fax machine next to it.

"The fax...the fax is gone!" There had been a fax coming in just before she left for Jake's two days ago. She planned to read it after she got home. A quick deep chill runs down her body.

"A fax? What fax?"

"Oh, Jake, it's something I can't bother you about." She had always wanted to keep these two parts of her life separate: the troubles of her old life and her new life with Jake. She walks over to the desk and looks around trying to see if the paper might have fallen. Nothing. Now Jake is up and looking around the desk also. He notices a bit of mud that Jamie missed earlier. Job sniffs, too, as if trying to help.

Jamie stares at the machine, thinking maybe it really didn't spit out news she didn't want to know. She knows otherwise. She feels violated. Physically and spiritually.

"Maggie, talk to me. Why is that fax so important?"

"I don't know! I didn't read it before I left to come to you. It was Thanksgiving and I wasn't going to be bothered by the business. Whoever was here must have taken it. That means it must have been important." Jamie takes one thumb into her hand and clutches to it as if she is holding onto something important.

"Why would someone want your fax, Magpie?" He hadn't called her Magpie in months. Why now? Jamie feels herself crumbling and begins to cry. Jake steps over to hold her. She hates felling like this! She has gotten through John's death. Has overcome her fear of this 'mountain man.' Has stood up to threats from faraway. And now this. A little piece of paper scares her to death, reducing her to tears.

After a few minutes, she releases herself from his hold and walks over to the window. Staring out to the ravine below, she wrestles with her emotions and how much to tell Jake. She also knows she has to get back to Stella today or tomorrow. But how to tell her what happened without sending alarm bells ringing back to the office and ruining her time here? Maybe her idyllic life is over...

"I don't know what to say, Jake..." She turns and looks at him. So young. So strong. Almost healed. How can she burden him now?

He looks back waiting. But he senses now is not the time to say anything. After a moment, Jamie gestures back to the couch. They sit, neither speaking. Jamie stares into the fire until she is settled enough to speak.

"Jake, I want you to listen. No questions. Just listen." She likes the firmness in her voice. She is ready to go on. Jamie then tells Jake the whole story of her past life and how it had encroached on her life now. He listens to her...the theft...the plot to try and overthrow the company. After an hour she is finished. Now he knows. And in the telling maybe she is figuring out what may have been on the fax and who came to the cabin. Jake has had his eyes fixed on Jamie this whole time.

"Why didn't you tell me this before, Maggie?"

"Because, Jake, it was my business. I need to figure this out on my own. This is my life. I came here to get away from my old life. I need to have a new life. But I can't just walk away and leave behind messes for others to clean up." She pauses. Then looks into his eyes with a love that is deep and profound.

"I have learned so much from you. I want to take what I have learned and use it in my life going forward. I just need to figure out how to make my break clean and without hurting others." Her voice is strong and calm. She likes that she's finding a way to chase fear away one more time.

"What are you going to do, Maggie?'

"About someone breaking in or about my life I left behind?" Jamie asks.

"Both. Do you think this person will come back?" Jamie realizes Jake can't protect her from paper. But he can protect her from the person who came looking for it.

"It depends if he got the information he wanted."

"Do you think he did?"

"I've been working through this, Jake. For months. I have a whole journal full of entries." Jamie walks over to her journal and hugs it to herself. "I am approaching it with the attitude of, 'Gotta Love 'Em,'" Jamie says. "I can't change what is happening. But I won't go back until I get what I came here for. I can only do what I can do."

"Gotta Love 'Em?" Jake asks. "After this guy stole from you? Stole from a children's hospital?"

Jamie lifts the journal into the air. "That is the conclusion I've come to. I'm not going to be scared out of this place until I'm ready... or nearly ready," Jamie answers as she sits back down by the fire and looks at the worried look on Jake's face.

"If you have a little time before you have to answer your emails, I'd like to tell you two things I learned in my Comparative Religions classes in college. For a beer, I'll share something that might help you." Jake breaks the tension with a shy smile.

Jamie laughs at the bargaining for a beer. She wants to hear the stories. Nothing he ever tells her is a waste of time.

"I'd love that, Jake. I have until evening to answer."

"Perfect. I'll stoke the fire and get some more wood inside for you. Maybe just for tonight you should lock the door."

"No one wants to hurt me, Jake. They just want to discredit me. Do you see the difference?"

"Yes. I see. I'll see even better with a beer." Jake's long body unfolds easily from the couch and he heads toward the door.

"Coming right up."

Jake brings in a large load of wood, carrying easily what Jamie couldn't bring in three loads. He stacks it neatly for her. This will last a while. Jake sits back down beside Jamie, takes her hand and starts, "There is a story in Buddhist lore that goes something like this: There once was a man who had a son and a horse on his farm. One day his horse ran away. All of the villagers came to him and said, 'Oh, this is terrible. You have lost your only horse. You'll be unable to till or plant or harvest. What will you do?' The farmer said calmly, 'We'll see.'" Jamie looks at Jake's animated face as he tells the story. Daniel must have loved his storytelling. How lucky he was to have Jake as a daddy for his short life.

"The next day, the runaway horse came home leading ten wild horses. The farmer and his son put all eleven in the corral. All of the villagers came to him and said, 'Oh, this is wonderful. You had just one horse and now you have eleven. You have such good fortune.' To this the farmer answers calmly again, 'We'll see.'"

After he has taken a swig, Jake continues. "The next day the farmer's son was breaking the new horses in when he was thrown from a horse and broke his leg. All of the villagers came to the farmer and said, 'Oh, this is terrible. Your son will be no help. You and your farm will suffer this year. What horrible luck.' To which the farmer answered, 'We'll see.'" Jamie is beginning to see the wisdom in this Buddhist story. There is no predicting what may happen.

Jake continues: "The next day the employer's army came to the village and conscripted every able-bodied boy for the war. When they saw the farmer's son had a broken leg, they left him behind. I'm sure you know how the rest of the story goes."

"Yes," says Jamie quietly. "Thank you, Jake. I can use that when I have to go back to my old life. I don't have to do battle with or even respond, really to whatever crosses my path. I've noticed that with a stray dog I sometimes meet on the trail. If I act to defend myself against her, she goes into growling and posturing. But if I just let us both mind our own business, she passes me by like some part of the scenery. What is the other story?"

"How about one more beer?"

As Jamie gets another beer, Jake relaxes in his chair, puts his feet on the hearth and lets out a long sigh. Jamie knows she could never tire of looking at this man. It is all she can do to not beg him to stay.

"Ready?" Jake draws himself up, sitting cross-legged facing her on the couch. He gets really serious when he is about to tell a story. She studies this serious face.

"Ready."

"This story comes from Taoism. It isn't exactly a story; it is just an idea worth thinking about. Taoism teaches that you need to be an empty vessel so that when something wonderful comes along you will be able to take it in. If you are filled with fear or hateful things, there will be no room for the wonderful things that life may bring."

Jake pauses and takes a long draw on his beer. "Think of it like having an empty spoon. You can choose what to put in the spoon. If you fill your spoon with negative things, then when the positive things come along there will be no room for them. It's an emptiness that gives the spoon its function. Do you understand, Maggie?"

Jamie thinks of beachcombing for shells and how when her pockets and hands become full, she can't pick up and enjoy the next shell even if it's more beautiful than the last. She sees how to hold and appreciate a thing; she must release the last one. "I understand most of it, Jake. Can we talk about them again sometime?"

Jake rises and carries his empty beer bottles to the kitchen. He puts on his boots and snugs the laces. Job is at the door beside him. "Sure, Maggie. Anytime. You know that. Now you listen to me. Lock your door for a couple of nights. If you hear anything, call for help. Promise?"

"Promise."

"I'll see you soon, Maggie. I've loved our time together and I am thankful for it."

"Me too, Jake. It was my best Thanksgiving ever. I love you Jake."

As he puts on his coat, he looks a little sad. "I love you so much Maggie. I'll see you soon. Take care." A big hug and a lingering kiss and Jake and Job walk off into the late afternoon. Jamie watches until they disappear. She locks the door and turns on the lights. The computer is waiting. She will email Stella to say there is a problem and can she call at eight tomorrow morning. Answering email is enough reality for today.

Before bed, Jamie picks up her journal. She wants to finish a thought she had last night just before sleep.

November 28th

I need to write now about Jake and me.

What is the meaning of 'cradle robber?' It is someone keeping another's youth for her/himself. Robbing another of all the joys and sorrows of making their way through the stages and discoveries, the journeys of adulthood.

Much as I revel in the youth and vitality Jake has stirred in me, I must not keep him for myself. Appreciate the gift we have each shared. Then say, 'Happy Trails.'

I remember the rewards of raising a family. Of helping John build a business. These did much to 'raise' and 'build' who and what I became in the ensuing years.

We are a life stage mismatch. How can I claim him for myself? How would I honestly answer the question of mating again after all the reasons for it (building family, achieving the wifely goals and fairy-tale endings, caring for-richer-for-poorer-till-death-do-us-part) are past? How can I revisit the anachronism of the exclusive relationship?

I want to explore the freedom of the trail and ALL the people who cross my path, rather than try again for some romantic ideal. This is the only thing that fits with my past experience and vision of what could be, or what I could become. Maybe life really is a beach! – strewn with beautiful things I can love, but not hold....

Tears pour from Jamie's eyes as she finishes the journal. Good night. She takes off her dirty clothes, but does not wash away any of the last three days. She will sleep with him on each part of her body. She does not have to give him up. Not yet.

Chapter 36

Ten More Shopping Days

Fall plummets quickly towards winter. Energies spent, animals and insects burrow into trees, rock and earth seeking protection and warmth. They slip into sleep, hoping to awaken when longer days and warming air call them forth into the spring of a new year.

Jamie, too, thinks of hibernating. But if she were an insect, she would be a bee and the hive of her life will not settle down. She gets Stella to resend the fax that had been stolen. What comes back is a copy of a small article in the Wall Street Journal speculating on the future of John's company. It quotes an "unnamed source" saying his widow had gone into hiding and that "her husband's friends and colleagues were concerned for her mental health and physical safety."

Jamie's hands shake as she reads the rest. She has a pretty good idea who this "unnamed source" is. He is making his move. Sending someone to spy or steal from her is part of his effort to flush her into the open and undermine her influence and credibility. Maybe the intruder took the fax hoping she hadn't seen it yet, keeping Jamie unaware for a while longer of the forces closing around her. The Thanksgiving snow had melted, revealing car tracks, but nothing else.

As she thinks about it, it might have been better that she was gone when the intruder arrived. She imagines him taking a picture of her with wild hair and rough clothes looking more mountain woman than millionaire as evidence to take back to his employer and her board. She considers calling the sheriff then decides against it. She really wants to keep the company and its troubles separate from the new life unfolding before her. Involving him would just bring more attention than she wants. Maybe it is a good idea. Maybe it isn't. But no response seems to be her best response at this point.

She faxes a quick note back to Stella thanking her and trying to comfort her. She has learned enough business lessons from John to see this for what it is. At some point she *will* have to confront it. But another snow guarantees that she won't be bothered by some city car trying to negotiate her hill anytime soon. Unlike Thanksgiving, this time the cold stays and the snow settles onto the hills as an owner not a guest.

Despite these gathering forces, or maybe because of them, Jamie is determined to continue her daily hikes. Checking the map one day, she is pleased to see she's covered enough ground to cross into Massachusetts near Springfield. She reads about a stone marker commemorating Shays' Rebellion. This was a short, but important, protest by debt-ridden farmers mainly in central and western Massachusetts led by Revolutionary War veteran Daniel Shays in 1787. More ground to cover!

Jamie steps out into foot-deep snow. With the onset of winter, hiking has become a chore. Sometimes Jamie doesn't have any idea why she continues this Appalachian "hike." Her daily six mile treks have slowed to four, then three, and then two as the snow deepens. She wonders if she will finish the A.T. by the time her year at the cabin ends in April. Still, she manages to get out virtually every day, even if it means just putting one foot in from of the other. Her hike south from the cabin down to the creek becomes a favorite, even if it is uphill on the way back. It is just over a mile down to where the path crosses over and starts up the opposite ridge where she had first seen Jake and Job. The trail is a favorite for animals, too. Deer emerge from their winter hideaways and follow the path down to water. She sees tracks of rabbits and squirrels. Jake also shows her the tracks of animals she would prefer not to meet. Coyote. A restless bear. And one that even gets Jake excited – bobcat!

One morning she peers into the water and sees three brook trout nosed upstream, gills opening and closing patiently in the near-freezing water. Had she been one of the predator animals, she would have lunged for them. As it is, she just wonders how they survive the winters. Do they find a deep hole farther downstream? Do they hibernate? Or just wait to become a meal for something hungrier and higher on the food chain? Nature is mysterious, but not unknowable. Jamie is glad for the lessons she's learning even now.

The mile and a half to Jake's sometimes becomes an overnight affair. He would insist on feeding her and then suggest in the waning light of mid-afternoon that she spend the rest of the day, and night, with him. As comfortable as he manages to make his cave, still she is glad for the extra blankets she insisted he borrow from the cabin. If nothing else, they make it easier to say yes when he asks. She also realizes this affair is a matter not of compulsion, but of comfort and contentment in his presence.

Christmas is coming. "Only ten more shopping days!" she laughs to herself as she nears the cave. In past years, she and her assistant, Rosa, would review the long list of people to buy presents for and then decide how much to spend and what to get for each. This Christmas will be much simpler and, she hopes, perhaps more meaningful.

It will be a day of very mixed emotions for both Jamie and Jake. Her first without John. Jake's second without Daniel and his wife.

Jamie arrives breathless at Jake's place. She and Jake discuss the upcoming holiday next morning, nestled deep beneath a pile of blankets. "Jake, I need to talk to you about Christmas."

"OK." He replies, with a touch of trepidation.

Jamie looks at the ceiling of the cave as she gathers her thoughts.

"I want to be alone." She pauses for a moment. "On Christmas Eve and Christmas Day."

"Why is that?" his voice perhaps reflects more relief than hurt.

Out comes a torrent of words, thoughts, emotions. "All my life I have been part of someone else, Jake. A child to my parents. A wife to my husband. A mother and grandmother to my children. I have been good to all of them. They have drawn strength and energy from me. And I have gladly given it. But all my life I've wondered who I am. I. Me. Who is Jamie? Maybe that's why I talk so much."

She looks at him wanting to see his reaction. His eyes are steadfast on hers. She feels good about continuing. "Maybe it's my way of not having to ask the hard question. But, Jake, I need to know. Who am I when I am all alone with myself? This time away has been good for me. I am getting to know me. I know I'm getting stronger...in *all* ways. I just think that if I can do Christmas all alone, maybe me and my God, that would give me the extra strength I'll need for my most alone times that will come when I go back. Times when there may be all kinds of people around me, but no one to count on...except me and..." Jamie remembers feeling alone in a boardroom full of people, each with his or her own agenda.

Jake pulls her close and puts his hand over her mouth gently. "Shhhh. I understand. I think I do anyway. If you're worried about hurting me, don't. I need that time alone too, to prepare for my own home going. Having you come into my life has been a blessing. My God may not be the same as yours, but between her and you, the hole in my heart has healed a great deal. The sorrow and anger that pushed me across the land like bits of dust before a storm have backed away. There is a peace and joy in me that I could foolishly deny myself forever."

Now Jake pauses. Jamie's eyes are wide. A tear gathers in each corner. "I do have a Christmas gift for you. I've been working on it since we met."

"Really?" Jamie asks after gently kissing his hand away, then brushing each tear away.

"Yes, really."

"What is it?" Sliding over him, trying to entice an answer.

"You have to wait until Christmas!" he laughs, rolling over her, loving how this woman can become coltish in a moment.

They kiss again. Then she says looking up at him, "Well I have a present for you too, but I want you to have it on Christmas."

"Well, how about this. You put my present out on your porch on Christmas Eve. I'm sure Santa will deliver it to me. How would that be?"

"That would be great. My present will need a rock to hold it down, so it will be under a rock on the porch. I have been working on it for a long while too."

"You can come the Saturday before Christmas and we can have a Christmas dinner of whatever Cora and Ellie May make for us," says Jamie.

"That's a deal."

The deal is sealed with more kisses and a wrestling match under the blankets leaving both exhausted and fulfilled.

Chapter 37

Winter Solstice

The Saturday before Christmas Jamie is up early. She needs to get to the store when it opens. The snow is still too deep for the Harley. It will take her a couple of hours to walk there. She wants to be home in plenty of time to fix up for a nice evening with Jake and Job. At 7 AM, she is out the door. The morning is brisk and clear. The sun is still an hour away. Today will be its shortest, the night its longest. Even with the starlight and a waning moon, Jamie has to use her flashlight to work her way down the drive. She laughs to herself thinking she must look pretty comical all bundled up for warmth and looking like nothing so much as the jolly old elf, her backpack and pockets spilling over with presents for Cora, Ellie Mae and the baby. She can't zip the backpack and a ribbon peeks out of her pocket.

Somewhere near the halfway point to Ram Cat, she realizes that this is the first time in her adult memory she is filled with the bright anticipation of Christmas – simple joy. Even as her efforts are impeded by the snow, she wonders if somehow the circumstances of her life have obstructed the coming of this spirit to her. She imagines the Christmas spirit as a traveler, a guest, struggling through the debris of her life, unable to make it to her door. Jamie resolves from now on to do whatever she needs to do to clear the path for Christmas to come, and fill her up just like this in the years that remain to her.

A little after nine she bursts through the door of the Ram Cat with a "Ho, Ho, Ho, and Merry Christmas!" The two women are at first startled by this early morning apparition, which turns Jamie's Ho Ho into real laughter. Cora recognizes Jamie and rushes toward her, Christmas apron tightly cinched around her ample waist. "Mercy me. You walked all this way in the cold? Let's get you unbundled and warmed up some."

Ellie Mae also sweeps in for a hug. She is looking radiant and healthy. The baby is still all in front of her. From behind she remains nubile and firm. "We was wonderin' if you would be by today. We figured you couldn't get out on your road," Ellie Mae takes Jamie's coat and folds it over her arm. "If you hadn't come we were going to bring you meals on wheels. Can't have Christmas without some of Ma's meatloaf, your favorite. And some garlic mashed potatoes. We fixed up some special cookies too."

As Jamie slowly sets down her backpack, she tries to keep the presents from tumbling out prematurely. She is ever more grateful for the caring and friendship from these two women. She makes a mental note to give them more time and space in her journal. She wants to be sure she never forgets what they have meant to her. They sit around the table and enjoy each other's company and some hot coffee and Christmas cookies. Ellie Mae updates her on the baby. She saw the first ultrasound last week. The doctor is pleased at how both mother and child are doing. "He said I was blessed with good genes and good raisin'," she smiled at her mother with these words. Cora covers Ellie Mae's hand with her own. Then Jamie covers theirs.

"You are blessed Ellie Mae. And so is your baby," Jamie says quietly. Then she looks at Cora and asks tentatively, "Have there been any more... you know...?"

"Spies?" Cora finishes her sentence with a crackle so abrupt they both laugh at the word.

"Yes...spies...secret agents?" Jamie knows her voice betrays her worry. But she needs to know.

"No. I haven't seen anyone strange around here. Except Buckshot. But he's local and he's *always* strange!" Cora and Ellie Mae laugh at this inside joke.

Then Cora, picking up on the question, turns serious. "Jamie, it's none of my business to meddle so I won't. But if there's anything you need us to help with, well, you know we would do anything for you. Sheriff too, if it came to that. Him I can vouch for."

Ellie Mae's eyes are wide, focused on her mother, a teenager trying to understand the adult world rapidly confronting her.

Jamie feels a sense of immense relief. She knows these women will protect her more fiercely than any of her husband's employees. And she appreciates that they have talked about her to the sheriff, still surprised anyone cares – though wishing, in truth, there was nothing to cause talk. But Cora didn't say anything about anyone suspicious being in town around Thanksgiving, so Jamie decides not to alarm her with the story about the break-in.

"Cora, and Ellie Mae, thank you. I want you to know that I'm not in any trouble. Not in any danger. But my husband, being a wealthy man, did have his enemies. With him gone, it's possible that one or two of them might try to do something to get at him through me."

"You mean try to kill you?" Ellie Mae blurts out.

"No!" Jamie replies, maybe a bit too loudly. "People like that don't try to hurt your body. They just try to steal your money. And maybe make you look bad while they're doing it."

Cora says, "Well, if anyone comes in here asking where you live, I'll just tell 'em I don't know for sure, but there's a crazy woman who lives about four miles out that way." – and here Cora points the other way out of town – "And I hear she's a crack shot." At this all three women laugh loud and long. Jamie decides not to follow up that comment with one about her own shooting prowess. Instead, she gets back to the business at hand... Christmas!

"Cora and Ellie Mae, I brought some presents for you. That's why I looked like Santa Claus coming in here four days early."

"I swear, you looked more like the Imbomnimable Snowman, or whatever they call it," laughs Cora.

Jamie reaches over to her backpack and pulls out the wreath she has made. "Cora, this is for you."

"Why, Jamie, you made this out of the ground pine by your place, didn't you?" Cora gets up and hangs the wreath on a small nail inside the door. She stands back admiring it. "It's beautiful!" She gives Jamie a kiss on the head and sits back down. "Thank you."

"It was nice getting ready for Christmas without all the usual riot of activity. I had time to do nice things like this."

"Aren't you missing your kids and grandkids this time of year?" asks Ellie Mae.

"Yes. That's the bad part. I feel very selfish being away from them this Christmas. But I hope it will end up being a good kind of selfish that will make next Christmas, and all the Christmases to follow, even more special."

Jamie leans forward in her chair, her hands wrapped around the warm coffee mug. "So, to kind of make up for my being here, I have been on the computer with the grandkids helping them each write an animal story. We finished last month and I sent the stories to an online printer to make into books for them. They should have them by now. I'll spend some good quality time with my girls when I get home in the spring. I know they still need me, too."

Cora and Ellie Mae take all this in accepting, if not quite understanding, it all. How does someone have enough money to *make* books, much less have time to write them? Jamie may be rich, but she's not like any of the other rich people who come snootin' into their store, acting like they own it and can't wait to get out at the same time.

"Ellie Mae," Jamie pulls out several pieces of beautifully carved red oak. "This is a cradle for you and the baby. See how it fits together?" Jamie shows how each board fits into the next, sliding the side pieces into one end, then snapping the other end into place. It balances easily on the floor's broad oak planks. Reaching back into the pack, Jamie continues, "I made a soft mattress for it out of blanket pieces I sewed together. And here's a little blanket for on top to match."

"Oh, Jamie, thank you." Ellie Mae's eyes fill with tears. "Where did you get a cradle up there in the woods? You never really go anyplace, do you?"

"I asked Jake, my mountain man, to make it for me. It is amazing what he can do with wood he finds. When he goes home in the spring he'll go back to being a carpenter I suppose. I figured you could send this along with the baby when the adoption comes through. Or you can keep it for when you start your own family."

Cora looks quickly at Ellie Mae. Neither misses the "my" attached to Jamie's "mountain man," only confirming that maybe there is more going on up in her hills than just some alone time. Jamie tries to ignore the glance and what they may suspect.

Now it's Cora's turn. She pulls a wrapped present out of her apron pocket and gives it to Jamie. "Something for you from the three of us," she says nodding to the third person inside Ellie Mae. Jamie unwraps a picture of the three women that they had had a customer take of them several months back. They were standing together on the porch of the Ram Cat, the older women with arms around the mother-to-be. Jamie had forgotten about it. It had a simple oak frame. All three are wearing the smile of a joy in each others' presence. "I will cherish this forever," Jamie now wipes tears from her eyes.

"It's the four of us, really," Ellie Mae chimes in. "I was pregnant when the picture was taken."

"That makes it even more special. Thank you both." She holds their hands. "Merry Christmas. I'm glad we have all become friends...the best Christmas gift of all. I'll start shopping for some groceries. It will take me a while to get back home," says Jamie.

Cora interjects. "You are *not* walking home. I don't care if you do think you're the Improbable Snowman. I'm going to take you in the truck up to the point where they stopped plowing your road. You're not walking all that way. And that's an order."

"Yes, Ma'am! In that case, I'll just have another cup of coffee. That will be a much shorter walk." After Jamie finishes, the three go to work quickly refilling her backpack with her shopping list of goods, plus the meatloaf and fixins. As she and Cora put their coats on, she notices Ellie Mae running her hand gently over the cradle, giving it an easy rock.

Jamie is very thankful for the ride back to her drive. The women are cozy in the truck. When they get to Jamie's road, Cora decides to try the snow-covered hill. But barely twenty feet in, the truck's tires begin to spin. Cora gives up and they agree Jamie has to finish on her own. As Cora helps her with the backpack she says, "If this old thing had four wheel drive I could take you all the way up."

"That's OK, Cora. Bringing me this far is a great help." They pause, looking into each other's eyes sharing warmth beyond words exchanged. Then a quick hug and more "Merry Christmases." Jamie waits for Cora to get turned around, waves once more, then starts up the drive trying to step into the tracks she made coming down.

Jamie makes it home in plenty of time to get cleaned up and get ready for the boys to arrive. She puts the picture on her desk, studying it once again. A friendship that might never have been. Wonderful women she met on her life path.

Jamie plans to ask Jake to stay the night. Brave as she feels about Christmas alone, she feels an ache for the touch of another – Jake's special touch – to help her through.

Chapter 38

Spirit Prayer

That night, lying in bed, Jamie tells Jake she misses having a Christmas tree. But at the same time she doesn't want to cut one down just for her. It seems too selfish somehow. Anyway she doesn't have the lights or decorations. Jake reminds her that the trees are already decorated with ice and snow. Jake compliments her on "learning the Indian Ways" by not taking something from the land without giving something back. He explains how Indian children learn that *every* day is Christmas. They are taught how to receive gifts with joy. When the gift, such as a doll or ball, no longer gives joy, the child is taught to give it to another child so they can enjoy it. He then says something that touches her deeply,

"As Indians we learn from childhood that the more one gives, the more spiritual, the more like our Ancestors, we become. We honor the giving spirit of Christmas not because the day is special, but because in our Land the spirit is with us everyday. What your Christ taught people in his Holy Land, our Spirits taught our Ancestors who have passed on, to us, and what we must pass on to those who follow. It is why we look at all lands as holy. It was a lesson I was trying to teach..." Then he breaks down and cries. He reaches for Jamie and she shelters him, letting the soul-ripping memory settle back uneasily into the scabbed boundaries of the past.

Hearing Jake's cries, Job comes in looking worried and sniffing. Checking first Jake, then Jamie, he senses the humans are really OK and decides he can return to his spot next to the fireplace. After more minutes of perfect quiet, Jamie shares with him her relationship with the Voice. She is hoping it will come at Christmastime.

"I don't know who or what the Voice is, Jake. I feel like it comes to me from somewhere out there. But I don't know where *there* is!" Jamie pauses and gazes up at the ceiling of her room. The ceiling fan is still, and the room falls into a complete and comfortable silence. "I was scared at first. Is this a ghost? John? A spirit? God? I still don't know the answer. But I do know this. I'm not scared anymore, Jake. I want the Voice in my life. It is real. I need it. Him. Her."

Jake asks, "What if the Voice is actually your own spirit growing? We are taught that your mind, your body, your heart and each of your five senses are like leaves on a tree. Your mind knows your body. Your senses feed your mind. But like leaves, they are connected to something larger. They take gifts from the sun and provide nourishment to the branches and trunk and roots. But without the roots and trunk and branches, the leaves cannot be." Even in her bedroom, Jake's mind goes to nature. The trees are just outside, and Jamie can also see herself as one, with leaves budding for spring, not bare in winter. "Your Voice," Jake continues, "may be your roots and trunk and branches speaking to your mind, your heart, your eyes and ears and nose and fingers and tongue. It may be You becoming All of You. This is a blessed thing."

Jake pauses for a second. When he speaks this time his voice sounds different as though the words themselves are coming from a different place. "You are becoming a Strong Spirit. A Spirit that can go to great heights. High. Higher than Owl. Higher than Crow. High where Hawk and Eagle live."

And now Jamie's mind goes to the sky. Beyond the ceiling fan and the ceiling itself is the expanse of sky. Jamie is under her comforter, nestled next to Jake, but she could almost smell the wind.

"When Eagle flies to the East," Jake continues, "this is our symbol for strength and endurance and vision. You have flown East to be here. You have gathered your strength and endurance. Now your Voice will speak with the wisdom of what you have seen and a vision of what you will see."

Jake pauses again. When he speaks, it is with a quiet softness. "This is what I have been feeling for some time. But your words have helped me find *my* words."

Jamie wonders aloud, "Has coming here been about finding my authentic self, finding the truth of who I am and bringing that to the world? She turns on her side and puts her arm around Jake. His body is warm and acts like a magnet to pull her close.

"Jake, it feels like most of my life has been being some *thing* to some *body*. A child to my parents. A wife, and then a caregiver, to my husband. A mother to my children. And now a grandmother.

"I'm not complaining. But I think women are expected to be in these different roles before we can be ourselves. Or maybe we are just expected to think about others first before we can think about ourselves."

Jake replies. "What if life is a thousand piece jigsaw puzzle that is only completed by each person showing up and sharing the gifts they were sent here to bring?" When Jamie looks at him not quite understanding, he continues.

"Like the story in your Bible, Maggie. The story of the loaves and the fishes. The followers of your Jesus did not know how to feed the large crowd that had gathered to hear him. They feared they would go hungry and so hid their bounty from each other. But a boy brought them five loaves of bread and two fish. And with that gift freely shared, he showed how a multitude could be fed – how we could feed each other."

Jake raises his arms, then puts his hands under his head, his elbows pointing up. He gazes toward the ceiling, as if skimming his thoughts from the air above them. "Your Christian leaders say the story is about the power of Jesus and the miracle he performed by feeding so many with so little. I think the story starts with the gift from the boy who believed that we'll have more than we need if we share what we've been given. To me it is a lesson from the Great Spirit that the People live through the gifts we bring to each other. Same with your parable of the Talents."

"Are you a Christian, Jake?" Jamie has never thought to ask this before, but she'd never imagined Jake knew so much about the Bible.

Jake brings his hands to his chest, then he turns on his side. He smiles. "No, Maggie. At least not in the ways that your Jesus was used to destroy our culture." There is sarcasm in his voice, but he softens quickly. "But I do believe that there is a Great Spirit who created these lands and who created the animals and the peoples to live on them and take care of them."

Jake sits up. He looks at Jamie, studying her face as he searches for the next words. "Jamie, we learn many prayers and songs. I want to sing one for you that I learned from my grandfather. I sang it back to him when he died. It is a prayer to our Great Spirit.

Jake sits cross-legged facing her. He clears his throat, then begins to sing:

"Oh, Great Spirit, whose voice I hear in the winds.

And whose breath gives life to all the world.

Hear me! I am small and weak.

I need your strength and wisdom.

Let me walk in beauty, and make my eyes

Ever hold the red and purple sunset.

Make my hands respect the things you have made.

My ears sharp to hear your voice.

Make me wise so that I may understand

The things you might teach me.

Let me learn the lessons you have hidden

In every leaf and rock.

I seek strength, not to be greater than my brother,

But to fight my greatest enemy, myself.

Make me always ready to come to you

With clear hands and straight eyes,

So when life fades, as the fading sunset,

My spirit may come to you without shame.' "

Jake sings his Spirit Prayer in a long, slow, deep cadence as though savoring the memories that each syllable brings. He seems entranced and Jamie feels carried along with him. When he finishes, she feels a union more powerful than even their lovemaking.

She wonders for a moment...is *he* the Voice? Have the past eight months been one long spiritual journey with him as her Spirit Guide? Is he really a man? Or one of those shamans, spirit men, she has read about? She feels adrift and anchored at the same time. What is going on? Then her eyes fill with tears. She reaches for him, wanting to feel his full embrace. His body uncurls gracefully and comes to meet hers.

"Thank you, Jake. For so many things," as she kisses him. "But that prayer, that song, I felt like you were taking me on a journey."

"We are on a journey, my Magpie. I became lost and broken on my journey. Then you flew in from the West and found me. And healed my wings. And cleared my eyes.

"At first, I thought you were just another person who came to these woods because you thought they belonged to you, that you 'owned' them in the peculiar way that some people think they possess the Eternal.

"But then I began to see that the one I mocked as 'Magpie' was only a disguise. I even asked the Great Spirit if he sent you to trick me, to lure me out of my den where I could be captured by your sheriff. Instead, the Spirit showed me something else. He showed me the anger and the hurt that I carried inside like a maggot-infested wound. And then he showed you as a powerful Medicine Woman. And he revealed your powers to heal. And he saw that we should walk the same path together."

Jamie cries quietly as he continues.

"I don't know where this path leads, Maggie. But I trust it. And I trust us to find our ways. And to use our powers and give our gifts. So when the time comes we can greet our Spirit and our Ancestors humble and unashamed."

Jamie stares back in wonder. Jake seems almost transformed. She will hold onto him now. She will hold on to this night forever.

Chapter 39

A Small White Pine

Jake and Job leave after breakfast. It is now three days before Christmas and Jamie won't see them, or anyone else, until after the holiday. This will be her time now. Her time of meditation. Of really thinking about the meaning of Christmas. Never in her entire life has Jamie been able to devote time like this to just contemplating why this day is holy. She misses John and her children and grandchildren. She knows her absence hurts them. Maybe someday she would be able to explain better to them why Grammy had to be away from them this Christmas.

Jamie takes her walk. The day is brilliant, but cold. She follows the same path into the woods that Jake and Job took back to the cave. Despite the snow, the trail was worn from their travels. The landscape is now simple colors of black and brown awash in sparkling white beneath a pristine periwinkle sky. Here and there a pine or fir tree fights for a spot amidst the oak, maple, birch and beech. She walks only as far as the top of the ridgeline. She wants to get back because, despite the absence of Jake or family, there is still much she wants to do. The sun has already crossed its apex, now sliding away hurriedly having fulfilled its short obligations for the day.

About fifty yards from where the trail ends at her clearing, she notices a small white pine. She had missed it before in all her hikes. She pauses for a moment, admiring its courage in trying to make a stand surrounded by mature trees. The cry of a hawk overhead ends the moment, almost a reminder to get going on the day's tasks. Before going in, she is drawn to the shed. She gets out the snow shovel and makes a clean path to her doors. She has no idea why. Maybe she is doing something physical, but it means something spiritual. If the Christmas spirit is a traveler – a guest – she wants to clean a path for him or her to come in.

Jamie has had plenty of time to write letters to all her friends and employees. She had time to reflect on their importance to her, or the company. She takes these correspondences seriously, believing in the importance of words. She will email them all out on Christmas Day.

Late afternoon comes early this time of year. The sun slants through the windows by four o'clock. Chores done, Jamie settles on the sofa with a glass of wine, a CD of traditional Christmas music (a favorite from her girlhood) and a book.

Then before bed she works on letters she will send to her children and grandchildren, also on Christmas day. She has saved these for last, wanting to write them as close to Christmas as possible. To her children she writes with an apology for being away from them this Christmas. She repeats her love for them and promises a special "Christmas" celebration when she returns in the spring. She mentions nothing of the company's troubles or of Jake. At the same time, she writes with a clearer sense of purpose, as though already trying to pass along the lessons she has learned. To her younger grandchildren, she writes shorter notes promising a very special Christmas when she sees them again in just a few short months. She especially likes the one she will send to her 13 year-old grandson, Drew. He is interested in science and how things work. She hopes he will understand what she is trying to say. Or perhaps he will save it until he does.

Dear Drew,

In school, you will learn about telescopes, microscopes, computers and something called science. These things are like flashlights that help us see in the dark (where those things live that we can't explain and do not know). These flashlights have helped us to see and explain things that our parents – and their parents – were completely in the dark about before. And the world is a better place for it.

But there was a time before flashlights; a time before even candles, when humans had only the light inside them to help them find their way in the dark.

And this is my wish for you: Know for sure, Drew, that you have a flashlight inside – in your heart and your mind – that can help you answer questions and help you find your way through this world and your life. With technology and science you may see light-years from here. But without the light in your heart and your mind, you'll be lost in the dark.

Find your light. Feed it. Look at what it shows you. And keep it burning.

With Love,

Grammy

Now it is time for bed. For the first time since her conversation with Jake, she thought about the Voice. Would it come to her tonight? Would it ever come to her again? Then as she settles under the covers she feels a desire to have Jake, or John, near. But she reminds herself this is what *she* wanted. Time for herself. And the Voice. Maybe.

Later Jamie awakes and gets out of bed to go to the bathroom. As she stumbles across the dark room, she sees a bright light from outside. 'What could this be?' she asks. The moon? An intruder? She steps carefully to the window. The light comes from the wrong angle to be the moon. Besides, she remembers how clouds came in as the sun set. No moon tonight. The light is too big and in the wrong direction for a flashlight or a truck or anything else that suggests an outsider. As her eyes adjust, she realizes that the one light comes from many small lights. Snow is falling in big fluffy flakes, but the little lights shine through it. She looks closely and what she sees brings tears flowing freely down her face. It's the small pine tree she had admired earlier in the day covered with tiny white lights. "Oh, Jake!" she sobs. "You got me a Christmas tree!"

As the snow covered the lights, it had to be the most beautiful Christmas tree she has ever seen. Where did he get them? When did he do this? How did he plug into the cabin without her hearing him? How perfect! She will keep it lit night and day till Christmas. She gazes at this little tree, a tree that had never fully grown because of the larger ones choking out its sunlight. Now it was a light in the dark. A gift to her.

"You are light. I am light. We are all light."

What?

"You are light. I am light. We are all light."

The Voice?

Jamie hears the words. Where are they coming from?

"You are light. I am light. We are all light."

It sounds like they're coming from the tree. Oh, Jamie girl, too much wine before bed!

"You are light. I am light. We are all light."

The glow from the tree seems to reach out and embrace her.

"You are light. I am light. We are all light."

"I think this is a dream," Jamie says to herself. "A good dream. But still, a dream. But in my dream I will write down what I have seen and what I have heard."

"You are light. I am light. We are all light."

The next morning, Christmas Eve, Jamie wakes late. No sun today. Only gray. And silence. She lies in bed a moment, feeling very rested. Then she remembers...the tree! The Voice! A dream...

She jumps out of bed and hurries out to the living room and over to the window, almost afraid to look. Three or four inches of new snow have almost covered the path she made yesterday. Then she looks into the woods. The tree! With lights! It hadn't been a dream!

Jamie throws her clothes on. Then boots and coat. And rushes out to see the wonder. Not more than four feet tall. Ignored through the spring and summer and fall. And now, in deepest winter, it sparkles. She reaches out to brush the snow off the lights and branches, then stops. No...this is perfection, she thinks. Her Jamie Christmas Tree. She kneels in the snow admiring its beauty. Wondering again how Jake, even in his Indian ways, had managed this surprise.

Then she rises, now seeing Jake's and Job's tracks in the snow and the cord leading to the side of the cabin. He had to wait until I went to bed, she thinks. And when did I get up? She doesn't remember. But they must have come after it began to snow because their tracks weren't as covered as the path she made yesterday.

"Oh, Jake!" she shouts into the woods. "I love you!!"

She walks back over to the tree, her tree, and touches her hand to her lips, then to the tip of the tree. This tree will have its full life. She will guarantee it. Even if it lives beyond her own years, she will protect it.

Then she remembers the journal. Did she really write anything? Or was the Voice part of an actual dream? She walks back to the cabin, shaking off the snow before going in. She will come back out later to re-shovel her path. In case her Christmas Stranger does walk by. She knows Jake will be in his cave. But maybe this is his way of saying they would still be together.

The journal is lying open, face down on the chair. Her pen is next to it. Nervously, Jamie picks it up, almost afraid to turn it over, prepared for disappointment.

"You are light. I am light. We are all light."

There they are. Written quickly, almost a scribble. And below:

"These are the words I heard tonight. I don't know who said them. Maybe me. Felt like they were coming from the tree. This is crazy! But Jake came back and strung lights around this little pine tree and plugged them into the cabin I think. What a night! Don't understand. Going back to bed now."

Jamie puts the book down. She knows if she tries to understand, this will just confuse her. The answer, if there is one, will come in another moment when she's not trying to play detective. She will write more later. For now, there are things to do!

The rest of the day goes by quickly. The fax machine stirs to life and makes Jamie jump. Not another crisis! Not on Christmas Eve! But it was just Stella faxing over a "Merry Christmas" in her very efficient way. Jamie appreciates the thought and faxes back a merry Christmas so Stella won't worry about her.

Now that Christmas Eve is officially here, Jamie puts on her Handel's *'Messiah'* CD. She has listened to it for decades, now knowing almost all of it by heart. She has her journal handy to write what she feels. The music comes to No. 43 in Part III, Soprano Air: "I know that my Redeemer liveth." A beautiful, flowing, reassuring, matter-of-fact offering rendered with confidence in the beloved. She listens to the rest, but this part about the Redeemer is what sticks. She starts to write.

What is redemption? Redemption is everything – or maybe I should say everything is nothing without it.

I think of redeeming a coupon or turning in those books of stamps way back when for merchandise. A Redeemer, then, is what makes those worthless scraps of paper worth something after all; a Redeemer is what makes these meaningless lives meaningful after all.

My take on redemption is that it's what makes the worthless and meaningless valuable and profound. I think the function of a Redeemer is to re-connect us with the cashier who sees the value and meaning in what the world has convinced us is refuse.

The world (others) will try to diminish us to give itself (themselves) greater influence, greater value, greater power. If we keep going to stores and jobs (those relationships) that give us less than what we're worth, we'll wind up broken.

If we go to the cashier (God) who always increases our value... well... I think I get it.

Our Redeemers are the teachers and friends who guide us to where the greatest value and meaning and wonder can be received for the gifts that we bear.

Another thing about redemption: a coupon is worth nothing unless presented at the issuing store – so give unto God what is God's... and get ready to dicker over everything else!

Where do all these thoughts come from? Maybe Jake is right. Maybe the Voice is my voice. A voice I can count on for the rest of my life. Maybe the Voice is inside me.

If the Voice is really inside me, I can do what needs to be done. I need to give myself the gift of the rest of my life. I won't save a thing...I'll use up my life... slide into Heaven broken...spent... stuffing gone. Saying, "I used it all. I ate the whole thing." Yes, this will be the gift to myself!

At 8:00 PM she puts Jake's present, wrapped in a piece of material she had used for the baby's cradle and sealed in a plastic bag, under a rock on the porch. She hugs it to herself before she lets it go. Is this present a mistake? She thinks not. It came to her one night and she got up and wrote it all in one sitting. The 'story' will either be the best present she could give or the worst.

Jamie goes inside and prints another copy. She pulls her chair to the window where she can see the tree and begins to re-read her words one more time before sleep. She doesn't have to hope that Santa will be good to her. He already has.

Chapter 40

Daniel Red Tail

My last day on earth wasn't a day at all. It was a night. Daddy and I went camping in a tent in the snow. He said I could stay up to see the moon and the stars and I tried to stay awake but fell asleep before the moon and stars came out.

Later I woke up but Daddy was snoring, so I left him asleep and went out to see if the stars and the moon were there. It was all really pretty, like Christmas. The sky was full of twinkle lights. The moon was floating like the Christmas star on top of the trees.

I walked a little. Then I laid down to make a snow angel and look for the man in the moon. And I found him. I really did! His face looked like Daddy's face – friendly and wise. It seemed like I could talk to him and the man in the moon could talk to me. But while I waited for him to answer me I must have fallen asleep.

When I awoke it was all bright and warm around me. "Daddy, Daddy," I called.

Someone answered me. It wasn't my daddy or the man in the moon that said, "Daniel, you are in Heaven now and I will be your daddy here." I think it must have been God.

"Daddy's grandpa went to Heaven," I said. "Will I get to see him? I have his picture at home."

"If you want to see him, you can do that," said God.

"What will I do in Heaven, Daddy?"

"Anything you choose" God said. "But I see in your heart you've already chosen to go back to earth as a new baby and live a very special life."

"May I go back to my Mommy and Daddy?" I asked.

"No, Daniel, you can't go to them. Home is where you're going, not where you've been. You can only be born into that family once."

"But that's where I want to go. I want to see my Mommy and Daddy."

"OK," said God. "I will get your great-grandfather to show you how you can look down from here and see them. But I must warn you they are very sad because you are not with them anymore. People do strange things when they are sad."

"Find my great-grandfather then, please. I want to see him."

Just then along came a spirit that looked like the picture I had of my daddy's grandfather. He was an Indian, a full-blooded Cherokee. He looked wrinkled and old and friendly and wise. "Hello, Daniel. You bring joy to my heart. I am so glad to meet you. I died just after you were born. I was there at your birth and after I died I watched from here as you grew."

"Please Great-Grandpa; I want to see Mommy and Daddy."

"OK, Daniel, but you may not find happiness there."

Daniel saw that his mommy was gone from his daddy. She was home living with Grandma and Aunt Mary. She had a job and another man was with her.

"Where is my Daddy?" asked Daniel.

Soon we saw him. He was walking in the woods. He had a beard and his hair was long. "Look, Great-Grandfather, Daddy has a dog! Daddy and I always wanted a dog. Mommy said no to a dog. Do you know the dog's name?"

"Job," said Great-Grandfather.

"I like that name. Where is Daddy's house, Great-Grandfather?"

"He has no house, Daniel. He walks the hills all day and sleeps in a cave at night."

"But why, Great-Grandfather?"

"Because he carries the sadness of losing you in his heart. He blames himself for you leaving the world, and sometimes your mommy blames him for your going away."

"But Great-Grandfather, we have to tell him it wasn't his fault. I walked too far to see the moon and stars. Can we tell him?"

"I'm afraid he wouldn't hear us, Daniel. Seeing him makes your Mommy angry and sad. Now they are apart. He decided to walk and live

in the woods until he felt better. Job found him out there. Job became your
father's first friend since you went away. But until your Daddy forgives
himself, he'll think no one will ever love or forgive him. Job is helping your
Daddy remember how to love – but only Daddy can let go of the hurt."

"Great-Grandfather, I have to help him. I have to be with him. Please
can I go back?"

"You would have to talk to God about that. Some people stay here,
some go back and start over. You can stay with me. Or you can be born
again and start over."

I held my great-grandfather's hand while we went back to see God
about my plan.

"God," I said. "I want to go be with my Daddy for a while. Then I
promise I will go to another family and start over again."

"Well," God said. "It's not done much, and it is doubly difficult when
it comes time to say "Goodbye" again. But if you really want to be with him
you could go back as an animal or a bird."

"My Daddy loves red tailed hawks, the best of all birds. May I go back
as a red tailed hawk? Then I could fly above him and Job and keep an eye
on them."

"Well," God said, "We could bend the rules if that is what you're sure
you must do. You must know you won't be able to talk to him, don't you?"

"That's OK God. It's what I really have to do. Oh, and Great-Grandfather, I'll be back. I'm sure I just need to be a hawk for a while."

Great-Grandfather said, "I'll watch out for you Daniel Red Tail. I
always envied the hawk's ability to sail through the wind effortlessly. You
can tell me all about how that feels when you come back."

"Great-Grandfather, why don't you come with me?" I asked.

"No, Daniel, this you must do for yourself. God and I will watch over
you."

I asked how soon I could go.

"You can go right now if you would like. Just remember it is only for
a while. And I can't promise he'll find the help you so want to give. But you
might be able to help him." said God.

"Thank you, God. Goodbye, Great-Grandfather."

Soon I was soaring through the sky over the wooded Appalachian
hills. I spotted Daddy and Job right away. 'Eyes of a Hawk' is what they say

and it is true. I could see everything. Daddy and Job were living off the land like I did as a bird in the wild. I soared overhead and kept watch every day. Daddy always looked lovingly up at me – and even when I knew he couldn't see me, he knew when I was nearby. I saw him carve beautiful things from wood pieces he found. His favorite thing to carve was me, the red tailed hawk. He carved my head into the handle of a fine walking stick.

Daddy and Job slept in a cave at night. It was fixed up with books and furniture and a fire for warmth. He loved reading his books...and he loved carving with wood.

One day my Daddy was hauling rocks back to the cave for his fire pit. He was getting the rocks along the side of a cliff. Trapped between my daddy and the cliff was a copperhead snake. Daddy didn't see him but I did. As the snake coiled back, ready to strike, I swooped in out of the shadows, grabbed the snake and flew off. My Daddy's heart nearly jumped out of his chest, it was beating fast. I decided I could drop the snake from high in the air and he would die, or I could take him miles away to let him go. I knew that's what my daddy would want and I did, too. I took him a few miles away and dropped him a few feet from the ground.

I flew close by my Daddy and Job all my days on earth as a hawk. I could see him start to forgive himself. He started to forgive my mother. I know he will be OK now. He will go home one day and have a happy life. I am sure of that.

In every red tailed hawk he sees, I will be there. He will never forget me. On my last day as a hawk on earth, I put this poem in his ear. He kept looking around so I'm pretty sure he could hear.

> *Each red tailed hawk*
> *Will make you think*
> *Of me.*
> *Soaring above the earth*
> *So high.*
> *Or in the old Oak tree.*
> *You never lose*
> *The ones you love.*
> *They are in your heart.*
> *If you get back*
> *To life, Daddy,*
> *I will have done my part.*
> *Forever yours, Daniel.*

Tears run down Jamie's cheeks as they did every time she re-read this story. When she returns home she will find an illustrator for this book and share it with the world.

The next morning, Christmas, Jamie jumps out of bed to see if Jake has come for his gift. The story is gone. In its place is something magical: a five-foot tall totem pole! Jamie stares, not quite believing what she sees. She is about to rush outside for a closer look, then decides clothes and coat and boots might be wiser – even on Christmas.

Minutes later she is on the porch running her hands over this incredible creation. It is the most beautiful wood carving she has ever seen. On the top, a hawk, beneath him a magpie, then a bear standing on his back legs and then the back of Job on his hind legs leaning against the bear. She looks carefully and sees letters carved into the wood. "Be silent, my Magpie." Jamie sits in the cold and snow and cries and hugs the totem, running her fingers over every part, especially the hawk and the words. Tracks in the snow show that Jake had pulled the totem on some kind of a sled. What a magnificent present! She is filled with the Christmas spirit like never before.

Chapter 41

Christmas Blessing

The rest of Christmas Day is a celebration. After finishing a special breakfast of French toast with real maple syrup, bacon and an orange sliced up, Jamie again dresses for the outdoors. She's tempted to hike over to Jake's cave, but remembers how serious she was in saying she needed this time alone.

The day is brilliant. Another spectacular winter morning when the sun throws everything into sharp relief, when shadows from trees and buildings have crisp, clear lines. Even with sunglasses, Jamie has to pause for a minute to let her eyes adjust to the brilliance of the snow. There is not even the hint of air moving.

She walks back over to the totem pole and runs her hands along it again. The hawk at the top seems to be protecting the magpie below. Supporting them, the bear with Job against his belly. She wonders if Jake has a story for it. If he hasn't already, they will write one together. For in the carvings there is a story – their story – here. And here that story will stay. Others will come to the cabin and see the totem pole and wonder who made it and why. Maybe they will make up their own stories. But *their* story, Jamie and Jake's story, will remain theirs alone.

Jamie walks over to her Christmas tree. She has kept the lights on, although they are barely visible because of the sun's brilliance. She kneels in the snow to be closer. She closes her eyes, thinking back to the magic of past Christmas trees...when she was a girl...when she was a bride... when she was pregnant...when she became a mother... and more recently, a grandmother. Will there be still more magic Christmas trees?

She feels stronger in her commitment to live consciously, more tuned in to nature and the things she has learned. She will try to remain indifferent to anything but the truth of her heart and her mission. What's the measure of truth anyway? She yearns to learn detachment from life's dramas. She will nurture her ability to draw sustenance and grow no matter what. There are still many things she wants to do with the rest of her life. But she also knows that life is what happens to you along the path. She will adapt.

Jamie stands and is about to start her hike when into the clearing steps a doe and her two yearlings. She watches as the three move gracefully through the snow, nibbling on branches. They come to within twenty feet of her when suddenly the mother realizes there is a human in their midst. Her nose flairs and tail twitches. Not sure what to do, Jamie and the doe eye each other carefully. Deciding this human is not an imminent threat, the doe turns and slowly leads her two back the way they came. Jamie feels blessed by this moment, too.

Returning to the cabin an hour later, she glances warily at the fax machine hoping it, too, is taking a holiday. It's not that she doesn't want to hear from her children and grandchildren, she does. But this Christmas is for her. She knows she will never have another one like it. And she knows how precious this time is. *Her time.*

She makes tea, stokes the fire and settles into the sofa with her journal. She leafs through the pages, reflecting, hoping that it will help tell the story of her year here. Eight and a half months have gone by. She smiles looking back at the first entries in April. And the different entries marking her progress along the A.T. But the ones she reads and re-reads are the ones involving the Voice. Especially the one from last night. She thinks for a minute, then begins to write:

December 25th

I started to write that this Christmas was special. But that's not right. All Christmases are special. Whether you believe in the story of Jesus or not. Which I do.

But this one is different. I am here by myself (I think). My first without John in 34 years. My first without the girls or the grandkids.

And my first without Jake. Will there ever be a Christmas with Jake? I don't think so. Even though he is with me in spirit.

With me in spirit. That's interesting. Maybe it's the Voice who is really with me in spirit.

I feel like I am being born over again...the new Jamie. I want to honor and appreciate that. To know what I've got before it's gone. I want the ability to live in real time.

So much of my life, I've just tried to get thru – to what?

What made past Christmases special? Childhood? Children feel worshiped at Christmas. Adults feel childlike. Is that it?

On previous Christmases there was never any room at the inn. It was filled with obligations and reservations. These Christmases were scripted and all about <u>making</u> Christmas happen versus giving it an open place to fill (letting Christmas gift us).

I feel the anticipation of something wonderful, a fresh start, looking to the future rather than the past – facing forward with the hope of great potential. Christmas allows us to start over no matter what we've done, no matter what's been done to us, no matter who was wrong or who was right. Anything can happen and everything is possible.

There may be weighty decisions ahead, but life will find a way – and love will find a way – to endure and prosper and grow... and anyone's welcomed along for the ride who will approach each day a little like it's Christmas morning.

I have left this Christmas open. I have left myself open.

I wonder why I didn't see this stuff before. Was life spooked by my clumsy approach, or did I simply overlook what was always there?

Jamie goes early and quietly to bed. Still reflecting. Glad that life is not just what you accomplish, but what you discover.

Chapter 42

Bumps Along the Way

The day after Christmas Jamie expects Jake and Job to show up on her doorstep. She does a little light cleaning, occasionally peeking out the window at the path hoping to see them emerging from the woods. She puts a pot of stew on, somehow hoping the aroma entices Jake from his cave. By mid-afternoon, the sun is already deep in the southwestern sky. She gives up hope and decides instead to take a walk. Rather than head north and east along the ridge trail that leads to Jake and the cave, Jamie walks south and west down the trail to the stream. This trail is less routine than the others and she makes her way slowly through boot-deep snow. Even though it is only a mile, it takes her a full forty-five minutes to reach it. The woods are quiet. Not even a flash of cardinal or finch disturbs the sleepy brown woods snug in its white feather bed.

Near the bottom, Jamie slips in the snow. She laughs at her clumsiness. Slipping was something that happened often in the spring. But as she grew stronger into the summer, her steps were surer. Jamie stands, slapping snow off her jacket and pants. She bats away a clump that threatens to slide inside her boot – but misses one now slipping into her collar and down her spine.

The sun is already behind the ridge, casting the valley into an early dusk. Jamie finishes the final hundred yards to the stream, partly because she doesn't like to cheat her hikes, partly because she's curious about what she'll see there. Ice now covers nearly the stream's entire width. But a small opening at the middle is a gurgling reminder that the ice is thin and she would step on it at the peril of ending up knee deep in it. Jamie steps carefully to the edge and peers through the opening, looking for the familiar striping of the three trout she saw earlier. But today they are gone. In the fading light, she can barely see to the gravel bottom. Are they lurking in deeper water downstream? Did they become a meal for raccoon or possibly even a bear? She hopes to see them again. But, too, she knows that life is fleeting and often ends violently.

Stepping back, she looks up the trail, realizing now that maybe she'd left too late in the afternoon. She thinks she can make it back to the cabin before it gets too dark. But there'll be no more dawdling. Jamie remembers retracing her steps as a child so it looked like only one set of prints. She does that now with a smile. Jamie climbs back up the trail, settling into a steady pace that breaks a sweat but with the easy cadence of an experienced long-distance hiker. A quarter of the way back, she pauses having stepped through a steeper part of the terrain that winds her. She has learned to breathe deeply as inclines approach. She could bank oxygen as the last leg of the trail approached. She wonders if that's something she should try in life after her recovery here: "breathe" more deeply so life's uphill stretches won't leave her winded.

There is still light in the sky. But now it won't reach to the floor of the woods. If she keeps climbing, though, she may yet catch sunset at the cabin. At least she hopes.

Jamie turns to start her way back up, then stops. There, not twenty yards away is a large buck staring at her and blocking the trail. Neither moves. Both exhale frosty breaths that drift and disappear. Jamie tries looking over the animal's shoulder to see if he has a doe or two in tow. She can't see anything. A glance to either side suggests he's by himself.

The deer is broad across the shoulders, thick through the middle. Jamie can count eight or ten points on his rack. Clearly this animal has survived several of these winters. And he's perhaps just as surprised to see a human here as the human is to see him.

Jamie's not sure what to do. She doesn't think he will charge. But she makes note of a thick oak about five feet off the path that she can get behind if he does. The buck's tail twitches. He dips his head as though trying to get a better scent. And then stares back at her, tail still twitching. It's clear both want to use the path and one of them is going to have to move.

"How are ya, boy?" Jamie offers a greeting, knowing he won't understand a word. But perhaps the tone of her voice will make her presence seem less threatening. Jamie takes a step back – and falls. She looks back up fearful he may yet charge. But the animal doesn't move. Jamie gets up slowly, brushing herself off. This time she can feel snow inside her pants, but avoids any shaking that might startle the buck. She looks back trying to read the buck's mind. The tail twitches again. She thinks he's figured she's not the kind of two-legged threat he's dodged successfully before.

Then, just as she wants to say something else, the deer takes a step to the uphill side of the trail and in three bounds is deep enough into the wood's fading light that only his tail is briefly visible. Jamie waits a moment more to see if he is coming back, or if there are others farther up the trail. Seeing, none, she re-starts her trek, clearing the path below for the buck to come back and work his way down to the stream.

Forty minutes later, Jamie is still a couple hundred yards from the cabin when all light is gone from the sky. She has to slow her steps. But she knows this trail well enough that she can feel her way back. When the trail levels out, she knows she's about thirty yards away and now she can see the small lights on the tree, a beacon leading her home.

By the time she gets inside, she realizes how hard she is breathing. Adrenaline triggered by a buck and approaching darkness gave her a boost she didn't know she had. Cold, wet and tired, she's very glad to be home.

Inside, she's anxious for a shower, then a glass of wine and a bowl of her stew for supper. She's a little disappointed that Jake and Job didn't show. Still, Jamie is glad for this day, until she glances at the bringer of bad news: the fax machine. There's a quickly scrawled note. Even at a distance she can see it's from Stella.

"CALL ME! URGENT!! STELLA."

She thinks for a second then decides, "Stella can wait. But these damp clothes and a hot shower can't." Later, warmed by the shower and her stew, Jamie again looks at Stella's fax. 'What could be wrong now?' she wonders. She has a good guess. The company. And Rich. She knows she will have to confront him sooner or later. Somehow she hopes that she can get through the holidays without facing the ugliness that he brings into her life. "Sharks never take holidays," John once told her. "They only swim and eat."

Wearily, she picks up the phone and calls Stella's cell. "Hello? Jamie?"

"Yes. How are you? What's wrong?"

Frantic and nearly hysterical, words come tumbling out almost incoherently, "Oh JamieI'msogladyoucalled!WehadareporterfromtheNewYo rkTimesinheretoday looking foryou.Itoldheryouweren'there.Butshekeptas kingquestions.'Where is she?''Is she sick?' 'Who'srunningthecompany?'All kinds of things Jamie.Shehadmeshakingtheremostoftheday.Idon'tthink youcanstayawayanylonger.Ithinkyouhavetocomebackanddealwiththis. Allofthis.Idon'tknow..."

Jamie interrupted, "Stella! Slow down! Slow...down." She hears a deep breath at the other end and an unconvincing "OK."

"Let's start this again." A second, less pressured, "OK."

"Now who came in today?"

"A reporter from the New York Times."

"How do you know she was from the New York Times?"

"She said she was."

"Did she give you a business card?"

"No."

"So maybe she wasn't from the Times?"

"Maybe. But Jamie she was asking all these questions like she knew EVERYTHING."

Jamie stares into the flickering fire. "OK. And what did you say?"

"I tried to be nice. I tried to explain that you were out of town for the holidays. Then she asked when you were coming back, and I said I didn't know for sure. Then she wanted to talk to someone else in charge. And I said there wasn't anybody."

"What did she say then?"

"She started getting agitated. She thought you were really here and hiding. Then I said absolutely not. Then she asked if you were in a mental institution because of your 'illness.' I said, 'What illness?' She said the word is all over Wall Street that you've become a crazy recluse since John died and that the company's going under because no one is running it."

That makes Jamie a little nervous, but she manages to ask evenly, "And what did you tell her, Stella?"

"I didn't know what to say, Jamie. All I could think to say was that it just isn't true. But I could tell she didn't believe me, Jamie." Terror was creeping back into Stella's voice. "Jamie, I'm sorry. Just tell me what to do."

After a long pause, Jamie says, "Well, first we need to make sure she really is a reporter. If you don't have a card or anything from her, then there's nothing we can really do, or want to do, until she comes back and identifies herself. Rich has already sent people *here* looking for me."

"He has?" another wave of fear invades Stella's voice.

"Yes. But I'm pretty sure they left without finding out anything." (Jamie plays the break-in and stolen fax close to her chest.)

"What does he want, Jamie?"

"The company. He's wanted it since before John died. And...he's wanted me, too." Jamie let that sentence hang a second.

"He does?" Stella responds with a sisterhood kind of curiosity that makes the plot become less sinister and almost more like "boys will be boys."

A half pause, then, "Jamie, did you....."

"Stella! Are you kidding me? Even when John was sickest I never, ever thought of another man. Of breaking my vows. Of hurting the man who loved me more than anyone. And besides...can you imagine me, or anyone else, with that shriveled up Scrooge of a man? Probably the only thing he takes to bed is porn."

At this Stella bursts out laughing. She loves Jamie's sometimes "earthy" humor. And she loves colluding with her at Rich's expense. When they both finish that good laugh, Jamie gets serious.

"OK, Stella, now listen closely. If this 'reporter' comes back, the first thing you do is ask for identification, got it?"

"Got it."

"Then, if she checks out as legitimate, you can tell her we've talked. You can tell her that John never paid attention to Wall Street gossip and neither do I."

"OK. I like that."

"Then you can tell her I will talk to her for ten minutes. And only ten minutes."

"You're going to come back?" she asks hopefully.

"No. I'm not. I know you don't understand now, Stella, but what I'm doing here is more important than whatever I could do for the company." Jamie throws another log on the fire. It catches immediately with a crackle. "But I'm *not* going to let the company fail, Stella. Believe me when I say that. I'm not going to let all John's work be for naught, or have his reputation ruined by small-minded men like Rich.

"But I will talk to the reporter. So you get her phone number. You can even ask what time of day is best to call. I can't put a stop to all the rumors. But I think I can convince her I haven't become a crazy old recluse."

Jamie pours herself another glass of wine and sips it slowly.

"Got that, Stella?"

"Yes, Jamie! I feel better." She sounds better and Jamie is relieved for that.

"OK. Things are good here, Stella. They really are. But I'll be back with you and everyone else before you know it."

"OK, Jamie. Thanks. I'm sorry I lost my grip! I'm...I'm really glad you called back right away."

"Good. Well, fax me when you know more. Right now, I need a second helping of stew." This was a white lie, but it was her way to wrap up the conversation and let Stella know she was eating properly too.

"I will, Jamie. I love you, Jamie."

"I love you, Stella."

She disconnects while the tone is up-beat.

'Well, that buys a little more time,' she thinks. And she really doubts that the woman was a reporter. But she knows, too, that the time is coming for a showdown, a real showdown with Rich. 'I'm hungry.' She surprises herself at the thought. Then she realizes it's a different kind of hunger. And laughs. She's hungry for another helping of Jake. Why isn't he here? 'Damn!'

She hears no Voice tonight and does not write in her journal. Maybe a dream or two. And her appetite will hold – until tomorrow – she hopes!

Chapter 43

Silent is the Magpie

The next day Jamie hears Job barking long before she sees them. She waits by the window holding the day's second cup of coffee, happy at their approach. Her walk for the day can wait. As much as she needed her Christmas alone, it also made her realize how bonded she and Jake have become. For a second, she wonders how she will manage the much longer separation that's coming. But then Jake and Job come bounding down the trail. Jamie opens the door and steps onto the porch her arms spread wide in welcome.

Job reaches her yards ahead of Jake, jumping up and almost knocking her over.

"Job! Good boy!" She gives him a good head scratch and bends down to accept his doggie kiss. Then he's down and barking his happiness. Jake strides behind, a big smile lighting up his face. He, too, almost knocks Jamie over, instead sweeping her up and swirling her around.

"Happy New Year, Magpie!" Jamie squeals in delight. Feet back on the ground she gives him a strong kiss. She *has* missed him. Yes she has.

"It's not New Year's yet, Jake," smiling and kissing him again.

"Well, it seems so long since I've seen you that I thought the old year must have ended. I forgot to rewind the grandfather clock and it stopped."

"What grandfather clo...?" Jamie catches herself mid-sentence and then laughs with him at the joke that he might have a grandfather clock in a cave. She loves when his eyes dance with mischief. This is a change she noticed back in the fall. She takes it then as a good sign. 'Yes, he is healed,' she thinks.

"Let's go inside. I'm getting chilled! I'll go for my walk later. Come sit by the fire for a while." Inside, they settle closely on the sofa. Job reclaims his familiar spot on the rug. Jamie runs her fingers through Jake's thick black hair. She thinks how he has so much hair on his head and practically none elsewhere. She pulls his head onto her lap. He wraps one arm around her thigh tightly. She can feel the way Jake touches her that he wants her. She wants him too. But not just yet. "Jake, you have to tell me about the totem pole! How did you…where did you? I mean, I have *never* been so surprised on a Christmas morning in my entire life!"

Jake smiles and looks up at her. "Maggie, I decided in the fall to do this. I didn't finish until a week ago. It took me time to find the right tree. Then cut it down and strip the limbs and bark. Let the wood dry a little. I kept it wrapped back in the deepest part of the cave, a place you haven't seen yet." Jake's eyes get serious…intense. "Totem poles are not part of my tribe. But I have always admired how the nations of the northwest told their stories through them. I thought I could tell ours."

Jamie leans down and kisses him. "You are one incredible man. So, what story did you choose to tell about us?"

"Our story is really the story of the Magpie. That's why I put her just beneath the hawk." Jake breathes deeply, before he continues. "In our tradition, we honor the Eagle. He is the Lord of the Sky. We respect the Raven, because he can trick and deceive but often with a good intent." Now Jake sits up and takes both of Jamie's hands. "But the Magpie, I don't know of anyone who has honored the Magpie. I called you Magpie because I thought you talked so much that you disturbed the animals and birds in these woods." His eyes are so intense that they seem to bore through her eyes and somewhere deep into her brain. "What I really meant was that you were disturbing me. You were making noises about things I didn't want to talk about. Things that were dead to me. Things that were dead *in* me."

Jake pauses. Jamie can feel tears welling. But she keeps them from her eyes, waiting for Jake to continue.

Jake looks into the fire, back at Jamie, then says, "Eagle speaks to our spirit. Raven speaks to our minds. But Magpie…Magpie, I found out, speaks to our hearts. She flies right next to us. And talks into our ears. And keeps talking until we can't hear anything else. And she keeps asking questions of our hearts until our hearts speak back. Until she knows our hearts. And until we know our hearts." Jake takes Jamie's face in both hands. "Knowing our hearts is the greatest gift. Magpie knows this. Which is why she won't stop talking."

Jamie's tears spill out. Jake continues. "When she knows that we see the truth in our hearts…and knows that heart won't be shut off from spirit and mind...and she doesn't have to keep asking questions...then she stops talking. Then Magpie is silent."

Jamie cannot stop the tears now. She leans into him sobbing. "Oh, Jake! How can you do this to me? How can you turn me into a blubbering fool? I don't know anything Jake! I am just an old woman. Someone just trying to find a little piece of truth that I can hang onto and carry through the rest of my life. Did you learn the story of the Magpie from your grandfather?"

"No, Maggie. That story came from my heart. Not all of our stories are ones that come down from my grandfather's grandfather's grandfather. Because of you, I am able to tell the story of the Magpie. And someday, when I am as old as my grandfather, maybe I will share it with others who should hear it."

A silence covers them like a wool comforter. Now Jamie leans on Jake. He hugs her tightly to him. After a few minutes, Jamie sits back up, wiping tears away and looking back at Jake, half expecting to see him transformed into a bear or wolf.

Jake wipes one more tear off her cheek. "Jamie, one more thing about the Magpie. One reason she talks so much is that she doesn't think she can fly as high as Eagle. And she doesn't think she's as smart as Raven. But because she knows the heart, she never gets old. Because the heart is where youth lives. Where we are refreshed. Even...healed. For this I honor Magpie alongside Eagle and Raven."

Jake wraps his legs around Jamie to pull her closer. "So when I think of our story, it really is the story of the Magpie who flew into these woods and spoke to my heart until it was strong enough to speak back.

"Carving our story into that trunk, I felt like we were speaking to all those who will come after us. Maybe they will look at Magpie and see nothing, hear nothing. But maybe Magpie will speak to them also. And maybe Magpie will heal another heart to speak truth again. And then fall silent, refreshed."

Jamie looks back at him in wonder. "Jake, sometimes when you talk, like now, your words are poetry. I don't know how you do it. But you mesmerize me. I have never heard anything so beautiful. You make my story about Daniel sound like gibberish."

"No, Maggie! No! You are wrong." He takes her shoulders in his large hands. "I could not have said these words if you had not shown them to me." Now Jake rocks Jamie slowly. "And your story...do not demean yourself with such a word as 'gibberish.' You, Magpie, flew with Eagle and found my Daniel. And you brought him back to me as Hawk. Hawk is our spirit of Spring. So of course he should be closest to me when Earth reawakens.

"Maggie, you have healed my heart. And I knew it was healed because I could read your story and see truth. No, Maggie, do not insult me or Daniel when you say your words are…gibberish. Truth is not gibberish. Love is not gibberish.

"Raven will make gibberish sound like truth. But Magpie speaks only truth. To those who will not listen, it may sound like gibberish. I did not listen at first. But when I did, I heard only truth pass from your lips. And now from your lips to your hand."

Jake takes her writing hand and kisses it.

Jamie speaks softly. "Your Christmas present is something I will cherish and cherish forever. Even if I can't tell people the whole of our story," promises Jamie.

"And yours to me as well," Jake says. "Now I can carry Daniel next to my heart for the rest of my days."

"Will you and Job come on New Year's Eve and spent the night?"

"Of course we will."

"I'll go to the Ram Cat and get something that Cora has made for our dinner."

"If you bring back a nice piece of meat, a ham or roast," offers Jake, "I'll cook it."

"OK! I like that!"

Jake and Job stay the morning. Then they head back to their cave.

The next afternoon after bundling up, Jamie takes a long walk. A hawk circles overhead.

Chapter 44

The Red Headed Stranger

Two days before the new year, Jamie is up well before sunrise. Dressed warmly, she scrapes a thin layer of crystalline rime from her bedroom window. A cold has settled in that clears the sky and makes the early morning stars look bigger and brighter than ever. The moon has waned, as though excusing itself to let the Galaxy's other suns congratulate this small planet's completion of one more orbit around its sun, the four billionth, give or take a hundred million orbits or so.

She remembers how much John loved the night sky. His training as a Scout included a ready knowledge of the constellations. He loved talking about how far these stars were from Earth. How far Earth was from the center of the Milky Way. How far the Milky Way was from its nearest neighbor, Andromeda. How far they were from other galaxies in their "neighborhood." And how far that neighborhood of galaxies was from other neighborhoods, other clusters. On and on until the distances and times became incomprehensible. And yet John could talk about them in ways that made them seem close, almost intimate.

"Are you out there, John?" she asks, somewhat longingly. There are times still when she feels slightly guilty that she does not think of him more often. She knows there isn't an answer to this question until it's her time to visit the stars.

She shudders remembering the bad dream of him staring at her in the café. What was that all about? She still doesn't know. She thinks about Jake and Daniel. She knows he was comforted by her story. But what if it wasn't just a story? What if Daniel could become a hawk and keep a protective eye over his father? And if Daniel could become a hawk, what kind of bird might John become? An owl? An eagle?

"But maybe I don't want John watching over me." Surely she wouldn't want him watching over her when she is with Jake. Or when she is with the Voice. Still, the problems with the company...and the years ahead when maybe her health won't be good and the children will be farther away than ever...maybe she would feel better knowing he was close by, in some form. To help. Guide. Just to talk to.

"Oh, John, I don't know if you're close or not. But if you are, and you can hear me, just know I love you. I'm not sure I can explain everything that's been going on since you left. Maybe one day I can. And if you have any great ideas of how to handle the mess at the company, I could use 'em." Then, silence.

Finally, Jamie looks away from the still night sky. The clock says almost 7. Time to get the day going, much to do! Jamie plans to walk to the Ram Cat again. She makes a shopping list of the menu Jake said he'd prepare for their New Year's Day feast.

Part of her had wanted him and Job to stay another night. But part of her wanted to be alone again. With her thoughts. Maybe with the Voice. And now this, with John. Maybe, too, she could feel herself getting ready for the parting that would be inevitable and come too soon.

Life's coming is full of joy. Its goings are full of sadness. She has had much of both in her 67 years. Her heart has never grown used to the bursting and emptying that is life. She hopes it never will.

She is anxious to see Cora and Ellie Mae again. And the baby. So pulling on boots and coat, gloves and back pack, she heads out into the cold, clear pre-dawn. Two hours later, she trudges onto the porch at the Ram Cat. She catches her breath before going in. She can see the two women moving about the store, Cora more quickly than the heavy-with-child Ellie Mae. "Knock! Knock!" Jamie announces. Cora and Ellie Mae are in high spirits.

"Jamie!!" Cora rushes – and Ellie Mae waddles – over to greet her with hugs.

Jamie, embraced by the warmth of the women and the store's wood stove, feels the cold melt away quickly. Removing her coat, she is ready for a relaxing couple of hours with her friends. In between customers, one or both women join Jamie and her coffee at the table.

The news comes quickly. The baby is doing great, Ellie Mae tells her. The doctor has settled on her due date: March 21. "The first day of spring," Cora chimes in from the counter where she is cheerily waiting on a customer. Ellie Mae is wearing a new maternity top now. She needs it. Her face is radiant. Her tiny body filling with another little life.

When they are both at the table, Jamie notices how mother and daughter sit close together, looking at each other, filling in each other's sentences, laughing often, Cora's weathered hand on Ellie Mae's child-like hand. She knows from her own experiences that something happens when a mother's daughter gets pregnant. The picking, the bickering, the tensions that always seem to be there fade. Instead, a bond of motherhood grows. The younger looking to the older for hints and help. The older reliving her own birth experience and wanting it to be as easy and loving as can be for the younger. Both uniting in hope for the next life to come into the world healthy and ready to grow.

These two women, already bonded by the store, have moved even closer, both out of desire and necessity, the absence of a male being felt and not needed at the same time.

"The baby is moving most of the time," Ellie Mae rubs her belly as if trying to calm the movement down some. "Here, feel." Ellie Mae puts Jamie's hand on herself to feel it. "Wow! This is one active baby. And the doctor says she's healthy?"

"Oh yes. Healthy and strong he says. Keeps tellin' me to eat more, feedin' for two." Both Cora and Ellie Mae sit between customers. "It's getting harder to do everything now. I don't know what I'll do when I get bigger!"

"It's funny," Jamie explains. "You get bigger a little at a time and you get used to the new stage before the next one is upon you. You'll see." Jamie takes Ellie Mae's face in her hands and looks her in the eye. "You are one hell of a woman, Ellie Mae. You are taking something that would devastate some and making it into a beautiful gift. I am so proud of you. You're a modern day hero."

"Jamie, you make me cry," Ellie Mae says with tears on her cheeks. "Sometimes I don't feel brave. I want someone else to raise my baby, but feel so protective of her." Ellie Mae wipes her tears on her shirt. "Something tells me this is goin' to be a girl. I want this baby to have the best life possible. Sometimes I dream of the baby's life. The other night I dreamt that the baby was adopted by a king and queen and she became a princess. Is that crazy?"

Jamie pulls Ellie Mae into her lap. She hugs her close like she is her own child.

"No, that's not crazy." Ellie Mae and Jamie's eyes meet. "Your baby will be a prince or princess indeed. You're doing the right thing. Bring this baby into the world healthy and strong. Then find someone you know will give her the life you can't give her right now. Then, when you're really ready, you'll find a man who you can raise your own family with. Think of this baby as your gift to the world."

Ellie Mae stares into Jamie's eyes, absorbing her words, seeing in her maybe a wisdom even deeper than her mother's. She will keep these words close. Another customer and the conversation shifts. Ellie Mae rises to get this customer while her mother sits for a while.

Cora says, "Jamie, I don't know how we do it, but this will be the best year ever for the store. It's not there's a bunch of people moving back into these hills. But the people who are here do come. They seem to like it here, I guess."

"Cora, they like *you*. And Ellie Mae. This place always feels warm and homey. You treat people right and they come back for more." Jamie cups her hands around her mug of coffee. "That's how my John was so successful in his business. There are all kinds of people to run money for others. John always said he was never the smartest in the business. But people knew what he believed in and he treated them fair. Even in the years when he lost them money, they stayed because they knew he would do right by them in the long run. And he did."

Ellie Mae settles back in her chair. She takes a slow sip of her hot chocolate and finally, broaches the subject the two women had wondered about and talked about between them daily.

"How was your Christmas, Jamie?" Not said was the alone-not-alone part.

"Oh, Ellie, it was more incredible than I have words to say. When my road clears, I want the two of you to come up and see what Santa Claus brought."

"Santa Claus!" Cora cried. "Santa Claus visited you way up there?" All three laughed at the mocking.

"Yes he did, Cora. And brought me more than I could ever deserve." Two more customers interrupt the conversation, both women leaving the table to tend to them.

Jamie looks at the clock and thinks about heading back. She hopes Cora will offer to give her a ride. She begins to fill her grocery list. Cora has made a large pork roast with sauerkraut and mashed potatoes. They have also found a large bunch of fresh asparagus for her to cook. She knows that her New Year's Eve dinner will be great. She thinks the women realize that she is sharing her dinners with Jake. The meals have become larger as the year progressed. "Cora, all this food! It looks wonderful."

"Well, me and Ellie don't want you starvin' up there Jamie. It'd be an awful scene if come spring someone found you frozen and starved holdin' an empty can of beans. I don't know who'd feel worse – you or us."

Jamie smiles and chuckles. "Oh, Cora! You are too much! But I thank you and Ellie Mae for helping take care of me. Honestly, I don't know if I'd have made it this far without you." The women embrace again.

"You need a ride?"

Jamie gathers her things and smiles at Cora. "And now you read minds, too, Cora! Yes I do, if that's not too much trouble."

"Heck no, we're through the morning rush. Ellie, I'll be just a few minutes running Jamie back home."

"OK, Ma," Ellie May says as she turns and walks back to the counter. "I'll start countin' our canned goods inventory," she says over her shoulder. "Think maybe we'll need an order put in so we have things on the shelves after the New Year."

Cora takes her coat off the hook behind the counter. "That's good. Go ahead and call Kennedy's. We'll need 'em here early day after tomorrah."

Cora helps Jamie get packed up and then they head out to her ancient truck.

"She's a good girl, Jamie. Pickin' up the store business right along." Cora puts the keys in the ignition, then turns to Jamie. "I don't want her gettin' a big head too early, but think she's a big reason we did better this year. She knows her numbers. And she could smile a frown offa Scrooge himself." She starts the truck.

"Like mother, like daughter!"

Twenty minutes later, Cora pulls into the bottom of Jamie's drive.

"Well, here ya are. Wisht I could take ya clear up the hill. But this old gal's four-wheelen' days are over."

"That's fine, Cora. I'm just very thankful you could give me a ride back this far."

"Jamie, I don't see no tracks here neither. That mean no one else is botherin' you?"

"No, Cora. No one's been up this drive since the snows came on. And Jake..." Whoops, Jamie let that one slip and immediately regretted it. Kinda.

The women sit silent for a minute. "He's kinda important in your life now, ain't he?" Cora asks tentatively, but maybe sensing it is time.

"Yes he is, Cora. He has been a big help. I think maybe I've been a big help to him in some ways. "

"Well, can't ask much more from a man than that."

Cora paused, wanting to let it all out what had been on her mind for months. Jamie didn't say anything, so Cora went on. "When he first showed up in these parts, I was skeered. Sheriff was too, tho' he's never let on. We've had our share of rough ones. But Sheriff's no one's fool. He's run 'em out afore engines cooled on their bikes. But not this one. Sheriff's content to let him stay up in the hills and keep close watch on him when he comes to town."

She pauses again. Jamie knows from looking at Cora's face that she is not done.

"This man o' yours, he's different. You ever listen to Willie Nelson?"

"Yes, some," Jamie answers surprised at the question.

"Years and years ago he came out with the greatest set of songs ever. Called it 'The Red Headed Stranger.' That's who your man reminds me of straight out!"

Jamie stares wide-eyed at Cora. This is a side to her she'd never seen.

"And what made you think that, Cora? I mean, Jake's hair is pitch black." She said it in a way that both women laughed.

"Well, there's something about him. Almost haunted like. When a man looks that way either he's kilt someone or his wife left him." She paused again waiting to see if Jamie wanted to respond. But Jamie was waiting for Cora to finish.

"Now, I don't think he's no murderer. Cuz I can see he's gentle-like under. Even Ellie Mae picked up on that right away. Said she could tell by how his dog acted. That's a loved-up dog, not a beat-up dog, if you know what I mean."

"Yes, I do, Cora. Job would give his life for Jake. Maybe even for me."

"So that's what made me think he's had woman troubles. And that's what made me think of Willie and his red-haired stranger. It's about a man whose wife left him and he goes crazy in sorrow lookin' for her."

Then without pausing Cora spoke-sang softly the refrain.

"Don't boss him. Don't cross him.

He's wild in his sorrow.

He's ridin' and hidin' his pain.

Don't fight him. Don't spite him.

Let's wait till tomorrow.

Maybe he'll ride on again."

When Cora looks back at her, Jamie's eyes are filled with tears.

"Oh Jamie, I'm sorry! I didn't mean to..."

Jamie wipes her eye on her coat sleeve. She takes Cora's hand in both of her hands. "No no, Cora, it's all right. I just can't believe how perceptive you are sometimes. Now isn't the time to talk about it."

Cora pauses not sure if she is pushing things too far. Then she plunges ahead. "If he was MY man, I'd make sure to keep him locked up in the bedroom where no other woman could lay eyes on him. Let him out to help with chores. But that stallion would ride this filly only. And I mean it!"

At this, Jamie roars with laughter until other tears were in her eyes. "Oh Cora, you are the best friend any woman could ever want to have!"

At this, Cora's eyes well a little, too. But she keeps the tears back. No time for those. "Well, you got a man to get ready for and I got a girl, maybe two, who need me back at the store."

Before Jamie gets out, she says, "Cora, you are the best possible Ma and Grandma. I know this is tough for you. She will need you so much when the baby is born. You are one of the women I read about in my books who are strong. Who stand by their family. Help their children do what they need to do. I am so glad I got to know you and Ellie Mae. My New Year's wish is that we can stay close somehow. Very different women, but having a special bond."

Cora hugs Jamie and now Cora cries. "I thought of you as someone I would never get to know." Cora sniffles. "Once I got to know you I see that we are similar women just passing through this life. We have made each other's lives better by knowin' each other. I really love you, Jamie."

"I love you Cora. Happy New Year."

"And Happy New Year to you Jamie. And to that man of yours! Dog, too."

Jamie climbs out of the cab, struggles with her backpack and waves as Cora backs the truck up and guns it into first gear. Despite the extra weight, the hike up the drive is an easy one. As though a burden has been lifted in the waning hours of the old year.

"And what a year it's been," Jamie says to herself. "What a year it's been."

Chapter 45

A New Year's Promise

The boys show up early on New Year's Eve. After Jake brings in wood and takes off his coat, he talks about the present she had given him.

"Jamie, I need to tell you that the story you wrote for me was absolutely therapeutic for me. I have never asked to see any of the children's books you have written, but now I must see them all." Jake says. "You must tell me when and how this story came to you. I can honestly say I have never read anything like it. Have you written anything else like it? How did you get your concept of Heaven? Where did this....."

"Shhhhh," Jamie says as she puts her fingers over his lips. "Just calm down and I will tell you where it came from."

Jake's body relaxes into Jamie's. They sit close together on the couch. Job, ever the sentinel, is on his rug by the fire. Jake is open to anything she has to say.

"Several months ago, after you had shared your story with me, I woke one night with the story in my head. This has happened to me before. I keep a lighted pen and paper by the bed. I sat up and wrote like a mad woman. Then I went back to sleep." Jamie strokes Jake's long black hair that she has guided onto her lap. "In the morning, I looked at what I had written and it was so beautiful that I cried. Then I got up and put it on my computer and worked on it the whole day until I had it right. I was afraid to give it to you, even at Christmas. But I knew I must do it." Jamie gently rubs her fingers over his eyes that are slightly damp with tears. "I love this idea of heaven. I want to go home and get my artist to illustrate it and publish it for others to see. Would that be alright with you?"

"You must, Maggie." Jake sits straight up and looks her in the eyes. "You must. I can't imagine that this wouldn't help someone else who has lost a child. Especially if they blame themselves. May I have a copy when it is done?"

"The first copy will be yours, Jake. I have most of my books here with me. While I get you a beer and some snacks, you can read them if you like. There is nothing like 'Daniel', but I think they are pretty good. I try to teach young children something with each book."

Jamie gets up and gathers several books. She places them beside Jake. She leaves him to his reading then readies a beer for him and some cheese and crackers for them to share.

Later that evening with dinner and a Jack Daniels for Jamie, she asks about things they have never discussed before. The plates are cleared and they are back beside each other on the couch...the fire bright before them.

"I would like to know about your wife, Jake. Do you feel like talking about that?"

Jake takes a long sip of his beer and looks at Jamie. "I met her in college. Sometimes I think she married me because of my looks. She thought we would make beautiful children together. If that is the case, then I can understand why she left me when Daniel died. As for me, I loved her deeply. We weren't alike. She wanted to live in the suburbs and have what she called a 'normal' life. I was able to overlook all of that to have her with me for my whole life. When I needed the natural world of my grandfather, I would go camping by myself."

"What do you think will happen when you return home, Jake?"

"I don't know, Maggie. When you gave me the phone months ago I called my parents and told them to call Laura to tell her that I was fine. I haven't called again since so I'm not sure what she said." Jake gets up and brings in more wood for the fire. Job follows him outside, always by his side.

Settling back beside Jamie, he says, "I do know that I will go back to my carpenter shop. That is what I am called to do. My parents said everything is just as I left it. That will be my life for a while."

Jake draws a long deep breath. He takes Jamie's hands and looks at her...almost through her. "I would love to take you home with me, Magpie. I feel like we've done something for each other that most people don't even know about. Would you go?"

Jamie looks into the flickering light of some candles that Jake had lit earlier. Her heart feels like it will split in two. Looking back at Jake, Jamie says, "Jake, you know that I can't. We are at two different life stages. We met for a short while and changed each other's lives, but it would never work. I need to go back and finish what John started. Then go and find what the rest of my life holds." Jamie holds her breath, waiting for his response.

"I guess I knew that is what you would say, Maggie. Could I make a suggestion so that we don't ever lose each other and what we have had together?"

"What is that?"

"What if we met here on the summer solstice each year? We would each come alone. We would share three or four days together at the place where we were each healed. I would commit that to you so easily. No matter what happens in my life I would always take the summer solstice alone with you to ground myself and have some time with you. I think if I knew we were going to do that, I could go back to my life and begin again. What do you say?"

Jamie begins to cry. Her heart is in her throat. "This sounds like an old movie I know. 'Same Time Next Year,'" she says. "Did you ever see that?"

"No, but I get the idea. Does that mean, yes?"

"That definitely means, yes, Jake. I was trying to think of something so I didn't completely lose you. This is perfect. We will know that once a year, we will get together to give each other strength. This will be our New Year's resolution. If I enter any other relationship, I will say that three days at the summer solstice are mine alone. Thanks for thinking of it."

"Our resolution then," he agrees.

Jake takes Jamie's hand and pulls her to the bedroom. He slowly undresses her and lays her on the bed. Then he undresses and folds himself onto her and soon they are one body...sealing their agreement with a promise never to be broken. Christmas like no other. Now New Year's Eve and a promise to be kept for all time.

Chapter 46

Hibernation

During the first weeks of the new year, Jamie cocoons. The days are short, made shorter still when clouds bank along the hills, refusing all but a dim, diffuse light to mark the sun's hurried arc across a hidden sky. Jamie wills herself up in the morning dark. She does her chores. She cooks. She reads. And doesn't feel the least bit guilty if the need comes on for an afternoon nap.

She can feel herself preparing for re-immersion into the life she left behind nine months ago. That would come in spring. Life she would go back to, hopefully stronger and more ready to face its conflicts and complications. But a life, too, with her family. One, she hoped, that was both embracing and less needy.

Jamie doesn't sleep in the cave, despite Jake's invitations. How he and Job managed there was a hardship beyond her strengths. The fires he built during the day kept the cave relatively warm and dry. But inevitably they would die down at night and on the couple of nights she tried, the cold penetrated through layers of blankets and clothing. She clung to him for added warmth. But even his heat wasn't enough.

Still, man and dog seem to thrive. Job has grown a thick coat of fur. Jake has too, but less so. His hair is now drawn into a long ponytail. His beard, never thick to begin with, covers enough of his jaw line and neck to give him a definitely scruffy look. Jamie prefers her men smooth-shaven, but she didn't have the heart to ask him to change, knowing it helped him a little with the cold. She imagines it adding to his wildness, that deeper, darker part of his soul she had seen and touched, and perhaps was helping him to heal.

There was an unspoken agreement that, while they didn't need to see each other daily, three days was the maximum between visits. Just to make sure the other was all right. And, Jamie thought, to keep her from developing a bad case of cabin fever. Weekends were theirs. Jake and Job stayed every Saturday and most Sunday nights. They would cook feasts that provided leftovers enough for both to last for days.

Jamie walks to the Ram Cat on Friday mornings. She welcomes not only the chance to be "in town," but also the tight family that has grown among her, Cora, Ellie Mae and the almost-due baby. She knows this bond is deep and permanent. Part of that bond, of course, is their shared responsibility in bringing new life into the world healthy and with a good home. Part of it is the wisdom in these mountain women that seems as old as these hills themselves. Jamie is drawn to it. She thrives in it. They, in turn, are drawn to her honesty and good humor and straightforwardness. Traits rarely seen among the other wealthy women and men, who need their store, but have no use for them.

The snow that came and stayed at Christmas will not quit. Every day it seems an inch or two will fall. Jamie keeps the porch and surrounding ground shoveled and swept. The trail between the cabin and the cave is worn, as is the trail behind, down to the stream. Elsewhere, it is piled nearly two feet deep. White. Clean. Soft. A virgin blanket pulled over the sleeping earth.

It is beautiful, but cold is beyond anything she could remember. In their younger days, she and John would come up here for hideaway weekends. But that was when he would call ahead to make sure the drive was plowed and there was plenty of firewood just outside the door. And plenty of food and drink inside. The cold hit only in short shocks from car to cabin and back again. Now it was part of each and every day.

It is coldest when, for a brief day or so, the clouds are swept away and the sky opens. At night, the stars dazzle, Orion dominating. But the cold would knife through the walls enough to make her worry about pipes freezing. She worries most for Jake and Job on those nights, regretting a bit their mutual desire for distance and independence.

To fight off the urge to cocoon all day, Jamie still hikes the main trails. She has more stamina than ever before. She can finish her six miles in all but the worst weather now. It takes longer. But three or four hours through the middle of the day is the perfect antidote to cabin fever. She surprises herself, but Jake and Cora even more. She is pleased that Jake still touches her with a sense of wonder.

When it snows during the night, she likes to see what other animals have used the trail before her. Deer, of course, tracking through their own trails out of the woods onto her "main highway." A stray rabbit. Then dog tracks. Fox? Coyote? Once on the trail down to the stream, she saw a track she didn't recognize right away. It was larger than any of the others. But didn't have the claw marks of a bear. Back at the cabin she tried to find one like it in her Field Guide. It was a cat. Possibly lynx. But maybe mountain lion. She shuddered at that thought. She stayed away from that trail for several days. When she returned, she looked again and was relieved when she didn't see them.

Still, Jake was worried when she told him. Of all the animals in these hills, he feared the mountain lion the most. It was unpredictable. And fearless. He urged her to sling the shotgun over her shoulder for protection. It was advice she chose not to take.

To make up for those few days when the weather is too bad to venture out, Jamie wills herself into longer hikes. She is determined to "finish" the Appalachian Trail before she leaves. By the middle of the month, she has logged enough miles to finish crossing Massachusetts and enter Vermont. Only a few hundred more to go before reaching the end in Maine atop Mt. Katahdin.

She thinks John would be proud of how strong and resourceful she's become. There was an old part of him that was wary of her innate strength and independence of mind. Jamie learned to mask these parts of her personality so as not to stir those twin passions of possessiveness and insecurity that move men to do irrational, dangerous and stupid things. Yet she knew, too, that John was attracted to her physical strength and courage. She knew how it played out in the dance of their physical attraction. How she could will him to greater desire. The hunter and the prey. And tables turned. The guard she could entice him to let down. And the greater pleasures that lay in defenselessness and innocence.

She reads in the guide about Vermont's growing bear population. Like many states east of the Mississippi, Vermont's farms have been abandoned. Reforestation has taken over. With the forests have come wildlife, including bears, in numbers not seen since the land was settled, cleared and cropped hundreds of years before. She thinks of the mountain lion tracks. And then of deer killed daily along highways. 'We want to be close to Nature,' she says to herself. 'But maybe not *too* close.'

John talked about the thrill of being a Tenderfoot Scout on his first long camping trip and seeing a deer "in the wild!" This was in the 1950s. Now she has to shoo them away from the bushes next to her home.

She runs her finger over the southern part of Vermont and

passes Old Job Shelter. Such funny names. Their origins lost, for the most part. She reads about Clarendon Gorge. The Mill River passes through here. Where it pauses to hollow out the Gorge, it also created a favorite swimming hole. A suspension bridge was built here in 1974 to honor the memory of Robert Brugmann, a resident who drowned while trying to cross the rain-swollen river.

Again, she thinks of John. How in their teens they attended separate summer camps. His with the Scouts. Hers with her church. How the camps were separated by a large lake, nearly a mile across. How miserable she was knowing he was so close, yet might as well have been a whole state away.

Then the night when campfire was ending and her group sang "Kumbaya" as they walked to their cabins. Out of the woods an apparition came alongside her and whispered "meet me at the canoes in fifteen minutes" and was gone before she had time to be frightened or scream. How her heart raced as she tried to figure an escape from the cabin. How needing to go to the bathroom with a stomach cramp offered an undeniable excuse. How, flashlight in hand, she turned in the opposite direction and made her way to the lakeshore. There, among the shadows, an urgent search for love's first flaming. She whispered its name. Her light danced across the overturned aluminum hulls. It searched into the lake. She could make out the Scout camp's lights on the other side, wondering if he really *had* come. Or if her mind was playing tricks because her body wished it so.

She remembers how she turned back and her moccasin stubbed a root and she almost fell. But an eager arm caught her and a hand covered her mouth. And in that moment of panic, she knew. John! She turned in his arm and they embraced. The rest of the memory was a rush of kisses and whispered 'How did yous?' and desires for more. Then more kisses and the inevitable parting, knowing too long from the cabin would bring the counselor looking for her. But she stayed long enough to watch him push his canoe noiselessly from shore and glide silently into the moonless night. Her Indian brave. Her brave Indian. It was his "damn the torpedoes" attitude she fell in love with and stayed in love with through all their years together. Even now she laughs remembering the counselor asking worriedly when she returned, "Feel better?" "Much!" she replied slipping under covers and into her dreams.

The reverie of winter slumber is shaken with a Sunday night fax from Stella asking Jamie to call tomorrow. She says they must do some work getting ready for Jamie's return and a meeting with Children's Hospital. Jamie calls early before Stella leaves for the office.

"Jamie! It's good to hear your voice again."

Jamie wishes she could say the same, but bites her tongue knowing Stella means well. Instead she listens as Stella's voice gains momentum. "I have an idea of a way we can get ready for the meeting we have to have with Children's as soon as you come home. When you have a date for your return call me and I will set up a meeting with our board that day or the next. If you agree, I think we should take care of the Children's problem first."

"I agree" Jamie speaks slowly trying to slow Stella down. She also realizes her annoyance at Stella's choice of words. "Come home" sounds slightly condescending, as though Jamie's been a runaway and Stella, ever the parent, has been willing herself through this episode in Jamie's life with excruciating patience.

Racing on ahead, Stella insists, "We need to document the chronology of those events leading to the gift of Nexcentury stock you and John donated to Children's."

"Wait, Stella. Slow down and tell me what you want me to do." Jamie interrupts, letting her voice rise with her annoyance.

"Well," says Stella, slowing down and quieting down some. "If you can write me something of how and why the gift happened, I can fill in the dates and what it was worth then and now. You didn't give the stock and the warrants at the same time according to my records. Just write anything you may remember and I will fill in the dates and other details that I know about for you."

"I'll try, Stella. You *will* have to fill in dates and numbers. Mine will be more of the story of the gift. That is really all I can remember. You know me and numbers. If you can do that part we will have the whole story."

"That would be great, Jamie. Just email it to my home computer. When I have it filled in, I will send it back in fax form so that you can begin to prepare for the meeting. How's that?"

Jamie smiles and takes a deep breath. Preparing for a meeting. She hasn't done that for a long while. Stella has no idea what Jamie is thinking of doing at that meeting. She'll probably want an outline of what Jamie will say and how we will handle the investigation going forward.

"Are you still there, Jamie?"

"Yes. Yes, I'm here. I was just thinking. Sorry. I'll get what you want. It may take a couple of days." Jamie looks out at the snowy morning, looking forward to her day's trek. She will think about this when she gets back.

"I'll watch for it, then," says Stella pressing the issue. "And, Jamie," pausing here, almost afraid to ask, "do you have any idea when you might return?"

Jamie sighs audibly. "Stella, it probably won't be until late March or early April. I know you would like a date and I may not know until close to the time, but you are the first person I will tell. I promise."

"OK. I'll let you know what happens at the office with the board. There is another meeting in two weeks. The reporter hasn't returned, but I'm keeping a watch out for her. Actually, it's been pretty quiet around here. Maybe because of the holidays. I hope not *too* quiet, if you know what I mean." Stella pauses for a breath and waits for a reply.

Hearing none, she knows it is time to end the conversation. "Jamie, take care of yourself. I can't tell you how much I miss having you here."

"You're doing a great job, Stella. I couldn't have had this time away without your help. I will be back to handle things before you know it. I'll get you what you want soon. Take care of yourself. The company needs you and I need you. Stay warm. Good-bye."

"Good-bye, Jamie."

Later that afternoon, Jamie settles at her computer to try to remember what she can of the events that led to the gift to the hospital. It was years ago. One of many, many gifts she and John made to institutions and individuals around the country. She loved John's generosity. He responded to simple need. There were no political or business calculations attached to his thinking. They wouldn't give to everything or everybody. There were certain things that were important. Children and their futures chief among them. John liked to give without fanfare. He didn't need to see his name on the side of a building. But if he gave money to fund a new building, he would often suggest naming it after someone who had been important to the success of the institution.

The gift to Children's Hospital had been done that way. A wing to establish a Child Advocacy Program to help everyone regardless of their ability to pay. But now greed and lust threatened to ruin a reputation and a business.

Meaning to title one page "Chronology," she finds she has instead written the Greek word "Chronos" and, seeing this, types "Kairos" without thinking. How strange. Jamie's mind flashes back to a talk she and John had shared when he went off to study at a Methodist seminary, before going into finance. She remembers him telling people later who wondered more about his first choice than his second, "I discovered I was a lot better at making money for people in this life than in getting them ready for the next. And there were a lot of others who were better at preparing for the next life than in making money in this one. It's worked out well for all of us."

Jamie stops her typing and, jumping onto the Internet, googles the two words together. In a couple seconds, she's reading "Chronos is the Greek god who, with his consort Ananke ("Inevitability") split the primordial egg and created the universe of earth, sea and sky. Chronos is the marking of time through the universe. The step-by-step progression from beginning to end.

"'Kairos' is a period of time not measured by the clock – a period of disruption to the normal flow of things. The old rules, methods, traditions, habits, ways of thinking and doing business do not seem to work anymore. It is chaotic. The ground seems to be shifting. The Greeks thought it was a special moment between the natural order of things. Something to be seized and taken special advantage of. Psychologists may call it 'a paradigm shift.'" Jamie turns from the computer to her journal.

February 6ᵗʰ

Why did the words "Chronos" and "Kairos" come to my mind today after all these years? Maybe it's the Voice nudging me – calling me out...or in. Sometimes we don't know what we're feeling until we put a word to it. "Kairos" Hmmmm.

John told me that part of the point of seminary students taking Greek is so the Bible can be understood in its earliest available form, the Greek texts. This is true with the term "life eternal," he told me. Life itself is endless, not an individual life. The connotation from the Greek is more like a life that is sacred, wonder-filled, and seemingly endless. By choosing to live in the flow of blessings rather than the isolated march of days, we inhabit eternal life.

How is this still in my brain after all these years? What is Spirit trying to tell me?

Too many questions – just keep writing, Jamie.

Maybe my time here alone is my "Kairos." I never had a physical knowing of, a gut experience with this other dimension of time – where I literally feel lifted and loved and carried by some benevolent flow of time, rather than time being something like 50 pound bags of stone to be dragged into tomorrow before sleep can claim me just ahead of tomorrow's demands that could interrupt my rest.

I only ever knew of time driven by obligations or deadlines. But now time is carrying me, rather than burdening me.

Is there a way to live this way... could it be my choice? Would life carry me if I stop trying to control it?

Oh, John, or whoever sent this thought to me, thank you.

I want to live like this, rising and opening and unfolding – not guarding myself against the biting and nipping away that is the hungry ticking away of each deadline and drama.

Maybe I am starting to understand. If I live to be 95 maybe I'll get the hang of it.

Maybe.

Jamie tables the Chronology for tonight. With dinner a fading aftertaste and the sky a blackened sea, she dresses warmly, douses every light and steps into the night to lie in the snow and cast her soul up to soar in an ocean of stars.

Chronos? Or Kairos? Is she on time? Or is she in time? Just who is the horse here – and who is the rider? Will time remain her burden or become her benefactor?

Chapter 47
Smiling Clouds, Angry Clouds

Wednesday morning arrives sunny and, for early February, warm. Jamie looks out to icicles melting off the porch roof. Long, lean, pointed. Drip. Drip. Drip. Like Chinese water torture, except for the welcome relief from three weeks of unrelenting cold and snow. The thermometer says 35 degrees. A big warm up from the teens, and worse, that had gripped these hills since Christmas. She can't wait to dress and head toward Jake's. Wednesdays have become an unofficial "date" day between weekends. A day to make sure the other is all right, if nothing else. Sometimes she cooks something on Tuesday so she can bring him leftovers. Sometimes he cooks trout with leftovers for her.

She heads out into the blinding sunlight, absorbing every ray of warmth she can. Eyes closed, she imagines for a moment her other life when February meant summer-like days in Florida with long walks along almost abandoned beaches. A cold breeze from the south caresses her cheek and almost makes her want to have those earlier days back again. This feels like a day of joy. And she steps onto the trail towards Church Rock and Jake's cave with energy and a girlish enthusiasm. Spots of color flit among the trees. Cardinals. Searching out seeds near the rhododendron. Higher along the ridge, she looks down and sees a doe and her two yearlings moving easily along their own path into a hemlock woods and stream beyond.

At the top of the ridge, she has broken into a good sweat, yet her breathing is measured and free. What a change from the first times she climbed this ridge! Then she had to stop once or twice to catch her breath. And her legs burned. She is delighted at the transformation in her body, feeling twenty years younger. "At least," she laughs to herself. She loves how Jake approves as well. Jamie is tempted to take the turnoff to Church Rock, but hurries instead to the cave. A few minutes later, she veers to the right, following the boot- and paw-worn path to the slate outcropping Jake and

Job call home.

"Hello! Are you decent?" she cries out fifty yards from the entrance. Job barks and comes out to greet her. This greeting has become an easy joke between them. Jake follows Job out of the entrance, a big smile warming the day more. In boots, jeans and flannel shirt he seems slightly underdressed even on this warming day. They embrace and kiss. "You're early!" Jake says.

Jamie glances toward the cave. "Oh, do you have someone else in there you have to get rid of before you can entertain me?" she teases.

"No!" shouting his innocence. "It's just I didn't expect you so soon... or at all."

"At all?"

He looks past her, toward the horizon. "Can't you tell? There's a big storm coming."

"A storm? On a day like this?" She puts her arms out, then lets them fall to her sides. "Jake, I think it's going to be close to fifty today. I saw bare ground on the trail for the first time in a month."

"Jamie, don't let that warmth fool you. Follow me." Jake leads her around to the top of the outcropping where they can see a little farther past the treetops.

"Look there." Jake points to the southwest, in the direction of the barely felt breeze. "See those clouds?"

Jamie squints. "Yes. Barely."

"My grandfather said those are smiling faces that hide much anger." They were thin wisps of cloud. Barely visible overhead. Perhaps a little thicker beyond. But not much. Certainly not enough to spoil a genuine day of thaw.

"Why did he say that?"

"Because they come so easily that you barely notice. And then the wind comes a little harder. And then harder. Until smiling clouds are overtaken by angry clouds. Clouds full of snow. Clouds that will stay for days. A bad storm is coming, Jamie. And as much as I want you to stay, you should probably head back to your home and make sure everything is secure. Can you survive a two or three day storm?"

"I don't know. I never had to. I guess I can. I mean, you know the cabin is well built. John always made sure of that. But what about you? You should come with me. I hate like fury to worry about you stuck out here."

Jake laughs. He always laughed when she expressed concern for his safety and well-being. It was a way of making her feel better. But it was also an expression of his confidence in his "Indian ways." "I appreciate the invitation. And maybe I will." Job licks his hand for attention. "Sorry, *we* will." Jake adds. He pets his dog, then says. "But actually I need to get to the Ram Cat and back before the storm hits."

"The Ram Cat? What for? I brought you some delicious meatloaf I cooked yesterday." Jamie was suddenly worried about the turn in the weather that was coming, drawing up images of Jake and Job caught in a blizzard.

"I need to get some more kerosene and a few other things. I think I can get down there and back before the storm hits. But let me see what you brought."

Jamie follows him down the outcropping and into the cave. She pulls the meatloaf from her backpack and the rest of a loaf of bread she and Jake had baked over the weekend. They each take a bite and give Job a bigger one.

Jake stands close to her. Jamie can feel him torn between a desire to get to town and back and a more primal one. Jamie can feel it too. But her maternal instincts for safety take over. "Well, if you have to go. I guess I have to also. But Jake, you have to be careful. Ask Cora to give you a ride back to my drive. Then you and Job come stay with me. OK?"

Jake moves a hand around her waist, drawing her closer. He kisses her hair, then her lips. "OK. That's a deal. But let's get going then." He slips on jacket and gloves and hat.

Jamie turns to him looking into his eyes for more knowledge of what's to come. Seeing none. She kisses him once more. "Are razor blades on your shopping list?" she asks innocently.

Jake laughs. "Noooooo....unless you think I look better without my beard."

"Oh you look fine. I was just asking."

"Come, let's go."

They walk down to the ridge line trail. There they must part. Jamie going left and back to the cabin. Jake and Job turning right and following the trail to a connecting trail that will take them west and end at the road just outside Ram Cat. They hug and kiss once more.

"Jake, be careful, please. And tell Cora and Ellie Mae I'll see them again Friday."

"I will, Jamie. Maybe this storm won't be so bad after all."

"You mean the angry clouds might smile on us?" she asks trying to lift her worries.

"Yes, maybe knowing you're there, they will smile and move on to the east. I'll see you in a few hours, hopefully."

"I love you, Jake."

"I love you, too, Jamie. Now, get home!" He pats her bottom for emphasis and a smile. And then heads his way down the trail, Job in the lead.

Jamie heads home, barely noticing the now wan sunlight and slowly thickening clouds above.

Chapter 48

A Guest

Inside, Jamie watches the afternoon light fade as the wind continues and snow begins to fall. Still, it doesn't seem like the blizzard Jake warned about. The thermometer has fallen to the upper 20s. The snow comes in small, almost granular, flakes. Even though it started hours ago, only three or four inches have fallen. "Maybe it'll miss us," Jamie thinks to herself. "Maybe Jake was just wrong."

She wills herself to go out one more time to the shed and pile up more wood on the porch. The wind and snow feel more like a caress than a bite. "This isn't bad." She puts down the last armload and stands straight into the storm. "Come on, you blizzard!" she yells and laughs into the wind and snow. "You're not as bad as my problems at home. I can handle you and I can handle them, too." Jamie stamps her feet and heads inside.

Within an hour, however, all light is gone and now she can hear the wind. She puts more wood on the fire; its crackling and spitting silence the blowing outdoors.

She sets a pot of tea to steep on the rough hewn sideboard and settles into the sofa with *Blue Highways.* She had 'borrowed' it months before. She had started reading it then, but had only picked at it a few pages at a time since. Now, she thinks, will be a good time to get through it. It will take her mind off the gathering storm and help her find the comfort of her own company. The book arouses her curiosity about the small nooks and crannies across this large country. Towns with funny-sounding names. Towns with histories. Like Ninety-Six, South Carolina – named by settlers for its distance on the Cherokee Trail from the Indian nation's capital of Keowee. And Dime Box, Texas, which got its name from the way the postal service collected letters and postage in boxes in the late 1800s. And, if the author had stopped in this area, Ram Cat Run, Pennsylvania. "What is a 'ram cat' anyway?" she asks herself. Cora will know.

Maybe she will spend this next phase in her life seeking out other small towns with funny names. Maybe she'll meet other Coras. Women who know much, but don't let on until you give a little. Like the towns they are born into, give life to and pass from into the Eternal. The world's informal historians. Passing from generation to generation the names of people and events that give a place its own seat at the human table.

A few hours later, Jamie wakes to darkness. And cold. And a roar! She has fallen asleep reading. In that time, the power had been knocked out. The fire had burned down to a still-hot glow of embers, quiet in the hearth. It waits patiently for more fuel to stir it back to life.

But the roar. A pack of hounds at each window and door. If Jake had been here, they would have had to nearly shout to be heard. A freight train hammering down her cabin walls. Close. Unrelenting. Deadly to any who dare face it. Stumbling to the window, she tries looking out. She can barely see a long drift building on the porch. But the flying, howling snow is invisible. She knows it's there. But this is no gentle Christmas snow. This is serious stuff. If the cabin didn't hold up…well, she wouldn't think about that.

She feels her way back toward the hearth and feeds more logs to the red-yellow coals. The first one catches almost immediately. Within minutes the fire is back to life, some reassurance from the monster outside. She curls back onto the sofa and stares into the flames. She tries not to think of the problems that will mount the longer the cabin is without electricity. She'll worry about them in the morning when the storm is over – hopefully. *If* the morning comes, that is.

She imagines Jake and Job huddled into one another deep inside the cave. They did make it back to the cave, didn't they? She refuses to think of them stranded in this weather. Maybe the entrance to the cave is drifted shut. But that would give them extra protection, wouldn't it? And Jake would be smart enough to have plenty of firewood stocked inside just like she has, wouldn't he? Almost as if in reply, another gust shakes the cabin making the blaze feel suddenly small…even impotent.

'What if they die out there?' The thought hangs in the air. She has no answer beyond the sharp stab to her heart of anticipated grief. 'Well, what if I die in here? Would that be so bad? The girls and my grandkids would be sad. For a little while anyway. But they have their own lives. And they're learning to live them. I've given them about all I can. The rest will be what they make of it.

'And Jake? I love him. But he has a lot more to do with this life before he's ready for the next one. And he can do it without me. He has to.

'John? Can you hear my thoughts? Are you here? Over there? Are you waiting for me? Or have you gone to the other side of the Universe disgusted with your faithless wife? John, I can't explain Jake to you. Maybe you don't care. But I hope you do. If you *can* hear me I do want to be with you. With *you*. We explored a lot here on Earth, you and I. If I make it to the other side, there has to be a lot more to see. And I want to explore it with you.'

Jamie gets up to place more logs in the fire. The room warms quickly. She thinks about making more tea, then remembers without electricity the stove won't heat. She'll just have to wait for morning. Instead, she makes her way into the pitch dark of the bedroom, pulls the comforter off the bed and brings it back to the sofa. Settling in again, she stares into the licking, dancing flames as if they were an old friend, or a new lover.

'John, what about the business? Do you care that I don't care as much about it as you did? I can let it go, John. I really can. Would that disappoint you? But I won't let it go to hell. Maybe hell only exists on this side.

'John, I'll leave it in good hands. I don't need much now. You made sure of that. And I love you for the security you provided me and our children. And our grandchildren too. But maybe that means I can't die just yet. Not tonight anyway. A little more time, John. A little more time. Just a little more...'

When Jamie wakes, it is morning. Or what passes for dawn on this blizzard-blown day. The fire has died down again, but warmth lingers. Jamie stretches out of the comforter and puts more logs on. There'll be no avoiding going outside at least to the porch. The logs will need to thaw before she can use them for warmth. Jamie thinks of the metaphor of the new fire within her that also needs tending.

The power is still out. The wind still howls. But looking out the window it seems the snow is not quite as driven as it was last night. She scratches ice off the window to look at the thermometer. It, too, has shrunk from the storm's fury. A degree, maybe two, below zero. Jamie can barely see the woods. The drift across the porch reaches nearly halfway to the roof. Beyond, the landscape is pure white. Any detail of earth or bush has been erased. Even naked young saplings have been covered, save for the tallest which now look like weeds sprouting from a winter garden.

'Well, I guess Jake earned his weather badge after all. Lord, I hope they're still alive. John, if you're looking after me, would you mind checking on them, too?'

Jamie gets enough water out of the bathroom tank to make another mug of tea. Attached to the hearth is a cast iron pot hanging from a swing arm. It had always just been a decoration. Something that Stella had found years ago thinking it would look 'cute' at the cabin. Now it has use again. Jamie pours the water and tea bag into the kettle and moves it over the fire. If the power doesn't come back on later, she'll have to melt snow for H2O.

By the time she finishes, the fire is already waning. Jamie only has 10 logs left. She knows she has to brave some minutes outdoors to replenish what she burned through the night. She hates the idea of opening the door and letting the storm invade. But she has no choice. She climbs into her snowsuit, part of a matching pair John bought for them years ago and had hung on pegs ever since. Ditto for the L.L. Bean boots. Well at least she wouldn't freeze to death outside. But she might inside later on if she didn't get more wood. Safely layered, she turns the latch. The door blows open and a foot of snow rushes inside. Jamie pushes her way into the wind and fights hard to close the door behind her. She wades to her left for the large woodpile. The wind is still strong enough to burn her face and membranes. And the driven crystals sting her cheeks. It may be letting up a little though. It's almost as though having scared to death her part of the world, this storm is beginning to have spent itself. Still, it's deadly to anyone foolish enough to taunt it. But perhaps not enough to crumble her cabin. And hopefully not enough to extend its icy fingers all the way into Jake's cave.

Picking up an armload of logs, she turns back to the door and stops. There not ten feet away is a buck huddled against her cabin. It is a magnificent animal. Massive across the chest. A full rack of antlers that can fend off marauding packs of coyote and attract the finest white-tailed babes. It doesn't look sick or wounded. It gazes at her without concern. Clearly, he's claimed this bit of shelter as his own and generously decided to let Jamie share the space.

Jamie doesn't move, looking back at the animal, trying not to show fear or alarm. Each studies the other with an intent that seems to belie the blizzard that has brought them together like this. She doesn't want to startle it and have him bound off into the dangers of wind and snow. Could it be the same buck that crossed her path a couple of weeks ago down by the creek?

"How are ya, boy?" Conversing with a deer seems a rational thing and Jamie hopes the tone of her voice will reinforce that she means no harm. But she can't spend the day like this. She moves slowly to the door. The animal watches her, not budging. She reaches for the knob and again the door blows open. She staggers inside and pushes it closed. Laying the wood down, Jamie pauses to catch her breath. She has many more armloads to bring in before she'll have enough to get through another night. Will the buck let her? Is he any threat?

She ventures out again, a bit more gingerly this time not wanting to startle her visitor. And with a bit more bravado as if the storm might be cowed by her confidence.

Back and forth she goes for nearly an hour. The deer watches her, but doesn't move. They have reached an understanding. He is a guest welcome to use her porch as respite. She is a different kind of guest welcome to his woods for allowing this bit of shelter. Weary now with the last armload, Jamie pauses before going in for the rest of the day. The buck has settled into an almost lazy indifference to her comings and going.

"Can I do anything for you?" It's the kind of insane 'conversation' humans try to have with animals. Jamie knows it's silly. Yet, somehow, she wants to communicate concern for the buck's welfare. "I'm going in now. For the rest of the day. And night too. I hope you'll be OK."

With that Jamie steps inside one last time. She's built a woodpile that spills across the rear wall and floor. She's sweating through and through and exhausted. She's about to step out of her snowsuit, when she remembers. She grabs the kettle and several large bowls and steps once more into the storm and packs them with snow. As an afterthought, she carries several shovelfuls to the sink. She wonders how much snow it takes to flush a toilet. One more glance at the buck and now she's in for good.

The morning nearly gone, Jamie knows there isn't anything she can do but wait. And read. And write. And boil some more tea. She walks over to her desk and there she sees a half page of paper sticking out from the fax machine. It must have come during the night, interrupted when the power went out. Wearily, she pulls it out and there is Stella's unmistakable handwriting, clearly done in a rush.

Jamie call me! Rich got Ted to call an emergency me......

That was all that got through. Clearly another problem with Rich and the company. Another effort to get rid of her and grab control. She looks at the time and date:

Feb. 13, 8:59

Jamie pulls out last year's calendar to check dates. The 13th was on a Thursday. So that means yesterday was Friday. Perfect.

"Happy Valentine's Day, Jamie," she thinks. Also perfect. Alone. A husband dead. A lover (is that what Jake is to me?) possibly dead too. And now her husband's former business associate wants to take over his company and destroy the reputation of the one who brought it all into being. 'Happy Valentine's Day!' she says sarcastically to the deaf-mute fax machine.

Jamie walks to the window. The storm is definitely losing its intensity although snow continues to fall. How much? A foot? Two feet? Three? She can't even tell. But even the thermometer is recovering a bit. 12 degrees. To her left she can see the buck's hindquarters. She admires the animal's coat, the haunches powerful enough to leap twelve foot fences effortlessly and outrace any would-be predator, except one. Its head is down, probably sleeping. She counts the points of his antlers. Ten. If she remembers right from what John told her, this buck would be three or four years old. And the rack has stayed the winter. Very impressive.

Where are his does? Tucked away in another part of the woods? Pregnant and waiting to give birth in another month or so? Somehow Jamie feels blessed by this animal's presence. Never has she been this close to a deer. Or any other wild animal for that matter.

She thinks how a few inches of man-made materials separate her world from his. How different each world is. Yet here they intersect, bound together a few hours by mutual need. This animal seeks refuge from a natural world of savage indifference, yet can't escape it. How she seeks refuge from an even more savage world of *things*, yet can't escape it either, it seems. How these *things* cause her species to turn on itself with a destructive bent that Nature can never match.

Jamie turns from the window and back to the half message on the fax paper. 'Rich is nothing if not persistent,' she smiles wryly to herself thinking of the light touch of his hand on her bottom *at the funeral.* Maybe she should just give it up. Let it go. Let Ted, Phil and the others deal with Rich and the future of Barlow. Let the hospital figure its way out of the multimillion dollar debacle, not its fault. Everybody would muddle through, like they always do. She'd make sure Stella was taken care of. Maybe somebody would curse John and his memory. But that, too, would fade. Life would go on. And she would be free from the faxes and frantic communiqués and fakery. It would be so easy to do that. So easy. Declare her own freedom. Find her own place.

She stares at the paper. Crumples it. Starts to throw it towards the fire. But something stops her mid-swing, something...."Damn you, John!

You won't let me let it go! Damn you! I have to deal with this, don't I? I have to go back. I have to face Rich and keep him from hurting more people. Keep him from hurting you. Damn you..."

She picks up her cell and calls Ted. When she hears a familiar, "hello," she says, "Ted? It's Jamie."

"Jamie? It's so good to hear your voice. Are you OK?"

"Yes, I'm fine." She turns toward the window. The snow is still falling with small, fine flakes.

"But we've all been so worried...."

"I'm *fine* Ted. Honest. You know why I'm calling don't you?"

"To wish me happy Valentine's Day, I hope," offers Ted.

Jamie glances at the fax machine. "No, it's not to wish you a Happy Valentine's Day. Ted, I know we have a mess on our hands. And I'm OK taking my share of the heat, having been away so long. But just because I haven't been there doesn't mean I don't know what's been going on. I know everything, Ted. *Everything.*

"I can explain things, Jamie."

"Please, Ted." His defensiveness is not what she needs.

"It's just been that...."

"TED," she interrupts. "Stop. Listen to me. When does Rich want you to call the board together?

"March 16th."

"March 16th? OK. You will tell him that the Board will meet on its usual quarterly schedule. April 16th. We are not going to get tongues wagging and make clients nervous thinking something's wrong by calling an early meeting."

"But Rich is insist..."

"I. Don't. Care. What. Rich. Says. I know what he's after as well as you do." Jamie is pleased with the authority in her own voice, and it had come so naturally.

"But, will you be there, Jamie?" Static fills the phone for a few seconds.

"Will I be there? Yes. We will have only two orders of business. My continued majority position with the company and renewing our loyalty to its mission and purpose. It will have been a year since John died. We owe it to the faithful clients *he* won to ensure the stability, continuity and success of the company. Don't you agree, Ted?"

"You're right, Jamie. But..."

"Wonderful!" Jamie cuts him off. "Now I don't care if you tell Rich that we've talked or not. But you just set the meeting for April 16th."

"What time, Jamie?"

"Ten o'clock is fine. I will be there. And we won't leave until everybody is clear on our direction. And *who* is in charge."

"It is so good to hear you sound so...*strong*, Jamie."

"Thanks, Ted. It's good to hear your voice again, too. It *has* been too long. But I look forward to seeing you in a couple of months. And Ted? I am stronger than you think. John isn't here to keep an eye on everything. But I learned at his side. I'm going to drive my agenda with John's best chops. Give my love to Carol, will you? Bye!"

A few cleansing breaths, then one more call. "Stella, hi it's Jamie."

"Did you get my fax?" she hears a familiar panic in Stella's voice.

"Yes."

"Did you get the surprise blizzard that we got here?"

Jamie glances at the window and watches snow blow from the roof. "Yes, we got hit pretty hard. The power's been out since last night. But I'm managing. Now, Stella, listen. I've just talked to Ted. There will be no special meeting of the Board."

"What?"

"That's right. I've reminded Ted that Rich does not call the board or set the agenda. Ted knows better than to listen to Rich. He just had to be reminded of that. So the Board will meet at its regular time. April 16th. Ten o'clock."

"Will you be there, Jamie?"

"Yes, I will be there. Promise."

"Are you coming home?"

"Yes. And that's all I can tell you right now. But I don't want you to say a word. To anybody. Yet. Promise?"

"Sure, Jamie."

"OK. Good. I have to go. But listen to me. We will take care of the

Rich-meister once and for all. I promise you that, Stella."

"I worry about you....."

"I'm fine. Really. Lots of snow and wind. But I have a big buck protecting me."

"A big Buck?"

"Nooool A *real* deer. Outside on the porch. He needed a place out of the storm, too. I have to go. You won't have to be my eyes and ears much longer, Stella. But you have been wonderful looking out for me. And John, too. I love you for all of that Stella.

"I'll see you soon, then?"

"Yes. OK. See you soon. Bye."

Jamie smiles. She "done good," as John might say. Storm or no storm. Time for some more tea or maybe a hot toddy.

Jamie spends the rest of the day feeding the fire, reading and checking on the buck. A thin layer of snow has settled along his back. She worries that maybe something is wrong. But later when she goes out for more snow, it looks at her with the same alert eyes that it had earlier. It also seems perfectly content to wait out the storm right here on her porch.

Back inside, she wonders if he's hungry. She imagines he is. But then animals go hungry when Nature won't let them eat. Should she try to feed it? What would she offer? Muffins? Hardly. Some of Cora's stew? Jamie, get real. Then she remembers! A few months ago she and Jake had spent an Indian Summer afternoon gathering nuts. Acorns. Walnuts. Chestnuts. It was fun, if backbreaking work. Jake knew he'd need them for the winter. He offered to split their take with Jamie, but she'd refused. Still, he insisted on giving her some and there they were in a wooden canister stuck back in the pantry. Not a lot. A couple of snacks for "Buck."

Jamie takes the container outside and spreads the nuts across the snow-covered deck. The buck's interest is real. But he doesn't move. 'There ya go, boy. You need 'em way more than I do." She goes back in and walks over to the window to watch. The buck doesn't move. But she can see him sniffing. Then, carefully, it stands and takes a step to the welcome meal. Jamie is amazed how much bigger the animal seems even now standing a few feet form her.

At first he eats tentatively, almost not quite believing his good fortune. He looks out into the whiteness as though looking for something, or someone. Perhaps remembering what happened to other bucks that wandered into a field offering a similarly surprising feast. Convinced this isn't a trick, he eats aggressively and Jamie knows she has done the right thing.

The wind has slowed to a breeze. The snow comes only in playful flurries. The storm is exhausted. Tomorrow, she hopes, she can start to dig out... and hopes Jake is doing the same. She can't imagine negotiating the trail between them. Maybe she won't see him again until the next thaw.

Thanks to her tending the fire, the whole cabin is warm now. The ice has melted off the windows and icicles now grow from the eaves. Tired and satisfied with how she's handled this blizzard-battered Valentine's Day, she is more than ready to settle in with her book and journal and a drink. She starts with the book. But then puts it down and picks up the journal. This was a day to be remembered and she writes all that has happened. Then she thinks about Jake.

This storm is a reminder. Sometimes I have wondered if Jake and I would ever stay together. John, forgive me, but sometimes I have wished it so. And now I know that we won't. I can't. He can't. (There is a larger issue here of pouring your gifts into a one-to-one relationship, or pouring these gifts into community: loving one, or loving many. Hmmmm.) Life's storms have tossed us together. And we have huddled and discovered and found new strengths. Like "Buck", we have to move on. But we can't hide those strengths. Others need us. We have a responsibility to use our strengths to keep building, to keep moving forward. But we can't do that together. He needs to continue on his path as I need to continue on mine. But life's path is rarely straight and true. Is the blizzard the wild life that awaits me? Is the buck something calm in the storm that I should pay attention to? Is the buck taking something from me? Is he bringing something to me? Do we have something to give each other? John. Jake. Buck. Hawk. Magpie. What a cast of characters! Now that I've learned to listen, there are messengers all around me.

Jamie puts her pen down. "What a cast of characters, indeed!" she says to the fire. The flames dance and the wood crackles almost as if they were children enjoying a nighttime story. Her nighttime story.

Jamie awakes to light and chill. She's disoriented for a second, then realizes it's still night but the lights are on. She can hear the hum of the refrigerator. She's happy the power is back. Yet somehow she feels as though she's broken some kind of charm, a guilty feeling for having broken the storm's spell and left the door ajar for mundane life to barge back in.

The fire has died down as well, as though retreating from vital necessity to vacation home accessory. The embers glow, but lack the intensity of the night before, dimmed by the glow from light bulbs. Soon the hearth will be dark again, save perhaps for a lingering coal here and there. Jamie stirs from the sofa, adding several more logs. Then she turns out the lights and returns to cushions and comforter. "I don't want this fire to end…just yet."

The next morning the storm abates. Jamie goes out for more wood and to feed her buck, but he is gone into the white wonderland of the forest. She smiles thinking that he had stayed with her during the storm. She wonders about Jake and Job. Could they have survived two days and two nights in that terrible blizzard?

She decides against a hike. Remembering her commitment to keeping paths clear for what guests may come, Jamie shovels the snow from the porch. This takes most of the morning with a single path leading to what would become the drive. As she works she hears the distant sound of snowplows far down on the road. She figures it will be days before she can venture down the drift-closed drive.

Jamie showers after her shoveling. She is glad for the electricity and hot water. When she goes out to get more wood for the afternoon and evening, she hears something like a snow plow on her driveway. A half an hour later, the Sheriff's truck with a snowplow on the front reaches close to the cabin. The sheriff gets out and walks to the front door. Jamie has only seen him once before at the store. He is taller and lankier than she remembered. Clad in a plaid wool coat and a hat with earflaps pulled down to envelop his ears, he all but orders her into his cab.

"Why?" asks Jamie. "What's the matter?"

"Get your coat and boots," he barks. "We're going to the hospital. In Uniontown."

"What…" she asks? Jamie's resolve to stay calm melts into the heaps of snow she had spent the morning shoveling.

"Get your coat. We'll talk on the way. Let's GO," he shouts.

Jamie gets her coat and boots on quickly. She doesn't take time to lock the door.

The Sheriff is in the cab when she stumbles onto the porch again. She stands frozen with panic for an instant then blurts "Am I under arrest?"

"No ma'am. Just get in and let's go, NOW," he shouts out the window. Jamie lurches forward to do as she's told. She scarcely closes the door as the truck pushes back through the chasm now gouged through her snow.

'What is this man not telling me?' Jamie thinks to herself. She looks to her escort and, seeing the set to his jaw and the cold intent in his eyes, realizes he'll tell her when he's ready and when he is, she's going to learn something she'd rather not know.

Chapter 49
Special Delivery

As the Sheriff eases his truck down the long drive to the road, he begins to fill her in. "Sorry for the hurry, ma'am. Been so many problems with this storm, I've forgotten my pleasantries."

"Call me Jamie, please," Jamie says looking in his direction while reaching in another for her seatbelt.

"Jamie, sure. You can call me Bob," his seatbelt hanging unused. Sheriff Kuhner is in his mid sixties, a tall man, still fit. He looks comfortable with his uniform and with the authority it conveys. He speaks in a laid-back voice, almost like John Wayne, but with a Pittsburgh accent. Perfect for someone charged with dealing in the tragedies of human life. Punching the gas for enough momentum to lurch over and through the plow drift, Bob launches the big Ford out onto the road. Even though plowed this morning, the road is barely wide enough for two cars to pass. The snow is piled high, rendering most curves blind.

Bob hits the flashers, but keeps to the 35 mph speed limit. If the twenty miles to the hospital had been an emergency, he might have driven faster. But he says, "I'm glad I can drive slowly. This mission will pass for my 'break.' " He drives with the kind of sure-handed calm that would have impressed John. Settling in, Jamie finally asks.

"So, what happened? How bad is it?" Jamie holds her breath, afraid of the answer.

"No, nothing bad. A couple surprises maybe. And a bit of luck."

That is more than enough to get Jamie's curiosity roaring. After a few seconds when Bob doesn't say more, she blurts out. "So, spill it, *please*," then following with a nervous laugh: "If we're going to the hospital, it *can't* be good."

"Cora was at the hospital visiting her sister, Dee Dee, after her gall bladder operation. Do you know Dee Dee? No? She's OK. Then the blizzard hit. And I decided to declare an Emergency Two. No one on the roads except emergency vehicles. So she was kind of stuck there. Not a bad place to be stuck in a storm, though."

Jamie nods impatiently, ready to reach down his throat and pull out the point of this painful narrative. Bob slows at a bend and waves at a pickup truck inching by him going the other way. "That's Forrest Findlay. Has the siding business in the Run. You know Forrest? No?"

"Bob, you're killing me! What happened?"

"Oh! Sorry, Jamie. Well, Ellie Mae was at the store covering the business. Your friend, Jake and his dog...now what's his name?"

"Job. JOB!"

"Yeah, Job. They showed up to get some fuel and some other supplies. I guess they were planning on heading back up to your hills, but the storm got too fierce even for your mountain man. So they hunkered in with Ellie."

Jamie's not sure if she likes how he said "your mountain man," but decides to let it pass. "Well I'm glad."

"Yeah, they were pretty lucky. That storm was a killer. 'Pike had a bunch of accidents. Three fatalities. Heard over the radio Tom Pullins – he's the sheriff over in the next county – he had to bring down four folks who froze to death in a place like yours."

Jamie thinks when he said "place...like yours" he meant rich people who'd snuggled into their third or fourth home imagining themselves immune to real-life dangers.

"Lost their electricity. Guess one died going out for wood. Lost his way back to the house in the white-out. Others just went to sleep and never woke up."

Jamie shivers at the thought. Not just at the story, but in the casual way Bob tells it. He doesn't seem uncaring. She realizes this is a man familiar with death and the quick, often cruel ways, it plucks people out of this world into the next.

The Sheriff slows a bit through some deep drifts formed almost as soon as the plows had gone through. It would need two or three more passes before it'll resemble a two lane road again. Feeling the pressure of her gaze, Bob gets back to the news.

"Ellie Mae's 'time' came early. The baby wouldn't wait. And she had a few problems. Good thing Jake was there to help with the delivery. The baby wouldn't have made it he hadn't been there, Jamie. Maybe Ellie neither. It was a miracle, I mean him being there to help."

"Was it a girl?" Jamie blurts out, her thoughts racing ahead with the good news.

"Yup, a girl. I helped get 'em to the hospital this morning. They wanted you there. Got something they need to talk about that can't wait. Think they were also worried how you made out during the storm. So I said I'd come for you."

"Thanks, Bob. I really appreciate it." Jamie breathes a sigh of relief as she looks out the window at shoulder-high drifts. She can't remember ever seeing so much snow.

"Jake. I'm glad he was there for Ellie Mae, but I gotta' ask you, what is he running from? I been worried about him since he showed up. Cora and Ellie Mae were kind of suspicious too. I was about to pick him up for vagrancy last spring when Cora told me you'd warmed to him. Said he was a friend of yours. Is that true?"

Jamie looks at Bob and sees that he is really interested. And there's no avoiding telling him the story, or as much of it as she was comfortable sharing. "To tell you the truth, I was scared the first time too. Wasn't at all sure what to make of him. But, yes, now he's a friend. He knew that storm was coming when it was still warm and the sun was out! I'm not surprised he helped Ellie with her baby." Then she adds, almost as an afterthought, "He had a son once. In Oklahoma. Lost him. In a snowstorm."

The Sheriff looks at Jamie hard, having flipped back to cop-mode with worst-case suspicions. But he decides not to pursue it for the moment, seeing sadness, not fear, in Jamie's eyes. Instead he decides to broach another subject of concern.

"I'm not sure it is connected, but others have been in town looking for you. Strangers. From out of state. What's that all about?"

Jamie tells him about the break-in, that it's possible others might show up, but she doesn't think so. Tells him it's related to her late husband's business. She says she doesn't anticipate physical danger.

"Jamie, that's not something you fool around with," he scolds. His instincts are not to be ignored. "When I get done dealing with the storm, we're going to have to talk more about this break-in. And I'll have to file a report. Even if you don't want one."

He lets that sink in for a minute, then asks the inevitable, "Was your husband in any kind of trouble? With people you don't want to have trouble with?"

"No, Bob!" She pauses, then asks, "Do you mean... like Mafia or something?"

They eye each other quickly. "You tell me."

"No!" she answers again emphatically; surprised that he would even suspect something like that. Then she continues, realizing that the Sheriff will need more than a simple 'No' to ease his suspicions. It's clear this has been on his mind for a while.

"Look, I don't know for sure, but I think this all goes back to a man who's been trying to get control of the company even before John died. The guy's on our board. With John gone and me here, he thought getting the board over to his side would be a pushover. But it didn't turn out that way. So now he's trying to dig up dirt, tell people I'm crazy and send his men over here to do some kind of mischief. Once you have money, some people will do anything to take it from you. Anything..."

Bob keeps driving, waiting for more. Jamie realizes he's not satisfied. "As far as the break-in goes, only thing he took was a fax paper. I wasn't home when he was there. That was the only thing missing."

"Where were you?"

"I was visiting...Jake."

"Where?"

"At his...cave. It's a deep outcropping. On our property. About a mile from the cabin. I can show you..." then she thinks better of it. She realizes the more she says, the more improbable it sounds.

The Sheriff lets it pass.

"How did you know there was only one?"

"I guess I don't for sure. But we only saw one set of footprints when we came back."

"'We'...you mean, you and...uh...Jake?" It was clear the Sheriff was beginning to form his own opinions about their relationship.

"Yes."

"And your intruder, you're pretty sure he only took a...a fax page?"

"Yes."

"Was there something important on it?"

"One of my employees was tipping me off about this...board member...trying another move on my majority position. I figure he took it hoping I hadn't seen it yet."

"How did he know it was there?"

"I don't think he did. How could he have?"

"Then why did he make the drive up to your cabin?"

"Snooping about? I don't know."

"You don't? I don't think he was bringing you flowers, Jamie."

She shivers, thinking of the possibilities.

Jamie suddenly feels painfully naive. "You don't think he was going to kill me?"

"Maybe. I don't know. Maybe he just wanted to 'talk.' Try and 'persuade' you into giving up ownership." Bob continues with a sigh, "Jamie, these hills may have been peaceful for you and John, but they've seen their share of killing too. Back in '69, a guy running for Mine Workers president was shot to death, along with his wife and daughter. On Christmas Day. It was a gruesome sight. In the '70s another guy was shot to death in a hunting 'accident.' Turns out he was a big shot with the Teamsters in New Jersey and had connections with organized crime."

"Did the killers get caught?"

"With the Mine Workers, yeah. But it took years. Gunmen were hired by the union president. He eventually went to jail and died there. But the Teamsters guy...no, never did. I don't want to scare you, Jamie, but you gotta watch out. You should have come to me. Right away," he scolds one last time.

They ride in silence for a couple more miles. Jamie feels guilty, because she knows the Sheriff is right. But how to hold on to her privacy... and her dream?

Bob seems satisfied, for now. Then he tells Jamie a surprising story. "I knew John when I was in Boy Scouts. I looked up to him because I was a First Class when he was the counselor."

"Yes! John loved Scouting. He learned a lot from it. He often tried to tell me how the Indians lived. Or about the stars. He told me he learned survival skills there that helped him in business."

Seeing her interest, Bob continues: "I was on a hike with John and the troop. I got too close to a ravine edge and fell. Broke my leg. John was the one who kept his cool, rappelled down the cliff, stabilized my leg and waited with me until the other scouts went back to camp and made a makeshift stretcher out of a door. John secured me with belts they sent down and the scouts lifted me to safety. They got me back to camp and took me to the hospital. I will never forget him."

Jamie is surprised that John never told her that story. She thought she knew everything about his young life. "When I heard that you and John were back in the area, I wanted to remind John of that, but felt he was too rich and powerful to be bothered. Didn't think he'd remember me anyway. Now I'm sorry because John is dead and I can't tell him."

Jamie's eyes well with tears. "I can understand that, but I wish you had come. He would have loved talking with you. I'm sure he would have remembered!"

They are just outside town. Houses line both sides of the road. The Sheriff turns off his flashers. Now Jamie see plumes of snow kicked up by snow blowers as people dig out slowly from what the National Weather Service will call western Pennsylvania's 'Blizzard of the Century.'

Bob pulls into the parking lot and drops her off in front of the hospital. He has just gotten a call about a car in the ditch and possible injuries in another part of the county. "Break time is over. Nice to have talked to you, ma'am...er, Jamie. I'm sure we'll talk again soon." He pauses, then adds, "I *do* have to file that break-in report. But I don't think anybody's gonna bother you while we have all this snow."

"Thanks for coming for me. I can't thank you enough," Jamie takes his hand in both of hers and squeezes it.

"Call me if you need a ride home. It's got all my numbers on it," handing her a business card.

"Thanks, Sheriff. *Bob*. Bye for now." Jamie springs from the truck and runs for the hospital entrance.

Chapter 50

Reunion

"Room 247," says the receptionist. She knows who Jamie is and why she's here without even asking. Word gets around fast, even after a blizzard. Jamie runs up the stairs, not waiting for the elevator. Cora is the first one to greet her. There is a big, tearful reunion. They are as relieved to see Jamie as she is to see them and the baby too. Ellie Mae is nursing, and both mother and baby look bonded. Jake's eyes are sparkling. Even Job is there, snoozing quietly in the corner until Jamie walks in. Now he's up too, tail wagging, waiting expectantly for her hug and a scruff behind the ears. Finally, when all are settled Jamie fixes on Ellie and Jake.

"OK. What happened?" Jamie asks. "I can't believe what I'm seeing here!" She truly is incredulous. To see Jake with Cora and Ellie Mae and a baby is something Jamie never thought she would see. A warmth flows over her at the scene.

"They wouldn't tell me anything until you got here," says Cora as she hugs Jamie for the third or fourth time. Jamie can hear the full range of a mother's emotions in her voice… a tinge of scolding, a bit of frustration, lots of relief and, underneath all, love and pride for her daughter and granddaughter.

"Ok, you two, tell us the story please," says Cora. "Cough up the details."

Ellie Mae begins. "I was on the phone to Ma when she was here with Aunt Dee Dee. Then the electric went out and the line went dead while Ma was tellin' me to stay put 'til the storm was done." Ellie Mae shifts her small pink bundle to the other breast. The newborn roots, then gurgles with contentment. Jamie sees Jake watching with an obvious happiness. Clearly, these two have also bonded in an extraordinary and wholly unexpected way over the last 72 hours.

"Right 'bout then, Jake and Job burst through the door. They were there for supplies. I was a little scared because I'd never been alone when they'd come in before." She smiles at Jake as she says, "But Job was so sweet that I relaxed."

Jake jumps in, "We made it to town just in time. I guessed wrong, Maggie. I knew that storm was coming. That's why I told you to get back to the cabin. And I thought Job and I would have enough time to make it down and back before it hit. As it turned out, we were lucky just to make it to town."

Ellie says, "I was awful lucky, too, Jamie. We were talking about how bad the weather was gettin' and how Ma told me to stay put. And now the power was out. Phone *too*. Then, BAM! I felt a pain like nothing never before. I was starting my contractions."

Cora said, "If I'd known she was gonna be early, I'd a never come down here to Dee Dee. Or, I'd a brought her with me."

"Ma, that's all right. You had no way of knowin'. Doc never said nothing 'bout me bein' early."

"That's true, honey. But I shoulda known better, you being so young and all. And... you came early too, remember." Mother and daughter look at each other a moment, sharing a memory and having their *own* thoughts at the same time.

Then Ellie gets back to the story, "Jake saw my stress. He asked if he should make a run for the doc, but I told him we got no doc in Ram Cat. Mine was all the way over here. I was like to freak, Jamie, but he was so calm!" Here, she glances and smiles at Jake again. Jake looks and then bows his head with an aw-shucks kind of embarrassment. "He said that he'd delivered a baby before... his *own*. He said he'd help me if I was OK with it. Like I had a choice?"

That provokes nervous laughter from Cora.

"So another contraction hits and I about panic. I begged him to stay."

Jake interjects, "She was a very brave woman through the whole thing. You have every right to be very proud, Cora."

Cora's eyes had been welling up. Now tears move slowly down her cheeks.

Jamie and Cora move their chairs closer, rapt and craving more. Meanwhile, the baby, belly filled, has fallen asleep on Ellie Mae's chest. "Jake, you tell 'em what happened next. I'm not sure I remember it all. I was in a panic."

Jake continues with almost a physician's level voice. Jamie recognizes the authority and intelligence she's seen and heard through many of their conversations. But even this part of him comes as a surprise. "Her contractions started about 20 minutes apart. So I knew we had a little time before delivery. Still, that storm was really picking up and I guessed we'd be off grid and on our own for quite a while. It was getting cold so I got blankets and set up a birthing place on the floor by the potbelly stove. I had Ellie lie there. Then I put water on top. I knew we'd need lots of it. I used bottled water first, but I knew I'd need to raid the tanks or melt snow later."

Ellie jumps in, "Job came over and lay right down with me! He was so good! Like he knew what was comin' and wanted to help. He was warm too." The humans look over at the dog, whose tail wags in recognition as he pretends to sleep.

Jake continues, "I knew we'd need a lot of wood too, maybe enough for a few days. Ellie Mae told me it was in a lot behind the store. But the blizzard was so fierce by then I didn't want to get disoriented. I knew too many stories of people frozen to death a few feet from their doors because they couldn't find their way." Jake stops and looks at Jamie, "I worried for you that way, too, Maggie."

She reaches out and squeezes his hand. "My story can come later. We need to hear the rest of yours."

"I found a good length of rope, tied one end to the back door and wrapped a loop around my waist. That way I could always find my way back. And I tell you. I needed that! My first trip out about knocked me over. It took me the better part of an hour just getting enough wood hauled in. I was always back for the contractions to hold her hand and coach her breathing. Once I had enough wood, I settled down to talk to Ellie and keep her calm." Now he reaches for Ellie's hand and they squeeze tightly.

"Her contractions stayed pretty constant through the night and well into the morning. I wasn't that concerned yet. She was holding up real well. But that first night of blizzard was fearsome!"

Cora came out with a "Hoo-wee, you bet."

"Jake. Tell them the story you told me... please. I want to hear it again", Ellie pleads.

Jake looks at her, and seems like he really doesn't want to. Maybe he thinks he owes it to Cora to lift the veil on part of his mystery. He looks at Jamie, wondering if she has shared this with the older woman. Jamie senses this and shakes her head once, meaning she has not. He looks back at Ellie who gazes back expectantly. Like he is more of a man in her eyes than anyone she has known in Ram Cat, including the boy who professed endless love, then left town as soon as he learned she was pregnant.

"Well, I shared with her the story of my own son's birth. My wife is a white woman. Or my ex-wife... or whatever she is now – wherever she is..." He pauses, getting lost in his own shadow world.

Jamie, knowing how hard this is for him, waits patiently. Cora shifts in her chair. Both Cora and Jamie, seeing the wave of Jake's complex emotions, feel something wash across their own inner beach.

"She wanted to know more about Indian ways. It always seemed like a tourist's kind of interest. Sometimes I felt even her love for me was kind of like something out of the movies, something you could see but not touch. It was hard to explain. But the closer she got to her time, the more she wanted to know. About our tradition. And about our God. One weekend about a month before she was due, we drove out to my grandfather's rez."

He caught the confusion in Cora's eyes.

"Sorry, 'rez' is short for reservation. Where our people were put after their homes were taken and they were marched from Georgia and Tennessee – the ones who made it, anyway..." Cora nods trying to understand.

"So we drove out there and she met Grandfather. He was kind of the rez medicine man. Even though we had a clinic, my people came to him for help because they trusted him. He had knowledge. And he blessed the birth to come. And then, my wife started her contractions! So, yes, I knew a little about early babies." Jake stops here. The women look at him with interest, each for her own reasons.

He continues, "My son was born on the rez. Grandfather called in the birthing women and they helped her through the delivery. I stayed also and saw the miracle of new life. It is our tradition now to give children born on the rez both English and Indian names. So we named him "Daniel," after the 'brave' in your Bible. And then we named him also after the warrior bird circling over when he was born... a red-tailed hawk."

He sees Jamie's eyes widen and, smiling a bit guiltily, adds, "Sorry, Maggie, you didn't know that part of the story. Maybe I should have told you."

Jamie sees this is another of those strange and wondrous experiences she has come to look for in her life.

Jake continues on with the rest of what happened at the store. "Ellie asked me why I was here when I had a wife and son in Oklahoma. I didn't want to tell her. I thought it would upset her. But... she insisted. So I put it all out there. The winter camping. Daniel wandering away while I slept. Me finding him...." His voice trails off at the memory and the pain of the retelling.

Instinctively, both women rise to comfort him. Cora looks at Jamie who finishes the sentence by the look in her eyes. All are silent for a moment. The baby continues to sleep as yet untouched by such a world.

"Jamie," Ellie Mae finally says. "He told me you knew the whole thing. He told me that you made a story for him about Daniel in heaven. He knew it all by heart. It's beautiful, Jamie. To hear him, I forgot my own pain."

Jake pulls himself back from his own shadows and continues with the rest of Ellie Mae's story. "In the morning, I realized something was wrong," Jake continues. "The contractions weren't coming faster, but they were getting more painful like the baby was struggling. I thought of all I knew about childbirth. I knew Ellie Mae and the baby were in trouble. I told her I needed to see and touch her to see what was wrong. She howled at me to do whatever I had to!" Again, Jake and Ellie's eyes meet. Only they will ever know the literal gut-wrenching of facing those hours. But it is clear that they have forged a bond that will transcend distances and lifetimes.

"That's when I felt the baby was in breach. She was coming butt first, instead of head first. I really didn't know what I was doing, but on her belly I could feel a hard head where a soft bottom should be. Somehow I pushed and turned the baby between contractions not knowing if I was doing the right thing."

"Oh, my Gawd Mama, that hurt worse than anything! I thought I was gonna burst inside out. But Jake, if he didn't know, he sure didn't let on. He was so good!" Ellie was smiling and crying at the same time.

"Ellie was the brave one. She had nothing going for her except she wanted that baby to be OK. But once I got her turned, seemed like her contractions were coming faster. And...more natural like. Within an hour the baby came out head first. She howled bloody murder as soon as she got free." Jake smiles now as he finishes the story.

"I don't remember all that," Ellie confessed. "But I heard her giving us both the 'what-for.' And I do know we'd a-been goners for sure if it weren't for Jake...and you too Job!" patting Job as he nuzzled the bundle. "Jake, tell them the rest...please."

"Well, she was a preemie for sure. I cut the cord and wrapped her in a blanket. I made sure the afterbirth got delivered and it seemed to be whole. I washed Ellie and the baby up as best I could. I told Ellie Mae that she could rest for a few minutes but then she would need to nurse the baby."

"I was panicked," Ellie Mae chimed in. "I hadn't planned on nursing. Jake calmly told me stories of how important it was for a baby to have breast milk. I told him I didn't know what to do and he said the baby would! He was so sweet and calm." Ellie shifts the baby kissing her softly on the head. Ellie Mae looks directly at Jamie. "Little Margaret Mae Kelley took to it on the first try."

The room was silent. "Margaret Mae Kelley"... what was that? Then Ellie finishes, "He'll call her Maggie Mae for short."

Now it is Jamie's turn to cry uncontrollably! She isn't even sure why. "What are you talking about?!" Jamie asks.

Ellie Mae speaks with tears in her eyes. "I have asked Jake to adopt my baby. If it wasn't for him she would have died. We named her together. He said he needs to think about it. Jamie, I am counting on you to talk him into this. He needs to be her father. We can put his name on the birth certificate. It would be perfect."

Jamie and Cora hold each other and cry for all good reasons. Jamie goes to Ellie Mae and takes sweet Maggie Mae in her arms. She cuddles in complete contentment. Jake and Job step closer. "What did you say, Jake?" written clear on Jamie's brow.

"I said I needed a few days to think it over," Jake chokes, welling with tears of uncertainty and joy. Clearly a bond was already set. He saved her life. But she might be the one to save his in turn.

Cora gets down to business. "I need to stay here with Ellie Mae and Maggie tonight and tomorrow. Would you two take my truck and go back to watch the store and keep it open for a couple of days?"

Jake says, "I've run a cash register before. I think we could do it. What do you say, Maggie?"

Jamie answers, "I don't know how to run a store! But...how much damage could I do in two days? I am one happy woman tonight. We'll gladly cover until you call to come and get you."

Cora gives Jake a big hug. "I need to thank you for more than you can ever know. Jake, you are some guy. You saved my little girl. And you brought this beautiful baby into the world. Jamie hasn't said a whole bunch about ya, but I know she thinks the world of ya. I haven't had the best of luck with men, but I think you're a keeper."

Jamie hands Maggie back to Ellie. "Jake, my guess is Cora's got some customers waiting for the store to open back up. Let's get back to the Ram Cat and let these girls get some rest."

Cora gives Jake the keys. Then another round of hugs.

"We'll see you tomorrow, Cora. And Ellie Mae. And Maggie Mae Kelley!"

As Jamie, Jake and Job head out, the floor nurse gives Jake an approving look. She, too, must have heard the story of the miracle birth up at Ram Cat Run.

Chapter 51

Decisions

Jamie sits close to Jake and holds his hand as they drive to the store. Job is curled up next to Jamie. The afternoon sun is already almost down. It has been a brilliant day. The road is wet and wider now the county plow has made another pass. "The roads are still bad. Especially the road to your place. I think we'll have to sleep at the store until we bring Cora back. OK, Magpie?"

"I think we can make do. Sounds like you had things positively cozy!" Jamie leans up to kiss Jake's cheek. Jake smiles and puts his arm around Jamie to pull her closer, while keeping an eye on the road.

"Jamie, I couldn't say it back there, but I honestly was scared for Ellie and that baby. I mean, I saw Daniel born. But it was the rez midwife who did all the work. I don't know how I did it. I mean, I really had to reach way beyond anything I knew to get Maggie turned around. And even then I wasn't sure the cord wasn't twisted…or worse. I honestly think someone else was watching out for us."

"Maybe someone was, Jake…"

"Maybe, Magpie. It was all so amazing. That blizzard. That baby. Cora not having a clue what was going on. You neither. No way to get an ambulance. I just did what I could. We were there two days until the Sheriff got around to checking on the store. Tell you what… that old guy is all right."

Jamie winces silently. "That old guy" is younger than she is. It's one of the few times she has felt that gulf between them. Both are silent for the next couple of miles.

She can literally feel the lid pop off an inner can of something she's pushed away, making her face that their relationship, however sincere, is improbable; a chapter in their lives, not an epic. Then, somehow, her doubts settle into a comfortable place in her own sense of self.

Finally, Jamie speaks up. "This is one of the most exciting days of my life, Jake. Are you really thinking of raising Maggie Mae?"

"I am, Magpie. I really am. It's way out of left field, but I feel like it might be what I'm meant to do next. What do you think?"

"It surprised me how I feel more comfortable with this than I have felt about anything for a long time. I think Ellie's rightly overwhelmed, though tougher than she knows. But she *has* made up her mind. It's *your* decision now. But if you take little Maggie, I can tell you, she'll have one great Daddy... and a rich chance for life beyond Ram Cat Run!"

Jake slows down as a car passes going the other way. Someone waves at the sight of Cora's truck. Jake and Jamie wave back.

"It's a helluva thing to think about. And I can't say I know all the legal ramifications, but I already gave Ellie permission to add my name to the birth certificate. She's strong like her mother. She could raise her just fine if she wanted to."

"She probably could. But she's just a child in many ways too. And if their store ever went under, I don't know what Ellie would do. She knows she has to finish high school and get to college. Even with Cora's help, that's an awful lot to do. And, speaking of Cora, is she OK with this yet?"

"Ellie was going to talk to her after we left. She was scared to bring it up. But she knows her own mind too."

"I don't think she could go through with the adoption, if it weren't you Jake."

"You really think that?" Jake brakes to a stop to let a frightened driver pass. She has a death grip on her wheel and probably wouldn't be out in this weather unless she had to be.

"I do. She had to sense something awfully strong in you to even give that a thought. When I've been at the store, we never discussed you much... and certainly not your qualifications as a father!"

As they pull into the Ram Cat, Sheriff Bob is coming the other way and waves them down. He is a little surprised to see Jake and Jamie. "Well, hello you two! I thought it was Miss Cora!"

Jake says, "She wanted to stay with Ellie and the baby. She asked us to mind the store until tomorrow or maybe the day after."

Bob smiled, "Well, I know there are people been askin' if the store was open."

He paused a second, then added, "Word's gettin' around what you done, son. That was pretty good work."

Jake replies, "Thank you, Sheriff. Means a lot coming from you. But I was telling Jamie, it almost felt like someone was watching over us, because I was only guessing at how to save our baby."

Ever in detective mode, Bob's face casts a question mark to Jamie at the words "...our baby." Jamie slips him a Mona-Lisa-ish smile.

Bob says, "Nobody had a clue, with the lines down and all. And if anything'd happened to her or the baby, it'd a' ruined Cora. She's had it hard enough as it is. All she's got is Ellie and the store. And now a grandbaby, too!" he laughed.

Jamie leans towards the window. "Bob, do know anyone who could get my road plowed? I don't need to get up there today. But maybe sometime tomorrow."

"Sure do. I'll send John Hagan over with his truck. You got a pretty long stretch there. He might hit you for a hundred bucks."

"A hundred would be fine, Bob. Tell him to stop here for a check before he heads over, if he wants."

"Consider it done!" Bob salutes her crisply.

"And Bob, tell folks if they're running short of cash, they can still come down to the store. I'll put them on account 'til they can get to their bank."

"I will, Jamie. That's mighty nice of you to offer."

"And we'll stay open 'til midnight, if that'll help."

Jake raises one eyebrow and mouths "Midnight?"

"Midnight! Miss Cora likes closin' up by seven, latest. So, yeah, that might help a few still getting dug out."

His radio crackles to life: "Base to Boss-Bob. Hey BigGuy, you copy?" crackles over his hand-set. "Well, that's for me. You two take care. I'll look for you tomorrow."

Jake pulls the pickup into a parking spot in front of the store. Snow is piled four to five feet high along the edge. The threesome climb over the drifts and work their way into the store, Job fairing a bit worse than the bipeds.

"Looks like I have some work to do," Jake says. "I think I saw a snow blower out back. You sure you want to stay open 'til midnight?"

Jamie shakes snow off her boots and pants and hangs her coat on the hooks by the door. "Jake, I think we have to, don't you? Like the Sheriff said, there're people who've been stuck inside for three days now. Seems like a small thing to do for them."

Jake comes over and wraps Jamie in a hug. "I know. I was just being...ah...selfish, I guess."

Jamie smiles and kisses him. "Oh, you! There will be plenty of time for that!"

"OK..." he says sheepishly. "Well, guess I'd better find that snow blower and get that walk cleaned off."

Jamie looks around. The store had been transformed into a delivery room. "I should get some things straightened up. I'm still trying to wrap my head around what happened here during that blizzard!"

A few people come in through the evening. All are surprised to see Jamie and Jake. But word about the birth has spread through town, so Jake ends up telling his story again and again.

True to her technophobia, Jamie elects not to fool with the cash register. She just writes down names and orders they bought. Hearing Jake tell the birth story again gives her a warm inner smile.

It's clear, too, these local folk have heard stories about him. She sees wariness melt into respect as Jake gathers them in with his unassuming warmth. She sees the same look come into the women's eyes as she saw in Cora's this afternoon. She realizes this look says "Now *this* is a man"... and realizes she feels the same way... but without any personal emptiness – the kind that could compel craving for this man or demand trying to possess him. She feels blessed to have Jake in her world, but not need him at its center.

Finally, it's midnight, the last customer an hour ago. Jamie flips the "Open" sign to "Closed" darkening the lot and the entry. She yawns and looks to Jake spreading blankets out in front of the wood stove with more enthusiasm than men usually afford to linens. He looks at her. "I think this is the best I can do. Not as good as yours, Magpie."

"But better than your cave! At least for tonight. Besides I'm so tired, I think that floor is going to feel just like my bed." They strip down to undies and ease themselves onto the blankets. She welcomes his arm around her. She also hopes his passion can wait until morning. They kiss and Jake stokes her hair lightly.

"What an incredible few days, Maggie. Even now, lying here, sometimes it feels like a dream." He snuggles against her shoulder. Now Jamie runs her fingers through his long, black hair. She is always amazed at how fine it feels.

"Jake, more than the day, it's what *you did* that was incredible. I can't tell you how worried I was for you and Job. I thought you would be trapped in the cave. When I lost power at least I was inside and had the fireplace. You just had your fire pit. I ended up sleeping on the sofa and cooking over the fire. And there was this buck that came up to the porch to get out of the storm. He stayed right there when I came out to get wood. He was beautiful Jake. Jake?" He hasn't heard a word she said.

Jamie smiles to herself. Kisses his hair. Closes her eyes. Quite a day, indeed.

Chapter 52

Waking Up

Jamie stirs in the morning light. She can feel a night on the floor in her bones and muscles. Jake's bed is five-star-hotel sumptuous compared to these boards, even with a couple of blankets underneath. Still, she was so tired she slept dreamlessly. She turns and reaches for Jake. Gone. So is Job. But the wood stove is roaring and there's the welcome smell of coffee brewing. As she makes her way to the bathroom in back, picking up clothes along the way, Jake and Job greet her with a blast of cold air.

"There you are!" She smiles and covers in one quick movement.

"Sorry. Job needed to go out. You were still sleeping like a baby." He leans forward to kiss her and is quickly rebuffed.

I'm freezing already! And I have to go to the bathroom."

Jake laughs at his 'indiscretion,' but still feels a primal male need to touch her bottom as she turns into the bathroom. "Jake!!!"

"I'll pour you some coffee."

In the crude bathroom Jamie washes her face and looks at the ancient shower. The showerhead protrudes from the pine board wall, a bent pipe ending in something robbed from a sprinkling can. The mismatched and unnamed hot and cold handles look dubious at best. The floor is stamped from galvanized tin with a well-crusted drain. The soap in the tray is used and there's a half bottle of a shampoo Jamie's hair swore off of in the 60's . There is even a fraying towel and washcloth on the wooden shelf.

"I could really use a shower," she thinks to herself. "Jake, too..." She'll just take a minute...After catching on to the reverse plumbing, she is pleased to find enough hot water to resemble a civilized shower. Relishing the creature comforts, she's grateful for this unexpected luxury. The water hitting the floor sounds like an offbeat rainstorm on an old tin roof.

It reminds her of a long-ago Bible camp where the water wasn't as hot. Where days were spent learning about how to resist temptations of the night. Where the nights were filled with newly-found moves and emotions. Where a heart ached for an absent boy...

"Coffee?" Jake's naked arm appears around the curtain with a steaming cup of coffee. Startled, Jamie looses a shriek.

"Jake! Honestly...I mean...sometimes you are *too* quiet."

Then the coffee disappears and the voice on the other side of the curtain becomes a body imposing upon hers. "Jake. Jake! Shouldn't... shouldn't...Jake...somebody... minding the..."

Teenage memories are swept aside by adult passions. The shower's rain-like pitter-patter is drowned out by the thunder-like rumpling of the overburdened and embarrassed sheet metal floor.

Hot water and human desire both spent, Jamie and Jake stumble out and try to share the single towel. Laughing, they embrace. Jake kisses her, "Thanks. I needed that."

"I guess you did!" Jamie kisses him back and smiles. "Me, too..."

Jamie sips gratefully from the now merely warm cup of coffee. Jake dries her backside with the tenderness of a satisfied man.

She can tell when a man wants her for love and when he wants her for sex. She knows this moment was sex. And she likes that too. It is lovemaking, but visceral and urgent. She had had to discover how to abandon herself over to this making of love.

All the things her mother and Bible camp counselors and high school teachers and even girlfriends held about how to respond to her body's needs pointed in the other direction. Sex was for marriage. Sex was for procreation. Pleasure was a side effect...OK within bounds.

Women younger than she were more open to the sexual flame. Sometimes, she thinks, they may have gone too far in the other direction and leaving the love part behind. John had "liberated" her in many ways, finding different places – and positions! – to try. Slowly, she had shed that church-contrived shell from around her own body.

At the same time she never could see sex as something recreational, something to be shared among lots of different people, like her "swinger" girlfriend, Marsha, who had felt a need to confess over coffee some years ago. But Jamie did like the way that Jake sometimes "took" her with little talk or foreplay. Like now... like the man he is, powerless against the woman she is, unable to resist the taste and the smell of her.

Dressed, they re-open the store for business. Jamie and Jake settle at the table with more coffee, some rolls, and bacon cooked over the wood burner. Job appreciates that they've cooked enough to share with him. "Do you think they'll send Ellie and the baby home today?" Jake asks as he eats hungrily.

"I don't know. With preemies, they want to make sure they're at a good weight so they don't get into trouble. Make sure their lungs are working well, that kind of thing."

Jamie realizes how nice it is for a man to make her breakfast and enjoys hers slowly, feeling warm and slightly spoiled.

"Yes. I should have remembered that. Even though Daniel was early, on the rez there is no special care for preemies. No room. Or money." Jake's eyes are again far away in that memory of Oklahoma. Jamie doesn't interrupt.

After a minute, Jake looks at her. "What do you think of this adoption idea, Jamie? I mean, what do you *really* think?"

Jamie eyes him carefully, knowing it's not what she thinks, but what he thinks. The whole idea is still such a shock that she is of two minds right now. "Jake, how far have you thought this through? I mean, I think it's wonderful you are considering Ellie Mae's request. But...what kind of home can you give Maggie?"

Jake looks at her with questions in his eyes, uncertainly poised for her words to come. He takes a long sip of his coffee.

Jamie presses her point. "Children need a mother or female in their lives... especially girls. How will you give her that?"

"I've thought of that, Maggie. If my mom is still healthy, she will be a great role figure for her. I have no right to imagine Laura in this picture, but maybe for Maggie Mae....'

Jamie knows she's on very sensitive ground. Jake's face darkens as he feels the seriousness of her questions. His beautiful eyes, that she has learned to love, penetrate her.

"I guess I don't have all the answers yet. I know I will find work and make money. As a carpenter."

"Or a furniture maker," Jamie volunteers.

Jake's face brightens at this idea. "Yes! I can do that. I've dreamed I could make beautiful tables and chairs and clocks and other things that would be more than just objects.

"We believe that when you make something, you give it spirit. A spirit that flows through your self into the table or chair or bowl or whatever. Some believe you are just uncovering the spirit that was already there. Maybe it's both." Jake seems to get himself into a kind of trance when he talks of spiritual things.

"I feel your spirit in the totem pole, Jake."

Jake reaches out and takes Jamie's hand. "Not my spirit, *our* spirit, Magpie. When I was carving that wood, I could feel my hands being guided by the story we've lived here. And, Maggie, I couldn't tell this to Ellie because I wasn't sure she could understand, but I felt this other spirit speaking to me through that wood. I didn't understand who it was. But Maggie," looking hard and deep into her eyes, "I felt like one spirit was Daniel *and* someone else – together. Daniel and Maggie? This was something I didn't understand until I held her that first night. Like somehow I was meant to be here with Ellie. Meant to help bring this new life, this spirit, into the world."

Jamie looks back at Jake with equal intensity as if to lift some veil and peer within. Could such things be? Spirits entering and leaving and re-entering this world? Coming and going as people, as animals, as both? Yet she too felt something while writing Daniel's story. While face-to-face with the buck. While she ran her hands over the totem and the walking stick.

"Jake, you've helped me see many things about our world that I never saw before. And I have experienced things here that are...almost magical... but maybe that's not the right world. Spirit-filled?"

"Jamie, I've told you before you don't give yourself enough credit. You are one of the most spiritual people I've ever known, maybe as much as my grandfather. You see things. You hear things. Like the Voice that speaks to you. And like the power you have to hear...."

They both eye each other – words shrinking in the presence of something larger.

Then a rude jarring door, a blast of cold air, and stomping of feet... the moment is broken and a shy spirit flees.

Chapter 53
Hero

It turns out that the Valentine's Day blizzard is the last big blast of the winter. The day Ellie and Maggie Mae are sent home feels like spring. The air is almost balmy. The sun is bright. The drifts that had people and towns in a death-like grip only days before, now become round and tame sending rivulets of gathering waters down drives, curbs and roads. Soon the streams throughout these hills will course with lives of their own, overflowing banks and filling the great rivers to the south and west.

Doc Stephenson pronounces both mother and baby healthy. But he has kept both in the hospital for almost a week to make sure Maggie Mae is gaining weight and Ellie mends after that potentially disastrous delivery.

Jake and Jamie mind the store again while Cora drives over to pick them up. Even though Jake is listed as Maggie Mae's father, Cora tells them there are already whispers that the baby belongs to the Shelton Boy that Ellie had been seeing. But the Sheltons have moved away – to save their boy from eighteen years of child support, some say.

Jake is seen as a hero. So the whispers are less of suspicion and more admiration – at least from the women – for this mountain man who has been living in a cave! On the Widow Barlow's property! Cora has heard through Tim Shardson, one of Bob's deputies, that the sheriff had called Jake a "mountain of a man" down at the Eagles club a couple nights before and that seemed to cement public opinion.

Jamie and Jake have just said goodbye to the day's last customer when baby, mother and grandma come tumbling in. They haven't seen Ellie or Maggie Mae since their hospital visit. Jamie can see already that Maggie Mae is robust. And Ellie shines with the compound glow of youth and motherhood.

"Here we are, safe and sound!" Cora proclaims. "I'm sorry we're later than I thought. But the hospital was a little backed up with their discharges. And Doc Stephenson wanted a few more words with us."

"He said we're both doing great," Ellie said proudly. "But he wants to see us again in two weeks to make sure she's making her weight." She pauses before looking at Jake and adding, hopefully, "He said you can come too, Jake, if you'd like."

While Jake dotes on the baby and her mother, Jamie and Cora exchange knowing glances, and wordlessly share a lot of joy and a little apprehension.

Job is curled next to the wood stove, eyes closed, but with one ear cocked in case he hears his name or the clink of his bowl.

Cora says to Jamie, but to Jake and Ellie as well, "He asked about the...birth certificate. Because of Ellie's age, I guess someone could make a fuss...about statutory and all."

Jamie's eyes widen. "You mean...a...rape?" She can barely get the word out of her mouth.

"Yes," Cora says evenly.

"But..but...why?"

"Because Jake agreed to put his name on the certificate. And she's underage."

"I guess I don't...understand." Jamie is bewildered and sounds it. How could something like giving Ellie's baby a father be turned into something so...sordid? Jake and Ellie listen closely now as baby and dog sleep.

"I told him that wasn't the case. I told him Jake was a good man, father or no." Cora looks at Jake as she says this. He returns her gaze appreciatively. "I said this baby was going to have a good home. Even if..." and here Cora's composure falters. "Even if...it wasn't me and Ellie... raisin' her." Cora's eyes turn red quickly at the thought. Instinctively, Jamie reaches out to hug Jake's arm, in turn, wraps around Ellie. All are quiet for a moment, waiting for Cora to reclaim her resolve.

"Me and Ellie, we know this baby deserves a better home than we can give her. At least now. She's got her schoolin' to finish and it's all I can do to keep this place running. So...so...I'm goin' to do what I can to see her adopted out to a good family."

Ellie cries large, silent, teenage tears. She looks at Jake. Then down at Maggie Mae. Then back to Jake. And finally back to Cora and Jamie. "Me and Mama, we've talked it all out. And I know it's the right thing. But it's just so...hard!" And here she collapses into sobs. Jake wants to lend comfort and looks to Jamie for an OK to speak. Seeing Ellie starting to calm down, she gives a slight nod, even though she has doubts about what she suspects he's going to say.

Jake clears his throat. "Cora. Ellie. I want to talk about something I've been thinking about a lot for the last week." He pauses. Cora and Ellie look at him expectantly wondering what is on this man's mind. Jamie eyes him steadily wondering how the other two will react to what he's about to say. "I'm...I'm going to be leaving here." Seeing alarm build on their faces, he adds quickly, "Not right away. But soon. A month. Six weeks latest."

Cora jumps in first. "Where you going, Jake?

"Home."

It hangs in the air like a foreign word. Cora never conceived of Jake having a home other than these hills. "Where's home?" Cora asks gently.

"You mean Oklahoma?" Ellie jumps in excitedly. "He told me all about it, Mama. How he lived in a city. But his people lived on a real live reservation! His grandpa was the Medicine Man. And he helped bring babies into the world. Just like...just like...he did...with me. And Maggie Mae."

Jake looks easily at Cora and continues. "My home is in Tulsa. My people are Cherokee. Our home is a memory. The reservation is a forced relocation. Most of our young ones have left for work in Tulsa or Oke City. The ones who want to, anyway. But my grandfather lived there until his death a few years ago. As I said at the hospital, we have midwives on the rez who help bring babies into the world. Sometimes he was asked to bless the pregnancies. Or help out, if there was trouble birthing. And...sometimes... bless the spirits of those who...couldn't make it." His words are flat and empty, tinged with bottomless sorrow.

The women wait for him to continue.

"I'm a finish carpenter. But I do lots of other things too."

Ellie jumps in with a teenager's curiosity. "You didn't tell me you were Finnish! You just said you're Cherokee. That doesn't make any sense!"

At this, the adults stare at Ellie for a moment before breaking out laughing together. Ellie stares back wondering what she said that was so funny.

Cora explains. "Honey, a finish carpenter is someone who does the finishing work on a house. He's the skilled one. Has to really know what he's doing." Still, she eyes Jake trying to draw her own conclusions about his home and his business.

"Ohhhh..." Ellie replies trying to sound in the know.

As if on cue, sensing a pause in the adults' conversation Maggie Mae wakes and yawns. All eyes turn to the newborn to awe in her innocence and bathe her in love. "Helllooooo there, Maggie Mae!" Ellie coos. She looks at the clock on the wall behind the cash register. "It's been over four hours, Mama. Think she's ready for a feeding?"

"I 'spect so. But you better check her for a changing first."

Again on cue, Maggie Mae lets out that small wail of a newborn cry for a clean diaper and food, preferably at the same time.

"I can change her over here on the counter, Mama."

Job wakes up long enough to figure out what this new noise is, eyes Jake standing next to Ellie and decides his skills are not needed at this point.

Cora eyes her daughter a bit uncertainly. "You need any help with that, honey?"

"No, Mama, I got it. Jake, bring me that diaper bag. There's a towel inside. Lay it out there. Good. Now, run into the bath and get me a wash-cloth with some hot water splashed thru it. Ohh! She got a full one, Mama!"

Cora looks back at Jamie. "OK – too many cooks, y'know."

"I'd say so, Cora." Jamie and Cora settle back in their chairs. The young ones can handle this problem. The grannies talk about the bigger issues.

"What do you think?" Cora asks.

"About?"

"About adopting her out?"

"Honestly," Jamie chooses her words carefully, "Cora, like Ellie said, it's hard. It's so hard." Cora nods silently.

"But...I think it's the right thing to do. For Ellie. She's got a lot of growing up to do. She'll be a real good mother. When it's time. But...not now."

Cora looks over at her daughter and Jake leaning over and talking to the baby. For a second, she lets her mind play with possibilities.

Jamie guesses and leans towards her friend, "Cora, I think I know what you're thinking. Sometimes, I think I'd like him to stay too. But he needs to get on with his life. And I need to get on with mine. And you and Ellie need to get on with yours."

Cora looks at Jamie earnestly now, sincerely looking for some guidance. "Are you leaving us, too, Jamie?"

"Yes."

"With...*him*?" Was there a tinge of jealousy behind that question?

"No. I'm going back to Pittsburgh. Back to my children. And grandchildren."

"When?"

"Soon. Maybe about the same time as Jake."

"Will you come back? Ever?"

"Yes! Of course. I love my cabin here. But...not like this last year. I can't stay here that long."

"Because of your husband's business?"

"No. Not that. Though it needs tending after. At least for a little while. For *my* family, Cora. I came here to learn something about myself. And I have. But they need me. And I need them, too." Jamie looks steadily into Cora's eyes, wanting to make sure she hears the next words. "Some of the most important things I've discovered have been because of you. And Ellie. You're family now too."

"Yes, and you're family to us too, Jamie. That's why it'd be nice if you stuck around."

"I wish I could, Cora."

"All done, Mama!" Ellie sits back down in her chair and starts hitching up her sweater.

Jake holds Maggie Mae. He sways gently as Ellie gets ready to feed her. Both women notice with maternal approval his ease with the newborn.

"Mama, he knows what he's doing around a baby! I never saw a man who could do that."

"Sounds like Mister Jake is full of surprises," Cora says smiling.

"Well, I have...had...one of my own, Cora." Maggie Mae's tiny cry foils the approach of an uneasy memory.

Jake hands her to Ellie and, after waiting for mother and daughter to bond one more time, sits down again looking to Jamie for guidance. Another nod lets him know he can proceed when ready.

"Cora. Ellie Mae. I've been talking with Jamie about something really important. Something that involves all of us."

Maggie gurgles contentedly. All four smile at the newborn. Cora looks at her daughter, only a mother for a week and already experienced and comfortable with her nursing.

Jake tries to continue. "Like I said, I'm headed back to Tulsa. I'm ready now. And I know I can get work as a carpenter."

"A *finish* carpenter!" Ellie interrupts.

"Yes," Jake smiles. "But I'm also going to start a furniture building business. I know how to do it. Make really good pieces. I think in three years I can build it up to where that's all I'll need to do. Maybe even hire an apprentice or two."

Cora looks at Jamie.

"I believe him," she says. "Cora, you have to see the totem pole he made me for Christmas!"

"A totem pole? Isn't that what Eskimos make? Thought you said you were Cherokee?" Another round of chuckles follows Ellie's question.

"You're right, Ellie. Well, not Eskimo. But tribes from the Northwest. So it's not something that comes from my people. I studied them and made a couple...in Oklahoma. I like how they tell stories. So, yes, I made one for Maggie. To tell our story."

Jamie blushes a little at this privacy made public. Jake catches this and casts her an "oops, I'm sorry" face.

Ellie is oblivious, watching the baby. But Cora definitely feels a twinge of something. It seems like suddenly she'd like to hold a piece of this man for herself. This man whose life now calls him elsewhere.

Jamie jumps in to save the moment. "So, I think if he puts his mind to it, he can make a go of this furniture business. I've already put an order in for a table and set of chairs."

"I *know* I can, Maggie."

"How're you gonna get home, Jake?" Cora asks.

Jake looks at Jamie and then answers, "I'm going to fly. Jamie's offered to take us on her plane. I might have to ask you for a ride to Latrobe, though," he finishes with a smile.

"Oh, I think I can do that," Cora replies. Then asks, "Us?"

"Well, it'd be me and Job. And Jamie. 'Less she follows behind on her bike."

Cora brightens, "Jamie, you got to give me a ride on that thing! I haven't had a good bike ride in ages."

Jake says, "Cora, make her take you down to Ohiopyle. There's a place we rode to last summer that was magical."

Cora said, "Well, I don't want to be magical in the same way it prob'ly was for you two!"

"Mama!"

"I was just sayin'..oh well...of course I'd be happy to give you a ride over. Jamie, you flying with him to...Tulsa?"

"Yes. But I'd be flying right back. To Pittsburgh."

Jake clears his throat again. "There's one more person I'd like to have go with me, Cora."

"Oh?" she says this more brightly than intended, perhaps betraying the fantasy that she may have let play out longer in her head than she should have ever allowed. "Who's that?"

Jake looks quickly at Ellie and the baby, then back at Cora.

"Maggie Mae."

The words hang for an intensely long time. Ellie and Jamie look at each other knowingly, but Cora seems not sure of what she has just heard.

Finally, Cora breaks the silence. "Maggie Mae? Are you plum crazy?"

"I might be, Cora. But I've actually given this a lot of thought. As Jamie knows."

Cora shoots a glance to Jamie who confirms what Jake said. She looks back at Jake and stares with maternal protectiveness. Ellie, too, looks at Jake but more with wonder than with disbelief. "And what, exactly, are those thoughts Mister Jake?"

"Well, Cora, as I said, I'm going home. To work. To start a business. I can provide. For her. For...a second chance at a family. For a second chance at...everything."

"You got a wife back there?"

"To be honest, I don't know. I did when I left. But I won't lie. Things were bad. She blamed me for...Daniel. And I blamed myself too. And I've been gone almost two years."

"You talked to her at all?"

"No. She might think I'm dead for all I know."

"You want to go back to her?"

Here Jake looks quickly at Jamie. "Cora, I don't know. We'd have an awful lot of making up to do."

"And you bringin' a baby to help along the makin'up. If I was her, you might be as welcome as a skunk with kittens under the front porch."

Jake smiles, "I know that, Cora. Jamie reminded me that a girl needs another woman around. My mother is still young and healthy and would be a great model for Maggie Mae. And I *have* called my mother at Jamie's insistence. If things don't work out with Laura...well, I can take care of myself pretty well."

"Oh, I don't doubt *that* a second, sonny. It's my grandchild I'm worried about."

The adults look back at Ellie and Maggie Mae (who'd fallen asleep again, contented).

Here Ellie jumps in. "Mama, the way he brought her into the world and saved me along with her, I think if Jake says he can be a good father to Maggie Mae...well, I believe him, Mama. It's not like we'd be giving her away to strangers and God-knows-what."

Cora eyes her daughter carefully,

Jamie, who'd promised herself not to jump in the middle of this negotiation, says nonetheless, "Cora, I've learned an awful lot about Jake. And I have to say, I wasn't at all sure I wanted him as a neighbor, or anything else at first."

"So. You think ...!?" Cora shoots back.

"Yes. But I didn't think so at first. I wasn't sure this was a good thing. For him. And especially for Maggie Mae. Cora, I believe in Jake. When he says he can give Maggie Mae a good life, I believe him. I believe he wants to give her the very best life in the same way you and Ellie do. And...I will... help."

Cora raises one eyebrow at Jamie. "How're you gonna do that?"

Jamie looks at Jake, then back at Cora, addressing both: "I will do for her as I've done for my other grandchildren and put money away for her college."

"You gonna move down there?"

"No. I can't do that, Cora. I think you know that. But I can make other...arrangements."

Turning to Jake, Cora continues, "Why don't you just stay here? I mean, not here, here. I mean *here*. In Ram Cat. I mean, not like with me and Ellie or nothin'. Oh jeez! I don't know what I mean!" Cora's confusion seems to relieve the tension among the adults, although it seems to spark a different ray of hopefulness in Ellie.

"Cora," Jake answers soothingly, "in many, many ways I'd love to. But Oklahoma is where my people are. And I think I need to be part of that. My grandfather's gone. I need to help out more on the rez."

"The what? Oh, right. Your...reservation."

"Yes. The reservation. We don't have enough young men there to do all the work to keep our people healthy."

"Where's your pa?"

"He is in Tulsa with my mom. He came to the rez years ago as an Irish preacher to save the 'heathen'. He fell in love with my mother. I get my blue eyes from him."

"So, you want to raise Maggie Mae on the...rez?"

"No. Not necessarily. The schools in Tulsa are a lot better. But... would you mind if she learned things about my people?"

"You mean how to make totem poles?"

Everyone laughs at this joke.

"Well, maybe. But we are a proud people, Cora. Just like you and your family here. We have a written language and books and wisdom to pass down. We have successful trades. We have everything the white people have...before...before we were forced from our lands in Georgia and Tennessee."

"It was awful, Mama. I read about that in school last year. They called it the Cryin' Trail, or something like that didn't they, Jake?"

"Yes. The Trail of Tears. But that was a long time ago. Now we have to make the best of what we have where we are. We're poor maybe in some things. But we still have our bond to the earth and the sky – and the Spirit of both."

"It don't sound too awfully different from what we have here in Ram Cat. Not a lot of things. But a lot of love. Sometimes too much... or maybe the wrong kind."

"Awwww, Mama. Now don't start on Jimmy again."

"I was just saying..."

Jake interjects, "Cora, Jamie and I have talked. We plan to meet back here every year. In June. Maybe I could bring Maggie Mae with me."

Jamie shoots Jake a quick look of disapproval. This was not included in their own agreement nor was that agreement intended public domain.

Cora studies him again. Then she looks at Ellie who in turn eyes Jake expectantly, then Cora offers: "Jake, I know where your comin' from and I appreciate that. But I have a feeling it'd be better for Maggie Mae if she was raised with a clean slate, so to speak. Maybe when she's all growed up you can tell her about her...home...in ...Ram... Cat."

Cora starts crying. Deep, unexpected heaves of tears. Jake and Jamie kneel quickly beside her to support her unburdening – of a hard life and a tough shell that grew while other girls discussed make-up and the fit of their clothes; of a daughter who came too quickly; and of a granddaughter who also came too quickly and now would leave abruptly. Jake's arms surround both women, their heads falling before a shared fate.

Jamie is comforted by his strength and is embraced by an unexpected moment of peace. Her jumbled thoughts about the baby and Jake, Ellie and Cora, settle into a sort of meditation. It feels like when she is reaching out to the Voice. But now her voice, silently takes the form of a prayer. She prays to a God who always seemed too distant to bother with her life, or she with His. She prays that such an air of confusion and conflict, of fear-tinged hope and saddened joys will never stifle the breath of this babe now asleep at Ellie's breast. She prays that in their rough communion her voice will be heard and Maggie Mae will be blessed by the love of these adults and Whoever lies beyond.

Chapter 54

A Dance in the Sky

Cora drives Jamie, Jake and Job back to the cabin. The bright, warm day has yielded to a cool, bright evening. A full moon arches into the southeast sky. Orion, winter sentinel, seems ready to slip away until called upon again at the end of the year.

There hadn't been much more to say back at the store. Jake and Jamie both knew Cora and Ellie would have to talk over Jake's proposal. There was plenty of time to sort out details. Ellie asked again if Jake would go with them to meet with Doc Stephenson. The ride is short, but silent, each lost in thought about what their futures might become. They will be separating, yet their lives will be forever bound together by this baby.

Jamie wants to say something to Cora that will somehow make all of this right for everyone. But she knows words won't work now. She also knows this is not her decision. She will need to support whatever the three of them decide is best for Maggie Mae.

Cora turns the pickup into the steep part of the hill and makes it farther than she did before. It has been plowed and has a day's worth of good melt. "Jamie, I swear, I don't know how you've made it through this winter alive up here," Cora breaks the silence. "That cycle's no good in the snow. And I still can't believe you *walk* all the way to Ram Cat." Cora pauses and adds, "You neither, Mister Jake."

Cora guns the truck to crest the final slope and brings it to a stop at the clearing. Job is the first one out, bounding to the door hoping for a spot on the couch by the fire.

"Cora, I don't believe I would have if not for you and Ellie keeping me fed and giving me rides. Living out here tests you, no doubt about it."

"Well, you won't have to worry about that much longer, looks like." Cora watches Jamie pull on her gloves.

"I still have some walks to the store left in me," Jamie replies. "I'm not ready to kick Harley out of hibernation just yet."

"I'm always glad to give you a ride back up here. I'd offer to give you rides, too, Mister Jake. But tough as this ol' truck is, I don't think she could find her way back to wherever that cave of yours is hiding."

Jake laughs, "Have to agree with you there, Cora. But I'd be happy to show you sometime."

"Naw, that's OK Jake. I'm a 'town' girl now. I don't need to be running around these woods anymore. That's how I 'found' Ellie, if you know what I mean."

Jake and Jamie laugh. "I understand, Cora," Jake says. Jamie opens the door and both slide out. Jamie leans back into the cab to say goodbye.

"Cora, we'll be down to see you in a couple days. But if you need any help with Ellie and the baby, or the store tomorrow or whatever, just come on up."

Cora looks her straight in the eyes. "Jamie, I appreciate that. Me and Ellie still have some talkin' to do over this baby. I think she's gonna have a harder time lettin' go than she's lettin' on right now. It's only natural. But maybe with Jake raisin' her, and you helping, maybe we can find a peace with ourselves. We just need a little time."

"I understand, Cora. I really do."

Cora looks past Jamie at Jake opening the door and turning on lights. "Well, I see he knows how to make hisself right at home."

Jamie looks back over her shoulder at Jake grabbing several logs to start the fire. Turning back to Cora, she says, "Yes. I guess he does. He's been an incredible...friend."

Cora smiles broadly while she runs her hand over the wheel. "Oh, Jamie, you don't have to dance around that stuff with me. I've seen how you two sometimes make the goo-goo eyes. Too bad there's not two of him. Good men're rare as a steady paycheck 'round here. And he must be workin' you pretty good, 'cuz you look twenty years younger'n' when you first showed up."

"Cora!" Jamie blushes deeply in the darkness.

"Well, it's true!" Cora says, revving the truck. "OK, I got to get back to my babies. I'll see you in a couple days."

"OK, Cora. And thank you. For everything." Jamie straightens up and holds the door handle.

"You're welcome Jamie. But maybe it's me that has the bigger thankin' to do."

Jamie closes the door and waves Cora goodbye. The truck circles around the clearing, pausing when the headlights catch the still half-buried totem pole, then heads back down the drive to the road and Ram Cat.

Inside, Jamie is thankful for the fire Jake has already stoked into a good blaze. Job has settled for his familiar spot on the rug. Jake and Jamie step into an embrace.

"Thanks for starting the fire," she says leaning her head into his shoulder. "Cora said you knew how to make yourself right at home!"

"Just trying to make myself useful! And I sensed there was some woman talk you two left undone."

"Yes. She has a lot on her mind, Jake. You could see that. She's a very proud and private person. I don't think she opens up easily, especially when something's bothering her." Jamie takes off her boots, gloves and coat. She takes Jake's hand and they walk to the couch to sit down.

"You mean me taking Maggie Mae?"

"Yes."

"You think she might give her blessing?"

"She will if she's convinced you're the best person to raise her grandchild."

Jake takes Jamie's face in both of his hands. "I'm glad you spoke up for me."

"I really didn't want to get in the middle of it. Didn't want Cora feeling like we were ganging up on her and Ellie and taking Maggie Mae away from them."

"We would never do that, Jamie!"

"I know Jake." Jamie pulls both of his hands down and looks Jake in the eyes. "But you have to understand that this is a whole lot more than you being able to offer a good home with your family. This is giving up flesh and blood. And even though they know in their heads that you will be a good father to Maggie Mae, in their hearts they want to keep her here. With her family."

"I understand."

"I think you do, Jake. No, I *know* you do. Without you, maybe we wouldn't even have Maggie Mae with us. Or...Ellie either."

Jamie pauses, then continues. "But in a way, you don't know at all. Because you haven't felt that life growing inside you. You haven't felt that push through your whole body to bring this person out into the world. And you haven't felt that bond when this brand new life looks at you while you're feeding it with your body. No man can, of course. Even though you've come closer to it than most."

Jake looks back at Jamie waiting for her to continue. She looks back at him with a deep appreciation for his patience and strength. She also wants to make sure he won't be hurt if the women decide to reject his offer.

"Cora's had a hard life. It was made hard when she had Ellie maybe before she was ready. It was made harder when her husband died without leaving them anything but the store, their house and a beat-up truck. But she's a survivor. And her Ellie's a survivor too. They'll make a go of that store. And I just know Cora's thinking they've made it this far without any help, so maybe they could make it with Maggie Mae too." Jamie kisses each of Jake's hands hoping he understands her.

"I won't press it, Maggie. I've said what I wanted to say. If Cora and Ellie decide they want to raise her, of course, I'm not going to get in the way of that."

"I know you would bring her up right and with lots of love, Jake. All you can do now is wait and see what they decide. Right now, I'm hungry. Which means you're probably famished. Let's see what we can do with those steaks and potatoes Cora sent home with us."

That night in bed Jake holds her tight deep in sleep. Jamie loves this closeness and knows she will miss it badly when they leave. She loves both Jake's independent and nurturing sides.

Some men are totally independent beings bringing wives or girlfriends into their lives only for sex or food or some other form of ego-driven desire. Others are subservient, like puppies, boys really, clinging to women as they would their mothers. In their overwhelming need to please, they lose themselves; lose any sense of what it means to be a man. To her, and maybe most women, this is unattractive.

Jake is a rare blend: wanting and able to do things on his own; comfortable being alone, but also connecting with her feelings and thoughts intuitively. How his wife could cut him loose, drive him away in their grief, she can't understand. She smiles thinking of Cora's way of putting it: Around here good men are as rare as a steady paycheck. It's also true back home though steady paychecks are easier to find.

Jamie pushes her hips and bottom back against Jake, nesting her body into his, draws his arm over her shoulder and his hand beneath her cheek. Her smile remains long after sleep has stolen her away.

The next morning breaks with more warming air and full sun. After breakfast, Jake says he wants to hike back to the cave to make sure some bear hasn't moved in while they were gone. Jamie asks him to come back before dark. She wants him here. And it will be easier for everyone if he and Jamie are in one place when Cora returns.

She walks out to see them off. Job runs out and makes straight for the trail, knowing where they're headed. Without saying a word, Jake and Jamie walk together to the totem pole and stop. Then they push away the snow to reveal its full length and story. Job, confused, returns to the trailhead looking expectantly at the humans.

"It's so beautiful, Jake."

"Thank you. It's my best work."

"So far," she prods.

"Yes, so far. If Maggie Mae comes with me, I'll make one for her. One that tells her story."

"I think that would be good, Jake. If you do, I'll arrange to have a tree from these hills cut and sent to you, if you want."

"Jamie, yes. That would be good. But I think it would be some years before she could ever be old enough to understand where she came from and why."

Jamie reaches and runs her hand over the newly carved wood. Starting with Hawk. Around eye and beak of Magpie, reaching to the face of Bear. "This is so beautiful, Jake. Before we leave, we'll have to make sure this is exactly where we want it. I've been thinking of writing a story. A story for children."

"What kind of story?"

"Oh, I don't know. Maybe a story about how Bear, Magpie and Hawk all met and had grand adventures. And when it was time for them to go to the Big Sky, Great Father immortalizes them in this totem pole so they could be together always."

"Maggie, you're starting to talk like my people!" Jake laughs. "But I think that would be a very beautiful story. A story I could read to Maggie Mae as she grows."

Jamie doesn't reply to this, holding back for a decision two others yet must make.

They stand together, Jake's arm surrounding her. Job settles onto the snow thinking he's been fooled by the promise of a hike, but always glad to be outdoors.

A sharp cry in the air breaks the moment. Jake sees it immediately. A red tailed hawk cutting circles out of the sky. "Look, Jamie. A hawk flying in big circles. That is a good sign. Sometimes that means he's looking for a mate."

Jamie looks up, shielding her eyes against the sun. At first she can't see it. Then its cry is over the ridgeline. She strains to see it above the trees. "I can't see it, Jake. Where is it?"

Another cry. "It's right there. Circling over that ridge."

Jamie strains to see. But the cry doesn't match where Jake is pointing. Her eyes shift to the south. She sees it!

"No, Jake, I see it. Over there. To your right."

"Jamie, are you looking at the same spot I am? I can see him right there."

"No, Jake, he's over there. Look to the left of the chimney."

Another cry.

"Jake, there're two of them! Look! He's flying over to where you were pointing. Now I see him!"

Jamie and Jake watch in rapture as the two hawks circle each other, flying higher into the sky. Now they can hear two cries. They fly so high Jamie loses sight of them.

"Can you still see them, Jake?"

"Yes, barely. Aren't they beautiful?"

"I've never seen a mating dance like that. Is that what they're doing, Jake?"

"Yes. He's showing off. And she's following, obviously impressed."

"Uh-huh. And how exactly do you know that, Mister Audubon?"

"Jamie, I've seen it lots of times. Not just red tails. Peregrines. Eagles too. It's what birds do when they're thinking about birds. And the bees."

Jamie laughs at his joke. She wants to say something about Daniel, but decides that might ruin the moment for him, for them both.

The birds circle back down to the ridgeline, then disappear over its eastern edge.

"Oh, Jake, that was marvelous! Is there any way we can invite them to nest here in our woods?"

"Hmmmmm...that I don't know about that, Jamie. You have the right trees. You want to start raising rabbits? They might take that as an invitation!"

"No!!"

The moment is over.

"You two go! I'm going back inside. Maybe I'll start writing my story now!" They kiss.

"OK. We're out of here." Job perks up.

"We'll be back by five. Promise." Jake's voice is already trailing as he strides into the woods with Job racing ahead.

After Jake and Job head down the trail, now melted down to the last inches of hard pack, Jamie heads inside, but not before trying for one more peek at the ridgeline and the hawks now gone. She loves having Jake and Job close. But she also loves her time alone, time that grows more precious by the day.

After catching up on other things, including an all's-well fax from Rosa, she opens her journal and makes some notes covering all the days since Sheriff Bob came for her. She leafs back through the pages, numbering well over a hundred now. A small book really. She wonders if she'll let anyone read it and thinks no. But she will gift it to someone. Just not sure who yet.

February 29th

Maggie Mae is almost a week old now. Her mother, Ellie, is a woman-child of sixteen. Her grandmother, Cora is not even 40 I don't think. And here I am at 68. I might live long enough to see a fourth generation follow me. A great-great grandmother! Ooh now that sounds old!

I feel warmth, some kind of sisterhood, and a new part of myself side-stepping the seemingly obvious social differences between me and the 'Ram-Cats'. I feel the intimacy of feminine bonding. Before, it seemed, I saw myself in competition with everyone else.

I am thankful that Cora and Ellie have let me into their lives. I know women who measure themselves against other women by how powerful their husbands are, or how much money they have. I could feel their eyes on me at lunches or parties measuring me worthy or not worthy of John's success. From time to time, I was guilty of that, too.

I think John liked comparing me against the others in our circle. He often said how "proud" he was of me. What did that mean? I know he was trying to say he loved me. But sometimes it felt like a love angled through the prism of our prosperity. I was a "good" wife. I was a "good" mother.

After the children came, I kept my shape. I could go out with John and his business friends and their wives or girlfriends – hold my own...play the game, not embarrass myself or my man. Our girls grew up without many of the money-related problems I saw creep into other families.

And when one of the other men, perhaps disappointed in his wife or family or whatever, tried to jump the fence, I never had a problem saying no. Nicely, but firmly. (Are you reading this, John?)

As young mothers we would compete through the lives of our children. We all wanted them to be as successful with their grades or their sports as our husbands were with their jobs. If one of them had an accident or got in trouble, then the mother was somehow sentenced in our eyes as well.

The awfulness of all this hit me the day Janice Stuckey killed herself. Her son got started into drugs when he was in high school. Then he got arrested for trying to sell them. I remember how we all tried to "help" Janice. But, really, it just gave us a chance to cluck about someone else's misfortune.

When her son got arrested again for stealing and got sent to prison it was awful. But it seemed like Bob, her husband, was no help to her.

Janice was never very strong I don't think. And when her world started collapsing none of us really tried to stop it. It was almost like a bomb had hit down the street and we gathered at the crater to look in and stare at the damage.

She just got smaller and smaller. So the day Bob came home from a trip and found her dead in bed (pills) we all acted horrified and cried big tears at the funeral and hugged Bob and his grief. But really it was just one more thing to talk about. And feel good that it wasn't ME they were talking about.

There was no sisterhood among us, even when a few of us burned our bras and went to consciousness-raising classes. We were too worried about our husbands keeping their jobs and getting promoted. And our children doing well and being popular.

When our children were grown and some of the men retired, where were those friendships that we'd had for years, even decades?

I remember going to a Garden Club party a few years ago and sitting around the table looking at these women I'd known for 30 years. They looked at me. We had nothing to say! Nothing! Oh, the usual about husbands retiring. Or divorcing. Or dying. Or the kids. (Now grandkids too.) But nothing really about US. How WE felt. If we felt anything at all. It seemed so sad.

And it made me think of Janice Stuckey. Alone in her bed. Taking all those pills. Knowing they were probably her last. And wondering what she thought then. Was she ending this life to go on to another? Or just ending it because this one was already over even though she was still breathing?

I had no idea then. I think I have a better idea now. I have Cora and Ellie to thank for that. And now Maggie Mae, too, in her own, one-week old way.

Can I explain how or what or why? Maybe...

Cora is what my grandmother used to call "salt of the earth." She hasn't had much education, but she's smart. She hasn't had a husband, or even much of a boyfriend from what I can tell, in most of her life. Still, she's managed that store and raised Ellie. She's tough. She knows who she is and she's not impressed by money or position or fancy cars. She takes people where they're at. If they are honest and good to her, she will return that double. If they aren't, then she has no time for them.

I feel blessed that she figured out who I was maybe even before I knew who I was. So she looked past John's money and our cars and saw something in me that said maybe we could be friends. Real friends. And that's what's happened.

Now she and I can just look at each other and know what the other is thinking. If she hadn't chosen to be open with me, I don't think there was any way I could force it.

After this winter at the cabin, if I hadn't had her looking after me I might well have given up and gone back to my other life defeated.

I can see the same strength starting to blossom in Ellie. I can write this without hesitation – I care for her as much as I care for my own girls.

That's why I hope Jake won't be too hurt if they decide to raise Maggie Mae. I hope, too, that Jake isn't looking to raise Maggie as just a substitute for Daniel. I don't think he is. But maybe I need to ask him just to make sure.

Lately I have been wishing I could spend the rest of my days right here. In this cabin. In these hills. Growing old with Cora and Ellie and Maggie. Riding my motorcycle in the summer. And getting an old pickup like Cora's for the winter. Writing and walking and exploring and LIVING to my heart's content. But then that would be a special kind of selfishness that would be too hard to explain to my girls and my grandkids. So I will go back. And I will try to bring this year's lessons with me.

Maybe I can help my girls and grandchildren find their own Voices. Maybe I can keep them from becoming women who only see life through their husbands' mirrors and then one day end up at a Garden Club luncheon not knowing who they are, or if they ARE at all. And, God help me, keep them from facing a morning like Janice Stuckey's last.

Jamie puts her pen down and stares at that last sentence. Then she starts to cry. Long, slow, silent tears. Tears she never shed for Janice Stuckey who deserved them more than anyone.

"I'm sorry, Janice. You deserved a better friend than I was then. I hope somehow, some way, you're in a better place now. If I see you again, I *will* be a better friend than I was then. I promise."

Jamie closes her eyes to the afternoon light streaming through the south-facing bay window. Had she opened them, she might have seen two red-tailed hawks perched on the large second limb of an old white oak fifty yards down the trail leading to the creek.

Chapter 55

Deadly Business

Jamie wakes from her nap. Almost three. The afternoon sun has made the living room toasty warm. She walks to the window to bask. The south trail is a swath of mud now, a clear cut through woods patchy with snow. It would be a slippery hike, but she wonders if trout wait for her at the bottom. Several minutes go by. Jamie follows the lazy dripping of an icicle melting from the eaves. A thought rushes in, and she hurries back to the journal to capture it:

From the earth to the clouds, from clouds to the earth, water does as water must. But water leaves beauty and nurtures life in its passing. I know I must do what has been given me to do – and maybe even leave something beautiful on the way. But what is it? It's like I have spent this year in school. What have I learned in school this year?

In my wildlife encounters, I did not react out of fear. Rather than flipping into attack mode I have witnessed these unknowns with respect... this teaching me that spirit and possibility lurk in the unknown. Try not to scare them (or yourself) off.

She pauses. Then continues.

I think my toughest job will be how to deal with Children's Hospital and my Barlow Associates commitment. How can I use what I learned to the life awaiting my return?

One thing I have learned on my bike, especially on the back roads, is the importance of not over compensating (important to be quick to respond, but not over-respond) and the importance of easing into a slide, befriending (so to speak) and giving up some control to the slide in order to maintain overall control.

I know I have to do something. But if I do the wrong thing, or even too much of a good thing, I could handicap the company, maybe even the hospital too.

Rich Larson at Barlow. That is a really tough one. How can I befriend his ambition and put it to work FOR the company? If I can figure that out in my last month here, I will be as ready as I can be to go back. He is a snake for sure. But he knows how to make money. John respected him even if he didn't like his business ways. Would he ruin Barlow? Would he make it even bigger and better than John had? I have to figure this out! Oh John, why can't you be here???

Maybe the rest of my time here should be a bit like the way I've learned to bank oxygen as my hike brings me to a steep hill – this has taught me to gather myself up, focus my wits and resources, bank up my strength – so I'll be ready and stronger for any challenge, business or personal.

I am starting to see that there are things calling for my notice beneath the noise of my day-to-day dealings…trying to give me the messages and the fullness life is trying to gift me. Maybe I've been doing it the hard way – on my own – maybe my spirit, or the Voice, or maybe life itself is trying to speak to me, guide me.

Jamie leans her head back, knits her hands behind her neck and closes her eyes.

Her reverie is invaded by the rumble of a truck pressing hesitantly along the ruts and heaves of her drive. Cora? Doesn't sound quite like hers, or Sheriff Bob's either. Who else could it be? She looks out the window as the front grill of a large black pickup pulls into view around the last turn into the clearing. It's not anyone she knows! Instinctively, she moves against the wall and looks from the side of the window as the truck moves slowly towards the cabin.

Heart pounding, Jamie steps into the bedroom and quickly removes the shotgun from its case. She grabs the box of shells and moves back to the window. Two men in leather bomber jackets, coveralls and knee-high rubber boots get out of the cab slowly, scanning the clearing and then assessing the cabin. The one on the passenger side has his right hand stuck in the coat pocket.

These are *not* locals. The clothes are all wrong and the sunglasses seem…*sinister.* Jamie can't quite figure it out, but she knows these two are trouble. She loads the shotgun while watching the men trade hand signals. The driver walks over to the totem pole and trailhead. The passenger walks up to the porch, pauses, trying to look in the window. Without even knowing how, she is certain this is the man who stole the fax.

The brief sheen of gunmetal gray drawn slowly from his pocket throws her. Jamie's heart is pounding faster than she ever knew it could. What to do? These are Larson's thugs, she's sure of it! They are not here for some of Cora's soup. And they're sure not the sort of men who negotiate. They have a mission. And that is for John Barlow's widow to join him. Now.

She can see the man on the porch nod and signal to his partner covering the back. Soon she will be trapped. The man on the porch walks to the door. Jamie sinks deeper into the corner's shadow. She hears the knob turning. A shaft of light stabs into her sanctuary. A pause.

"Miz Barlow?" The voice is rough. Factory-educated. If that. Or less, probably.

"Miz Barlow, you home?"

Jamie knows she dare not answer. The door opens an inch wider.

"Miz Barlow, we know you're here. We're just here to talk."

'Sure you are,' she says to herself.

Her shotgun is lowered now at waist level, its butt planted against Jamie's right hip.

"Miz Barlow, we're comin' in. To talk. That's all."

Silence.

Then the door pushes open swiftly. A step. A thundering shot! A howl! And a body falling heavily to the floor.

Jamie is stunned. Did she shoot the gun? Did her shot hit the man now lying and bleeding in her house? Life accelerates. She moves as through a dream. Swift and slow simultaneously.

Jamie looks out to see the second man run and jump into the truck. She lurches from the shadow to see the fallen man bleeding heavily from his left leg, but still alive, cursing his misfortune and stupidity. Without thinking she leaps over her would-be assailant and onto the porch as the truck starts up and gets kicked into gear, tires spitting mud furiously. She runs into the daylight yelling at the driver to stop. He replies with a wild shot through the passenger window that misses Jamie, but shatters the cabin's window. Turned around, the driver tries another shot from his window that misses both Jamie and the cabin and ricochets into the woods. Then he punches the truck into second gear trying frantically to get down the hill and not giving a thought to his partner wounded – or dead – left behind.

Dropped prone on the porch, Jamie sighs, exhales, and returns fire with her remaining shell. She hears an impact, but then truck and driver disappear and roar off down the hill.

The silence that suddenly returns disguises eerily the last seconds of mayhem. Heart still trying to make its way out of her chest, Jamie staggers to her feet. Sweat slides down her face. Her hands shake uncontrollably. Slowly, time and reality reestablish themselves. What just happened?

Then another moan reminds her of unfinished business splattered inside her doorway. Jamie steps back onto the porch, eyes the man with a mix of fear and pity, then steps over him and almost onto the gun lying inches from his extended hand. She kicks it several feet away, walks over and picks it up. She holds it away from her body with two fingers, afraid it, too, is still alive. The longish barrel looks like it has an attachment. A silencer? Maybe Sheriff Bob can tell her. Sheriff Bob! She needs to call him and tell him about the getaway truck.

Her hands still shaking, Jamie dials her phone.

"Sheriff's office."

"This is Jamie Barlow. I need to speak to Bob right away!"

"He's not here now. This is Deputy Ricks. Is there some way I can help you?"

Stupid her! Should have called his cell phone number first. She didn't want to get others involved. Not yet. No choice now.

"Yes! You need to call him right away and tell him two men just broke into my cabin. I shot one, but the other got away in a black pickup truck."

"You said you SHOT a man? Is he dead? Do you need an ambulance? What was your name again?"

"Jamie Barlow. B.A.R.L.O.W. I live two miles south of Ram Cat on Fire Tower Road. Yes. I need an ambulance. Or he does. He's still alive. I think he is. But Sheriff Bob's got to catch the truck." Jamie could feel the adrenaline rushing through her voice now. Talking too fast, but she couldn't help it.

"Bar-low. South of Ram Cat. On Fire Tower Road. You that rich lady got that mountain man who saved that girl and 'er baby's lives?" The man's drawl highlighting his ineptitude.

She is in no mood to argue or whatever. This is maddening! "YES!" She tries deliberately to slow down so Deputy Whoever knows it is time to stop talking. "Now, please call Bob and find that pickup. I couldn't tell for sure, but I doubt he's headed toward Ram Cat. And get an ambulance out here quick! Or just send a hearse whenever you want."

"Could I have your number? It's showing UNLISTED on our screen. That was a heckuva thing he done."

"724 666 1345."

"724 666 1345. Got it."

"Deputy, call your sheriff NOW. Tell him I'll be waiting here with MY gun and my prisoner who may or may not be dead if you don't get help here right away." She disconnects and walks over to the man lying in a growing pool of his own blood. He is barely conscious. Could she let him bleed to death? Would serve him right. But if he dies maybe there would be no way to connect him to Larson. Especially if the other guy gets away. But she doesn't know anything about first aid. John knew everything. As an Eagle Scout he could splint a broken limb, suck out snake venom, and tie a tourniquet.

A tourniquet! She can't remember much. But instinctively she gets a rag from the pantry. Kneeling next to the man, she wraps it above the wound, fierce in its redness and gushing. She ties it off. She needs to twist and tighten it. The wooden spoon is on the counter. She stabs it through the knot and twists it tight until the pulsing flow lessens, then only seeps. Well, if he dies, it won't be for her lack of trying. Or that deputy's "gift" for gab. Now she can hear a siren in the distance. She hopes it is for her. Or her 'prisoner.' Who seems now to be completely unconscious.

Then she hears a dog barking. Getting closer. What the? Of course.... She looks through the doorway to see Job bounding across the clearing. In three more leaps he is next to the man's feet barking furiously.

"Job! Job! It's alright! I'm OK!!" Then he springs again into her arms and licks her face.

Seconds later Jake appears in the doorway completely out of breath. "MAG..GIE!"

She stands and pushes him back out to the porch with her hug. His body is rigid and he looks like he is in attack mode. "Are...you...O...K?"

"Yes. But he's not."

The siren grows louder. Definitely on its way. Would be here in a minute. Maybe less.

"What...what happened?" He stares past her at the shattered window, as though that suggested even greater violence than the man sprawled on the floor.

"I think...I think...I think Larson sent them...to kill me."

Just then the enormity of what happened overwhelms Jamie and she breaks into sobs against Jake's coat. The siren has turned into the drive.

Still holding Jamie in a protective hold, he looks at the man on the floor. "Is he...dead?"

"No...not yet. I don't think," she manages between sobs. "Oh Jake!"

The ambulance whirls into the opening and pulls next to the porch. Job starts to bark and bare teeth, but one look from Jake lets him know this is not danger. The two EMTs jump out and in seconds are working on the downed man, not even bothering with questions.

Jamie and Jake retreat to the southern end of the room. They stare out the window, saying nothing, seeing nothing. Jamie is still in shock and leans heavily against Jake's chest, his arm holding her up.

After another eternity of minutes, they hear another thump. Turning, they see a gurney being set up and watch in silence as the EMTs lift the wounded man. Then they wheel him to the back of the ambulance.

Almost robotically, Jamie follows Jake's lead towards the doorway. They step onto the porch as the ambulance door is slammed shut. One EMT jumps into the driver's side and starts up the engine. The other walks over with a clipboard, needing some quick information.

Jake asks Jamie's question. "Is he going to live?"

"Yeah, he's going to make it. Took a lot of buckshot. Just nicked the femoral artery though. If she'd cut it, not sure he would've." The EMT added, "Nice tourniquet. Where'd you learn that?"

"My ...my...husband. He's...was...an Eagle Scout."

"OK. So you're not her husband?" This EMT looks so young. Like a teenager. And in great shape.

"No," Jake responds. "Just a friend."

"OK. We got to get him to the hospital. But I need some quick information. Then Sheriff'll be here and he'll follow up."

Jamie gives him her name, phone number and a brief description of what happened. The EMT gives here an admiring look when she explains how she shot the intruder.

"That's pretty impressive, Miz Barlow. He was carrying a serious weapon. I think he was going to do you in." Jamie shudders and moves closer against Jake.

As he leaves, the EMT reminds them not to move anything until the Sheriff gets there. Then the siren is on and the ambulance circles around and heads down the hill and to the hospital.

Jake leads Jamie to the sofa and both slump into it. Again, no words. Jamie cries again silently. Then she stretches out, laying her head in Jake's lap. His fingers stroke her hair gently, easing her into a light nap.

Job, sensing the seriousness of what's happened, assumes a protective position at the base of the sofa, away from his usual place on the rug and closer to his humans as well as the door.

Bob shows up an hour later at the beginning of evening light. The sound of his truck awakens them both. Jamie feels a jolt of panic before realizing that this truck is not a threat. They all walk out to greet him.

As the sheriff gets out, he scans the scene with a professional's eye. He pauses when he sees the bullet hole through the front window, then walks over and shakes Jake's hand and gives Jamie a hug. "You al'right?" The sheriff is definitely in detective mode. He looks tall, straight and very serious.

"Yes, I think so."

"Those boys came here for serious business. You're a lucky lady. And a decent shot, looks like also."

"Bob, I've never been so scared in my life!" Then the words come spilling out. "I saw his gun and he called for me and said he wanted to talk, said he was from Larson and the other guy was going around the back. I just hid in the corner and when he stepped in I closed my eyes and pulled the trigger. Bob, I didn't want to hurt him. I just wanted to scare them out of here. I'm so sorry. Is he going to live?"

"Whoa, Jamie! Slow down. First, yes, he's going to live. But I suspect he's going to spend a lot of years behind bars cursing the day he messed with you. His sidekick, too."

"You caught him?" Jamie's eyes, still big, now focused on the sheriff for the first time.

The sheriff seems to get taller with this question. He has a look of pride on his face. "Yes. Your second shot was a hit, too. Caught his rear quarter panel and sprayed buckshot into the left rear. He went flat about three miles down the road. We got him trying to put the spare on. Tried to give us a story about the flat. But we saw the marks and the holes. Then saw his gun under the seat."

Bob looks worriedly at Jamie. "That wasn't meant to scare you, Jamie. That was meant for a quick, silent hit."

With those words, Jake's arm tightens around Jamie. It's beginning to dawn on all three that this day could have had a much more tragic ending.

"Do you have the other gun, Jamie?"

"Yes, inside."

"Is that what messed up your window?"

"NO! He never shot. That was from the guy trying to get away. He took another shot, but I think it went in the woods."

Bob walks back to his truck and gets a camera. He takes a picture of the window. Then the blood stains in the doorway. "This is as far as he got?"

"Yes."

"EMTs said you even tried to stop his bleeding." Standing up, Bob smiles. "You've had quite an afternoon, Jamie."

"Well, one of these is enough, thank you very much!"

Bob walks over to the south wall, looks closely at the window. Jamie and Jake follow him over thinking he sees something. Then his hand traces the wall, first up, then down. Finally, it stops close to the corner next to the fax machine. He pulls out a pen knife and digs into the wall. Turning, he holds up a bullet.

"I think this will be helpful evidence in case our getaway guy tries to weasel out of his participation in today's 'activities.'"

Bob walks back outside and takes a few last photos in the fading light. He tries to make out the tire tracks from the black pickup, hoping to match then with the tracks at the site of the flat. Walking back to Jamie and Jake, he says, "Jamie, I need you to come down to the department tomorrow and fill out a report. It's possible an assistant D.A. will want to talk with you too. We'll want to keep these guys on ice until they come to trial."

"Do I have to press charges now? Jamie asks.

Bob and Jake both look at her with disbelief. "Why'd you want to wait at all? He meant for those two to kill you."

"Well, we don't know that for a fact." Jamie looks from one man to the other, knowing they can't believe what they're hearing. "Look, I may need to wait. Can you figure how long I can wait to press charges?"

"Jake, maybe you can talk some sense into this woman."

Jake is still holding Jamie. "I'll sure try," he says.

"I shot someone. I can't believe I shot someone." Jamie seems to finally realize what she did. "Are you going to charge me with anything?"

"No! Don't go getting all willy-wally on us, Jamie. You defended yourself is all," Bob reminded her. "It was him or you." Bob turned toward his truck. "Look, I need to follow them to the hospital now. I'll be back tomorrow. Jamie, you can forget about coming to the department. We'll try and handle it from here. I forgot your only transportation is your feet and your Harley. Jake, take good care of this woman tonight."

"Sure will, Bob. Thanks for the good work."

Jake cleans up the blood on the floor and fixes supper for them while Jamie takes a shower. He gets a beer for himself and a 'Jack' for Jamie. They sit and talk quietly by the fire until the whiskey achieves its therapeutic levels. Jamie's eyes – and brain – lose their focus. Jake carries her to bed. His eyes flood with tears, as likely his guard falls and his heart and head become flooded with the real possibility of this day's alternate ending.

Standing over her, he whispers hoarsely, "Magpie, if they had silenced you today, I don't know how long I could have survived."

Jake begins chanting in Cherokee. Jamie listens to the music of the words. "O-gi-do-da ga-lv-la-di he-hi...." The words come in a smooth, careful rhythm. After he finishes, he tells her, "That is the Lord's Prayer in Cherokee. It's all I can think to say."

Chapter 56
Path Interrupted

The days after Jamie's "unwelcomed guests" are filled with the sheriff, detectives and all manner of intrusions. She has to let Stella know what happened and that, atop Jamie's legal procrastinations, prompts an hour-long phone call to her attorney. The first of many, no doubt.

The would-be assassins provide sexy, sinister, front-page news in the local weekly paper, *The Echo*. Crime is not unheard of in these hills, usually of the petty sort. But attempted murder! Dark rumors of hit men! Countless speculation of who – and why? Then, most improbably of all: the widow Barlow shooting straight and true to maim one and help capture the other. Well, this is almost too much! A sell-out for the weekly. A story that sets the hills and valleys buzzing loud enough to be heard almost all the way to Pittsburgh.

Truth be told, Ellie's "Blizzard Baby" story pales by comparison. Jamie gets word of her notoriety first from Sheriff Bob. She is not altogether thrilled that her life has become the talk of the county, however unavoidable it is. She knows that her supposed wealth by itself is an easy source of gossip. John had prepared her for this endless publicity and she learned both not to listen to it, nor to be a source for it. But he didn't prime her for this tabloid status.

Although Sheriff Bob talked to Bill Hearst, *The Echo's* publisher, who agreed to keep his reporter and photographer from bothering Jamie, it is still front page news in the following week's paper, but below the fold and mostly a summary of the previous content. A fire of suspicious origin at the VFW replaces it for the lead.

Despite, or maybe because of all the intrusions – warranted or not – Jamie feels an overwhelming need to escape. Not from, but deeper into, her woods. She manages a long hike each day to take her mind off of this mess and look for signs of another spring and a sense of her own renewal. Fortunately, the signs are everywhere. Patches of daffodils. Dogwoods budding up. The creek flowing full and clear.

Without even knowing why, she doesn't ask Jake to go with her. She wants these hikes to be hers alone. She is grateful that Jake senses this and doesn't push to go with her, instead retreating with Job to his cave to face the business of pulling up stakes.

Nearly eleven months of hiking the property has put Jamie within a hundred and fifty miles of her virtual destination: the northern end of the Appalachian Trail – Mount Katahdin in Maine. "Katahdin." It has an almost mystical sound to her. "Greatest mountain" in the language of the Abenaki. A holy place to them. Just as these forested hills and valleys and rocks and streams have become holy to her.

Will she have enough time to finish her two thousand-plus mile hike? She doesn't know. But she's learned so much on this trail. About nature and about herself. How far she's come, from those fist tentative steps down to the creek and the fear that drove her back (up the path) to the cabin's safety that first time she saw Jake and Job. Now she knows these lands as intimately as John and Jake. And she knows both of them better in context of the habitat that holds them. These lands have spoken to her in shouts and whispers. Often she heard them only in the darkness of her nights and in the unguarded silences of her mind. And she wonders: had they been calling to her for years?

Now she hears them in clear, strong voices. Voices. Voices. The Voice.

Her Voice?

She feels something present and alive with each step, each breath, each detail emerges from a once-foreign, now deeply intimate landscape. Jamie steps through arbors of rhododendron, reaches for the soft caress of hemlock and white pine, feeling the supple give of cool, damp earth. She moves as one with all that surrounds, not hearing, not seeing, not smelling, not touching, not tasting. Yet hearing and seeing and smelling and touching and tasting all. She feels the deep pang of disappointment when the trail leads back to the cabin, as it always does – as it always must.

Jamie is just coming out of the woods when a truck pulls up. Jamie's heart starts pounding at the sound of a truck and she freezes by the edge of the woods, close to her totem pole. Then realizing it is Cora, she moves into the clearing and waves. Cora throws the truck into park, jumps out and runs over to Jamie. They hug each other and cry for minutes before speaking.

"The whole county's *still* talking about that man you shot! And the one you almost shot! They were going to KILL you, Jamie!!" Cora takes both of Jamie's hands in hers and presses them against her heart. "The sheriff is sure proud of you. Ellie Mae and me too. But it helps to just lay eyes on you. I don't know what I'd a done if they'd...if...they'd...." That thought triggers another round of tears and hugs.

"But Jamie, I got so much to tell you. Probably things you haven't heard about yet. Bob said you wanted your peace and quiet, and I understand that. But I had to come up. I brought you some food. And, oh Jamie! I was just so *worried*! Ellie too. So I had to come up. Had to!" She looks at Jamie to see if she might have made a mistake coming by so soon.

"I'm so glad to see you, Cora. I'm really glad you came." Jamie stretches her long arms around Cora again. She really is glad to see and feel the simple fortitude of her friend.

Cora takes Jamie's hand and pulls her toward the truck. "Come help me unload some groceries. Made a big pot of our favorite stew. Enough for you and Mr. Jake for a couple days. I sure hope he is staying here watching your back." Then she giggles and adds, "your backside too."

The women carry the food into the house and put it away. Cora looks around carefully. "Wow! I wondered what your cabin looked like inside. It looks down-home cozy. Fits you perfect."

Jamie makes coffee and they sit. Jamie fills Cora in on her part of the drama.

Jamie figures Cora and Ellie must have found out details of the shooting from Sheriff Bob when he asked them to look at some photos, hoping to jog their memories. He suspected that the would-be killers might be the same ones who came to Ram Cat last fall asking about Jamie. But he was disappointed that the two women didn't recognize either of the men.

"I'm sorry, Jamie, but the photos was of two of the meanest looking men I've ever seen. But they wasn't the same ones who come asking after you."

Bob had told Jamie that the new suspects confirmed his worst suspicion – this was probably a murder for hire. Unless he could find a way to make his prisoners talk, it would be very difficult to trace back to the actual person who planned Jamie harm.

Jamie shivers at this. Both because she fought off professional killers, and because she has good reason to know exactly who was behind this. She also knows he is smart enough to leave not one bit of evidence or circumstance linking him to this crime.

"Are you sure you are OK?" Cora wants to know again.

"I've settled down Cora. I think I was more shook up the day after it happened. I've done a lot of walking these past couple days." Both women hold the hot mugs in their hands to warm themselves. Each is different. Each one has a special meaning for Jamie. She has collected them for years.

Cora takes another sip from her Tabasco mug and continues. "Bob said Jake got here before he did."

"Yes. He heard the shots and came running. It scared him something terrible. Even Job was ready to attack."

"He's a good man, Jamie. But not the kind of man you want to cross, if you know what I mean." Cora raises her eyebrows knowingly.

"Yes, I think I do, Cora. I was very glad he and Job showed up when they did. I'm kind of glad they didn't get here earlier. The guy in the truck might've shot them!"

"You don't think..."

"Yes, I do."

Cora stands and takes her mug to the kitchen area, running her hands across things and looking at the pictures and books lying around. Jamie smiles to herself, realizing that Cora's probably never seen such a "well-stocked" cabin.

Jamie stands to follow her. "Cora, I'm going to have to go home for a few days to try to find out who paid to have this done. As much as I hate to leave before my year is up, the sheriff won't put this off. There is only one person who would have done this, but I'm not sure he would have paid someone to kill me...just discredit me." Cora turns toward Jamie with a questioning look.

"I'd like to get my hands on whoever would do such a thing. I hope you can get him arrested." Cora takes both cups and washes them in the sink. "Another thing, Jamie. Ellie Mae and me have talked it all out. 'Bout Maggie Mae, I mean. We're going to let Mr. Jake take her and raise her good. Ellie Mae could surprise me and change her mind, but I don't think so. She was sure of it the night Maggie Mae was born. She's still sure."

"Are *you* sure?" Jamie looks long and searchingly at Cora.

"Yes. Yes I am. It's hard to give up blood. Especially my first grand-baby. But I am convinced that Mister Jake will be a good Daddy to her. And you tell me if I'm wrong, but I have a suspicion you'll be keeping an eye on her too."

Cora puts her coat back on and starts toward the door. "Ellie wants a chance at a education. She knows she has to have something because the store won't carry us forever.

"And she wants to find a man who will marry her. She wants to have children with him. She seems pretty sure that Mr. Jake is meant to raise Maggie."

Jamie opens the door part way and says, "He will need to spend some time with Maggie Mae before I take him back to Tulsa. How about you four stay here at my cabin while I'm home? You can work during the day and spend the evenings and nights up here to let Jake bond with Maggie Mae and see how it feels to him to be her daddy."

Cora eyes her steadily and with appreciation. "That's a great idea, Jamie. Thanks so much."

"You brought enough food for all of us. Why don't you, Ellie and Maggie come on by after you close the store and tell Jake the news? I won't be leaving for a few days. I have to get my plan in place for when I go home and the sheriff has more he wants to talk to me about. When I'm done, I'll come back for a week or two to spend a little more time with Jake. Then I'll take Jake, Job and Maggie Mae on home to their new lives." At this, Jamie's eyes well with tears. That this most wonderful time of her life is about to come to an end is more than she dares to think about just now.

Cora and Jamie hug each other again and Cora hustles on out to the truck. She turns and calls back, "You find out who tried to do this. No one is going to try to hurt my good friend and get away with it." Cora's voice cracks. She is shedding a few tears, too. "See you a little after seven tonight."

Jamie goes inside for a shower and to get started planning her return home on March 8th. She had called Stella and Ted to move the meeting with Barlow Associates up to March 11th. She made it almost eleven months. With all that has happened that seems a pretty good run: a full measure of whatever she came here for.

Jake and Job should come back in an hour or so. Company for dinner. "Hmmmmmm," she says to herself. "I guess this is the start of going back to real life."

A life that has forever changed.

Chapter 57

Maggie Mae

Jake and Job show up right on time. For a man who refuses to wear a watch, Jake has uncanny punctuality. Jamie walks out to greet them as they emerge from the greening woods. The early evening air is sweet with coolness and fragrance. The sun seems reluctant to surrender its brilliance and spring warmth. A cardinal sings in a nearby oak, hoping to attract a mate. Even Job is distracted from his usual greeting, dazzled by a cacophony of scents that humans can only guess at. He accepts a quick scruff across the head before bounding behind the cabin in search of something new that's just caught his nose.

Jamie and Jake hug and kiss. Each can feel these embraces are now numbered. As they hold each other a few seconds longer, Jamie can also feel a distance developing, an emotional separation that comes before the physical one. It saddens her, as she's sure it must sadden Jake as well. She had felt this before as John entered the final months of his sickness. She thought she would never feel that emptiness again, yet here it is less than a year later. An emptiness as inevitable as death itself. And life too…she keeps reminding herself.

She presses her head tighter into his shoulder, almost a shudder, as though she expects The Voice to return, this time with a far less gentle message, one from which she wants to hide. All this rushes through her in just a moment.

She guides Jake to the totem pole. "Will this be OK here?" she asks. "Or should we move it closer to the cabin where it's more protected?"

"Where do you want it to stand, Magpie?" Jake asks back in that slightly toying tone of voice he uses when something she says strikes him as a bit silly, like asking if the bed looks better in this corner or that corner.

She knows this, feels an annoyance rise, and just as quickly lets it slide away. "Well, I just want it to still be here and in good shape when we... when we...come...back." Jamie looks at him expectantly. She knows she's looking for reassurance that they will, that he will, come back.

"I'd like to paint it. Next year." He replies enthusiastically as though he'd been thinking the same thing. "So maybe it'd do a little better on the porch against the house." Jake gives the answer she hoped to hear.

"I think painting it will be lots of fun!" she says. "Here let me help you carry it over."

Jake draws himself up to his full height, feigning insult. "No! Me Tarzan. You Jane. Tarzan carry tree long way. He carry little more." Jamie laughs out loud at her "Indian Warrior" playing "Jungle King." Then Jake stoops, wraps the pole slightly below its middle, swings it onto his shoulder and carries it triumphantly to the porch. Jamie jogs ahead, pointing to the spot between the door and the window that she'd already picked out. Jake eases it down with Jamie's steadying hands. It rests comfortably on the boards.

They stand back to admire. "It looks like the cabin's guardian," Jake observes.

"A guardian of all the untold stories hidden inside," Jamie replies teasingly.

"And a few outside," Jake says as he grabs her around the waist playfully, hoisting Jamie onto his shoulder the same way he'd just carried the totem, swinging her out to the grass. It's clear he'd like the totem to watch one more untold memory unfold.

"Jake! Not now!" Jamie shrieks. "Cora and Ellie and the baby will be here any minute! I invited them to dinner."

Jake swats at her backside and tugs at her flannel shirt playfully. Then he relents, knowing there will be time to play again later. He sets Jamie down gently. Jamie pushes her hair out of her face, tucks her shirt back in and turns to him. "You're an animal!" she admonishes smiling.

"No! Me Tarzan! Cheetah animal! And Job. You still Jane." They break into laughter and another embrace. Then in the distance they hear the now familiar sound of Cora's truck downshifting as it slows and readies its turn into and up the drive.

Arm in arm they wait as Cora guns the truck a little to make the final rise before turning into the clearing. The revving of the motor sends a slight shudder through Jamie, bringing back still-fresh memories of a week ago. Jake's arm tightens slightly, sharing the memory and the terrible thoughts of what-if. Then the truck is in the clearing and Ellie is waving with one hand and holding the baby in the other. "Hellooo!"

Job comes from around the back confused, barking half in warning, half in greeting. Then seeing the women his tail starts wagging furiously. The three get out and there are hugs all round. Jamie notices Cora giving Jake a little longer one.

Ellie is all eyes for the cabin as she holds the baby. "This is soooooo beautiful, Jamie! Mama talks about it all the time. But I never imagined it'd be like this!"

"Thank you Ellie. My John wanted something simple. But he also liked things nice. So we built something with a little of both."

"And you own ALL this?" she asks turning in a complete circle.

Jamie laughs and then says, "NO, not all. That ridge over there belongs to someone else. A newspaperman."

Ellie's eyes get big at this. "You mean that John Scharf who delivers the papers? How'd he get enough money to buy all that?"

Jamie laughs louder at this, as does Cora. "No, honey, the man who owns that property also owns a newspaper. A big one. In Pittsburgh."

"Ohhhhh," Ellie answers trying to comprehend wealth and power reaching from far away into her Ram Cat world.

Cora stares into the woods looking for something and starts to ask, "Where's the ...? Then she turns once more and sees the pole on the porch. "There it is! Jamie, I thought for a second you'd gotten rid of that pole."

"Oh no, Cora. That pole is staying. For a very long time, I hope," she says glancing at Jake who smiles back.

Now Cora looks at Jake, her curiosity piqued long ago, "You *made* that, Jake?"

"Yes. Yes I did."

The group walks to the porch. Cora first touches, then runs her hand over the carved wood. Cora and Ellie Mae are wearing freshly pressed clothes. "It's beautiful, Mister Jake. But...well...what IS it?"

"It's a totem pole, Cora. Haven't you heard of those?"

"Yes. Yes, I heard of 'em Mister Jake, just never *knew* of 'em. I never knew what they were about. Just funny lookin', that's all."

"I learned about them in school. First in art. Then tried making one in woodshop."

"So what's them funny faces about?" Ellie Mae shifts Maggie Mae to her other shoulder, bouncing her all the time.

"They tell stories, Ellie Mae. Could be about something important that happened to a family or a clan. Or could be a way to talk to God."

Here Jamie breaks in. "Let's go inside. If I'm not mistaken I think that baby has a diaper needing a change."

Everyone laughs and then Ellie says, "Oh, Mama, I'll get her bag out of the truck. Here, will you hold her?"

"I think maybe Mister Jake might want that responsibility now." Cora responds.

"Of course," Jake says smiling. "And I'll make the changing too, Ellie, if you want." Ellie hands Maggie to Jake. Cora smiles approvingly at Jake's comfort with the cooing, but sodden bundle.

Jamie leads the way. She watches as Cora and Ellie Mae take in the simple splendor. She thinks how for years the only people who saw the inside were she and John. Then it was Jake. Now, in a week, a would-be killer, the Sheriff and his deputies, and Cora and Ellie have seen what John sometimes called his "sanctum sanctorum." Things would never be the same. *As though they ever were,* she smiles to herself. She wonders for a second what The Voice might have to say to all these intrusions.

"Where can I change little Maggie?" Jake asks.

"Oh, you can take her in the bedroom, Jake. There are towels and wash clothes in the bathroom if you need them" Jake, Ellie and Maggie disappear.

"So when did you and your John build this?" Cora asks, ever inquisitive, somehow never seeming nosey.

"About twenty years ago. He had been an Eagle Scout and always loved being close to nature. At first he wanted kind of a mansion in the woods. But I convinced him less was more. It became the perfect place for him to get away from all the pressures of the business," Jamie explains. Then she added, almost to herself "And it's been the perfect place for me, too, this last year."

"I 'member when you started stopping in at the Ram Cat for groceries and all. There's lots of rich folks come up here. But I could tell you were different. Right from the start. You never acted around like you could barely stand to be in there. Or tryin' to boss me around. Or askin' for foolish things that no grocery store 'round here would ever have on their shelves."

"Well, I'll take that as a compliment and thank you for it, Cora."

"But it looks like you got 'bout everything you need. It's cozy!"

Jamie smiles back at her friend. Then Cora's eyes go past her to something else. She just stares, not sure if it's something she wants to know about or not. "Is…is that…is that your shotgun? The one you winged him with?"

Jamie turns and looks at the gun standing butt end in the far corner of the room. She'd actually forgotten she'd put it there.

"Yes it is." The simple sentence hung in the air silently reverberating all that had happened the week before. Jamie could see that Cora's curiosity was almost killing her. She could also see that Cora was looking at it with a trained eye. She felt another strand in the fabric of their bond: two women who knew what it felt like to fire a weapon with intent…to pull the trigger or relinquish her own life.

"Here we are! All clean and ready for something to eat!" Ellie leads the way out of the bedroom with Maggie in her arms. Jake follows with the soiled diaper. Job noses up to him, then quickly thinks better of it.

The women look at each other with another glance of understanding. The gun will wait.

"Jake, would you like t'give her a bottle?" Ellie asks, half aiming the nipple Jake's way.

"I thought you were breast-feeding her, Ellie." Jamie and Jake look surprised.

"I am. The doc gave me a pump so's I could get some rest and Ma could feed her, too. I pumped a bottle for you to feed her tonight if you like, Jake."

Jake settles into a chair with Maggie Mae and the bottle.

"You have kids, Jamie?" Ellie Mae asks.

"Two daughters. And six grandkids, too."

"Six Grandkids! Whoooo-eeeee! You don't look old enough for no grandkids!"

"Hey, I heard that!" Cora pipes in from the kitchen, where she is getting dinner ready.

"Did you breastfeed, Jamie?"

Noticing Jake's eyes have joined the others, awaiting her reply, "My first one, yes. For about a year and a half. But my second one was colicky. And it didn't make sense fighting that. So we worked the bottle as best we could."

Cora starts the next round of conversation. "So when are ya going back to...your other home?"

Jamie answers with a hint of resignation, "Tomorrow." She pauses, then continues as if to explain: "I need to go back for a few days. Maybe four. Or even five. But then I'm coming back."

"You gonna move up here?" Ellie interjects hopefully. "I mean for permanent?"

"No, Ellie, I can't." Jamie glances from her to Jake as she says this. "I have my family – and business – responsibilities to take care of."

Cora picks up on the "business" reference and asks excitedly, "You gonna take your shotgun with you?"

Jamie laughs at this suggestion. "Nooooo, I'm not Cora. But some of the 'business' I have to take care of *is* connected to what happened last week."

"You sure you don't need some protection? I can handle one of those too, you know."

Now Jamie smiles appreciatively at her friend, understanding her concern is genuine. "Thank you, Cora. But I think I can do what needs to be done peaceably. At least I hope I can."

"Well all I know is you don't put your hand in a bear's den unless it's holdin' somthin' that can take care of Mister Bear right quick."

"Yes I know what you're saying. My John had to go through plenty of fights with his business. And he had more 'friends' do him wrong than enemies. Through them all, he said something that always stuck with me. 'Don't get mad. Get respect.' And even though somebody tried to do me very wrong last week...actually for many months now...I'm not mad. But I do intend to serve some comeuppance." Jamie says this so coolly that Cora, Ellie and Jake just stare at her, impressed into silence. She surprises herself at how the words come out.

The baby's soft burp breaks the moment. "All full are we?" Jake coos at Maggie Mae. "Let's see if we can coax one more burp out of there." Jake's voice is a surprise itself. "I have a bit of experience with this, too."

"Here, take this towel for your shoulder," Ellie offers. "In case she... you know."

"Yes, I do. It's happened to me a few times."

Jamie sees how easily and gently his large hands cradle the child. She notices Cora watching closely as well. Both of the older women are comforted by this. Ellie, as she has from that stormy day almost a month ago, continues looking at him with a mixture of awe and teenage crush.

"Mister Jake," Cora starts decisively. "I think we got some settlin' up to do."

Jake smiles back at her, but Jamie can see a line of apprehension across his brow. "OK, what do we need to settle, Cora?"

Here Cora falters for a second. "Well," she looks now at Ellie, then back at Jake. "Ellie and me we've been 'talking.' And I know. And she knows...at least I think she knows..."

At this Ellie covers her mother's hand with her own. "I do, Mama."

"We both know she's not really ready to be a mama yet. I mean a GOOD full time mama. And this baby here deserves a GOOD full-time mother ...or, uh father..."

Again, words hang in the air.

Jamie sees Jake who, relaxing a bit now, feels where this conversation is going and tends the task at hand. With more reassurance than words could bring, his hand spans Maggie Mae's back giving it small rubs. "Brrrruhp."

Chapter 58

Children's Hospital

Jamie is glad for a great day to ride home. She leaves Jake and Job at the cabin. Cora, Ellie and Maggie will come up in the afternoon to spend the four days Jamie will be away. Cora and Ellie will work the store during the day, leaving Jake and Job to take care of Maggie.

The ride down from the cabin has been exhilarating – mostly. The bike rouses from its long winter's nap after being stored in the shed nearly four months. The transition continues – the familiar ever falling before the unknown. Hmmm: what was it someone said about life happening while we make other plans?

Jamie and Jake's parting that morning had been bittersweet. Each knew their time together had now shrunk from weeks to days. Jamie had put on a brave face for Jake, as she could see he had for her. Even their goodbye kiss had been awkward as she revved the bike and it had slipped into gear a second before intended and she lurched away from them, starting down the drive.

She had stopped at the Ram Cat for just a minute. She was happy to see Cora, Ellie and Maggie all smiling and the women saying the right things about taking care of Jake in her absence. She noticed (or hoped she did?), a serenity on Cora's face not seen before, as though she could now see a future for the baby that gave comfort to them all.

Then she is off. Past the old barn on Rt. 381, past the horse fences, past the two hundred year-old stone foundations that no longer hold a purpose, past all that has been her life for the last year. She guns the bike, leaning into the last curve before the straightaway that ends at the state highway just as Sheriff Bob comes around the other way tossing a wave that both said hello and a reminder that the speed limit is 50, even for Jamie Barlow.

She enjoys the feel of the road again on the highway. She even gets used to traffic as she and her bike begin to inhale urban second-hand air. She doesn't even mind the come-on honk from the eighteen-wheeler she has passed. A quick look in her review mirror reveals a young man closer to Ellie's age than Jake's. Is it her leather jacket and jeans? Her long ponytail of gray-mistaken-for-blonde hair?

She pulls into the drive of their Pittsburgh home with a pang of panic. Does she really want to be here? Is this where *she belongs.* So much to do. Soon, too soon, her privacy will crumble. But there is work to be done. Matters to be settled. And, yes, another life to resurrect. Hank left the garage door open as she had asked. She parks her bike in the large garage. The garage door grinds closed on a previous life. Then she goes through the connecting door and the short hallway to the kitchen. Everything looks the way she left it, save for the neat stacks of sorted mail and Fran's large, loopy handwriting on a note welcoming her "home."

Jamie walks into the dining room. She runs her hand along the edge of the walnut burl table. The house seems simultaneously strange and familiar. She cries a "Hello?" just to make sure Fran, Hank or someone else isn't waiting for her. She feels a slight disappointment when her word just hangs in the air. She half expects John to come wheeling around the corner. Or her girls screaming at each other and herself for instant attention and adjudication of their latest spat. But that was years ago, wasn't it? Decades? The time...the time. A life of time.

"Hello?" She calls out again. This time more to hear her own voice, to let it begin again to occupy this space...to clear away silent echoes gathered like cobwebs and dust-bunnies. She wanders back into the kitchen, not wanting to open the mail. It's not that much in reality, Fran having chucked or handled all but the things she might actually want to see from the last year. Then she sees the large white envelope looming beneath the others. She knows what this is. She pulls it from the rest and walks through the dining room and living room, turning down the long corridor to her bedroom. She wants to read the contents, but can't decide if she wants a shower first – or if she'll need one afterwards.

Jamie plans to have a couple of days here before she meets with the Children's Hospital board. She will see them the day before all the Barlow Associates meetings.

Stella asked the hospital to set up an emergency meeting of the board, but refused to tell them what it was about. Jamie knew that the mystery of her absence, plus the call for an emergency meeting, would be enough to guarantee a full house. She'll need that time to get familiar with the details of the problem she must discuss with them.

The date for the quarterly Barlow meetings has been moved up at Jamie's request. She knows everyone there must be on pins and needles wondering what she plans to do. Will she resign as chair and turn control over to Larson? Will she stay on and try to run something she only knows the bare outlines of? Will she be a figurehead, keeping the name on the door as a sort of comfort to skittish clients, leaving the day-to-day operation to others (much as the past year has gone)?

She knows that her rebuff of Larson's attempted takeover is well-known both inside and outside of Barlow. Even "Heard On The Street" mentioned it in passing with a "tip of the hat to John Barlow's widow, Jamie, who has reputedly staked a hideout somewhere deep in the Blue Ridge mountains, but who obviously keeps close tabs on her late husband's empire." There is nothing she can do to make them feel better until the meeting in three days. But she hopes that just being in town gives them some peace, most of them, anyway.

Fran has gotten some personal things ready for her. Jamie needs a hair cut before she can see anyone. Fran set that up for four o'clock today. A couple of hours yet. Enough time for a shower! She pulls the band from her hair and shakes out the ponytail. Then she strips off her shirt, jeans, undies. Looking in the mirror she sees a truly changed woman. Thirty pounds lighter. She turns to admire the tone from her butt down through her legs. Even her breasts seem to have more firmness, although, God knows, gravity is wicked to all women. Her hair is an easy six inches longer. Mostly gray now with just hints of her youthful blondeness. But the gray itself is lively, not the drab she feared when it first appeared in her late forties. Her face...tanned, taut. A few wrinkles. But through her Indian great-grandmother, she has been blessed with smooth skin over high cheekbones. Maybe Cora was right, she did look a lot younger than when she'd left here a year ago. Maybe the trucker saw something to honk about after all!

A shower. Long and hot. Closing her eyes, she floats back to memories of ones shared with Jake. Then maddening minutes searching for clothes that fit! She settles on a pair of nice jeans at least one size too big and a Claiborne tee shirt that John liked her wearing because it was tight across the bust. Now it seems to fit perfectly. Finally, she's ready for the drive across town to her favorite hairdresser. This time she takes her five year-old minivan.

Jamie's hairdresser, Cordell, waits for her. He is always ready to get, or give, the latest gossip. But he's not prepared for the Jamie Barlow who steps through the door. His eyes widen in disbelief. His arms reach out as though trying to keep her from taking another step. "Excuse ME? Do you have an appointment? I'm expecting a very important person here at four o'clock!"

"Cor-DELL! Now you damn well know it's me!" Jamie plants her feet inside the doorway, taking pleasure at his disbelief in her transformation.

He stares for another second before relenting. "Mizzus Barlow? That you? Crazy woman who's been runnin' up and down mountains and scarin' people half to death? I do not believe my eyes! My arms must do my seein' for me!" He gives her a bear hug and then looks her up and down. "Woo! Girlfriend, you is feelin' GOOD *allll* over! I want the name of that spa you been at! Someone's been *workin'* you righteously!"

Jamie worries for a second, wondering if he somehow knows about Jake. But then figures even that bit of news could not have made it down here. Or hopes so anyway.

Then his eyes stay on her hair with the look of cool professionalism. He runs his hands through it from scalp to tip almost as though it were his own. "Except whoever was cuttin' your hair musta been usin' hedge shears. You take a year away from Cordell and look at this! If you stayed away any more, I don't think even Monsieur Cordell could have helped you."

Jamie laughs at his French affectation. "Well, I'm here and I need you to work your magic on me, *Monsieur Cordell, tootsweet!*" she says mimicking his French accent. "I think I'll get just a cut – no color. I've gotten used to it natural. Gray doesn't look so bad, does it?" Jamie says.

"Bad idea," Cordell answers calmly and quietly. "Very bad idea. You have important meetings where you need to be heard. If you don't get color, people will be looking at your hair rather than listening to you. You already look different enough from when you ran away from home."

"But..." Jamie protests as she laughs at Cordell's view of her year away.

"Trust me on this one, Jamie. Let me put some color in. Then later, if you want to go natural we can do it slowly. Slowwwww-ly." This is the Cordell she loves and confides in, although not nearly as much as others probably do.

"OK, Cordell. You are probably right. Just fix me up." As Jamie watches the transformation of her hair, she has time to really look at herself in all those mirrors. She does look younger. She looks very alive.

Ready to start her new life. She looks 68 years young.

Throughout, Cordell pumps her for information. Where has she been? Why did she go away? Is she missing John? Is it true someone tried to push her out of the company? What is with her shooting an intruder?

Jamie gives him just enough to convey that she was a new widow who needed time away to work through her grief. She also said enough about the past year at Barlow Associates so he can tell others that he was right all along: that Jamie Barlow knows how to run a company, too, even though her John is dead. She knows before the week is out that Cordell will have performed his service of reinstating her reputation among his clients – and their husbands. When she runs into these women later, there will be the ritual of fake hugs and air kisses and then her words to Cordell coming right back to her in the form of innocent questions and "I heard...."s.

Finished, she concludes Cordell has been right. The cut and color make her feel even surer of herself and of what she has to do. And now she *does* look twenty years younger! Before she leaves she makes a touch-up appointment for three weeks. Then with another hug from Cordell, she's back in the minivan heading for home. No need to worry about honks from horny truck drivers when she's in this "Mom-Car" as her daughters call it.

When she gets home, she doesn't linger next to the mail or call out to empty rooms. Instead, she heads to the sliding glass doors leading to the large deck and grounds beyond. She and John had built this house on a heavily wooded lot and made sure that most of the best trees were saved, including two majestic white oaks. She walks to the one at the farthest end of the property. Its trunk is massive, a good three feet in diameter, stretching a good seventy feet up. Its limbs create a canopy a hundred feet across. Little grows underneath, almost out of respect for the guardian of this spot of earth.

Jamie runs her hand over the bark, then walks around to the backside. Getting down to her knees, she has no trouble finding what she's looking for: A crude, weathered carving in the bark. Cut there more than twenty years ago when the house was new and life was newer, too.

She and John had carved it a week after moving in, by flashlight, when the girls were asleep, having made love quietly in the thick grass. They never told anyone about it. Even the girls didn't discover it until years later. But John always called it their 'rendezvous point' as his code for meeting there later on summer nights when the girls were asleep.

"Oh, John, give me the strength to do the right things in the next few days. I'll make sure the girls and the grandkids are taken care of. But after I talk to the board, I'm just not going to have as much money as you wanted me to have." Jamie lies down beneath the great oak tree. She gazes up to the tallest branches with a little sky showing through. "And, John, I am going to make sure Larsen pays for what he tried to do to you...and to me. Why you put up with him all these years is beyond me. You were always so good about people. I just don't know how you could have gotten him so wrong. So, I'll have another look. Maybe you saw something that I missed all these years." With that, Jamie runs her hand over the carving again and leans forward and touches the ancient bark with her lips. Then she stands and heads back into the dark house.

Tuesday morning starts with a call from elder daughter Caitlin. "Hi Mom! Hope I'm not calling too early," sounding genuinely happy to be talking with her.

"Hi Cait. No, not at all. I've been up a good forty-five minutes." Jamie is sitting at the kitchen table with a large window to the back yard. Her coffee cup is steaming.

"So, we're still on for eleven? Sarah and all the kids can't wait to see you!"

"Yes! I can't wait to see all of you too. So much to catch up on."

"You got back yesterday?"

"Yes. But I had to let Cordell see me first, so you all wouldn't think your mother had turned into some kind of witch up at the cabin."

A slight pause. "Mom, you're OK, right? We went crazy when we learned you had to defend yourself from intruders."

Not knowing what all lay behind that question, Jamie answers evenly, "Yes, Cait. I'm fine. Lots to tell you."

Another pause. "Mom, word got out that Larsen tried to take over Daddy's company. But you didn't let him."

"Yes, Cait. That's true. But it's a lot deeper than we have time for here. And I can't really tell you all of it when you come over. But...

everything is going to be all right. I think Daddy would be proud of me."

"I miss him, Mom."

"So do I, honey." A shriek in the background brings the conversation to a close.

"Sounds like Kerry and Lonnie haven't changed a bit!"

"No, Mom! GIRLS! Stop it! OK, Mom gotta go. See you in a few."

"Bye, Cait. Love you." But the line was already dead.

The rest of the day becomes devoted to a family reunion, of sorts. Her girls show up in separate cars and late – as usual. The house quickly becomes a chaos of hugs and kisses and "Hi-Grandmas." Except for Sarah's youngest, Kai-Lee, who was adopted from China only six months before John died and Jamie went away. The three year-old seems on the verge of tears until Jamie understands why...she doesn't recognize her Grandma! She talks to her very quietly after the rest of the kids start on their explorations. Jamie raises Kai-Lee's hand to her face and hair, letting her touch and using that to help get reacquainted. Finally, the child smiles shyly, climbs off Jamie's lap and runs to join the other children.

Jamie is amazed how much they all have grown in the year she's been away.

Evan, Caitlin's eldest, is on the edge of puberty. It seems he's grown several inches and his voice is starting to change. Everyone laughed when he announced, "Grandma, you're SKINNY! Did you starve to death up there?" Then the kids are off to explore the insides and outsides of Grandma and Grandpa's house, full of mysteries and treasures, and much larger than their own homes.

Now mother and daughters have a few moments to catch up. Caitlin and Sarah are amazed at their mother's transformation. "How did you do it?" Sarah asked. She is acutely aware of her own weight and usually the latest diet fad is part of any conversation with her, as though talking about losing weight was enough to make it happen.

"I walked a lot. About six miles a day."

"Six. Miles. A. *Day*?" Sarah asks incredulously. Clearly this was not included in any of the diets she had read lately.

"Yes. Maybe not so much in the worst of winter. And I kept a journal that made me believe I was hiking the Appalachian Trail."

"Mom, I think you look *fabulous*," Caitlin chimed in, ignoring whatever the Appalachian Trail was. "And Cordell did wonders with your hair."

"Yes. And I didn't want you to see it before he worked on it. You might not have thought I looked so fabulous then!"

She could see Caitlin about to ask another question...Just then the kids come screaming through the living room, including Kai-Lee – happy now that "Grandma" is really Grandma. Jamie knows it's time for lunch.

The rest of their three hours is spent in small talk about the kids, getting their sandwiches ready, wiping up one, then two, glasses of spilled milk, ending one crying spell and watching Sarah nibble at parts of three sandwiches not her own.

Jamie tries the best she can to talk about the highlights of living alone for a year.

Caitlin interjects, "Mom, I can't get two minutes alone. I'd probably go crazy with a whole year!"

Sarah picks up on that, "Mom, didn't you think maybe you were going a little crazy up there with no one to talk to or anything? Makes me think of that movie with Jack Nicholson where he goes crazy at this big house in the middle of winter that's full of ghosts and he tries to kill his wife and son..."

" 'The Shining,'" Caitlin finishes helpfully.

"Yes! That's the one! Mom, didn't you ever feel like someone was going to come with an ax and cut off your head and everything?"

Jamie has gotten used to Sarah's vivid imagination and so takes her question in stride, even though she felt the involuntary shudder remembering what *did* happen just a week ago.

"No, honey, your daddy made sure I knew how to handle a shotgun if I ever needed to. Plus, I made friends with a woman and her daughter who run the little grocery store in town and they keep a pretty close eye on strangers coming to town. And the sheriff there is a good one. Not that I didn't get lonely and miss you girls like crazy!"

This seems to satisfy their curiosity and the conversation ends with hugs and we-missed-you-too-Moms. Then it's time to bundle up the kids and get them home for afternoon naps, although all the moms know they'll be asleep five minutes into their drives home. "Bye, Mom! We'll see you soon!" Caitlin and Sarah each wave from their twin Hondas, John's last gift to them.

Inside, Jamie sighs: the house is dead quiet again. She notices how this quiet is different from the cabin's quiet. Quiet there is the natural order of things. Quiet here seems out of place.

This home had never been quiet. It was always full of John and the girls, then a crescendo of John's friends (even an occasional enemy or two) and sometimes her friends, then teenagers and boyfriends, then husbands and babies, all building over the years until illness, then death, brought this unnatural quiet...as though the house itself had died. What will she do here? Will she learn to live with this quiet? Or will she, too, retreat, reduced to peering out the window several times a day, like too many of the older widowed women she knew and heard about, hoping against hope that the girls will pull into the drive unexpectedly and bring their momentary chaos with them? Will touch-ups at Cordell's become more frequent, giving her the rare excuse to get out of the house, away from the quiet?

"No!" she shouts into the emptiness, surprising herself, as though shouting at her fears. "No! No! No! No!"

Her cell phone rings. It's Fran. "Hi," the other voice begins a little warily. "Is this a good time to call? Are the girls still there?"

"No, it's fine," Jamie answers maybe a bit too brightly, feeling a slight embarrassment at being "caught" yelling into air, at walls. "They left about ten minutes ago."

"Did you have a good visit?" Fran was a master of banalities.

"Yes, we had a very nice visit."

"Awww....that's nice." Now, down to business.

"Are you ready for tomorrow? Is there anything I can do?"

"Think I'm fine. Stella will pick me up at one? I'm going to read through the file now so I know my stuff and no one on that board will be tempted to have me admitted to the booby hatch right then and there."

"The booby hatch? What's that?" Jamie had forgotten that Fran's appreciation of the English language was wholly and completely literal.

"Oh, that's a just a term for a psych ward."

"Do you think someone's going to try and have you put away?" Now her alarm was genuine.

"No, no, no." Jamie responds gently. "Just me thinking how someone tomorrow might think I'm crazy for what I'm offering them."

"Ohhhh."

"At 1 pm tomorrow I will be ready to go knock the socks off that hospital board!" Jamie said brightly, signaling the end of their conversation.

"Okayyy," Fran draws out her answer hoping for maybe a few more minutes of conversation, but she can't think of anything else to say and Jamie stays silent at her end. "I'll call again after the board meeting. Good luck."

"Thanks a lot, Fran. Talk to you then!" Jamie snaps the phone shut before Fran could think of another question.

She really does need to study the documents Stella pulled together. They will describe the problem John's "friend" created for them in excruciating detail. A problem that was meant to surface after John had been laid to rest six feet under. A problem meant to ruin the lives and reputations of John and Jamie and many, many others the perpetrator would never know.

She feels badly for having been a little short with Fran. Jamie can't have a better assistant than her. She has been a star at keeping things going. Maybe she's just feeling a little cranky because of all that's ahead of her, starting tomorrow. She makes a mental note to do something extra nice for her before leaving for the cabin again.

The night slips away dreamlessly. She is actually surprised to open her eyes and see daylight pouring through the bedroom window. After reading the materials in the envelope and fixing a light supper, Jamie had turned in fairly early. She half expected visits from John or The Voice or both. She feels vaguely disappointed her "ghosts" hadn't come to comfort her in the wee hours. Now it's almost seven thirty and time to start The Day.

Walking into the living room she sees her phone blinking. Who could've called so late, or early? "Hi Grandma!!! Hi Gran'ma!!!! Weeeeee lovvvveeeee youuuuuuuu!!!! Hi, Mom, sorry if we called too early, but the kids were up and wanted to see if you were awake, too. We really had a good time yesterday. Kai-Lee said, 'Gran'ma looks sooooo bewful!' Isn't that cute? OK, see you soon! Love you, bye!...And, Mom, I'm really glad no one cut your head off. Bye!"

Stella arrives at the strike of 1 pm, ready to take Jamie to Children's. All efficiency and tidiness, she looks the part of perfect lawyer or paralegal, including the expensive briefcase. "Do you want to go over any of the papers about the warrants? I've got the originals in case we need to show them to the board. "

"We don't need to go over them now, Stella. I do appreciate you having them for me to read last night. Pretty ugly stuff. I have my plan in my mind. If I need details I'll call on you for those. I'm glad you're also on the board – a friendly face will be nice."

"What are you going to tell them? I mean, this is going to hurt the hospital a lot. The last board meeting, the financials were so bad that Bob Connell said if things don't turn in the next three months, he'll have to do layoffs. Then Rob Doolittle asked if the rumors were true that General was after us for a merger."

"What did Bob say?"

"At first, he didn't say a thing. He turned white instead! Then, finally, he said he had heard the rumors too. But he said there was nothing to them. No one had contacted him." A pause. "But, Jamie, when you tell them this what else can they do? Or maybe nobody would even want them and then we'd die a slow death."

Seeing the stress in Jamie's eyes, Stella thinks she's made a mistake, John's last months still fresh in her mind. "Oh, I'm sorry, Jamie! I didn't mean it that way."

But Stella was misreading Jamie. The stress she saw was really anger. This was more than abstract numbers and anonymous greed. These were real lives that were going to be hurt. *Children's* lives! How could anyone be so heartless? Jamie is angrier still that the perpetrator is dead, beyond her reach. Because if he were still alive, he might not be for long, given how she feels right now.

John had always counseled, "Don't get mad..." But now she couldn't even do that. She looks at the clock, a minute past one-thirty. She decides to lighten the mood a bit. "C'mon, let's get going. We have enough time to stop at Starbucks? I'm craving a Skinny Mocha. Couldn't get one of those up at the cabin!"

Stella smiles weakly back at her. "OK. I'm ready. Got everything?"

At 2:30 the board gathers in the room that hasn't been this crowded since the announcement of Bob Connell's hiring a decade ago. Everyone says how sorry they are about John's passing. They thank Jamie for the donation of the Nexcentury stock. They tell of all the good it will do. Everyone sits down, and the room goes quiet. Jamie stands. She is shaking. She hasn't spoken to a group in a year. She forgot how much she dislikes public speaking. She takes a deep breath and starts slowly.

"I am happy for all the good that the Nexcentury stock has done already. John would be very happy about that. But there is something you should know. There were also warrants for Nexcentury that were to come to the hospital as well." Jamie goes on to explain what a warrant is and how when they came due they were worth $10 million.

"Before John died, the warrants disappeared. None of us knew they were gone. When the warrants became so valuable, Stella noticed they were gone. She called me at the cabin. No one else at Barlow knew about them as John had them earmarked for Children's as a donation if they became worth anything.

"Stella and I investigated the crime ourselves (with Stella doing most of the work). We have proofs that John had nothing to do with it and of who stole them from us. The person who took them died several years ago and most of his fortune went to charity.

I feel no need to destroy his name for his surviving wife, children and grandchildren. They think he did great good with his money – and he did.

"However, that doesn't change things for you and for my responsibility to get you the $10 million. You can use it for the good you do every day in this community. Therefore, if you will give me a couple of years to do it, I will get the money for you myself and leave his name in peace."

Jamie has stopped shaking. She glances at Stella who has tears streaming down her cheeks. She knows Stella is moved by this. "I think John would approve, and it is the only way I can feel good about myself.

"I'd like nothing to leave this room. I'd like no one to speculate on who stole the warrants. I'd like nothing in the paper about my pledge. I'd like to quietly begin to downsize my life. I will donate things or the money from them to you. While I was away they discovered a huge gas well on my property. My percentage of whatever they find will also help me pay this off. Seems when I was crushed by this theft by a "trusted colleague" of John's, a door was opening with the gas discovery.

"If you agree with my plan, I'd like to see a show of hands. Then Stella and I need to get moving, as we have promises to keep." Every hand in the room goes up. People get on their feet, some crying, in a standing ovation. Jamie smiles and blows the board a kiss, picks up her purse and heads for the door.

When they get to the car, Stella hugs Jamie. "I have some paper to shred," she says.

"You do? Would you run my purse home for me? I'm going to walk."

"But, Jamie, it's at least ten miles! What if someone *sees* you?" Stella worried.

"It will clear my brain, Stella. I need to clear this away to get ready for tomorrow's meetings. I'll be fine. I have my phone. Just give me a minute to change my shoes. I stuck a pair of sneakers in my purse."

"OK, Jamie. I guess I'll see you tomorrow, then. Have a nice walk. Call if you change your mind."

"Thanks, Stella. I'll be home in a few hours – if I don't decide to just keep walking."

Chapter 59

Barlow Associates

Jamie sleeps well again. Part of it is getting things right with Children's Hospital. The financial hurt she will suffer will be more than compensated for by the great good she will be able to do. Part of it is feeling good about getting reacquainted with her daughters and grandchildren. She knows even better now that they need her, and she needs them. Part of it, strangely, is the absence of nocturnal visits from The Voice. She thought, given the silence and emptiness in the house, that this would be the perfect time for another conversation. But The Voice seems to choose the time and place for those. Just not here. Yet.

Her longing to hear The Voice has been made worse by the deep ache in her gut for Jake and Job. Will that ever go away? She is amazed that the feelings are as intense as her first teenage heartbreak. Her heart races thinking they'll be together again tomorrow, if only for a few days more. She's up early searching her closet for some business clothes that will fit her new body. She has always kept several sizes. She hopes to get into some of her favorites that were too small. It's like having all new clothes.

Jamie has set up an appointment with Rich Larson first. She needs this toughest business of the day out of the way first. Whoever commissioned the hit on Jamie had covered their trail like a pro. According to the intruder, the thugs were contacted by phone and there were never any names. Still, only Larson would have the motive and the means to launch such a plan, and the smarts to make sure he couldn't get caught. Jamie couldn't believe Rich would ever go so far as to kill her...discredit, maybe, but kill no. She had gone over and over all of this in her mind. How would she handle this knowing she would never be able to prove anything?

Sheriff Bob had pleaded with her for names. She had not given any so far. She told him she would go home and see what she could find out. She had the Sheriff working on the other person who had been nosing around and broken in at Thanksgiving. "What are you waiting for?" Bob had asked her. "I can't protect you when you go home. The paper was full of the story because of who you are. It isn't safe for you there. If he had the juice to hire guys to find you out here, you'll be a sitting duck when he knows you're back home. Alone."

Jamie knows the sheriff wasn't trying to scare her intentionally. It was just his experience with the darker side of humanity, the strength of our impulses to rob and kill. "I'll bring civil charges if I have to, Bob. But for now I want to use that threat as leverage to get something else. I'll be back in a few days. If I don't get what I want, then you and I will have a little talk."

The sheriff wasn't happy. Jamie feels bad about that. She knows he can't keep his prisoners indefinitely. But she wants to handle this her own way. After her meeting with Larson, she will meet with the whole board. After that will be the employees at Barlow Associates whom she loves and missed so much. She has planned the rest of the day with them and will have lunch brought in.

Her first meeting is at 8:00. Stella and Rosa are waiting for her. Both give her big hugs and smiles. Rosa has the same kind of incredulous look that she's seen from Cordell, her daughters and Stella. Adding to Jamie's presence is one of her favorite business suits, a red light wool, with a cream blouse underneath. It'd been stuck in the back of the closet, two sizes too small when she'd left last year. Now it hugs her body perfectly. She can see both women regarding her with the kind of deference she had only seen them give to John. While this makes her a little self-conscious, she knows that she is expected to exude the kind of confidence and power that drew people to John, trusted him with their money and more.

They walk back to John's office where she'll wait for Larson. "Can I get anything for you, Jamie?" Stella asks helpfully.

"No, thanks, Stella. But when Rich arrives, tell him I'm on the phone. Then wait about three minutes before buzzing me to tell me he's here."

The women leave and Jamie takes a minute to survey John's office. Not a thing has been moved since his death. She feels both closeness and an emptiness being here. But there isn't time to linger with those feelings. Larson should be arriving any minute, and she needs to focus for what will be a short, but tense, encounter.

As expected, Rich shows up just on time. At three minutes after eight, Stella buzzes, asking if she's ready to see him now. Fifteen seconds later, Rich Larson stands in the doorway, a big smile masking whatever concern he might have for this unusual meeting. He is wearing what Jamie calls a Mafia suit – black with bold white pinstripes. A white shirt and black tie finish the ensemble. She stands to shake his hand.

"Jamie, it is so good to see you! How have you been? You certainly don't look like you've been hiding away with your grief for almost a year!" Jamie notices his perfect smile except for one tooth that overlaps another. His wrinkles are more pronounced. They come from years of smoking. She always wondered how he kept his teeth so white.

Larson is arrogant, rich and used to getting his way. So much so that he has no sense of boundary with his speech. Or with his actions. He reaches for a deep embrace from Jamie and seems genuinely puzzled when she rebuffs him with a stiff handshake and an invitation to sit down across from her at John's favorite conference table.

Jamie brushes the discomfort with him away. She takes a deep breath. She needs to be stronger than she has ever been for what she has to say. "Rich, let's get started. Hopefully, this won't take long." Another breath. But she can see she has Larson's attention with the seriousness in her gestures and in her voice. Even through his moussed dullness, he can see this woman means business.

"Rich, I'm sure you read about me in the paper. There is only one person that I know of who would like me out of the way, and that is you." She pauses a second for effect, then continues, "I just have a hard time believing that you would have me killed to get what you want."

Rich stares at Jamie for the briefest of seconds before deciding she must be bluffing. "Jamie, come on. We have been friends for a long time." He leans forward with an even bigger smile, as though consoling this still-grieving widow who, despite her obvious physical health, is still not yet of sound mind. "Think about what you're saying. Yes, I saw the small item in the Trib and my first reaction, honest to God, was that this couldn't be true. Someone trying to kill Jamie Barlow? If that's what this meeting is about, then let's put it to rest now and let me take you to The Baguette for breakfast. We have so much to catch up on!"

Jamie studies Larson carefully as he makes his speech. She thinks his eyes betray a fear his voice and smile had been trained never to. A flicker. A blink too quick.

She decides to push ahead. "Rich, stop. This is too serious and, frankly, your bullshit is just a bit too much this early in the morning."

Rich straightens at her profanity. She can see him recalculating quickly. Maybe this woman has something more to her than just being

Barlow's widow. "I know about the spies. I know about the fake reporter. I know about the attempted takeover. And, yes, I know about your hit men. What the paper didn't report was that I shot one of them. Almost killed him."

She watches Rich's eyes widen with each statement. Even the smile couldn't stay in place. "They botched the job, Rich. And that's why I'm here this morning. And why you're here. And why before you leave, you can confess your crime to me and take my punishment. Or you can wait for a jury and take theirs."

Now Larson's eyes narrow, the smallish brain trying desperately to calculate the odds that the widow is bluffing also. What could she know that would put him in a court room? The paper said two men, one badly wounded, the other caught and jailed. What could they have said that would implicate him? He shifts to the wounded animal act.

"I would never put out a contract on anyone, much less you, Jamie! I hope you believe me." Rich's eyes cloud over and his lower lip is trembling. "Please let me tell you what I did do. If you blame the hit on me, they'll send me to jail for the rest of my life."

"I'm listening, Rich."

"Just before Thanksgiving, I paid a private eye to spy on you. We were worried that you had gone crazy and we did have the company to think of. The guy I hired was unable to get any pictures or anything else on you...like the mountain man they said you were living with up there." Rich took out his handkerchief and wiped his eyes. "I had paid him half down and I said I'd pay the other half when I got something I could use."

Rich is on the edge of his seat – very tense. He looks desperate. Maybe the wounded animal isn't an act. Jamie plays another card.

"I have the sheriff looking for someone like that," Jamie breaks in. "He did break in over Thanksgiving while I was away. I didn't even report it at the time as I wanted to be left alone. Because of all that was going on back here, I figured it was you trying to make me look crazy or despondent or something."

Rich looks at her with surprise. She can see he didn't expect her to connect the dots as strongly as she has. She knows she has him. It's a position Rich is used to putting others in. Now she wonders how he'll react.

"I have tried to figure out where the other two came from," Rich continues. "I am going to tell you the truth here, Jamie, because I have nothing to lose. Either you believe me and let me off the hook, or the rest of my life is ruined."

Rich looks directly into Jamie's eyes and proceeds. "I refused to pay any more as I never received anything but pictures of you hiking alone in the woods.

"They asked what it would take to get paid and I said that I needed something that would prove you unviable to lead Barlow Associates. I had never dealt with people like this before, Jamie, honest." She's not sure she entirely believes that, but Rich is squirming in his seat. "When I read in the paper what happened, I was in shock! I thought I was just hiring a private detective... not a "full-service" operation.

Jamie's not sure what a "full-service" operation is exactly, but she can pretty much guess. She hopes Rich didn't see her shudder. Instead, he seems to shift into a full confessional mode.

"I thought of ending my life when I read it, but I was too much of a coward. I decided to face you instead and tell you what probably happened. I will never get over this Jamie – never! I am putting myself in your hands. You can turn me in today if you wish. I'll just go with you. I just wanted a chance to tell you how horrible I feel... that all this is probably my fault."

Rich sits quietly, his head down. Jamie feels a wave of compassion that she never expected to feel. This is an unexpected consequence of a bad idea gone sour. Her mind is churning. Rich has literally put his life into her hands. How can she turn this bad situation into something good for everyone?

Jamie sits quietly and closes her eyes. 'Lord, give me strength to do the right thing,' she says to herself. Not knowing what to say, words come from deep down inside her that she didn't know were there. Maybe this was the moment The Voice (her voice) had awaited to speak.

"Rich. This is a horrible mistake grown even worse. My head says turn you in and let you rot in some godforsaken place. But my heart, and maybe something else, says not to."

She pauses. Rich looks at her quickly, then looks down as though awaiting his sentence.

"Rich, I have decided to forgive you. Power and greed do things to people." Jamie feels pulled from her impulse to 'get even'. Something reminds her that John trusted the man now melting before her.

"But you are *not* getting off scot-free. Here is what we are going to do. You and I need to stop this group of people from hurting anyone else.

If you think they can't trace the original request back to you, I need to tell the sheriff I found the guy with the camera who broke in originally. The sheriff can take it from there. You will need to give me his name and where we can find him."

"I can do that, Jamie. There is no way someone can trace it to me… no way except through you. I will do anything you want. This is one of those things that is life changing…like a near death experience."

Jamie continues. "Here is what you are going to do. John always liked your opinions and thought you were smart. I was going to ask you to resign from the board, but now something tells me I would like you to stay. You need to put your brain in gear the way John's was in gear. You probably knew him business-wise as well as anyone. At the board meeting later this morning you will hear what my plan is. I want you to stay on to help make this happen and to help Barlow make it with John gone. You can do this without grabbing power. This is how you pay John and me back for the mayhem you have raised."

Rich is sniffling a bit as he realizes he may have a second chance when he thought he had none. His body straightens in the chair for a minute.

"Jamie, I can't believe you will forgive me and give me another chance. If you don't ask me to leave the board, no one will suspect it was me who made this near-fatal mistake. You are giving me a new chance at life. I promise you will be proud of me. I will dedicate the rest of my life to helping this company grow as if John were still here – and I will become a philanthropist in the shadow of what you and John have and will do."

Now Rich is sobbing and has his head in his hands. Jamie feels a combination of sympathy, pity but also some revulsion at the site.

"Rich, you need to get cleaned up for the meeting in a few minutes. For this to work it can't look like anything is wrong. Somehow I feel like this is the way John would have wanted me to handle this, too. I will be going back to the cabin in a few days to wrap things up before I come back to my life here. I'd like to take information on the so called 'Private Eye' you hired."

"I'll go and clean myself up. I never figured this would turn out like this. I just knew for once in my life I needed to take the responsibility for my actions. Putting everything in your hands was all that I could think to do. Thank you so much for trusting that I will do the right thing going forward. You will not be sorry you forgave me. You will not be sorry you let me have a chance to do things right. I'm 61 years old. I don't have that much time left. I will get it right from today going forward."

Jamie smiles at him for the first time that she could remember. "Go get ready, Rich. This company needs to get going. I'll see you in a few minutes."

Rich comes around the table and takes Jamie's hand. He presses it to his lips and whispers, "Thank you."

"Get going," she says softly. "We have work to do."

The meetings all go well. Jamie is welcomed back. The board is somewhat surprised to hear that Jamie is selling the business to the employees. She reads them the letter that she and John wrote in the event that they both went together. It was notarized too. The board agrees the company has prospered with John gone and Jamie in hiding. They feel confident Barlow Associates will go on in some form.

"You might be interested to hear that in John's and my will, it says that the company goes to the employees. John said that I could run it for my lifetime if I liked, or I could start the process of turning it over to the employees when he died. I've decided this is not how I want to spend the rest of my life. After I meet with you, my lawyer and I are meeting with the employees to get the process started. Ted will be at that meeting to represent the board."

At lunch with the staff, Jamie shares some of her time away with them. They all want to know what Jamie is going to do with the rest of her life. "I think I might write a book about my time away," she tells them.

"Maybe it should be a diet book," Stella offers. "All that hiking and no fast food and look at you! You look gorgeous!" Jamie and the rest laugh and agree with Stella.

"I'm sure I'll write more children's books and help the charities I love. I'll be in here with you all some, to help out until you feel comfortable without me. Mostly, I will walk the path of the rest of my life and see what I find... and see what finds me."

Chapter 60
Anybody Home

Jamie is surprised at how tired she is when she pulls into the garage. Still, it's been an eventful day. She confronted her would-be murderer and turned the company over to John's employees...all in one fell swoop!

A year ago could she have summoned the courage to do either one? She could see in the eyes of Rich Larson, as well as those of the "associates," that they were looking at a new Jamie Barlow. Well, maybe they were!

Stella asked if she could come over for a while. But Jamie really felt like she wanted to be alone for now. Tomorrow would be another busy day riding back up to the cabin and wrapping up details for Jake and Maggie's flight to Oklahoma. She told Stella to stop by at eight in the morning for some last minute instructions. She could see Stella was both relieved at not having to come over now and happy at being needed first thing tomorrow. Jamie knew this suited Stella's own clock perfectly.

The bright morning has given way to an early evening high overcast. Showers are predicted and Jamie hopes they don't linger and slow her trip back to the mountains. She walks through the house with casual purpose, no longer needing to call out to people not there.

The living room feels more comfortable now, both person and space adjusting to each other's presence. She runs her hand over the cracked leather of John's favorite chair. The touch brings back memories of how he would pull her onto his lap if she walked too close, hands everywhere as if to say "mine, all mine." She leans closer to smell its warmth and familiarity and remembering how it felt to be really wanted by one man for so long.

She smiles thinking of John's decades-long desire for her. Even in his last illness, the desire to give and get pleasure remained strong. She loved him for his large appetites...in love, business, sport...in *life*. Then she thinks of all the women who'd confided in her over the years of lost interest and extramarital affairs. Then the divorces and remarriages. Sometimes repeated once, or even twice.

What were they searching for? Physical or sexual perfection? All-consuming love? Validation? Worship? After years of listening to countless stories Jamie still doesn't know. But the sadness was too great and the happiness too small. She knows she's lucky. But she also thinks that it's more than just luck. Maybe it's because she and John never let "things" get in the way of "them." Or their children.

Jamie sighs then thinking of her girls' failed relationships. How she wishes she could have helped them choose more wisely! Then she thinks of her grandchildren and how precious each one is despite not having fathers active in their lives. John filled some of that void, of course. But she worries what impact that will have on them later on.

She walks into Caitlin's bedroom. Now in her late thirties, the room hasn't changed since college except for toys strewn across the floor. This is her grandchildren's favorite playroom. She opens the toy chest and starts putting the cars and dolls and plastic Slinkies back. How often has she done this same chore over and over after they've come and gone? Soon, too soon, they will outgrow these toys and crave more sophisticated power objects…video games and MP3 players and all the technology gadgets that kids obsess over these days.

She wonders how Jake will raise Maggie. Will she, too, want what her friends have, what the TV says she must have? Will he let her watch much TV? Or play on the computer? Does he even have either of these? So many things are so different from her own growing up and parenthood. Her girls raising children with fathers absent. Jake about to start raising a girl without a mother around to help and teach. And she knows they are not alone.

What will it mean when this newest generation becomes adults? Will two parent families look like something out of the Stone Age? Or the Victorian Age? Jamie has no idea. But she senses that with John gone somehow she'll be needed to fill both grandparenting roles. And she will do her best to keep an eye on Maggie, even if it's from far away.

Jamie walks back out to the living room, then thinks to check emails before grabbing a bite to eat and getting ready for bed. She walks into John's office – it was always *his* office, never hers, even though they both used it a lot – and turns on the computer. Then she walks to the kitchen to fix a sandwich and mix a drink.

A few minutes later she's picking through the few emails that have come in since she's been back. The first is from Stella. Sent less than an hour ago. A checklist of things they need to go over tomorrow morning. Good, efficient, always loyal Stella.

1. Arrangements for the plane that will fly to the small regional airport twenty minutes drive from the cabin.

2. Extra cash that Jamie had asked for.

3. A schedule of appointments for the week after she's back for good.

She writes a quick note of thanks.

The next is from an ever-snooping "friend" of hers...Martha Jefferson. "I JUST FOUND OUT YOU WERE BACK!!!" In addition to trying constantly to pry details of Jamie's life, and then insinuating herself onto Jamie's calendar, she adds one more annoying habit: typing her emails in all capital letters. It felt like she was shouting out at Jamie from the screen, which is often what she did in person, violating Jamie's person and her peace. The rest of the note was a compendium of WHERE-HAVE-YOU-BEENs and ARE-YOU-ALRIGHTs and HAVE-YOU-HEARDs.

Jamie skips a reply. She will write when she gets back. She is too tired to think carefully about what she wants to say. But not too tired to make the mistake of writing what she really wants to say.

The third is a surprise. From Rich Larson.

"Dear Jamie,

Although I am the last person you want to hear from today, I just had to write.

First, I want to thank you for believing me this morning.

I am many things, not all of them good, but a murderer I am not.

I thought I could control things and do what I thought best for John's company.

But I could not and something almost happened that would have ended my life as surely as it would have ended yours.

Second, I have made arrangements through my associates to have their contacts compensated in full, along with something of a bonus to make sure this goes no further.

I understand through channels that you are reluctant to press charges. If you can hold to that, I will be forever in your debt, as though I'm not already.

Third, attached is my letter of resignation from the Board. Copies have also been sent to Kevin Bragg and my attorney. While I cannot agree with your decision to turn John's company over to a group of employees far less talented than he, I am in no position to quarrel.

Fourth, I, too, have decided that a little time away from the hurly-burly will do me good. So for both financial and personal safety reasons, I will repair to my Caymans condo for the next six months at least.

Finally, I want to say that John was one of the most astute, savvy and ballsy investors I have ever known. I miss him.

He was one of the few, maybe the only man, who gave me a run for my money.

I underestimated him only one time before. It cost me one million dollars.

Now I have underestimated him a second time. Little did I know until this morning that he had chosen a mate every bit as astute, savvy and, may I say, ballsy as he. This time it has cost me much, much more than one million dollars.

My hat is off to you, Mrs. Barlow.

May we meet again in calmer times.

Yours,

Richard Larson"

Jamie stares at the words for a long time. She is unsure how to respond. Then writes quickly,

"Dear Rich,

Thank you for your note.

I appreciate your frankness.

I'm sure the Board will accept your resignation without complaint.

Best wishes for enjoying your sabbatical.

Sincerely,

Jamie Barlow"

Satisfied that she was sufficiently succinct and neutral in her reply, she lets the screen go blank. The others would have to wait another week or so. Now she is truly exhausted. Turning off the room lights, she makes her way to the bedroom. She can hear a soft rain falling. The patter is rhythmic on the roof and deck. A quiet, steady, comforting beat. As she undresses she thinks how nice it would be to have Jake here. Then, she catches herself. No, it would not be right. Not here. This is still John's home. She couldn't be comfortable. And she knows Jake wouldn't be comfortable.

Jamie shudders at her 'infidelity.' Then she climbs into bed and, before turning the light out, makes up for it by kissing the photo of her and John taken years ago at the cabin with Caitlin. "I miss you, John." The cool satin welcomes every inch of her skin and within seconds she is asleep.

When she awakes, it doesn't feel quite like morning yet. But there's a dim light suggesting a too-early dawn. And another light straying in from the living room. Did she forget to turn one off? She gets out of bed to investigate.

It's the reading lamp next to John's chair. How she could've missed turning it off, she has no idea. She reaches to click the switch.

"I've missed you, too, Jamie."

Jamie screams, "John!!"

John Barlow is sitting in his leather chair, dressed in the plaid shirt and jeans that were always his favorite outfit at home or at the cabin. His face is ruddy, his smile cock-eyed as usual. His brown-gray hair is neatly combed, with that one unruly shock falling forward. He looks at Jamie with the same kind, intelligent blue eyes she had always loved.

Abruptly, she feels her nakedness. Her hand crosses her midsection as she finds a seat on the sofa across from...*her husband.* "John...John...I... I...don't understand. What..."

"What am I doing here? Why shouldn't I be? Isn't this...my home? Isn't this...my chair? Aren't you...my wife?" John's tone is casual, slightly amused.

Jamie stares at her husband. This cannot be! She must be dreaming. But the slight chill up her back and across her breasts suggests otherwise.

"John...I mean of course this is your home. But...but..."

"But how is it I'm a year dead and talking to you?"

"Yes!" Jamie steadies a bit now. Is she talking to an apparition?

"You could have talked to me at the bake shop, but you seemed in a hurry to leave."

"Oh, John, I'm sorry! But you scared me..."

"...half to death?" John finishes her sentence, smiling.

"Yes!"

"Guess I'm sorry for that. I thought you'd be happy to see me."

"I am! It's just so...unexpected. I mean it is *you*, isn't it?"

"Whom did you expect, a ghost?"

"John! Now come on! Don't tease."

"Sorry." A pause. "Jamie, I must say you're looking better than ever!"

Jamie is even more self-conscious, although for no real reason. She was always comfortable with nudity around her husband, even as her body aged. But now she shifts on the sofa, another arm crossing breasts to rest on her leg.

"Thank you. Hiking the property this last year has done wonders, John."

"Your young man, too, I think."

Jamie is stunned into silence. He knows about Jake! But how? Now the chill becomes a hot full-body flush of guilt and embarrassment.

"John...I..."

She stares at her husband. This can't be happening, can it?

"John, I'm so sorry..." The words came spilling out now. "John, it just...it just happened. John, I was missing you so bad. I mean, you were... are?...dead. And Jake..." Here the word sticks in her throat. Now tears start at the corners of her eyes.

"Oh, John, I'm so sorry. I didn't mean to hurt you."

"Hurt me? How could you *hurt* me, Jamie? I *am* dead, aren't I?" Here John pauses.

Jamie stares back at him, wild-eyed, disbelieving, yet so wanting it... him...to be her husband.

Maybe this was some excruciatingly good actor hired by Rich Larson. Maybe this was one last effort on his part to rip the company away from her. Maybe somebody had a camera taping the entire 'show' of the widow Barlow, naked, off her rocker, thinking she's talking to her ghost of a husband. She looks around the room for a red dot of light that would betray this wicked scheme. She wants to get up and grab her robe, but she feels glued to the sofa. Jamie looks back at John who continues to smile at her.

"Besides what could I do about that? Seems like a nice man. Half Cherokee, yes? Kept you company all those months away. And now he's going to take that baby and raise her as his own."

Lord! He knows *everything*! But how could he? Not even Rich knows about Jake and Maggie.

"Besides, if you'd been the one to go first, would you have wanted me to become a monk and go into hiding?"

"No, John, I guess not."

"Well, then, enough of that. I don't blame you, Jamie. I'm just glad you didn't give in to some of those limp dicks like Larson when they came sniffing after you."

"You knew?"

"Of course, I did! The only one I worried about was Kevin Bragg. He never tried did he?"

"Never," Jamie assured him.

"I know I got a little crazy at the end. That's because I knew Larson was making his move and there was nothing I could do about it."

"Knew what, John? I know you didn't trust him much. You always said he could make you money, but you had to watch him like a hawk so he wouldn't steal it and more."

"I always thought he'd go for the company soon as I was gone. I thought he'd go for you too. Didn't think he'd go as low as murder, though."

"John, how do you know these things? I'm still not sure if he hired those guys to kill me or just to scare me into giving up the company."

"Those guys weren't there to scare, Jamie. They meant real business. Good thing I taught you how to handle that 30 aught, huh?"

"I just closed my eyes and fired, John! I didn't want to hit him! I just wanted them off the property!"

"Well, you done good, girl. Don't think I could have done better myself. You sure you want to let Larson off that easy?"

"Yes, John. He's not going to bother you, me, or the company anymore. Besides, I guess he's already taken measures to make sure they don't talk any more than they have. And I don't want the spectacle of a trial and all that press coming down on that little town. They might start asking questions about...the baby."

"I wanted to ask you about that. You're going to fly this...Jake...and that baby to Oklahoma? And then leave them there? How are you going to pull that one off?"

"It's all set, John. The mother...she's just 16...and her mother, you know them, run the Ram Cat? They've agreed this is best for everyone involved. Especially that baby. Jake will be a good father to her."

"And who's going to be her mother? You?"

"No, honey! You know I could never do that. I'll make some provisions so when she comes of age she can go to college. But Jake has family there. I'm sure they'll take good care of her."

Jamie looks at John closely. The smile has slipped. The eyes look wan, almost vacant. He looks...tired.

"You did...the...right...thing...with the hospital. I had...no idea."

"I know you didn't John. But you know I had to do the right thing and make sure they got the money you wanted them to have."

"I...know. But you...and...the girls...you'll have...enough?"

"Yes. You always took very good care of us. Always. And I am forever grateful." Jamie smiles now, this time with another wave of tears coming.

"OK. You do...what's best."

"I will, John. I will."

"OK. I'm...sleepy."

"Me, too, honey."

"Help me to bed?"

"Of course."

RING!

RINGRING!!

RING!

RINGRING!!

Jamie stares into her bedroom space.

RING!

RINGRING!!

"What? What's that noise?" she says to herself.

"John, who's making all that racket?"

RING!

RINGRING!!

His side of the bed is empty. Maybe he's gone to see what's wrong.

RING!

RINGRING!!

"John! Who is it?"

Then, as if from her old pocket transistor, another voice: "Jamie! Jamie!! It's me! Are you all right?"

Jamie bolts upright in bed. She looks at the clock, 8:00.

RING!

RINGRING!!

"Oh my God, it's Stella!"

Chapter 61
Stella

Jamie stumbles out of bed, throws on a robe, and staggers to the door.

"Ring...ring." Then a muffled "Jamie?!"

"I'm coming!" The light coming in the east window is blinding. Jamie shades her eyes. Opening the door, she meets the wide eyes of Stella, a look torn between relief and scolding.

"Are you alright? I was getting worried something had happened. I was about to call the police." Stella is dressed in her usual business suit. Casual days are lost on her. She always looks professional.

"I'm fine, I'm fine. Come in. I just overslept, that's all." Jamie brushes hair off her face. She knows she must look hideous. Nothing to do about that just now. She leads the briefcase-laden Stella into the living room. Stella's heals click along on the wood floors. She stares at the chair and sofa, wondering if she should invite Stella to sit where...where...

Stella sits down on the sofa.

"Jamie? Jamie?"

The voice sounds distant. Then Jamie sees why. Competing images and voices: Stella shares that same spot on the couch with a shadow, an echo. Jamie was there last night, *wasn't she*? Jamie sits in the chair. Stella sits on the couch in the exact spot where she had sat when talking with John last night. That *was* last night, wasn't it?

Stella leans in close, searching Jamie's face for a clue. Jamie stares back at her, not quite ready to talk. "Are you really all right? You look like you've seen a ghost!"

Stella has a tendency towards the dramatic, but maybe she was right this time. Jamie looks again at Stella, her sense of here and now finally taking root. "A ghost? No. I just overslept. That's all. Really."

Still, her eyes survey the sofa for some sign that she'd sat there last night and talked with John. She pushes back into the chair slightly as though trying to feel the presence that had been there just a few hours ago. Nothing really feels different.

Disappointed, she thinks, 'Maybe the bed!' Maybe after Stella leaves, she'll see where she used to help John lay down, where her husband used to sleep next to her.

"I think I brought everything."

"What? Oh, yes! Just put them on the table. I'm going to start coffee. Would you like some?"

"No, that's all...wait! Yes, I guess so. Thank you, Jamie."

Jamie uses the few minutes making coffee to get her bearings again.

This is the day after I confronted Larson and told John's employees what I was going to do with the company.

In the next room Stella patters on about the documents she's brought.

This is the day after the night when I sat in that living room and talked to John. We talked. He was there! Or I am really losing my mind.

"Is that OK with you?" Stella's voice calls from the living room. Again a shard of reality pierces her cloudiness.

"I'm sorry, Stella. Missed that. Forget...do you take cream?"

"Yes. Thank you." Stella continues, "I was saying, do you want to sign these here? Or take them with you back to...the cabin?"

Jamie brings two cups of coffee out. Handing one to Stella, she sits back down in the chair. Three neat stacks of paper are laid out for her. Finally, she is able to focus on matters at hand.

"I'll take them with me. But I think after yesterday, things are pretty well in hand, don't you?"

Stella *loves* being asked her opinion, Jamie knows. The question will buy her a few more minutes as she starts to sort how the rest of this day will go. "Yes I do! Everyone was talking at the office after you left. They really can't believe it, Jamie. They can't believe you are really you. You've changed so much. I mean...on the *outside*. I know you haven't inside. But, you know, there have been some times this past year when we..." Here Stella stumbles a bit, searching for the right words. "...Well, we were just worried about you, Jamie. And then all the things Rich was pulling. We thought you'd come back and there'd be no more company. It'd all belong to him and there'd be nothing left from John. Or for you. Or for..." Here she stops, thinking she's already said too much.

Jamie finishes, "...or for everybody else. I understand what you're saying Stella." She looks steadily at the woman who's been her lifeline in many ways since she left for the cabin. "This was something John and I discussed many times, even before he got ill at the end. He knew all about Larson and the tricks he might pull. But even he was surprised Rich would stoop to attempted murder."

Stella stares back at Jamie, searching her face for some other meaning.

"Jamie," here she replies slowly, choosing words carefully. "Were you thinking about someone else? I mean, John doesn't know what Rich tried to do...up in the mountains? I mean..."

Here Jamie catches the slip of her tongue and tries to backtrack quickly. "Did I say 'John'? I'm sorry, Stella. Feel like I didn't sleep a wink last night. No, of course not! John did warn me many times that Rich would try and get the company away from me. What I meant to say was John told me Rich was capable of about anything, including murder, but he said that for exaggeration."

Seeing an opening, Stella pushes asking, "Did you try and kill him?"

Jamie looks at Stella not quite understanding for a second.

"Kill Rich?"

Stella's eyes get wide at the thought.

"Oh! You mean, the men who...came for me?"

Stella's eyes get wider even at this thought. Jamie can see as much as they've worked together, they've never really had *this* kind of conversation. She just nods at the question.

Jamie again looks at her friend with a mixture of astonishment and genuine love. Have they ever really talked to each other before? "No. I did not intend to kill them. I only wanted to scare them and get them off my property. But the one was coming into the cabin, and I was backed into a corner and I just closed my eyes and shot the gun. Not even the way John showed me. I got lucky. I mean, I'm glad I didn't kill him. Even if he was maybe going to try and...kill...me."

Both let those words hang in the air. Each staring back at the other.

Then Stella bursts out, "Jamie!! He was going to *kill* you! You don't have to sound so....so...*saintly*! "

Jamie is stunned by the strength of Stella's words. She can't recall her speaking so directly to her before.

"I...I didn't think of myself as saintly, Stella. I was just trying to protect myself. I fired the gun. I hit him in the leg. He fell down. That was all. I didn't even think about what I was doing."

"What about the other one...in the truck?"

Obviously, Stella has been waiting for the right moment to ask all the questions she's kept bottled up inside. For a brief moment, Jamie panics and wonders what other questions she might have that she's been too afraid to ask. About Jake. About the baby. About the flight to Oklahoma. Jamie realizes she trusts Stella with an awful lot, but often doesn't tell her the whole story behind her requests.

She reaches out and runs her hand absent-mindedly along the edge of the walnut burl coffee table separating her and Stella. Then she continues, her voice more distant now as images from those deadly moments flash by.

"That whole part of it is such a blur I don't think I remember much. I guess I ran outside. I remember the truck kind of coming at me. I thought he was going to try and run me over. Then it turned and started down the drive. I guess he fired a shot, I really don't remember. And then I shot the gun again. I didn't even know I'd hit it until the sheriff told me they'd caught him later because a tire had gone flat."

Jamie again focuses on Stella, as though coming out of a bad dream. "I'm sorry, Stella. Maybe I should've told you more. But I've been trying to put it out my mind. It happened. It's over."

"You don't think they – or Larson – will come after you again?"

"No. Of that I am definitely sure."

Then, putting an end to this conversation, Jamie taps her hands on the stacks of paper. "I'll take these with me and have them read by the time I get back."

Stella, realizes their time is about over and ventures one more question to Jamie.

"When will you be back? Soon, I hope. I mean, you're not planning to..."

A pause.

"Planning to?"

"Planning to stay. In. Oklahoma."

Jamie notices that Stella can barely squeeze the words out of her throat. Maybe she fears she is overstepping the bound between the women.

Jamie relaxes and again smiles warmly at her friend. "I'll be gone four days. Max. Promise! So, no, you don't have to worry about me running off to Oklahoma or wherever."

She tamps the piles again for emphasis. "Besides, you've given me some pretty serious homework assignments that have to be turned in soon, don't they?" At this, Jamie stands up. Stella stands, too, knowing this meeting is over.

"Yes, I guess I have. So, you'll be back…Saturday?"

"At the latest. And tell you what…ask the girls to come over in the afternoon. We'll do a cookout. And why don't you and David come too? I don't want to impose, but he still knows how to run our grill, doesn't he?"

Stella brightens at all this. An invitation to Saturday dinner! With her husband as cook! Nothing could be better! Jamie can see her compiling a list already.

"Oh that sounds like a great idea! Thank you, Jamie." She reaches out impulsively and hugs her. "It's good to have you back. Back *home*. Again."

Jamie hugs her in return. "It's good to be back. Or, it will be. By Saturday."

They walk to the door. She senses Stella wants to ask something else, but Jamie doesn't let her.

"Call me with anything urgent. Otherwise, I'll see you, David and the girls, and the grandkids Saturday!" Jamie says this overly brightly, and knows it, but wants to be alone. Stella, feeling comforted and needed again, smiles and leaves.

Jamie waits for the car to be down the drive and out of sight before closing the door and leaning heavily against it. "Oh my God…"

She closes her eyes, letting the silence gather around, feeling comforted by the stillness. She's afraid to open them, thinking somehow John will be standing right in front of her. Instead an image floats before her still-closed eyes. Jake. Hair pushed slightly by a breeze. Shirt unbuttoned.

Smiling his I-want-you smile. Looking like the cover model for some Harlequin romance novel. "Jake..." she says softly, yearning.

The image evaporates as soon as she says his name. Now – a deep breath. Eyes open. And back to reality. "Time to get going..."

Jamie walks back into the living room, picks up the half-empty coffee cups and carries them to the kitchen. She thinks how the next time she's here it will be pandemonium again with grandkids spilling over adults and other grandkids. She smiles at the thought. She walks back into the living room, looks at the neatly clipped piles of 'homework' deciding to take them in her briefcase instead of stuffing them into her too-crowded handbag. John had bought her that briefcase many years ago when she started accompanying him on business trips...John...John!

Her heart jumps into fifth gear. How could she have forgotten?! Is he here?!

"John!" "John!!"

She sits on the sofa, on the exact spot where she sat last night and talked with her husband. She looks deeply into the chair where he'd sat, looking for some trace, some evidence that he'd been there. But what to look for? A hair? She'd just been sitting there herself minutes ago with Stella. The bedroom!

Jamie races into the bedroom. "John!" She jumps onto the bed, half expecting to roll her dead husband over on his back so he can talk to her. She grabs at the blankets, the pillows. She stares at the sheets on his side of the bed, running her hand over them, searching for lingering warmth of a body having slept there. Can she feel it? Can she feel...*him*?

"John..." Now less a shout than a complaint? "I must be losing my mind. He *was* here. We *did* talk. I *touched* him...John?" Jamie splays herself across the bed, fingers curling over the mattress edge. "Maybe he'll come back if I just stay silent...silent as a...magpie." Now she laughs softly, Jake coming back to her again.

Jamie rolls over, robe falling to the sides. Eyes closed still. The men in her life. The men *of* her life. One a ghost and gone. The other a dream about to be gone. How will she manage? Man-age. Man. Age. They certainly do!

She laughs now at her play on words. She runs her hand lightly across her body.

"Jamie Barlow, you sure have come a long way. Yes, you have." Her hand slides lower, poorly mimicking the touch from the men she loves to need, and needs to love.

Eyes open and one last look at the other side of the bed. "Time to go. John, you come see me any time. Jake, I'm on my way! You be waiting for me!"

Now up and into the shower. Twenty minutes later, she's dressed, packed and into the garage where the van waits for the drive back to the cabin. And Jake. And the rest of her life.

Chapter 62

Ni-hi. A-ga-li-ha

The drive back to the hills is quick and uneventful. This is one of those trick days of April, where it feels like June or July. Even though the trees are still bare, it's hot and Jamie turns on the air conditioning to cool the van as it zips along the winding roads.

Jamie can't believe how much of a hurry she's in to get back. After a year when each day had its own pace, one that she could control, the last two weeks have been a blur. Even those things she had planned seem to have whirled beyond her grasp on courses of their own.

She has to keep reminding herself that she really did commit the bulk of her personal fortune to making good on a promise made by her late husband – a promise stolen by someone now beyond the grave. And she really did confront Rich Larson. And she believes that he will no longer be part of her life, or of the life and fortunes of Barlow or anyone else's life at Barlow Associates. And she really did put in motion the things that would turn John's company over to his employees. She knows this will be a transition in need of her guidance. And...and...she really did "have and hold" her dead husband last night. But how could that be? This will be something she'll have to figure out on her own. Just not right now. Because she has another family waiting for her in the hills to start down its own life path.

She's in Ram Cat Run in another fifteen minutes. She thinks about stopping at the store, but she's in a hurry to get to the cabin. Jamie knows she risks being rude, but she'll see Cora and Ellie soon enough. Even if they happened to see the van driving down the road, she knows they won't recognize it or its driver. Five minutes later, Jamie makes the turn up the drive. For the first time she notices the still-fresh tire tracks in the mud off to the side. Tracks from the would-be killer who almost got away. She shudders slightly, then guns the van for the steep climb up to the clearing. Stepping out, she's slightly disappointed no one seems to be here to greet her.

"Hello!" No answer.

"Jake?" Silence.

She knows he's not here. Job would've been barking before she turned the engine off. A chill of disappointment descends, a momentary distraction from the day's heat, now at its apex. "Oh well..."

She walks to the door and pauses. "There's no one here!" she shouts, hoping maybe still Jake would open the door wide, Job would come bounding out and, Jake would sweep her into his embrace. Silence. Then she glances at the totem pole. Comforted, she turns the knob and steps into the cabin's dark coolness.

Even on this hot spring day, the cabin seems to embrace Jamie with its certain calm and stolidity. The violence of two weeks before is pushed to dim memory. The cabin is very empty and very clean, but not unlived in. A box of diapers sits on the kitchen counter along with several jars of Gerber's. A baby's blanket is folded neatly on the sofa.

Walking into the bedroom, she's pleased the bed is made up. Maybe not quite as neatly as she prefers. But at least an effort. Something's not quite right, though. Clothes are piled on the dresser. Hers and John's. Her heart races at this disorder. What is this? And why? A bungled burglary? Did Rich, or one of his hired goons, come back looking for something? Is that why Jake is gone? Did they kidnap him and the baby? Jamie turns in a half panic towards the far side of the room, takes a step around the bed and hits her foot.

"Ahhhh!!!" Looking down, it's the bottom drawer from her dresser. Made up with blankets. A bed for Maggie... The clothes piled on the dresser were from this drawer.

"Oh my God!" Jamie shouts half in relief and half laughing at her self-inflicted frenzy. She kneels down to feel the blanket, imagining the baby lying there, Job at the foot of the bed for protection, Jake sleeping above. The new family.

"Oh Jake...you will be a good father to Maggie. Maybe she will have a mother someday too. But I know you are strong enough for both," she says to herself.

She glances around the room. "John, can you hear me again?" she asks. "Listen to me. I want you to keep an eye on this man and this baby too. You will have some help. From his son. He's up there with you too. I will do my part down here. But this man has gone through hell. He has earned some happiness in this life. And a lot of that happiness will come from raising this baby into a fine woman. We can do this, John. We can do this." She runs her hands again over the blanket, then gets back to her feet.

Now Jamie feels that ache to want to be with Jake again. Should she wait? Is he in town with Cora and Ellie? Possibly...but then the thought hits her...the cave! He is probably there, putting things in order, cleaning out, whatever. She needs a good walk regardless. If he is in Ram Cat, they'll be back soon enough and wait for her if she's not back. But if he's at the cave, she can surprise him.

Jamie changes quickly into her jeans and favorite hiking shirt. Pulls on her boots and heads out the door to the trail she's come to know so well. Within minutes she's worked up a sweat climbing the ridgeline. Her pace is steady, but determined. Her breathing is normal, a testament to the conditioning she's worked herself into over the past year. Cresting the line, Jamie pauses to take in the oncoming spring. Down the western side of the ridge, spots of color poke out from the browns and grays of fallen leaves and trunks of trees. A patch of narcissus has taken hold about fifty yards away. Did she miss that a year ago? Her eye is led to another patch maybe fifty yards farther on. A rhododendron is in swollen bud, purplish flowers still a week away from full bloom. White dogwoods are also budding. The summer-like heat will push them along nicely today. She will miss their flowering here. For a moment, this makes her sad.

The deer run down the slope is a dark, muddy path. But no deer are seen today. The pregnant does are ready to birth. She will miss seeing their fawns. Maybe later, when she returns, she'll catch sight of them camouflaged against the dark greens and light browns of the summer forest. Looking up Jamie sees oaks and maples starting to bud also, the faintest hints of green tipping the ends of their branches. She walks over to the trees and runs her hand over the bark of a thick walnut. This one will wait until nearly June before leafing out. And it will be the first to drop its leaves in the fall, too. But its nuts will feed a forest of animals through the late fall, winter and into early spring when other food is scarce.

A bob of red catches her eye. A male cardinal. She loves how they fly as though bouncing on little waves of air. A flutter of wings and up. Then a glide. Then a flutter and up again. Time to get moving! Jake's cave is still a mile away. She hopes he's there. But even if he isn't, she'll have one last look at a place that's become such an important part of her life. She knows it will never be the same after this. Even these hills, ancient as the continent itself, won't be the same.

In all the years she and John motored over these trails, she never knew the cave existed. She knew about Bear Cave, of course, but that is just a small outcropping. And bears were just a figment in her grandchildren's imaginations. Jake's Cave, as it would be known forevermore, was a *real* cave! Hard to find. How did he find it? Do these places draw seekers to themselves? Big. Deep. Probably home to real bears. Home to the first Americans too. Now home to the man and dog who had come into her life so fearfully at first, who now leave having added their chapter to its own untold history.

Into a good rhythm now, Jamie remembers something Jake said back at Christmas as they were sharing memories of holidays past. "Our gift from the Great Spirit is to walk this Earth. Only the Spirit knows how long our path may be, whether it will be crooked or straight. But we honor the Great Spirit when our path is clear, well-marked and one with the ground that others may follow." Did this mean that when we change the ways that we live in the world, we change the ways of the world we live in? Jamie was confused by the "one with the ground" part. She knew part of it was "being grounded," a saying from *her* culture. But she also knew Jake meant something more. More than just muddy shoes!

Today she thinks maybe she is beginning to get it. It's not just the walking. Not just the scaling of steep ridges. Not even the sense that every step is a bonding with earth, grass, roots and rocks. It's more. It's not even this hike. Or the destination.

It's the sense that the path she leaves behind is as important as the one she walks into. That her walk, all of her walks, in the forest, on the street, in the offices, even those in her mind – all of those merge to become *her* path. Jamie's path. A path that others will see and some will follow.

A path that, in Jake's words, should be made to honor the Great Spirit. Or in her words to honor those values, those people, even those things that are important to her and hopefully important to others as well... those things that amount to growth of what Jake's Great Spirit has planted here. How did Jake say it? "A path that starts with Sky. Blesses Earth. And returns to Sky." Jamie hadn't thought of those words for a long time.

She thinks, "If I closed my eyes now, I could stay on this path and find my way to Jake's Cave. And maybe just keep walking all the way to Sky!" She laughs at this. But is comforted, too. In one year: so much loss and challenge and...joy.

A loud CRASH! rips into her reverie. Through bushes, the unseen animal is on her before she has a chance to react. She stumbles against a small oak tree. The animal is up against her.

"Job!!!!" Tail wagging and tongue licking furiously, Job is as excited to see her as she is surprised to see him. Running a few steps behind the dog comes Jake.

"Jamie!! I didn't expect to see you out here!" The lovers embrace. Jamie holds Jake tight even as he tries to catch his breath.

"I got back to the cabin and no one was there and..."

Jake pulls away long enough to put a hand lightly across her lips. Then removes it and parts her lips with his own.

Jamie pushes into him trying to press every bit of her self against him, into him.

And Jake's arms seem intent to consume her. How can she let this man go? They kiss until Job barks, as if saying "Break it up!"

They unlock lips and, laughing, look down at the dog that is again up on his haunches leaning against both and wanting his share of attention. Satisfied with mutual scruffs across his head and neck, Job gets down and starts nosing down the trail towards the cave.

"I missed you!"

"I missed you!"

"I was down at..."

"I hoped you were..."

"So much..."

"I wanted..."

Their words tumble over each other until Jamie says, "Wait! You first!"

Still embracing, Jake smiles his gleaming smile, pushes a strand away from Jamie's cheek and kisses her lightly on the lips.

"When did you get back?"

"Not long. Maybe forty-five minutes. I was a little surprised you and Maggie weren't at the cabin. But I didn't think you could be far away. So I came looking!"

"I was there until a few hours ago. But I asked Cora and Ellie if they would help me by taking Maggie for the rest of the day. I...I wanted to pack things up...at the cave."

"Have you been there already?" Jamie asks, disappointment creeping into her question.

"No! I went down to Church Rock. To meditate." Jake kisses her again.

"I ran my hand over the exact spot where you were...that first day."

Now Jamie kisses him back. "I guess you really were missing me!"

"I was. And I will." Jake runs his hands down her back and across her buttocks.

Jamie has learned unmistakable signs of his desire. Her body is responding with its familiar ache of anticipated pleasure.

"Then I sat and closed my eyes. I wanted to remember all that has happened here. I came here not even knowing where 'here' was. Now I know. These hills, that cave, your rock – they are holy to me now."

Jamie's fingers trace the strong muscles in Jake's back. "They've become holy to me too." She kisses him again.

Job comes back barking his impatience.

Jake smiles, "I think he wants to get back to the cave."

"So do I."

They walk with arms around each other the hundred yards or so to the narrow path leading back to the cave. Then Jake moves in front. Jamie looks at the lean strength in his buttocks and legs. The taper in his back. The hair flowing easy and straight to his shoulders. *I am so going to miss this man.*

Job is waiting for them when they reach the first overhang. Stepping into the coolness of shaded stone, Jake turns and says, "I only want to take..."

This time Jamie steps up and puts her hand across his lips. Silenced then she kisses him. Her eyes adjust slowly to the dark cave with its cool, grey, damp walls. The bed is still made inviting them to its warmth. Arms around again. The deep embrace of yearning for union.

"Jamie..."

"Hush."

She unbuttons his shirt with fingers and kisses. Jake's bronzed skin is glistening and smooth, alive to her touch. Shirt off, Jamie bends to trace the lines of his ribs with kisses and licks, then brushes his abdomen with her face and hair. Her lingering grasp gathers up the firm roundness of his beautiful behind then circles forward, squeezing his inner thigh.

Jamie kneels and unbuttons his well-worn jeans. More skin. His scent. A cherishing caress and kiss. A snap opens. A zipper parts. His hands working to part Jamie's clothes. Female skin laid bare to man's lips, to man's hands. Woman's hands hold and caress filling maleness.

Now lips taste lips again. Hard. Hot. Soft. Wet. Pleasured by her pleasure.

Aroused by his arousal. Self aching for other. Other craving self. Senses blurring in upward spiral. The flavor of her touching. The sound of his pulse in her hand.

Brightening colors. Boundaries falling. Swirling color of needs turning to gifts.

Welcomed invading. Welcoming. Mouth at neck. Pleasure cascading. Lips stay tasting female sweat.

Nuzzling flesh. Fingers raking through hair. Hands pushing. Pulling. Desiring. More. Eyes fixed deeply together as invasion finds welcome.

Knees buckling. Cool bed sheets, rolling, lying. Pressing. Worshipping.

Darkness. Forgetting even to inhale, then deep, heaving, animal breaths.

Gripping. Searching. Tasting. Lifting. Coolness touched by warmth.

Move into deeper darkness. Familiar softness.

Male on female. Arms on arms. Lips on lips. Thighs on thighs. Toes remembering each others' touch. Separation finds closure. Vulnerable to oneness.

Ecstatic surrender swathed in darkness, bathed in light.

Then light. Flash of light. Flash of dark. Light and dark.

A galaxy of lightness and darkness. Swirling miasma of color and light.

Rising and falling. Falling and rising. Maleness and femaleness. Twined and turned. Water and seed. A flood.

And cries deep into that darkness. Holy cries. Spirit cries. From Sky. To Earth.

Earth spouting to touch sky. Full union. And deep.

Male and female. Lost in each other. Found in each other.

Breathing slows. Arms relaxing. Grips released.

A blessing of Sky. Bright sun. And dark stars.

A blessing of Earth. River eternal. Carrying all.

Present. Future. Past.

A blessing of Silence. Deep.

A blessing of Voice. Deeper.

Jamie's head is on Jake's chest with his arm around her. Gently, tentatively, a song rises from Jake's throat but resonates mysterious and deep beneath her ear in his chest.

> *"Ni-hi.*
>
> *A-ga-li-ha*
>
> *A-da-nv-to*
>
> *U-li-he-li-s-di*
>
> *U-gi-tsi-s-gv*
>
> *Di-tsi-ga-to-li*
>
> *Ka-nu-yo-la-di."**

"Was that Cherokee?"

"Yes."

"What does it mean?"

"It's a Cherokee love song:

> "Joy
>
> Of my dawn.
>
> My eyes
>
> Become mist
>
> At
>
> The thought
>
> Of
>
> Your love."

Jamie allows herself to think of the next day. She knows how it will be. There will be goodbyes, then tears, the lump in her throat, the uncertainty, the baby, the promise to meet at the Summer Solstice. But for now she is with Jake, as close as they have ever been. They lie together hidden in their cave...the sun beyond, the birds and the animals too. But all she wants is Jake's arm around her. She rubs her hand on his chest. She wants to hear his voice resonate in his chest again; vibrating into her as though his voice could merge with hers.

"Please sing it again. Let me hold it again. Let it be ours. Forever." she asks.

Jamie welcomes the sound and the truth of this moment as it fills her once more. She hopes it will carry and sustain her to the end of her days. She and Jake...unending ripples in Life's unending sea. *"Ni-hi. A-ga-li-ha..."*

Epilogue

"Ram Cat Grocery, Cora here."

"Ummm... hello. I am trying to find someone and this phone number is the only clue I have. Would you be able to help me?"

"Shoot, sweet heart. I'll answer if I can."

"Well, I am trying to get in touch with someone. Her name is Maggie. My father had this as the only contact number when he would go away on the summer solstice. I would like to know if you know who this Maggie is."

"What is your name, hon?"

"My name is Margaret Mae Kelley, ma'am. My father Jacob Kelley died and I am trying to fit my life together." Silence.

"Jake is dead? What happened?"

"He was killed in an accident with his dog in his truck a month ago. Did you know him?'

"Yes, darlin'. I knew him. Go on."

"I am trying to find a Maggie who he knew. He always left this number when he went away every year at this time."

"The woman you are looking for is Jamie Barlow." Silence again.

"Did you say Jamie Barlow?"

"Yes, darlin', I did."

"Could you hold the phone for a minute, Cora? I have to look at something."

"Sure, I'll be right here, Maggie Mae."

Margaret sets the phone down. Her body is shaking as she runs to her father's study. A book sat beside his reading chair for as long as she can remember. She picks it up, tears rolling down her cheeks. It is a children's book he had read her often. She looks at it: *Daniel Red Tail* written by Jamie Barlow. She clutches it to herself and runs back to the phone.

"Yes, yes, Cora. It is Jamie Barlow I want. Why did I think it was Maggie?"

"His pet name for her was Maggie. But she is Jamie Barlow and that's for sure."

"I need to find her. Can you tell me where she is? It is very important that I find her now. I will come to Pennsylvania next week. Can you give me an address where I can find her?

Cora picks up a small address book. "I will give you her address, Margaret. Write this down. She lives at 312 Newburn Drive, Pittsburgh, Pa. I don't have the phone number, but if you put the address in one of them new GPS things, you can find her. If you can't find her you can call here again and ask for Cora. Do you hear me, Margaret?"

"Yes, ma'am. I hear you. I will call you back if I have any trouble. Are you sure this woman is at that address?"

"Sure as I can be, darlin'. Now good luck to you and call again if you need anything. And Margaret?"

"Yes ma'am?"

"I'm so sorry about your daddy. And you take good care of yourself... you hear me?"

"I hear you Cora, and I will call you again after I find Jamie."

"One more thing, sweetheart. Could you tell me what you look like?"

Postscript

I'd like to share with you some of how I wrote this book. It might help *you* tell a story or two. I believe there are important personal and communal benefits of telling and hearing each other's stories. I hope this will give you some tools and confidence to step forward with your own voice/s.

This novel took me four years to write. I wrote it in little snips of time that were my own – usually between four and six in the morning while the world of distractions and demands still lay sleeping!

I tell you this because often that's how writing goes. Few of us have the luxury, or the stamina, of being able to spend whole days at a time writing. We snatch the moments we can and push on. In fact, I think I can offer only one bit of real advice to would-be-writers and it is this: just do it. But do it every day, if you can. Even if it's only for a few minutes in the middle of the day. Or a couple of hours early in the morning. I found it to be very much like exercise. The more you do, the more you're able to do. And the more you're able to do, the better you get at it.

The other little bit of advice I have is this: Ask others to help. Even though I wrote most often in the wee hours, I don't think I could have finished this without the moral support, editing and just great ideas I received from family, friends and professional writers.

The popular image is of the writer squirreled away in some lonely corner of the world. Reality is much different. We write what we know and sometimes about *who* we know. Writing is work, sometimes hard work. But it doesn't have to be a form of penitential suffering. Enjoy the experience and share it with others.

I thought it would only take me a year to write 'Magpie', so I decided to put on a step counter like Jamie did and simulate walking the

Appalachian Trail. The Trail, or "A.T." as it's called stretches 2,174 miles from Georgia to Maine. I confess: I have never walked even a few miles of it. But hiking the A.T. is a dream Jamie and I share. So I used monthly planners to map my progress and in four years I walked the equivalent of its entire length four times! (That's more than 8,500 miles, but who's counting?) I lost a total of 31 pounds and 15". I can look back at my calendars and see what was happening as I wrote. Jamie didn't quite finish the trail, which made the walking about the journey and not the destination. Telling Jamie's story got me a whole lot more fit physically *and* mentally!

I used the "Appalachian Trail Thru-Hikers' Companion – 2007", put out by the Appalachian Trail Conservancy as my guide. I also read Bill Bryson's book "A Walk in the Woods." I recommend both of these books if you're thinking about hiking the A.T., or even if you're just thinking about writing about it. You will learn tons about how the Trail was built, the wild (and not so wild) areas it sneaks through and some very, very interesting history.

If you actually do walk some or all of it, drop me a line and let me know what you experienced. You can reach me at info@newburndrive.com.

Some have asked me, "What's next for Jamie? What happens to Jake and Maggie?"

I am starting to answer those questions now. Check back in a year or so- and I hope to have a sequel ready. But here's a hint. I think Maggie's going to grow into a woman that Jamie will be proud of. And hopefully by now you've figured out that Jamie is a woman who will search and experience and grow until she draws her last breath. And then...who knows?

Finally, like many authors, I fell in love with most of my characters and I miss them now that I am finished. I really like Cora a lot and asked some friends to send me a good, "down home" meatloaf recipe that Cora would use as one of her many meals that she and Ellie prepared for Jamie (and Jake!).

I picked one of Fran's. Fran is a longtime friend and an excellent cook. She had her husband try many of her meatloaf recipes. He finally sent me an email that said, "Pick Already!!!" Following is my favorite. It's Cora's too.

"Cora's" Meatloaf

Recipe by Fran

1-pound ground beef

1-teaspoon salt

½ teaspoon black pepper

½ cup chopped onion (1 medium onion)

½ cup chopped celery (1 stalk)

1 egg, slightly beaten

8 ounces chopped tomatoes with juice

½ cup quick cooking oats

Topping

¼ cup ketchup

1-tablespoon brown sugar

Preheat oven to 350 degrees.

Mix all meatloaf ingredients well and place in a baking dish.

Spread the ketchup/brown sugar mix over the top
of the meatloaf and bake for 1 hour.

Dig in!

Feeds 4 hungry people. And one hungry dog, if he behaves.

Vanita Oelschlager is an award-winning author of nearly two dozen children's books. Born in Pittsburgh, she has lived her adult life in Ohio. Mother of two and grandmother of six, Vanita has written extensively for children about sensitive and complicated subjects ranging from adult disability to childhood fears to same-parent households. She has also written a book of poetry based on her experiences as a caregiver to her husband.

She is a graduate of Mount Union University where she currently sits on its Board of Trustees. She is also Writer-in-Residence at The University of Akron.

Silent Is The Magpie is Vanita's first novel.

CPSIA information can be obtained at www.ICGtesting.com
Printed in the USA
BVOW021849210212

283459BV00001B/3/P